HOMER
THE ODYSSEY

HOMER
THE ODYSSEY

Translated by
LEE AUSTIN THOMPSON

GAVIDIA PUBLISHING LLC
Santa Fe, New Mexico

THE ODYSSEY BY HOMER

Published by
Gavidia Publishing LLC
P. O. Box 178
Tesuque, NM 87574

www.gavidiapublishing.com

ISBN: 978-1-7325666-1-3

Book design and cover artwork by Sara Glaser

"Mask of the Cyclops"
Square Mausoleum from Fourchevieilles (Orange)
1st Century AD, from a Roman cemetery
Théâtre Antique & Musée d'Orange
Photograph by Lee Thompson

This book is set in ITC Legacy Serif.

Printed in the United States of America

For Raquel,
muse, partner, wife:
your suggestions and comments
always inspire me,
your understanding of the process
and support for this project
have been absolutely
critical to its success.

For Felino
who left us too soon.

Contents

Introduction

A NOTE ON THE BEGINNINGS OF THIS TRANSLATION

So he spoke. And all kept still, bound
in silent enchantment in the shadowy halls.
ODYSSEY BK 13:1–2

A spark ignited a fire.

Reading and translating from Virgil's Aeneid in high school Latin class launched my passion for ancient epics. And then I encountered Homer. I felt as though I were there in the palace bound in silent enchantment as the bard sang the tale, listening to the rhythmic chanting and lyre while torches flickered in the smoke-filled, shadowy halls.

So I began studying Classical Greek in college and had in mind to read the Odyssey in the original because the work had touched something deep within me. Now, many years later, having read it multiple times in Greek, I feel I have finally been initiated into an ancient bardic ritual: a performance of the Odyssey at first hand within my own imagination. A desire to share this wonder and enchantment drove me to translate this poem.

A NOTE ON THE TALE

Odysseus' journey is not just an adventure story. It is a deeply painful and personal account of a hero's suffering and endurance as he attempts to return home from a war he tried to avoid. His own hubris causes a great deal of the difficulties he encounters on his journey, but he does finally return to his wife, his son and his island kingdom.

Upon his return to Ithaka, he finds a country locked in intrigue: 108 suitors are vying for his wife and his throne. He must use his stratagems and skills to find a way to win them back.

The Odyssey is one of the two surviving tales sung by the ancient bards in the palaces of the great lords during the dark ages of ancient Hellas (Greece) after the collapse of the Mycenaean civilization. They were sung by generation after generation of bards, and in the process were honed into arguably the finest poetry Western civilization has produced.

> *By epic convention the narrator cannot go back in time.*
> M. L. WEST

The structure of the Odyssey is clever in that it appears to break the convention of not going back in time. The events in Books 1 to 4 about Odysseus' son Telemakos convey the impression of happening at the same time as the events in Books 5 to 12 when we first meet Odysseus. A careful reckoning of the days shows that they do not coincide, but the narration and the cut between stories serve to help us think that they do. Odysseus returns to Ithaka and joins the swineherd in Books 13 to 15. Once Telemakos and Odysseus meet in Book 16, the two stories converge, progressing in clear chronological order for the remainder of the poem.

The Odyssey opens with an invocation of the muse. Then, in a Council of the Gods, Athena and Zeus discuss how to free Odysseus from the nymph Kalypso who wants to keep him as her mate forever. The rest of Book 1 and the next three Books describe how Athena helps Telemakos search for news about his father. Meanwhile, happening in seemingly parallel time, we meet Odysseus in Book 5 as Hermes relates Zeus' command to Kalypso to let Odysseus leave her island. Books 6 through 12 narrate his time among the Phaiakians and his telling them of the previous ten years of his life—his travails after leaving Troy and arriving at their island kingdom. The final twelve Books relate how Odysseus arrives in Ithaka, retakes his kingdom and regains the trust of his wife Penelope.

A Note on *Xenos*

> *In the desert every newcomer is an*
> *enemy till you know him to be a friend.*
> GERTRUDE BELL

The Homeric epics describe an age in which Viking-like cattle raiders and feudal warlords battled constantly to control their fiefdoms. As a result, everyone was suspicious of everyone else. In the lexicon of the Odyssey this concept is reflected in the word *xenos*.

The ancient word *xenos* meant both stranger and guest—or the knife-edge between the two, a concept we can barely fathom today. From this concept derived the ancient custom that required a just host to bathe and then feed a stranger/guest and, once the meal was finished, the stranger could be asked who he was, where he was from, and who his family and tribe were. And then perhaps the host would consider the stranger a guest, and, upon his departure, would give him guest-gifts. The host would then visit the new guest-friend and receive his guest-gifts in turn. Thus in this bartering culture were alliances formed, marriages arranged, and peace kept—such peace as there can be in a warrior society.

A Note on Oral Epics and This Translation

Answering him, artful Odysseus then spoke:
"Lord Alkinoös, renowned of all people,
truly this is beautiful to hear, a voice
such as this bard's, this voice like to the gods!
For I say there is no more pleasing fulfillment
than when joy takes hold of all the people,
guests in the palace listening to the bard,
sitting in rows alongside tables filled with food
and meat, the wine-pourer draws out the wine
from the mixing bowl and fills the goblets:
this seems to me in my heart most beautiful."

ODYSSEY BK 9:1–12

The Iliad and the Odyssey were oral poems sung by bards much like Phemios who sings in Odysseus' palace (Book 1 and later) and Demodokos who sings at the Phaiakian palace of King Alkinoös (Book 8 and later). The Homeric poems as well as other poems in the Epic Cycle, in fragments or whole, were passed down from singer to singer, over a period of some 500 years from the fall of the Mycenaean world, traditionally dated circa 1170 BCE, before they were written down as the epics we know today circa 700 BCE.

The groundbreaking work by Millman Parry and others has helped us understand how these poems were sung. They are full of repeated text called formulas. These formulas are replete with specific metrical units (or complete lines or even multiple lines) that are repeated many times to allow the audience to savor their haunting beauty and the singer to summon the next lines. The most common of these are the epithets (*Pallas* Athena, *sensible* Penelope, *artful* Odysseus, *well-benched* ships, etc.) and entire lines or groups of lines describing repeated actions such as the washing of hands, the serving of food, the coming of day, etc.

This is counter to our modern approach. Instead of repeating descriptive words and phrases, we strive to find different ones each time. So as you read, if you think you have seen a passage before, you most likely have, for this translation repeats many of the formulas throughout the text.

The Odyssey consists of more than twelve thousand lines divided into 24 books corresponding to the 24 letters of the ancient Greek alphabet. It is written in dactylic hexameter, or lines with six dactylic feet. A dactyl has one long syllable followed by two short syllables. In ancient Greek, a long syllable was long in duration, like a half note in music, and the short syllables were like quarter notes, giving a regular rhythm to sung or chanted performances of this epic. Furthermore, the final foot of a line is two long syllables (two half notes), taking the same time but slowing down the cadence at the line's end. Thus when the lines are spoken there is an inherent musical rhythm.

This is not a verse form well suited to English. Iambic pentameter fits the rhythms of English much more naturally. Virtually every English verse translation of the Homeric epics uses a version of iambic meter. I have mainly used iambic pentameter and hexameter lines, with trochees often at the beginning of a line to push it onward.

My translation attempts to map to the text line by line. There are occasions when the lines are in a different order because English lacks the flexibility of Greek syntax. To accomplish this line-by-line mapping, I have cut the frequency of the epithets as well as some adjectives while attempting to keep the story line strongly bound to the original. Readability has been uppermost in my decisions about line order and rhythmic patterns.

A NOTE ON THE *NOSTOI* OR RETURNS

The Greek word *nostos* (plural *nostoi*) means journeying to a specific place, and in the Odyssey the specific place is home. Because the Trojan War was fought across the Aegean Sea, retuning home involved a sea voyage and all that such a voyage implies: storms, shipwrecks, troubles at home on arrival, etc. The Odyssey contains several *nostoi*, or Return stories and not just that of Odysseus, though his is by far the most complex—and the most entertaining.

One such story is the Return and Murder of Agamemnon by his spouse and her new lover told in Book 1 and elsewhere. There is the benign Return of Nestor in Book 3 and the prolonged Wandering and Return of Menelaos in Book 4. There is the failed Return of Aias shipwrecked and drowned in Book 4. There is also the Return of Telemakos. In Book 4 there is the planned ambush of Telemakos by the Suitors on his Return, and in Book 15 his escape and safe Return to Ithaka.

So the word Return throughout the Odyssey carries with it a sense of the loss felt by families waiting at home with no word of loved ones far away. It contains the dread felt by warriors returning home after a long, brutal war and the fearful uncertainty of surviving a sea crossing. In his Return story, Odysseus felt the added bitterness of enduring ten years before he finally reached home.

A NOTE ON NAMES IN HOMER

Virtually every translation struggles with Homeric names. The most familiar of these names have arrived in English via Latin and are often far from the original. To keep the Viking-like flavor of the epic, I have, for the most part, left the Greek names in a simple transliteration. The Cyclops appear not as the Greek Kyklops because I believed this would be too confusing to modern readers. Penelope retains four syllables because the five syllable Greek version was difficult to fit into the translation. The other well-known names will look familiar but may have some different consonants and, occasionally, different vowels. When a name first appears in the Odyssey I have cited this in the glossary of names at the end of the book; if there is a common Latin or better-known spelling, that is listed in parentheses after the Greek transliteration.

The endnotes (listed by book and line number) may help elucidate some words or passages in the text. An asterisk * at the end of the line in the text indicates there is an endnote.

A Final Note

Whether chanted for an audience or frozen on a page, every translation is a performance. When asked why I undertook this translation, I think of why a musician performs the "Goldberg Variations" by Bach even though the work has been performed marvelously many times before and will be performed marvelously again. So why do I offer another version of the Odyssey? Partially I do it for the sheer joy in the making of this translation and partially because I read with a different ear and I speak with a different voice, my voice. I humbly offer this translation as my performance of this monumental opus of ancient Greek literature.

While I have consulted many texts and commentaries, any mistakes in this translation are mine.

LEE AUSTIN THOMPSON
Santa Fe, New Mexico
January 2019

BOOK ONE

Invocation and Council of the Gods
Athena inspires Telemakos to search for news of Odysseus
The suitors of Penelope feast in Odysseus' palace

Speak, Muse, tell me of that brilliant man,
who wandered—lost—after he sacked holy Troy!
He saw the towns of many men, learned their thoughts,
and his heart suffered much on the barren seas
struggling to stay alive, see his men safely home.
But those men he could not save hard though he tried:
they were destroyed through their own recklessness.
Fools! They ate the oxen of Helios the Sun.
He it was who ended their homeward journey.

Goddess, from some such point begin, tell us! 10

By now, all the others who had escaped hard fate
were home, safe from death in fighting or on the seas.
But he alone, longing for his return, the woman,
the nymph lady Kalypso, bright goddess,
held in her hollow caves, wanting him as mate.

But when through passing seasons the year arrived
the gods had spun for his return home
to Ithaka not even there would he elude
sore tests among his people. The gods all pitied him,
but not Poseidon: he raged relentlessly against   20
Odysseus until he reached his native land.

But he was far away, among the Aithiopians,
farthest away of men. They live in two tribes,
one where Helios rises, the other where he sets.
A hecatomb of bulls and rams they offered him.*
There he sat enjoying the feast. The other gods
were together in Zeus' halls on Olympos.
The father of gods and men began with these words,
reminded in his heart how far-famed Orestes,
Agamemnon's son, slew handsome Aigisthos.   30
Remembering him he spoke thus to the deathless ones:

"How indeed these mortals blame the gods!
They say all evil comes from us! They themselves
through reckless acts suffer pain beyond their due!
Now Aigisthos has ignored his fate and wooed
and wed Atreus' son's bedmate and slew him*
when he returned—a hard death—though we warned him
sending Hermes, keen-eyed Argos-slayer, who told him:
'Do not kill him, nor dare to wed his bedmate!
Orestes will bring vengeance for Atreus' son   40
when he becomes a man, longing for his own land!'
So spoke Hermes. Though speaking well he did not
persuade Aigisthos who has now paid the price."

Then the goddess bright-eyed Athena answered him:

"Oh Kronos' son, our father, supreme lord,
that one, Aigisthos, lies in death deservedly.
And so should any other die who does such deeds!

But my heart weeps thinking of wise Odysseus,
ill-fated, who long has suffered, far from friends
on that wave-washed island, the navel of the sea.   50
The goddess dwells in her halls in that forested land,
child of wondrous Atlas, he who knows the depths
of every sea, he who holds the tall pillars
that keep the land and the skies apart.
His daughter restrains that grieving, sorrowful man.
She tries to charm him with her mild, winning words
so he'll forget Ithaka. Odysseus
yet longs for home, to see the hearth smoke rising.
Or else he longs to die. Why is your heart not moved,
Olympian one? Did not Odysseus give you   60
the holy offerings by the Argive ships
in wide Troy? Zeus, why do you hate him so?"

Answering her, cloud-gathering Zeus said:

"My child, such words escape the fence of your teeth!
I? Forget? About godlike Odysseus?
His mind is best of all mortals, best with gifts
to the deathless gods who hold the wide skies!
But earth-embracer Poseidon keeps his ceaseless fury
because Odysseus put out that Cyclops' eye,
godlike Polyphemos, whose strength is greatest   70
of all the Cyclopes. The nymph Thoösa bore him,
Phorkys' daughter, when she mated in
a hollow cave with Poseidon, lord of the seas.
Because of this, earth-shaking Poseidon, though he
cannot kill him, makes him wander far from his land.
But come, let's all consider now his return
so he can leave. Poseidon shall, must, cease
his wrath. Even being so enraged, how could
one stand against the will of all of us?"

Then the goddess, bright-eyed Athena, answered him: 80

"Son of Kronos, our father, supreme lord,
if this action is now dear to the happy gods
that brave Odysseus return to his home,
send messenger Hermes Argos-slayer
to reveal to the fair-haired nymph
our immutable plan: Odysseus
will leave Ogygia Island and return home.
I'll go to Ithaka to urge his son on
and put such mettle in his heart that he
will call the long-haired Akaians to meet,*   90
speaking out to all the suitors who keep killing
his herded sheep and shambling, spiral-horned oxen.
And then I'll send him on to Sparta and sandy Pylos
to learn if there's news of his father's return.
Thus he'll earn respect in the eyes of men."

So speaking, she put on her perfumed sandals
of shining gold, which would bear her with a breath
of wind over both sea and boundless earth.
She took up her strong spear, huge and heavy,
its bronze tip sharp. Lord Zeus' daughter used this   100
to tame the ranks of men, heroes who angered her.
She went darting down from Olympos' peak
and stood in the land of Ithaka, at the gate,
threshold of Odysseus' house. Bronze spear in hand,
she took a stranger's likeness, Mentes, a Taphian lord.
She found the valiant suitors amusing themselves
playing board games with stones and dice, sitting
by the door on skins of oxen they had killed.
The heralds and attendants were kept busy:
some mixed the wine with water in the wine bowls,   110
some with sponges washed the tables which they placed *
in front of them, and others cut up the meat.

Godlike Telemakos saw him at once, for he
was seated among the suitors, his heart troubled
thinking about his father: if only he
would come, scatter these suitors from the halls,
win back his honor and rule from his palace!
Sitting with them, thinking such, he saw Athena.
He went straight to the forecourt, his heart upset seeing
a stranger left standing by the gate. Approaching,   120
he took his right hand, accepting the bronze spear
and addressed him with these winged words:

"Be glad, stranger, for you are welcome here. And when
you have enjoyed a meal, you can say what you need."

He spoke while guiding him. Pallas Athena followed.
They went within the high-ceilinged house.
He carried the spear, stood it against a tall pillar
in a polished spear-rack where there were many
others, the spears of great-hearted Odysseus.
Leading him to a well-wrought, cloth-covered   130
chair, he bade him sit, a stool for his feet.
Near it he put a carved bench for himself,
away from the suitors' noise lest the stranger
be put off his meal—and also so that he
might ask about his long-absent father.
A maid brought in a golden pitcher and poured
water over a silver basin for them to wash
their hands and drew polished tables up to them.*
The modest housekeeper carrying bread
served them a broad selection, the best at hand.   140
The carver gave them a platter of mixed meats
and set beside them golden goblets. A herald,
going back and forth, poured them some wine.

Then the valorous suitors came in. They sat

themselves down in their usual chairs and benches.
Heralds poured water over their hands,
slaves walked among them with baskets of breads,
young boys filled their cups to the brim with wine.
They reached their hands out for the ready food.
When desire for drink and food was sated, 150
the suitors felt in their hearts the need
for singing and dancing, the crown of a feast.
The herald put a golden-toned lyre in the hands
of Phemios and he was made to sing for them.
Touching the strings, he began an epic song.
Then Telemakos spoke to bright-eyed Athena,
bending near so others might not learn of it:

"Stranger, will what I say here offend you?
They are interested in these things, the lyre and song.
It's easy since they eat without compensation 160
the goods of a man whose white bones rot in rain
lying on land or are rolling in great sea waves.
If they should see him return to Ithaka,
they would all pray to be swifter of foot
than remain here wealthier in gold and clothes.
But now he's lost to evil fate and it
gives us no gladness if any man on earth
should say he'll come. The day of his return is lost.
But come, tell me this and speak only true words:
among men, who are you? Where from? Your town? 170
Parents? What type of ship brought you? How did the sailors
come to Ithaka? Who did they claim to be?
For I do not imagine that you came here on foot.*
Tell me these things truly so I may know well
whether you are newly come, or were my father's
guest once, when many others used to visit
our house when he went about among men."

The goddess, bright-eyed Athena, answered him:

"I will indeed tell you truly of these things.
I tell you I am wise Ankialos' son   180
Mentes. I rule the oar-loving Taphians.
I came here with my ship and companions,
sailing the dark sea to foreign-speaking Temese
after copper; the cargo I carry is iron.
My ship waits along the coast away from town,
in Rheithron cove under woody Mt. Neion.
Our fathers were mutual guests: let us be too
from first meeting. The old man will tell you,*
the hero Laertes, who they say no longer
comes to town but stays in the country in pain.   190
An old woman servant brings him his food
and drink when that weariness comes to his joints
and makes him struggle up his vineyard slope.
Now I am come because they told me your father
was home. But no, the gods are blocking his way.
Good Odysseus still walks upon the earth,
yet, though alive, he is held back in the wide sea.
Men keep him on some sea-washed island, harsh
savages, who hold him back against his will.
Now I will make a prophesy. The deathless ones   200
put this in my heart and I believe it true
though I am no seer nor can I read bird omens:
not much longer will he be absent from his
own land, not even if iron chains hold him.
Artful as he is, he'll find a way to come.
But now, you tell me and tell it truly
if Odysseus can have such a fine son!
The head and eyes are strangely like his own.
We used to meet each other often then,
before he went away to Troy with the others,   210

the best Argives who went in hollow ships.
Since then I have not seen him, nor he me."

Then discreet Telemakos answered thus:

"Therefore, I, stranger, will tell you truly:
my mother says that I am his, but I
know not, for no one knows of his own birth.
I would be happy were I the son of a man
overtaken by age on his own estate.
But now, when you ask me this, they say I am
born of that most unlucky of mortal men."   220

The goddess, bright-eyed Athena, answered him:

"The gods did not put you in some obscure clan:
yours will continue since Penelope bore you!
But now, tell me this and tell me truly:
What feast is this? Who this throng? What need is it?
A wedding feast? It is no communal meal.
What do they think, so arrogant, wantonly
feasting throughout the house? Any prudent man
would be angered seeing such presumption!"

Then discreet Telemakos answered her: 230

"Stranger, since you ask and question me
I will tell you. Our house was once wealthy
and fine when that man still was here at home.
Now the gods plot otherwise: with evil plans
they make him invisible among all men.
I would not grieve so for his death if he had died
among his companions in Troy or with
his friends after the war had finally ended.
All the Akaians would have heaped a barrow for him
and his fame would carry to his child in aftertimes.*   240

Now storm gods have snatched him away in secret:
he went unseen, unheard of, leaving me in pain
weeping for him. But I grieve not for him
alone. The gods have caused me other troubles.
As many lords as there are who rule the islands—
Doulikion, Same, and wooded Zakynthos—
and those lords here in rocky Ithaka,
that number court my mother, consuming our wealth.
She neither refuses the hated marriage nor can
consent to it. Meanwhile they keep eating, destroying   250
my goods. Soon they will bring me to ruin."

Stirred to anger, Pallas Athena answered him:

"What? You do have strong need of that absent one,
Odysseus! His hands would strike these shameless suitors!
Would he were home and set himself at the first gate
with shield and helmet, holding two strong spears,
as the man he once was when I first met him
in my home, drinking and enjoying himself.
He had just come back from Ephyre with King Ilos.
Odysseus went there in his swift ship in search   260
of a man-slaying herb so he might smear it on
his bronze-tipped arrows, but Ilos would not give that
to him because he feared the ever-living gods.
But my own father gave it because he loved him strongly.
That Odysseus against these thronged suitors:
they'd all find quick deaths and bitter marriages!
But these things lie in the hands of the gods,
whether, having returned, he takes revenge in his
palace or not. I urge you to think on how   270
you might drive the suitors from the palace.
But will you let this go for now and heed my words?
Tomorrow call the Akaian lords to assemble and
give them this speech, the gods standing as witnesses:

order the suitors to disperse to their own homes,
and your mother, should her heart bid her, to marry.
Let her go back to her mighty father's great palace.
They will make the wedding feast, prepare the gifts,
very many, as should follow a beloved child.
For you I'll urge this thought, if you will be persuaded.
Fit out a ship, twenty oars, one of the best.   280
Go and ask about your long-absent father,
whether any mortal has talked of him or heard
Zeus' rumors—those carry most weight among men.*
Go first to Pylos and ask of noble Nestor.
Then ask in Sparta of auburn-haired Menelaos,
for he returned last of the bronze-clad Akaians.
If you should hear your father lives and will return,
then, though hard, you can endure another year.
But if you hear he's dead, that he is no more,
then return home here to your father's land,   290
heap up a marker, gather his best-loved goods,*
his due, then give your mother to another man.
When you have completed these things and all is done,
think then in your mind and heart how you might
slay the suitors in your palace, openly
or by deceit. It's time to put off childish ways.
No more! You're no longer of such an age.
Have you not heard of that acclaim Orestes won
among all men once he had killed that wily
Aigisthos, the man who killed his famous father?   300
And you, young man, I see you're strong, well-built.
Be brave so those in aftertimes speak well of you.
And now I must go down to my swift ship and my
companions, who must be tired of waiting for me.
And as for you, take care and heed my words."

Then, full of spirit, Telemakos answered thus:

"Stranger, you speak of these matters with knowledge
as a father to his child. I will not forget.
But stay though your journey urges you on.
When you have bathed and cheered your heart, you will hold   310
a gift when you leave on your ship, your heart's delight,
a precious, worthy gift from me: a treasure
such as hosts give their guests though they're strangers."

The goddess, bright-eyed Athena, answered him:

"Do not detain me here since I'm prepared to go,
but give me such a gift as your own heart bids you
when I return. I'll carry it on the homeward leg,
something lovely: your gift will be matched by mine."

So speaking, bright-eyed Athena went away
flying like a bird. But she put strength   320
and courage in his heart, and she put in his mind
yet stronger thoughts of his father. Thinking of this,
he marveled in his heart: he knew he'd seen a god.
A new, godlike man now went among the suitors.

The famous bard was singing to them. They sat silent,
listening. He sang the Akaians' bitter return
that Athena caused them when they left Troy.*

And from upstairs, she heard his divine song,
Ikarios' daughter, thoughtful Penelope.
She came down the high stairway from her own room,   330
but not alone, for two handmaids came down with her.
When she, most radiant, reached the suitors,
she stood by the column supporting the strong roof.
Holding a linen veil in front to hide her face,
with one maid standing on either side of her,
weeping, she addressed the divine bard thus:

"Phemios, you know many soothing songs
of mortals, deeds of men and gods, famous songs.
Sing one of them for these men sitting here as they
drink wine, but cease from this sad song that always   340
bears me down, a pain in my own heart, its grief
never to be forgotten. It touches me the most.
When I call to mind that man whose fame spread wide
in Hellas and half of Argos, I miss him so."

Then, full of spirit, Telemakos answered her:

"Mother, why don't you let the faithful bard
sing the songs that come to his mind? Bards
are not to blame. Blame Zeus who gives toiling
men, each one, whatever fate he wishes!
Let him sing the curse of the Danaans' cruel fate: 350
for men hold closest and dearest that song
they've heard most recently, the newest to make the rounds.
Let your heart endure it, your mind listen.
Yes he, Odysseus, will not come home
from Troy, as many others won't who perished there.
Go back into your room, tend your own work,
the loom and spindle, and order your maids to do
their work. Words belong to men, especially me
since the power in this house now rests with me."

Astonished, she went back up to her rooms,   360
her child's stinging words lodging in her heart.
Going upstairs among her serving women, she wept
for her dear mate Odysseus until the goddess
poured sweet sleep on her eyelids, bright-eyed Athena.

The suitors were making a din in the shadowy halls,
and each prayed that he would lie in bed beside her.

Full of spirit, Telemakos said this to them:

"Suitors of my mother, full of arrogance,
let us enjoy our feasting but make no clamor,
since hearing such a song, whichever one,   370
is to hear a voice like to the gods.
Tomorrow, go to the meeting ground and sit.
I shall invite you openly to quit my home,
to go and do your feasting, eating your food,
passing from one house to another. But if it seems
better, yes, and more convenient to eat
the wealth of one man and give no recompense,
then eat away. I'll cry to the deathless gods
that Zeus may pay back such arrogant acts, that he
might kill those in my house with no recompense." *   380

So he spoke. Biting their lips, all were amazed
at this Telemakos who spoke so boldly.

Then Eupeithes' son Antinoös answered:

"Telemakos, the gods themselves must have taught you
to be a boaster and to speak thus boldly.
May Zeus never let you rule in sea-washed
Ithaka though it be your right by clan."

Full of spirit, Telemakos answered him:

"Antinoös, will what I say anger you?   390
If Zeus grants it, I might wish to rule here.
Do you say this is the worst thing for a man?
It is no bad thing to rule. It brings wealth
to the household and ever more honor.
But there are many Akaian lords, and many
others here in sea-washed Ithaka, and one
may rule this land after Odysseus is dead.
But I will rule my house and slaves, those whom
noble Odysseus won as his rightful share."

Then Polybos' child Eurymakos answered: 400

"Telemakos, these things lie in the gods' hands,
which Akaian shall rule sea-washed Ithaka,
but you yourself should hold these goods and rule your house.
May no man come who might by force wrest your goods
from you while men yet live in Ithaka.
But come now, I wish to ask you of that stranger,
where he came from, what sort of land was it?
Who are his tribe, where is their tilled land?
Did he carry news of your father coming home?
Or did he arrive here to further his own needs?   410
Starting up, he left at once, without waiting
to be made known, yet he seemed not a bad type."

Full of spirit, Telemakos answered him:

"Eurymakos, no hope remains for my father.
I no longer trust in news, wherever from,
nor do I care for prophecies which my mother
commands, asking a seer into the palace.
He came here from Taphos to see my father.
He claimed to be wise Ankialos' son
Mentes who rules the oar-loving Taphians."

So he spoke, though his heart knew it was a god.   420

The suitors, turning, enjoyed once more the dancing
and lovely song and waited for night to come.
When the darkening evening dimmed their pleasure,
then, in order to bed down, each went homeward.

Telemakos' well-built room was high up
with a good view, overlooking the courtyard.
There he went to bed, his heart pondering much.
For him she carried good torches, trusty

Eurykleia, daughter of Ops, Peisenor's son,
she whom Laertes bought as his property.   430
Being young then, he paid twenty oxen,
and treasured her like a good bedmate in his halls
but had no sex with her: he feared his woman's anger.
She carried the torches before the boy. Of all
the slaves she loved him best, for she had nursed him.
He opened the strongly made chamber door
and sat on the bed pulling off his soft tunic,
and put it in the wise old woman's hands.
Folding the tunic, handling it with care,
she hung it on a peg beside the slatted bed.*   440
She left the room and closed the door behind her.
With a curved, silver rod she pulled the bolt across.*
All the night through, covered in fine sheep wool,
he planned his path, the one Athena had pointed out.

BOOK TWO

Telemakos summons the assembly in Ithaka
Telemakos asks the suitors to leave
Telemakos sets sail for Pylos

When early-born, pink-fingered Dawn appeared,
Odysseus's son rose from his bed,
pulled on his clothes, strapped the sharp sword over
his shoulder and bound sandals on his oiled feet.
Like to a god he went forth from his room.
At once he bid the strong-voiced heralds call
the longhaired Akaians to assembly.
So they were summoned and gathered very quickly.
Once they had come together in a group,
he set out for the meeting place, a bronze spear   10
in his hand. His two white dogs followed him.
Athena made him look yet more handsome
and, as he walked, all the people looked at him.
He sat in the king's seat and the elders withdrew.
Then that hero, great Aigyptios,
wise but stooped in old age, spoke first.
His own son spearman Antiphos—killed by

the fierce Cyclops—followed Odysseus in*
his ships to Ilios, land of horses. He was
the last man devoured in that hollow cave.   20
Three other sons he had, one with the suitors,
Eurynomos, and two worked their father's land.
Grieving, he could not forget his lost son.*
A tear flowing down his cheek, he said:

"Hear me now, Ithakans! Mind what I say!
We've had no assembly nor other session since
Odysseus went away in those hollow ships.
Who summoned us? What need brought this on?
From some young man or from an older one?
Has someone heard news of the army returning?   30
Then tell us plainly whoever learned it first.
Or is this some public matter to tell us of?
He must be a helpful noble man. May Zeus
let him speak whatever his mind ponders."

Hearing these words Odysseus' son was glad.
He did not stay seated but rose to speak
in the center of the meeting. Peisenor,
the prudent herald, handed him the scepter.

Then he spoke, first fixing on the old man:

"Old sir, he who summoned you is here: 40
I did. My grief drove me to summon all.
I've heard no news of the army returning home.
If I had heard of this, I would tell you plainly.
And I have no public matter to make known,
only my own business. A two-fold ruin has fallen
on my house. My noble father is lost, he
who ruled you all as a kindly father would.
But now there is something larger which soon
will ruin my house entirely, destroying my wealth.

Suitors assail my mother against her will,   50
the sons of you who are best among us.
They seem to fear going to her father's house,
Ikarios', so that he might betroth his daughter
and give her to whom he wishes, whom he favors.
Instead they come and go in our house every day,
sacrificing our oxen, sheep and fattest goats!
They revel in recklessly drinking our wine!
They are consuming everything! And there's no man
such as Odysseus was to save our wealth.
We can't keep them away: no, we would make   60
a pitiful stand and we know not the ways of war.
I'd drive them off myself if I had the strength.
The acts they've done are not endurable. My house,
once beautiful, they've ruined. You yourselves should be*
indignant, ashamed of these men, our neighbors who live
near here! You should fear the gods' wrath lest they,*
astonished at this evil, turn their wrath on you!
I pray both by Olympian Zeus, and Themis,*
who calls and closes assemblies of men:
friends, hold back. Leave me alone to suffer my   70
hard grief—unless somehow Odysseus
acted hostilely against you well-armored
Akaians for which you now punish me in anger,
urging the suitors on! For me it would be better
if you, the people, ate up my goods and livestock.
If you ate my goods I might have recompense;
for we would ever dun you throughout the town
until we had our just compensation.
But now you bury my heart in overwhelming pain."

So he spoke in anger and threw the scepter down,   80
weeping, and pity then seized all the people.
All were silent and no man could endure
answering Telemakos with harsh words.

Antinoös alone, answering him, spoke:

"Telemakos, bold talker, wildly brave! You speak
to us of shame? You wish to put the blame on us?
We Akaian suitors are not the guilty ones.
It's your mother who knows many tricks.
For three years now, soon to be four, she dallies,
deluding the hearts and minds of all of us.   90
She leads us on, but she holds back each man,
sends messages, but thinks on other things.
And she thought up this last trick for us.
On a loom in her chambers she started to weave
a very large, fine cloth, and she spoke to us thus:

'You, my suitors, since noble Odysseus is dead
and you are eager for my marriage, wait till this shroud
is finished lest my weaving count for nothing.
It's for hero Laertes' burial, when his
terrible time shall come, when he's laid low by death.   100
Let no Akaian women be angry with me that
I let a wealthy man lie without a shroud.'

So she spoke and our hearts were convinced.
By day she kept weaving at the great loom.
At night, with torches placed near, she undid the thread.
For three years this trick convinced us all,
but as the hours passed and the fourth year came,
one of her maids who knew the ruse told us,
and we surprised her undoing the fine loom work.
Thus, though not wanting to, she had to finish it.   110
So we suitors answer you that you may know
in your heart, and all Akaians may know as well:
send your mother home, bid her to marry
whom her father commands or who pleases her.
But she keeps tormenting us, Akaian sons,

and plans to keep on—she whom Athena gave
such wondrous skill in crafts and such a brilliant, noble
mind. For we've not heard of such things even
from ancient times among fair-haired Akaian women:
not Tyro or Alkmene, nor Mykene with her garlands.   120
None like to Penelope for true thoughtfulness.
But in this endeavor she has not thought well.
We will eat through your goods and livelihood
as long as she keeps to this, which the gods
must have put in her breast. Her fame is made
great, but your livelihood is being lost.
We'll not go to our farms or anywhere else
until she weds one of us, the one she wishes."

Full of spirit, Telemakos answered him:

"Antinoös, I can't push her out of her home.   130
She bore and reared me. My father, in another land,
died or lives. It would be hard to pay back
Ikarios if I sent my mother unwillingly.
I'd suffer pain from her father, and if she should
leave the house some god would grant my mother
vengeance on me from the horrible Erinys.
All men would blame me. Never will I say those words!
If your hearts are angry at what I say, then go
from my palace, attend other feasts,
eat up your own goods, house by house.   140
But if it seems agreeable and better to you
to destroy the livelihood of one man, then
eat on. I call upon the ever-living gods
that Zeus may grant a fit revenge on you:
to die within my house with no blood money."

So he spoke. Then far-thundering Zeus sent
two eagles flying from a high mountain crest.

They soared along on a breath of wind a while,
their out-stretched wings nearly touching, but when
they reached the middle of the loud assembly,   150
they whirled about, wings beating the air rapidly,
and looked on the heads below, their eyes deadly.
Their talons spread, each tore the other's cheek and neck,
and sped off toward the right, away from homes and town.*
All were astonished at the sight of such birds,
and their hearts wondered what might come to pass.
Halitherses, old hero Mastor's son, spoke to them,
for he exceeded the wise old men in knowing
bird omens and the hidden meanings of prophecies.
He spoke, considering his words carefully: 160

"Ithakans, here now what I say to you
revealing all. I'll speak mostly to the suitors,
for them great woes roll in: Odysseus
is not far from his friends, but he is near,
and he is sowing murder and death for all
of them and for the town and others who dwell
in sunny Ithaka. He brings evil. But let
us help them cease before he arrives—or you
yourselves should cease, for this is far better.
I speak no mere prophecy, but what I know well.   170
For I told him all that would come to pass
through prophecy when the Argives went to Ilios,
and with them went artful Odysseus. For I
told him then he'd suffer much, his men would all
perish. In the twentieth year, unrecognized
he would come home. All this now comes to pass."

Eurymakos, Polybos' son, then answered him:

"Old man, come now! Go prophesize to your children!
Tell them to stay home or they'll suffer later.

In response, I foretell these things for you:
many birds fly under the glare of Helios,
not all are charged with meaning. But Odysseus
died in distant lands! Would that you had withered
with him! Do not speak such prophecies
expecting gifts that he might give you lest
you anger Telemakos and unleash his wrath.
But I tell you this and it will come to pass:
if an old man knowing much advises a
young man, urging him on to wrath, for that
young man it will be very bad and he will
only bring yet more grief on himself.
But we'll charge you a penalty, old man, that your
heart will find hard to pay: a harsh pain for you.
And I myself put this to Telemakos:
bid your mother go back to her father's house.
They'll arrange her wedding and gather bridal gifts,
many, such as should follow a beloved child.
For I think the Akaian sons will not stop their
hard wooing until that happens. We fear no man,
not Telemakos though he speaks fine words.
Nor do we care for the unfulfilled prophecies
that you utter, old man. Better to leave off.
More of his goods will be devoured with no thought
of recompense so long as she puts off the suitors
and her marriage. Day after day we wait,
rivals for her merits. We don't go after other
women though each could find a suitable bride."

Full of spirit, Telemakos answered him:

"Eurymakos and you other noble suitors,
no more will I beg you or speak of these things,
for now the gods and all Akaians know my plight.
But come, give me a fast ship and twenty men.

Let them take me on my journey, there and back.
For I go to Sparta and to sandy Pylos
to learn of my long absent father's return,
if any mortal can tell me, or if I hear rumor
from Zeus, for rumor carries news among men.
If I hear my father lives and will return,
though I'm worn out, I can endure another year.
If I hear he's dead and he is no more,   220
I'll return here to my native land
and build a barrow, perform the funeral rites,
his due, then give my mother to another man."

So he spoke and sat down. Mentor then rose
to speak. Odysseus, when he sailed
in his ships, turned his household over to
this old man's guidance, to watch over all.
He spoke, addressing them with well-considered words:

"Ithakans, listen to what I say.
Let no scepter-bearing king be cheerful, nor good   230
and mild, nor know right thoughts in his heart!
No, let him be harsh and act unjustly
since no one now remembers King Odysseus
who ruled his people like a kindly father.
But I do not blame the well-born suitors
who do violent acts with bad thoughts in mind.
They risk their heads eating up the wealth
of King Odysseus. They say he won't return.
What most angers me is all you others
sitting in silence, saying nothing to them.   240
You are many! You could stop these suitors!"

Then Euenor's son Leokritos answered him:

"Abusive Mentor, your heart is crazed! You speak
such words, urging us to quit? Who would fight us

over a feast? Think: we outnumber you!
If lord Odysseus himself should come
to his own house while we well-born suitors feast,
his heart planning to drive us out of the palace,
his woman would find no joy in it though wishing
him at home! You know he'd bring about his own   250
death fighting so many. You don't tell his real fate!
But come, people, disperse, each to your own home.
Mentor and Halitherses will see the boy off,
for they are long-time friends of his father.
That boy I think will bide his time in Ithaka,
waiting for news and never make this journey."

So he spoke, and all quickly left the meeting
and dispersed each toward his own home. But
the suitors went to great Odysseus' palace.

Going to the shore, Telemakos rinsed   260
his hands in the gray brine and prayed to Athena:

"Hear me! Yesterday a god came to our house
and bid me go by ship on the misty sea to ask
about the return of my long-absent father.
The Akaians delay this plan, most of all
the suitors—those men so evil and arrogant!"

So he spoke in prayer. Athena came near him
like to Mentor, both in build and voice.
Speaking to him with winged words she said:

"Telemakos, you'll never act thoughtlessly   270
or badly if you are blessed with your father's strength,
for that one stood by his acts and his words.
Your journey will not be useless or in vain.
But if you are his child and dear Penelope's,
I hold hope you will complete what you have planned.

Few children are equal to their fathers.
Most are worse, fewer yet are better.
But you will not be a bad or thoughtless one.
Always carry the wisdom of Odysseus
with you and there's hope you will complete these things.   280
Leave behind you the advice of the suitors,
foolish ones. They are neither thoughtful nor just.
Nor do they know of the black pain and death
that come near them, for all will die on the same day.
But no longer delay the journey you have planned!
For I am your father's friend and I'll
equip a swift ship and go along with you.
As for you, go home. Mingle with the suitors.
Arrange provisions and put all in containers:
wine in two-handled jars, barley—men's marrow—   290
in tightly-packed leather bags. I'll go through
town to gather men. Of the many ships
in sea-washed Ithaka, both new and old,
I'll choose the one that is the best, the fastest,
and once equipped, we'll push out into the wide sea."

So spoke the maid Athena. And Telemakos
delayed no longer once he'd heard the god's voice.
He set out for the palace, his heart troubled.
He found the suitors in the halls, with half-flayed goats
and hogs being singed in the courtyard.*   300
Antinoös, smiling, approached Telemakos,
clasped his hand and addressed him with these words:

"Telemakos, boaster and most headstrong,
harbor no other evil act or word in your heart!
Eat and drink to please me, as you did before.
We Akaians will fit you out with all these things:
a ship with excellent oarsmen so you'll soon reach
sacred Pylos to hear of your famous father."

Full of spirit, Telemakos answered him:

"Antinoös, I cannot eat in silence, content   310
and cheerful with you who overreach yourselves.
In the past I was a child when you suitors
went through much of my food and wealth.
I'm stronger now and have learned, listening
to others' words. My spirit has grown within me.
I will try to harm you, whether in going
to Pylos or from here, waiting among the people.
But go I will and my trip will not be fruitless.
Having no ship, no men to row, I'll go
as passenger, since this I think was your wish."   320

So he spoke, pulling his hand from Antinoös'
with ease. The suitors kept on eating in the hall.
But they mocked and teased him in their talk.
Here is how one over-proud youth spoke:

"Quite openly Telemakos ponders our murder.
Perhaps he'll bring back from sandy Pylos or from
Sparta some friends. He is completely set on going.
Or if he wishes, he can go to Ephyre,
most fertile, to find some life-destroying drug
to toss in the wine bowl and kill us all!"   330

Another of the over-proud youths spoke thus:

"Who knows? Traveling in a hollow ship perhaps
he'll die far away, just like Odysseus.
Terrible! More work for us to do,
dividing all his goods and giving his house
to him who takes his mother when he weds her!"

So they spoke, but he went to his father's wide,
high-roofed room where lay heaped up gold and bronze,

clothes in close-packed chests and fragrant olive oil.
Tall jars of well-aged wine sweet to drink   340
stood there lined up against the wall, holding
the sacred, unmixed drink until Odysseus,
though having suffered much, should come home.
Close-fitting double doors shut the room up tight.
Eurykleia, the woman housekeeper, daughter
of Peisenor's son Ops, was often there
both night and day and she watched over all.
Calling her to the room, Telemakos said:

"Come, Nanny, draw me rich wine into amphorae,
the most refreshing of those you guard for that   350
unlucky one in case he comes, having escaped
his death and cares, Zeus-born Odysseus.
Fill twelve jars full and fasten lids on them.
Pour barley into leather bags strongly stitched.
Let there be twenty of ground barley corn.
Tell no one of this as you gather them.
I'll take them in the evening after my mother
has withdrawn to her room and gone to sleep.
I leave for Sparta and sandy Pylos to learn
of my father's return and hope to hear of him."   360

So he spoke and dear nurse Eurykleia wailed
and, lamenting, spoke these winged words: *

"But why, dear child, why was this plan put in your head?
Why do you wish to go over the wide earth,
you the only son? Zeus-born Odysseus
died far from home in land known only to others.
With you away, they'll devise evil plans for you
to die in their trap and they'll divide your wealth.
No, sit yourself down and stay here! Why go
to wander—and to suffer—on the wide sea?"   370

Full of spirit, Telemakos answered her:

"Be not afraid, nurse, my plan has a god's help.
But swear not to tell my mother of this
until the eleventh or twelfth day has passed,
unless she misses me and hears of it,
so her weeping may not mar her lovely skin."

So he spoke. The old nurse swore the gods' strong oath.
And when she'd sworn and finished the oath,
she started pouring wine into two-handled jars
and then the barley into well-sewn leather bags.   380
Telemakos went back and joined the suitors.

But bright-eyed Athena hatched another plan.
In Telemakos' shape, she went throughout the town,
standing near and speaking to each man,
bidding them gather that evening by the swift ship.
And she asked Phronios' glorious son Noemon
for a fast ship which he gladly gave her.

When the sun set and all the pathways darkened,
she went to the swift ship, pulled it into the sea,
and loaded all the tackle that well-benched ships carry.   390
She moored it at the harbor's edge. Around the ship
the men gathered. She filled each one with courage.

Then bright-eyed Athena had another thought.
She went to brave Odysseus' house
and, there, poured sweet sleepiness on the suitors,
dazing the drinkers and knocking goblets from their hands.
And they sat there no longer, needing to sleep in their
own beds for sleep fell on their eyelids.

Then bright-eyed Athena addressed Telemakos,
calling him out from the comforts of the palace,   400

appearing like to Mentor both in form and voice:

"Telemakos, now your men sit ready,
their oars waiting for you to urge them on.
Let's go! Do not delay your journey longer!"

So speaking, Pallas Athena led the way
and quickly; he followed in the foot tracks of the god.
When they came down to the sea and the ship, they found
the longhaired men on the strand by the ship.
God-protected Telemakos spoke to them:*

"Friends, come. Load the supplies. They're in a heap   410
in the palace. My mother of this knows nothing,
nor any of the maids save one who keeps my secret."

So speaking, he led and they followed him.
Carrying all to the well-benched ship, they loaded
all as commanded by Odysseus' son.
Telemakos boarded, but Athena went first,
sitting in the rear of the ship; near her
sat Telemakos. The men cast off the ropes
and went aboard, sitting at their oars.
Bright-eyed Athena sent a following wind,   420
a brisk westerly, humming on the purple sea.
Telemakos, urging the men, told them to make
ready and they obeyed willingly. They stepped
the mast of fir, attached the tie ropes, and they
tied down the mast's forestays. Then they hoisted
the sail and bound it with ox-hide ropes.

The wind bellied out the sail and the great waves
heaving along the keel hissed as the ship went on,
speeding forward over the waves on her journey.
Once they'd tied all down in the black ship,   430
they set out mixing bowls brimful of wine

and poured libations to the deathless gods,
most of all to the bright-eyed child of Zeus.
All night and through the dawn the ship sped on her way.

BOOK THREE

Telemakos visits Nestor
Nestor tells Telemakos about the return of heroes from Troy
Telemakos and Nestor's son travel to Sparta

Leaving Okeanos' fair stream, the Sun rose
in the coppery sky to shine on the deathless ones
and mortal men in the wheat-growing fields.
They'd come to Pylos, to Neleus' well-built town.
There on the shore a sacrifice of pure black bulls
was being made to the dark-haired Earth-shaker.*
There were nine groups, five hundred sitting in each,
and each group held before them nine bulls.
The crew saw the innards tasted, thighbones burnt
to the gods, and then they lowered the sail,   10
bound it, moored the ship and disembarked.
First went Athena, then Telemakos.
The bright-eyed goddess Athena said to him:

"Telemakos, you need not feel unworthy or
in awe. You have crossed the sea to ask about
your father, whether buried or some other fate.

But come now! Go straight to horse-taming Nestor.
Let's find out what he advises in his heart.
You yourself ask him so he will speak truly.
He tells no lies, for he is sound of mind."   20

Full of spirit, Telemakos answered her:

"Mentor, how should I go? How embrace him?
I am not practiced in thought-out speech.
I'm young! I am in awe of such an old man."

The bright-eyed goddess Athena said to him:

"Telemakos, some things you will know in your heart
and other things a spirit will give you: you were
not born and raised contrary to the gods' will."

So speaking, Pallas Athena led the way
quickly. He followed in the foot tracks of the god.   30
They came to a group, a throng of men in Pylos.
Nestor sat there with his sons and companions
ready for the feast: roasted meat, more on spits.
Seeing the strangers, they all went to them, taking
their hands, welcomed them and bid them be seated.
Nestor's son Peisistratos strode to them,
took both their hands and seated them at the feast
on the sandy beach, on the softest fleece,
by his brother Thrasymedes and his father.
He gave them part of the innards and poured wine   40
into golden cups. Greeting them, he said
to Pallas Athena, aigis–bearing Zeus' maiden:*

"Pray you now stranger to lord Poseidon,
for this feast you've come upon is his.
When you've poured your libation and prayed,
as is right, give that one the cup of wine

for his libation, since I think he also prays
to the deathless ones: for all men need gods.
But he is younger, much of my same age,
so I'll give you the golden goblet first."   50

With this, he put the cup of rich wine in his hands.
Athena was glad and full of spirit at this just man
because he gave her the goblet first.
Then she prayed earnestly to lord Poseidon.

"Hear me, earth-embracing Poseidon! Do not
deny us and our prayers! Fulfill these words!
First send glory to Nestor and his sons
and then give kindly recompense to all
these thronging Pylians for glorious sacrifices.
And give Telemakos and me safe sea-crossing   60
that we might reach home in our swift, black ship."

Thus she spoke though she would bring all to pass.
She gave Telemakos the two-handled goblet.
The son of lord Odysseus echoed her prayer.
They pulled off roasted outer meat, dividing it
among themselves, and feasted on the good food.
Desire for food and drink now sated, Nestor
the Gerenian horseman addressed them thus:*

"It's better to ask of strangers who they are
once that they have been made glad with food.   70
So who are you? Where from on this sea path?
Do you come for trading or are you roaming
aimlessly as pirates on the salt sea, staking*
your lives and bringing evil to those in other lands?"

Full of spirit, Telemakos bravely answered—
Athena herself had inspired him thus
so he might ask about his long absent father

and that he might gain great fame among men:

"Nestor, Neleus' son, the Akaians great glory,   80
you ask where we are from and I will tell you.
We've come from Ithaka that lies under Mount Neion
for my affairs not the affairs of the people.
I come for my father's wide fame, to hear
news of noble, steadfast Odysseus who,
they say, fought with you in the sack of Troy.
Of all the others who fought at Troy we've heard
report: where each died a sorrowful death. But
Kronos' son hides Odysseus' death.

No one can say clearly where he died,
whether overcome on land by hostile men,   90
or in the sea among the waves of Amphitrite.
Therefore have I come to beg you if you would
be willing to speak of his forlorn death if you
have seen with your eyes or heard news from another
of his wandering. His mother bore an
ill-starred child. Don't pity me or use soft words,
but tell me plainly when you met my father
face to face. If ever noble Odysseus
promised you at Troy where Akaians suffered,
promised by word or deed and did fulfill it,   100
remember that now and tell me honestly!"

The Gerenian horseman Nestor answered him:

"My friend, you call to mind the sorrow we wild Akaian
sons endured in battle frenzy in that sad place
when we sailed in our ships on the shrouded sea
with Akilleus leading us, looking for booty.
Or when we fought around lord Priam's large
city where so many of our best were slain.
There warrior Aias and Akilleus lie.

There Patroklos, godlike in wise counsels.   110
There too my dear slain son, both strong and noble,
Antilokos, a warrior who moved so swiftly.
But we suffered terribly in that place. Which one
of us could tell of all the men who died there?
Not if you stayed five years—or even six—
to ask what the noble Akaians suffered there.
No, wearied, you'd soon return to your native land.
Nine years fighting we tried all kinds of strategies,
but Zeus ended the war only with our pain.

There, no one wished to vie against noble   120
Odysseus in counsels since he was best at plans
and all sorts of tricks, your father—if you
truly are his son. Awe holds me seeing you!
Indeed, your words ... so fitting ... like one mature,
in such a young man ... to speak like your father!
During that time Odysseus and I never
disagreed, not in assemblies nor in councils.
We shared one thought in both our minds in our
wise plans, by far the best thing for the Argives.
And when we had destroyed Priam's lofty city,   130
we sailed away, but some god scattered us.
For Zeus intended a mournful homeward journey
for the Argives. Not all of us were thoughtful
and just! The fierce wrath of Zeus' maiden*
fell on many of them—a most dreadful doom.
She caused a quarrel between the sons of Atreus.
They called all the Akaians to the assembly
with no good reason, rashly, when the sun was setting.
They came, heavy with wine, the Akaian sons.
The two spoke, telling why the army was gathered.   140

Menelaos bid all the Akaians to plan
their return on the broad back of the sea.

This did not at all please Agamemnon.
He'd planned to keep the army and make a holy
hecatomb to heal the fierce wrath of Athena.
Fool! He did not know that she would not listen!
Not so quickly is a god's mind changed!
The two stood, bickering with harsh words.
The well-armored Akaians jumped up shouting
loudly. Two groups formed, one around each plan.   150
The hard night passed, the groups turned against
each other. And Zeus made ready his terrible plan.
At dawn, we dragged our ships to the bright sea
and loaded our goods and the captured women.

Half the army remained, waiting with the son
of Atreus, Agamemnon, the army's shepherd.
The other half boarded and we swiftly sailed away;
a god smoothed the deep hollows of the sea.
Going to Tenedos, we made a holy offering
to the gods to send us home, but Zeus, steadfast,   160
refused us, rousing fierce strife a second time.
Some, turning back, went in their curved ships
with lord Odysseus, skillful and very clever,
to find favor with Atreus' son Agamemnon.
But I with all my ships—and others followed—
escaped, knowing this god intended evil.
Tydeus' son escaped, having roused his men.*

Later auburn-haired Menelaos met us
at Lesbos as we considered our sailing route:
whether we should sail north of rugged Chios   170
past Psyra island, holding it on the left,
or south of Chios, along windy Mimas.
We begged our god for a path and he showed one,
bidding us to flee danger quickly and cut
across the middle of the sea to Euboia.

A shrill wind arose, blowing strong. The ships
ran quickly over the sea to Geraistos,*
running all night. For safely crossing the open sea,
we offered many bulls' thighbones to Poseidon.
On the fourth day the curved ships reached Argos.   180
Horse-taming Diomedes' men moored
their ships, but I held for Pylos, and the wind
never dropped from when the god first made it blow.
So I returned with no knowledge of those others,
whether Athena saved them or if they perished.
Whatever I've heard seated in our halls you'll learn
as is right. I will hide nothing from you.

The spear-fighting Myrmidons returned home.
Great-spirited Akilleus' son led them safely
back as did Philoktetes, Poias' son.   190
Idomeneus led all his men to Krete—
those who had escaped the war. The sea took none.

You've surely heard about lord Agamemnon,
when he returned, Aigisthos planned his death.
But his son repaid him ferociously.
It's good to leave a child when a man has gone:
he can repay the murder of his father as
Orestes slew Aigisthos who had slain his father.
And you, friend, I see you are handsome and tall:
be brave so those in the future speak well of you."   200

Full of spirit, Telemakos answered him:

"Oh Nestor, son of Neleus, great glory of the Akaians,
yes, Orestes took strong revenge. The Akaians
will carry his fame far! Those hereafter shall learn it!
May the gods wrap me in such strength that I
might slay the overbearing suitors who cause such pain,
who recklessly run riot and plan my death.

But the gods have spun no such gladness for me
or my father. Now, all must be endured."

The Gerenian horseman Nestor answered him: 210

"My friend, your words have reminded me of this.
They say there are many suitors for your mother
in your palace who stay against your will.
Tell me, are you held, mastered by them, or do
the Ithakans hate you, a god's voice plying them?
Who knows if lord Odysseus may repay all
by force alone, or together with the Akaians?
If bright-eyed Athena should wish to befriend you
as she looked after renowned Odysseus
in Trojan lands where we Akaians suffered so—   220
I've never seen gods helping one so openly
as Athena did, standing by him in public!
If she befriends you thus, troubled in their hearts
will be those suitors, forgetting all thoughts of wooing!"

Full of spirit, Telemakos answered him:

"Sir, I can't see how your words will come to pass.
You speak of great things; I'm held in awe. But I
cannot hope thus, though the gods should wish it so."

Then the bright-eyed goddess Athena said:

"Telemakos, what words escape the fence of your teeth!   230
A god can save a man though he be far away!
I would rather suffer much on the hard voyage
and come safely home than come back
to be destroyed at home as Agamemnon was
by a trap of Aigisthos and his own bedmate.
But death comes to all. Not even the gods
can save a man when hard leveling fate

takes him down, bringing the lasting pain of death."

Full of spirit, Telemakos answered him:

"Mentor, though grieving, let's no longer speak of this.   240
There is no truth in his homecoming. For him
the deathless ones have shown the darkest pain.
Now I wish to speak of other things, to ask
Nestor since, beyond all others, he knows what's just.
They say he's ruled for three generations—
to me he seems one of the deathless ones!
Nestor, Neleus' son, tell me truly:
how died lord Agamemnon who ruled widely?
Where was Menelaos? What death for him
planned wily Aigisthos who had slain a king?   250
Was Menelaos not in Argos, but sailing elsewhere
when wily Aigisthos found the courage to slay him?"

The Gerenian horseman Nestor answered him:

"Well then, child, I will tell you all the truth.
Indeed, you can surmise what would have happened
if fair-haired Menelaos, coming back from Troy,
had found Aigisthos living in the palace!
For Aigisthos there would be no heaped up mound
marking his grave, but rather dogs and birds
would devour him lying in far off fields. Nor would   260
Akaians weep for him for such a wicked deed.
We stayed there at Troy fighting many battles
while Aigisthos in the horse-grazing fields of Argos
enchanted Agamemnon's bedmate with his words.
She refused this shameful act at first, well-born
Klytaimnestra, for she was good at heart.
There was a man, a bard, whom Atreus' son,
leaving for Troy, asked to guard his bedmate.
But when the gods bound her to Aigisthos,

he drove that bard to a desolate island 270
and left him to be the spoil and prey of birds.
Then she willingly followed his lead homeward.
On an altar he burned thighbones to the gods
and hung many glorious offerings of gold and cloth
for having fulfilled what he had not dared dream of.

Leaving Troy, we sailed together, Menelaos
and I, knowing each other well, but when we reached
Cape Sounion, Attica's farthest tip,
Phoibos Apollo approached and with gentle
arrows slew Menelaos' pilot—rudder* 280
in his hands guiding the ship—one Phrontis,
Onetor's son, who surpassed the race of men
in steering ships when storms drive them on.
So there he stopped, though the journey weighed on him,
to perform the funeral rites, give death gifts.
Then Menelaos sailed on over the purple sea.
Running swiftly, he reached the steep cliff Maleia.
There far-seeing Zeus planned an evil path
and poured down on them a blast of shrill wind
and stirred up huge heavy waves high as mountains. 290
Then Menelaos sent half his ships to Krete
where the Kydonians live near the Iardanos river.
There a sheer and mighty cliff juts out—
Gortys—far out into the shrouded sea.
The south wind heaps huge waves on the left
of Cape Phaistos, where small boulders block the surge.

There they came, the men hoping not to die,
their ships broken by the storms and waves.
But five of his blue-prowed ships sailed on
to Egypt, the wind and seas driving them onward. 300
There he roamed, gathering much of goods and gold
in his ships among that foreign-speaking race.

Meanwhile Aigisthos was planning his crime at home.
Seven years he ruled gold-rich Mykene once
he'd slain Agamemnon, and the people obeyed him.
In the eighth year noble Orestes brought him trouble.
Returning from Athens he slew this father-killer,
crafty Aigisthos, he who slew his famous father.
Having killed him, he made a funeral feast with those
of Argos for his hated mother and weak Aigisthos.   310
That very day, Menelaos sailed into port
with many goods—as much as his five ships could carry.

And you, friend, do not wander long or far from home,
leaving your goods and those men in your palace—
so arrogant, devouring everything, dividing up
your wealth—lest this journey prove a mistake.
Yet I urge and bid you go to Menelaos,
for he has recently come from distant lands
of men where he could never hope to come back from.
For the raging storms drove him far across   320
a sea so great not even birds could return
the same year, so wide and fierce was the sea.
But go to him now with your ship and men.
Or if you go by land you'll have a chariot
and horses, and my son will be your escort
to Lakedaimonia, to fair-haired Menelaos.
You yourself ask him, so he will speak truly.
He tells no lies for he is sound of mind."

So he spoke. The sun was setting and darkness came.
The goddess spoke then, bright-eyed Athena: 330

"Old man, you have recounted these things well.
Now cut the sacrificial tongues, mix the wine,*
and offer Poseidon and the other deathless ones
a libation. And we should find our beds—it's time.

The light has sunk in the west. It's not fitting
to sit so late in a feast to the gods. Let's leave."

So spoke Zeus' daughter. They heard her words and
heralds poured water on their hands,
youths filled the mixing bowls with wine,
handing out the drinking cups to all. Standing   340
they threw the tongues as offerings in the fire.
When they'd poured the offering, such as their hearts
wished, Athena and godlike Telemakos
were setting out together for the hollow ship
when Nestor detained them, speaking these words:

"May Zeus and the other deathless gods prevent
that you go back to your swift ship while in my land
as one poor and in need, without clothing,
as if there were no cloaks nor rugs in my house
for me and my guests to sleep in comfort!   350
I have cloaks and beautiful rugs at hand!
The dear son of that man, Odysseus,
shall not bed down on a ship's deck while I
yet live and my sons remain in my palace
to receive guests, whomever may come to my home."

Then spoke the goddess, bright-eyed Athena:

"Indeed well spoken, good sir! It's right that he,
Telemakos, obey when you speak so well.
He will follow you that he may sleep
in your palace, but I'm going to the black ship   360
to hearten the men and tell them what they need to know,
for I alone claim to be the eldest of them.
The others are all younger, those who follow him
in friendship, of like age as Telemakos.
There I'll bed down alongside the black ship.
In the morning I'll go to the Kaukonians

where a debt is owed me, not a new one, nor is
it small. But you, when he leaves your palace,
give him horses, the fastest and strongest you have,
and a chariot, and send your son with him."   370

Thus spoke bright-eyed Athena and flew upwards,
appearing like a vulture: awe seized all who saw her.
The old man marveled when his eyes saw her.
Grabbing Telemakos' hand, he spoke these words:

"Friend, I cannot see that you'll be bad or weak,
though young, if gods accompany and escort you:
None other than one of those who hold Olympian homes—
Zeus' daughter, most noble Trito-born,*
she who honored your father among the Argives.
Goddess, be merciful! Give us noble fame: 380
to me, my children and my revered bedmate!
I'll sacrifice to you a yearling broad-faced cow,*
unbroken, one no man has put under the yoke,
and I will have her horns gilded in gold."

So he spoke, praying, and Pallas Athena heard him.
The Gerenian horseman Nestor led his sons
and sons-in-law to his splendid palace.
And when they reached his famous palace, they seated
themselves in order on the couches and chairs.
Once they were settled, the old man mixed the wine,   390
sweet to drink, for the housekeeper had loosed the top
and opened a jar of wine aged eleven years.
The old man mixed this and with much praying
poured a libation to Zeus' maid Athena.

After the offering they drank as much as their
hearts wished, then each went home to sleep.
But then King Nestor told Telemakos,
Odysseus' son, to bed down there on a

slatted bed in the echoing portico
near Peisistratos, spearman, leader of men,   400
yet unmarried and living in the palace.
He himself lay down in a bed his bedmate,
mistress of the house, had prepared.

When early-born, pink-fingered Dawn appeared,
the old Gerenian horseman Nestor arose
and, going outside, sat on the hewn stones.
They were set in front of the lofty gates,
white and shining from oil. In earlier times
Neleus had sat there, like to the gods in counsels;
but now, his heart vanquished, he'd gone to Hades.   410
Now Nestor sat there, guardian of the Akaians,
holding the scepter. His sons thronged around him,
leaving their rooms: Ekephron and Stratios,
Perseus and Aretos, and Thrasymedes.
And with them came the sixth, lord Peisistratos.
He led Telemakos, whom they bade sit.

To them began the Gerenian horseman thus:

"Quickly, dear children, do as I wish that I
might appease Athena before the other gods:
she came as a man to yesterday's feast.*   420
But go now to the plain for a cow, quickly,
and have the overseer drive the cow here.
Another go to great-hearted Telemakos'
black ship and bring all his men, leaving two there.
Another go and bid the gold-smelter Laerkes
come hither that he might gild the ox horns.
The rest of you wait here. Tell the maids
to ready a feast in our great palace,
put firewood and seats nearby, and bring clear water."

Thus he spoke and they all busied themselves. A cow   430

came from the plains, the men came from the swift, well-balanced
ship of Telemakos. And the smith came,
holding in his hands the tools for the craftsman's art:
anvil, hammer and well-made fire tongs
with which to work the gold. And Athena came
to accept the gift. The old man, horse-driver Nestor,
gave the gold. The smith then gilded the horns
so that the goddess would be glad seeing the work.
Stratios and Ekephron led the ox by the horns.
Aretos came from the chamber carrying a basin   440
for washing hands and a basket of barley grains.*
And trusty Thrasymedes held the sharp axe
by the cow ready to strike. Perseus
held a basin to catch the blood. Then Nestor sprinkled
water and barley grain praying to Athena
and from the cow cut head hairs and threw them in the fire.

When they had prayed and sprinkled the barley grain,
Nestor's high-spirited son Thrasymedes drew near
the ox. The axe cut through the neck sinews and the
strength slipped from the ox. The daughters and   450
daughters-in-law, and Nestor's bedmate Eurydike,
famed Klymenos' eldest, raised the ululation.
Then the men lifted the cow from the field
and Peisistratos, leader of men, cut its throat.
The black blood spurted out, the spirit left the bones.
They split the body, cut out the thigh pieces,
all in due order, and with folded fat
covered the savory pieces, placing raw meat on top.
The old man cooked them, pouring bright wine
over them and the young men readied their skewers.   460
When they had cooked the thighs and tasted the innards,
they cut up all the rest, pierced it with spits
and roasted it, holding the spits in their hands.

Meanwhile, Polykaste, the youngest daughter of
Nestor, Neleus' son, bathed Telemakos.*
After he had been washed and rubbed with oil,
she put a tunic and a well-made cloak on him.
He stepped then from the tub looking like a god.
Approaching Nestor, the people's shepherd, he sat.

When they had pulled the cooked meat from the skewers,   470
they sat and feasted. Noble men attended them,
pouring the bright wine into their golden cups.
When they'd satisfied their desire for food and drink,
good King Nestor began with these words:

"Children, for Telemakos' long journey,
yoke the strongest horses to a chariot."

So he spoke and they heard him and were persuaded.
They quickly yoked horses to a chariot.
The housekeeper put out wine and cooked food
such as a king nourished by Zeus might eat.   480
Then Telemakos mounted the chariot.
Nestor's son Peisistratos, leader of men,
mounted the chariot beside him taking the reins.
With his whip, he urged on the eager horses
who left the citadel and flew over the plain.
All day the swift horses shook the yoke that held them.

Then the sun set and all the pathways darkened.
In Pherai they reached the home of Diokles,
Ortilokos' son, grandchild of Alpheios.
there they passed the night treated as guests.   490

When early-born, pink-fingered Dawn appeared,
they yoked the horses and climbed into the chariot
and left the echoing portico and gate.
With his whip, he drove the horses who dashed ahead.

They came to a wheat-filled plain and there
they neared the journey's end, so well their horses ran.
Then the sun set and all the pathways darkened.

BOOK FOUR

Telemakos arrives in Sparta
The wanderings and return of Menelaos
News of Odysseus; the suitors plot to kill Telemakos

They came to mountain-ringed Lakedaimonia
and drove on to the palace of great Menelaos.
In his house with many clansmen they found him
giving a wedding feast for both son and daughter.*
Her he gave to mighty Akilleus' son*
at Troy; he'd promised her to him, approved
the wedding and now the gods were bringing it about.
He gave her horses and chariots to take
to the Myrmidons' famous town where he ruled.

And he brought Alektor's child from Sparta for his   10
beloved son—slave-born, strong Megapenthes.
The gods did not let Helen bear another child
once she'd borne that lovely girl Hermione,
she who was like to golden Aphrodite.
Thus they feasted joyously in the great,

high-roofed halls, neighbors and clansmen of glorious
Menelaos. A godlike bard was singing, and
two acrobats began to tumble among them,
dancing about and whirling in their midst.

There, before the door, stood young Telemakos   20
and Nestor's noble son with their two horses.
Being near, busy Eteoneus, servant
of great Menelaos, saw them. He went
across the palace to the people's shepherd *
and, standing near, spoke these winged words:

"Two strangers have come here, lord Menelaos,
two men who seem like those born of great Zeus.
Tell me, should we unyoke their sweating horses
or send them to another who may befriend them?"

With anger auburn-haired Menelaos replied: 30

"You weren't before so foolish, Eteoneus,
but now you speak as foolishly as a child.
We two ate many times as guests of other men
before we reached our home again at last. May Zeus
keep us from such sorrows! Go, unyoke
their horses and bring them in to join the feast!"

So he spoke. The herald hurried through the halls
and bid the other servants come along with him.
They loosed the sweaty horses from the yoke
and tied them in the horse stalls, throwing them wheat   40
mixed in with white barley. The chariot they tilted
against the bright inner wall and then they led
the two men into the palace. Seeing it,
they marveled at the home of this Zeus-cherished king.
A radiance as from the sun or moon shone on
the high-roofed house of great Menelaos.

After their eyes had feasted on the palace,
they went to bathing tubs where they were bathed.

When slave girls had washed and rubbed them with rich oil,
they dressed them in tunics and in fine woolen cloaks   50
and seated them alongside lord Menelaos.
Carrying a golden jar, a handmaid poured water
into a silver basin to wash their hands.
Alongside them she put a smooth table.
The revered housekeeper brought bread and placed
much food beside them, whatever seemed good to her.
The carver brought a board with many kinds of meat
and placed alongside them golden goblets.
Then fair-haired Menelaos, greeting them, said:

"Welcome! Eat well! And when you have finished   60
your feasting then we will ask you who you are,
of what lineage, for your begetters were not lost
in you who are of the race of sceptered kings
nourished by Zeus. Base men could not beget you."

So he spoke and, taking in his hands the roast
ox chines carved for him, set them beside their drinks.*
They reached for the good food put out before them.
When they had eaten and drunk, sating themselves,
Telemakos called to Nestor's son, leaning
his head near him lest the others notice: 70

"See there Nestor's son, friend dear to my heart,
the lightening flash reflecting through the palace
of bronze and gold, of amber and of ivory!
So must it be within Olympian Zeus' halls—
unspeakably splendid! A holy awe holds me!"

Auburn-haired Menelaos heard him and spoke,
addressing them in these winged words:

"Dear child, no mere mortal can hope to vie with Zeus,
for his palace and wealth will last forever.
Of men, another may equal me, or perhaps not.   80
But I suffered much and wandered much,
coming home in my ships after eight years
wandering from Phoinikan Kypros and Egypt.
I saw the Aithiopians, Sidonians,
Erembians, and Libyans, where lambs mature
quickly and the ewes give birth three times a year.
There neither lord nor shepherd goes without
cheese or meat or sweet milk, and always
there is plenty from milking throughout the year.
While I wandered there and got my great wealth,   90
a man slew my brother by stealth, his bedmate's trap!*
Ruling here now gives no joy for all my wealth.
You may have heard of this from your fathers,
whomever they are, how much I suffered, and how
my palace that held much treasure fell into ruin.
Would that I had my wealth's third part but had
stayed home and those men safe in horse-grazing Argos,
those who perished in the broad fields of Troy!

But often when sitting in our great halls,
lamenting and grieving for all of them,   100
at times I satisfy my heart with weeping;
at times I pause, sated with cold tears.
Of all of those that I lament and grieve for,
there's one who, when I think on him, I cannot eat
or sleep since no Akaian labored more and did
as much as did Odysseus. Suffering
is his lot, mine pain, never forgetting
him who has been gone so long. No one has seen
him living or dead. They grieve for him now,
old Laertes and true-hearted Penelope,   110
and Telemakos left newborn at home."

So he spoke. A longing for Odysseus
swept the boy, tears flowing, hearing of his father.
Lifting his purple cloak he held it before his eyes
with both hands. Menelaos saw this and
was anxious in his heart and mind whether
to allow him to think on his own father
or whether to ask him of these things now.

While he pondered this in his heart and mind,   120
from a high-ceilinged, sweet-smelling chamber she came,
Helen, like Artemis with her golden distaff.
With her came Adreste, who placed a chair for her,
and Alkippe with a soft woolen rug,
and Phylo with a silver basket which Alkandre,
Polybos' spouse, gave her, who lived in Thebes,
in Egypt, where great wealth lies about in houses.
Polybos gave Menelaos two silver bathing
tubs, two tripods, and ten talents of gold.
Moreover, his bedmate gave Helen more lovely gifts: 130
a golden distaff and a basket on silver wheels
finished off with gold worked about its rim.
This basket, filled with fine yarn, the maid Phylo
brought in and put beside her, and on this
she put a distaff with dark-colored wool.
Helen sat in the chair, her feet on the stool,
and began asking her husband about these things:

"Zeus-nourished Menelaos, do we know
who these men claim to be who've come to our house?
Will I be wrong or not? My heart bids me speak.   140
For I think I have never seen such a likeness
neither in man nor woman—and it holds me in awe—
so like the son of great-hearted Odysseus,
Telemakos, whom that man left newborn at home
when, for my shameless sake, the Akaians came,

stirring up bold war under Troy's high walls."

Answering her, fair-haired Menelaos said:

"Now I see him as you make him out to be:
he has his feet and has his very hands,
the look of the eyes, the same flowing hair.   150
And just now as I was speaking, remembering
how much Odysseus suffered toiling for me,
just then he let fall a piercing tear from his eye
and held up his purple cloak in front of his eyes."

Nestor's son Peisistratos answered him:

"Atreus' son Menelaos, leader of men,
of him this son was born, as you have said,
but he is modest and feels shame coming here,
announcing himself first in front of you,
so much we were in awe of your godlike voice.   160
Thus the Gerenian horseman Nestor sent me
along with him as escort, for Nestor wished to know
if you might suggest some acts or words for him.
With his father gone, a boy has much trouble
in his halls with no one else there to help him.
Such it goes now with Telemakos with no
others to help ward off the ruin of his home."

Then answering him spoke fair-hared Menelaos:

"So, the very son of that dear man has come
to my home, he who toiled so much on my   170
account! I told him that I hoped to show above
all others my thanks to him if far-seeing Zeus
granted us both a return home in our swift ships.
Would he lived in Argos! He'd have a home and town!
He could bring his goods and child here and all

his people! I'd even sack one of my towns that he
might live around it and stay and rule with me!
And being here we'd meet often and nothing
would divide us from friendship and pleasure
until death's black cloud should cover us.   180
But god himself will not let us exult so:
he gave that wretched one alone no return."

So he spoke and they all began to weep.
She wept, Argive Helen, born of Zeus.*
They wept, Telemakos and Atreus' son.
Nor could Nestor's son hold back his tears,
remembering Antilokos, his brother,
whom the radiant son of bright Eos slew.*

Thinking of him he spoke these winged words:

"Son of Atreus, when we talked about   190
which mortals were wise, old Nestor named you
when we spoke of such things in his palace.
If such may be, then be persuaded now by me,
for I do not enjoy weeping at dinner.
Early-born Dawn will come, a proper time
to weep for him who has died and met his fate.
These honors we can give the wretched dead:
cutting our hair, letting our tears flow.
My brother was slain there, far from the worst
of the Argives; it may be you knew him.   200
I neither knew nor saw him but they say
Antilokos was quick and most warriorly."

Fair-haired Menelaos answered him thus:

"Friend, when you speak thus you speak as a
prudent man speaks and acts: as one first born.
You speak as your father does, a wise man.

Your acts show you of his lineage, for whom Zeus
spins out happiness in birth and in marriage,
as even now he gives King Nestor right through all
his days, as he grows old in his great palace,   210
and sons who turn out wise, among the best with spears.
But let there be no more weeping beyond this
and let us remember our meal, pouring water
for our hands. We'll tell stories in the morning,
Telemakos and I, telling them to each other."

So he spoke. Asphalion, the busy
servant, poured cleansing water on their hands.
They reached out for the feast spread before them.

But then Zeus-born Helen thought of something else.
To banish their pain and anger, she poured a drug in   220
their wine so they forgot the bad times.
Whoever drank that drug once it was mixed,
throughout that day no tears would fall to the ground,
not even if his mother or father should die,
not even if his brother or dear son were slain
with bronze while he watched it with his own eyes.
Zeus' daughter had these powerful drugs.
Egyptian Polydama, spouse of Thon, gave these
to her, for there the earth is most fertile
for drugs and plants, good ones and those bringing harm.   230
Each man's a healer, knowing more than other men,
for they are of Paieon's tribe. Once Helen
had put this drug in the wine she bid it poured
for them and once more spoke with these words:

"Zeus-fostered Menelaos and you sons
of noble men: Zeus gives to one and all
both good and bad, for he can do all things.
Now, as you eat in the hall enjoying

speeches, I'll tell a thing fit for the evening.
I can neither tell nor name all the feats   240
that noble Odysseus carried out, but that man
performed and endured many toils in
sacred Troy when the Akaians suffered so.
Bruising himself with terrible blows, he threw
a ragged cloth over his shoulders. Like a servant
he entered that broad town of enemies.
Disguised, he seemed to be a beggar man
to others—not like he was on Akaian ships!
So he entered the town of Troy. No one
said anything. I alone knew him and kept   250
questioning him: quick witted, he avoided me.

But when I washed and rubbed him with rich oil,
and had put clothes on him, I swore a strong oath
that I would not make him known to the Trojans
until he should return to the hollow ships,
and then he told me all the plans of the Akaians.
When he'd slain many Trojans with his bronze sword,
he went back to the ships with important news.
Then Trojan women shrieked loudly with grief, but my
own heart rejoiced for my thoughts had turned toward home,   260
ruing the madness that Aphrodite gave me*
when she led me from my land, from the girl-child
I left alone in my bedroom and from
my spouse who lacks nothing in heart or form."

Then auburn-haired Menelaos answered her:

"Woman, what you say is right and true.
I've come to know the will and plans of many men
whom I've met traveling in many lands.
Of those great heroes I've seen with my own eyes,
not one was such as great-hearted Odysseus.   270

Such a strong man, he toiled and suffered much
in that hewn horse that carried the best Argives,
bringing death and murder to the Trojans.
Then you, Helen, went to the horse. A god bid it,
one who planned glory for the Trojans,
and godlike Deïphobos went with you.*
Three times you circled the horse, touching it,
calling to each of the Danaans by name,
your voice like the voices of their Argive bedmates.
Tydeus' son and I and good Odysseus   280
were sitting in the middle and heard you call out.
We both wanted to stand, to jump out of the horse
or answer you at once from deep within.
Odysseus restrained us, kept us from jumping out.
All the others, they waited in silence, all
except Antilokos who wished to answer you.
Odysseus seized his jaw with his strong hands,
never letting go. He saved the Akaians!
He held him until Athena led you away."

Then wise Telemakos answered him: 290

"Lord Menelaos, leader of the people,
how much worse that he could not keep death at bay,
not even with that iron heart he had.
But come now, let us go to our beds so that
we may enjoy the sweetness of sleep."

Thus he spoke and Argive Helen bid her slaves
put beds and good red rugs in the portico
and spread them with blankets, rugs and cloaks,
spreading out the woolen ones on top.
So they left the hall, torches in hand,   300
to prepare the beds. A herald led the guests
to the forecourt that they might lie down there,

Telemakos and Nestor's splendid son.
Menelaos lay down in a nook of the vast house.
Long-robed Helen, most radiant, lay beside him.

When early-born, pink-fingered Dawn appeared,
battle-voiced Menelaos rose from the bed,
pulled on his clothes, strapped the sharp sword over
his shoulder and bound sandals onto his oiled feet.
Like to a god he went forth from his room.   310

Sitting beside Telemakos, he said these words:

"Telemakos, tell me what need brings you so far
over the wide-backed sea to Lakedaimonia.
Affairs public or private? Speak the truth."

Then wise Telemakos answered him:

"Lord Menelaos, leader of the people,
I've come to learn of any news of my father.
They fill my house, those hostile men, eating
my goods, destroying my wealth! They kill my flocks,
slaughter my ambling, spiral-horned oxen!   320
With overweening pride they woo my mother!
Therefore have I come to beg you if you would
be willing to speak of his forlorn death if you
saw it with your eyes, or heard news from another
of his wandering. Oh his mother bore an
ill-starred child! Don't pity me or use soft words,
but tell me plainly when you met face to face.
If ever my father, noble Odysseus,
promised you at Troy where Akaians suffered,
promised by word or deed and did fulfill it,   330
remember that now and tell me honestly!"

Greatly troubled, fair-haired Menelaos spoke:

"See now how these weak men wish to use
his very bed, the bed of a strong-hearted man!
As when a doe leaves in a mighty lion's lair
both her suckling, newborn fawns to sleep while she
searches the mountain spur and grassy hollows for
a place to feed, the lion, returning to his lair,
then sends those two fawns to their hard fate—just so
Odysseus will send those men to their hard fate.   340
By father Zeus, by Athena and Apollo,
would he were as he was in Lesbos! He stood
for a challenge and wrestled Philomeleïdes,
threw him down hard—the Akaians were glad—
so may Odysseus come among the wooers!
They'd enjoy an early death, a bitter wedding!
You beg and ask these things and I will not
swerve from the telling, nor deceive you, but will
tell truly as the Old Man of the Sea told me:*
I'll hide no word from you, conceal nothing.   350

Though I strove to leave Egypt the gods stopped me:
I had not offered them the sacrifices.
Gods always remind us of their commands.
There is an island in the stormy sea
just off Egypt, they call it Pharos. It lies
as far off as a hollow ship sails in
a day with a stiff, following wind.
There's a harbor good for landing, where ships
are launched and good water can be drawn.
The gods held me there twenty days without   360
a wind blowing from the land to speed our ships
onward and forward on the broad back of the sea.
When we had eaten all the food and my men
were weak, a god had pity and saved me—the daughter
of Proteos, the Old Man of the Sea,
Eidothea—for her heart was moved for me.

She met me while I wandered, far from my men
who roamed the island ceaselessly fishing
with bent hooks, for hunger seized their stomachs.*

She stood near me and spoke, saying these words: 370

'Are you a fool, stranger, and very thoughtless?
Or do you hold on to your suffering and like it?
You have stayed long on this island and you can't
find a way to end this while your men lose their courage.'

So she spoke. I answered her with these words:

'I will tell you, as you are a goddess.
I'm held back not of my own will, for I must have
offended the deathless ones who hold the wide sky.
But tell me now, since you gods know all things,
which deathless one binds me in chains from my path,   380
and tell me how to sail home on the fish-full sea.'

So I spoke. The most bright of goddesses said:

'Then I will tell you, stranger, and very truly.
One comes by here, the Old Man of the Sea,
deathless Egyptian Proteos, Poseidon's true
servant who knows the depths of all the seas.
They say he is my father, that he begat me.
If you wait in ambush, you can seize him here
so he'll tell you your path, the length of your journey,
your return home as you sail on the fish-full sea.   390
He'll tell you, Zeus-nourished one, should you wish,
what of good and bad has happened in your palace,
and going home, how long and hard the way.'

So she spoke. Answering her, I said:

'Explain how you will trap an old man, a god,

lest he know of me beforehand, know my aim.
It's hard for a man to overpower a god.'

So I spoke. She most radiant then said:

'Then I will tell you, stranger, and very truly.
When the sun reaches the middle of the sky,   400
the Old Man of the Sea emerges under
Zephyros' breeze, hidden in the wind's dark ripple.
Going from there, he lies down in a hollow cave
with seal pups born of the sea goddess sleeping
around him, breathing out that sharp smell of deep-
sea beds having come out of the gray sea.
I'll lead you there at break of dawn, laying
you down in a row. You must choose well three of
your men, the best from the well-benched ship.
I will tell you all the tricks of that old man.   410
First he will approach the seals and count them.
Looking at them, he'll count them in fives,
then lie down, a shepherd among his flock of sheep.

Then, as soon as you see he's gone to sleep,
mindful of your own vigor and strength, hold him
even when he fiercely strives to escape.
He'll keep on trying to escape, becoming each
kind of beast on earth, even water and fire,
while you, unshaken, grasp him, holding him down.
When he asks you about yourself in words   420
and you see him back in the shape he lay down in,
then free the Old Man from your strong-held grip
and ask which god is angry, blocking your way,
and how you should sail on the fish-full sea.'

So speaking, she dove under the waves of the sea.
I went to my ships on the sandy shore,
many dark thoughts roiling in my mind.

When I reached the sea and ships, we readied
our evening meal, for fragrant night came quickly on.
Then we lay down beside the foaming surf and slept.   430

When early-born, pink-fingered Dawn appeared,
then I went along the shore of the broad sea,
praying to many gods, leading three men,
those I relied on most for any task.

Meanwhile, having dived into the sea's broad lap,
she brought back from the sea the skins of four seals,
all newly flayed. She planned a trick on her father.
Now, having scooped their beds out in the
salty sand, she sat waiting and we came near.
She laid us in a row, a skin fit on each man.   440
This was a most terrible trap, for the stench
of those sea-reared seals oppressed us mightily.
Who would want to lie beside a sea monster?

But she saved us and gave us a great aid. Bringing
ambrosia, she put it under the nose of each,
and the sweet scent destroyed the sea monster stench.
We waited all morning with long-enduring hearts.
The seals came from the sea in throngs and lay
down in a row beside the pounding surf.
At noon the Old Man came forth from the sea and found   450
the fat seals, approached them, counting the number.
He counted us among the first sea monsters
and his heart saw no trap. Then he too lay down.
Springing up we ran toward him and held him down
with our hands. The Old Man forgot not his arts
and tricks but changed first to a thick-maned lion,
and then into a snake, a panther, a giant pig,
then into flowing water, a towering tree.
Steadfast, we held him, our hearts enduring all.

But when the Old Man tired of his deadly shapes,   460
then, speaking these words to me, he asked:

'Atreus' son, which of the gods conspired with you
to ambush me against my will? What do you need?'

So he spoke and I answered him in these words:

'Old Man, don't dodge. You know already what you ask.
I have been kept long on this island and know
no reason why. My heart is dying in my breast.
But now speak you, for you gods know all things.
Which god has chained me here, blocked my path?
Which god keeps me from leaving on the fish-full sea?'   470

So I spoke, and he quickly answered me:

'You greatly offended Zeus and the other gods,
embarking with no sacrifices that would let
you quickly reach your land sailing the purple sea.
For it is not your fate to see your loved ones and
reach your lofty home and fatherland
until you go to Egypt's river, rain-fed from Zeus,
and use the water in holy sacrifices
to the deathless ones who hold the wide sky.
Then they'll give you the homeward path you want.'   480

So he spoke and my very heart broke
because he bid me go back on the shrouded sea
to Egypt, a long and hard way to go.
Even so, with these words I answered him:

'Old Man, as you bid, I will complete these things.
But come now, speak, and tell me truly
whether those Akaians sailed safely home,
those whom Nestor and I left behind at Troy,
or if any found bitter death in their ships

or from friends' hands when they wound down the war.'   490

So I spoke and he, quickly answering, said:

'Atreus' son, why do you ask these things?
You have no need to know this nor learn my mind.
If I speak, you won't be tearless learning all.
For many were slain, many left, but only two
of the bronze-clad Akaian kings perished
on the voyage home. Of the war, you know.
One, yet living, is held back in the wide sea.

Aias perished. His long-oared ships were lost.
First, Poseidon drove him onto the huge   500
rock of Gyrai but saved him from the sea.
Though hated by Athena, he still might have escaped
were it not for his boasting, his foolish shouting:
he said he'd fled the sea's great depths despite the gods.
Poseidon heard his shouting and came with his
huge trident in his hands to that same rock,
Gyrai, where Aias still sat in his reckless folly.
That rock the god split in two. The god
waited until that block toppled into the sea
carrying Aias into the sea's boundless depths.   510
Thus he died, drinking the bitter, briny water.

Your brother escaped death, fleeing in his
hollow ships, for Hera saved him. But just
as he came to Maleia's sheer cliff, a storm
seized his ships and he was driven on
the fish-full sea to the edge of his own land—
the gods had caused a wind change so he reached home.
There Thyestes used to live in his palace,
but now Thyestes' son Aigisthos lives there.
So it seemed he'd have his homecoming unharmed.   520
Rejoicing, he set foot on his native land

and, taking some dirt, kept kissing it, shedding
many hot tears, so glad he was to see his land.
From his lookout an idle watchman saw him land.
Aigisthos had stationed him there, paying him
two talents of gold. He had kept watch a year lest*
the king arrive unnoticed, remembering his strength.
The watchman ran to the palace to tell Aigisthos
who immediately devised a cunning plot.
From his men he took the twenty best and set   530
an ambush where he had a feast laid out.
Then, planning a shameless act, he went by horse
and chariot to fetch King Agamemnon. Knowing
nothing of his ruin, the king was led back
and killed while feasting, as one slays a barn-held ox.
Not one of Agamemnon's men was left, nor any
of Aigisthos' men. They all died in the halls.'

So he spoke and my own heart shattered.
Sitting on the sand, I wept. My spirit now
no longer wished to live or see the sun's dear light.   540
When I had had enough wallowing in my tears,
the Old Man of the Sea told me—and truly—this:

'Atreus' son, no more of this unceasing crying.
We will achieve nothing by this. But quickly
endeavor now to reach again your fatherland.
You'll find Aigisthos living, or, if Orestes
has already slain him, you'll find the funeral feast.'

So he spoke, and my heart and manly spirit,
though still grieving, were warmed again.
Addressing him, I said these winged words: 550

'I know of those two, but you named a third man,
who, yet living, is held back in the wide sea,
or dead: though grieving, I wish to hear of him.'

Thus I spoke. Quickly answering me he said:

'Laertes' son, who had his home in Ithaka,
I saw him weeping big tears on an island,
in the palace of the nymph Kalypso—she who
holds him by force. He can't go to his native land,
having neither oar-ready ships nor men
to carry him over the wide back of the sea.   560

It's not decreed for you, great Menelaos,
to die and meet your fate in horse-grazing Argos.
The gods will send you to the Elysian fields
at world's end, where fair-haired Rhadamanthys is.
There men have an easy life, for there's no snow,
no harsh winter, and no rain, and Zephyros
always sends a clear breeze, raising it up
from Okeanos to refresh men. You'll go there
since Helen connects you to Zeus by marriage.'

Having spoken, he dove into the sea's swells.   570
I went at once back to my ships and godlike men,
many dark thoughts roiling in my mind.

When we were back among our ships by the sea,
there we made our meal and fragrant night came on.
Then we lay down beside the foaming surf and slept.
When early-born, pink-fingered Dawn appeared,
we dragged the ships into the glittering sea,
stepped the mast and raised the ships' sails.
The men sat down at their assigned oarlocks;
they sat in rows, their oars splashing the gray sea.   580
At the Zeus-fed river of Egypt, we anchored the ships
and sacrificed the hecatomb completing our task.
When the ever-living gods had ceased their wrath,
I heaped a mound to Agamemnon's glory.
And after finishing this, we left. The deathless ones

gave me a wind and sent me quickly to my land.

But come now, stay awhile in my palace
until eleven or even twelve days have passed.
I'll send you off well, give you glittering gifts:
three horses and a chariot of polished metal,   590
a lovely cup for the deathless gods' libations
that will remind you of me all your days."

Then wise Telemakos answered him:

"Atreus' son, don't urge me to stay here long,
though I could pass a year sitting beside you.
Nor would longing for home or parents seize me,
for I'd enjoy mightily hearing your words
and tales. But my companions are impatient there
in sacred Pylos, for you've kept me some time here.
Whatever you might give me, let it be as treasure,   600
for I can drive no horses to Ithaka. Keep them
for your own delight. You rule over vast plains,
filled with lush clover and tall sedges,
where wheat and broad-eared barley grow abundantly.
In Ithaka there are no wide tracks nor meadows.
Though lovely, it's more suited for goats than horse grazing,
None of the islands has broad meadows, none is fit
for horses and most unfit of all is Ithaka."

So he spoke. Noble Menelaos then smiled,
caressed his hand and calling out, said: 610

"My child, you are of noble blood that you speak so!
I will exchange these gifts for you because I can.
Great treasures of gifts are stored in my palace.
I'll give you the best and the most esteemed.
I'll give you a well-wrought mixing bowl made all
of silver, with the rim finished off in gold,

like work of Hephaistos. Sidon's king, warrior
Phaidimos, gave me it when he sheltered me
on my return voyage. I give it now to you."

Thus they spoke to one another as the guests   620
came to the palace of the godlike king.
They drove in sheep, brought wine—the joy of men.
Wearing lovely headbands, their bedmates brought the bread.
Thus they worked, preparing the meal in the palace.

Meanwhile in lord Odysseus' grounds, the suitors
enjoyed hurling discus and hunting spears
on level ground with their usual wantonness.
Antinoös was seated with Eurymakos,
the suitors' leaders, far away the best in sports.
Coming near them, Phronios' son Noemon,   630
fastening on Antinoös, said these words:

"Antinoös, do we know for certain when
Telemakos will come back from sandy Pylos?
He left, taking a ship of mine. I need it now
to cross to the broad fields of Elis where twelve mares
are suckling strong yearling mules yet untamed.
I want to pick out one of them to tame."

So he spoke, amazing them! They'd never thought
he'd gone to Neleus' Pylos but was somewhere
here on the estate with the flocks or swineherd!   640

Eupeithes' son Antinoös replied to him:

"Tell me truly: did he go then? What youths
followed him? Selected from those of Ithaka?
Or slaves and freemen? He could have done that.
Tell me plainly so I understand it well.
Did he seize your black ship against your will

or when he asked, did you lend it, a gift?"

Phronios' son Noemon answered him:

"I lent it as a gift. What would any man do
when such a one with cares heavy in his heart   650
asks this? It was hard to refuse giving it.
Those who followed him were the best among
the people after us. In the lead I saw
Mentor embarking, or a god. It seemed like him.
But I wonder. I saw Mentor here yesterday,
at dawn, yet he was on the ship bound for Pylos."

Having spoken, he left for his father's house.
But the bold hearts of both were greatly troubled.
They stopped the games and had the suitors sit.
Eupeithes' son Antinoös addressed them.   660
Troubled, his heart darkened and filled with anger.
His eyes shone as from a fire lit within:

"A great feat was done by that arrogant
Telemakos—the trip we said he'd never take.
In spite of us, the young child went, just like that,
launching the ship, choosing the best crew from town.
Such a beginning will mean trouble later. May Zeus
destroy his strength before he reaches manhood!
But come, give me a fast ship and twenty men
and I'll stand guard and ambush him in the straits   670
between Ithaka and rugged Samos, and thus
his sailing for news of his father will end."

So he spoke and all approved and urged him on.
They stood at once, entering Odysseus' palace.

For a long time Penelope was not aware
of this since the suitors planned it secretly.

Medon the herald told her; he'd learned of the plan
outside in the courtyard while she wove indoors
and at once he took the message into her.

As he crossed the threshold, Penelope said: 680

"Herald, why did the suitors send you here?
To tell the maidservants of lord Odysseus
to stop their work and make ready their feast?
May they woo no more and ever meet elsewhere!
May this be their last feast here—their final feast!
You are often with them, consuming the goods
and wealth of wise Telemakos. Did you all hear
nothing from your fathers when you were young,
among those who bred you, of great Odysseus?
He never did or said anything unjust   690
to the people as many divine kings do:
one man they hate and another they love.
But he did no injustice to any man!
This shows how bad you all are in heart and deed!
There is no kindness for past work done well!"

Then wise Medon replied to her again:

"My queen, would that this were the worst of it.
But much bigger and much more painful is
what the suitors plan—may Zeus prevent this!
They long to kill Telemakos with their sharp swords   700
as he comes home. He went for news of his father
to sandy Pylos and holy Lakedaimonia."

So he spoke. Her knees buckled, her heart broke,
and, speechless, words failed her. Both her eyes
filled with tears, her voice blocked in her chest.
At length, she answered him with these words:

"Herald, why did my child go? He had no need
to board a swift-moving ship, which for men
are horses of the sea, driving through the brine.
Did he want to die nameless among men?"   710

Then wise Medon answered her once more:

"I do not know whether some god stirred him,
or if his heart urged him to go to Pylos to know
of his father's return, or what fate he met."

So he spoke and left, going through the palace.

Life-killing pain poured over her; nor could
she sit on any of the many chairs. She sat
on the raised threshold of the well-made room,*
moaning pitiably. Her handmaids cried
around her, all who were in the house, old and young.   720

Though weeping ceaselessly, Penelope then said:

"Dear ones, Zeus gave me suffering
beyond that of women born and reared with me.
First he killed my noble, lion-hearted spouse,
who surpassed all Danaans in excellence,
that noble man, wide-famed in Hellas and Argos.
Now some storm has taken my dear son from home
with no news and I heard nothing of his going!
Cruel ones! Not one of you had in your mind
a thought to rouse me from bed, though each knew   730
of it when he left in that black hollow ship.
For if I had known he pondered such a journey,
he would have had to stay though longing for the trip,
or left me behind, dying in the palace.
One of you call Dolios now, the old
slave my father gave me when I came.

He tends the garden's many trees. Send him
at once to sit beside Laertes, telling him
these things in hopes that he may weave a plan,
complaining to the people how the suitors now   740
wish to kill the heir of brave Odysseus!"

The dear nurse Eurykleia answered at once:

"My child, kill me with ruthless bronze or let
me stay in the house: I will not hide my thoughts.
I brought him those things that he urged me to,
sweet wine and food. But he made me swear a great oath
of silence until you asked, or the twelfth day had come,
or if you should miss him, or hear of his going
so you would not mar your fair skin with weeping.
But bathe, wrap your body in newly washed clothes.   750
Go to the upper rooms with your handmaids,
pray to Athena, child of aigis-bearing Zeus,
For even from death she can rescue him.
Do not distress the old man with bad news, for I
do not believe the happy gods entirely hate
Arkeisios' offspring. There will be one to rule
this high-roofed palace and the rich, far-flung fields."

So she spoke. Penelope calmed and dried
her eyes. She bathed and wrapped her body in clean clothes,
and went to the upper rooms with her handmaids,   760
placed barley in a basket and prayed to Athena:

"Hear me, aigis-bearing Zeus' child, Atrytone,
if ever good Odysseus burned fat thigh-bones
of ox or sheep to you in his palace,
think of them now for me and save my son.
Ward off the evil arrogance of the suitors!"

So she cried out and the goddess heard her prayer.

The suitors in the shadowy halls were boisterous.
One of the younger, arrogant ones said:

"The queen readies now to wed one of us,   770
knowing nothing of the murder of her son!"

So one spoke, but no one knew what lay ahead.
Then Antinoös spoke, addressing them:

"Fools! Avoid such bold and daring talk
of all kinds lest someone report this inside.
But keep our silence. Let's complete our plan,
the one that had pleased our hearts before."

So then he chose twenty of the best men
and went down to the shore to the swift ship.
First they dragged the ship to the deep water,   780
stepped the mast, put the sails in the black ship,
and they fitted the oars in the leather oarlocks.
When all was ready, up they stretched the white sails.
In high spirits, attendants brought their weapons aboard.
In deep water they moored the ship and then they came
ashore. They had their dinner there, waiting for nightfall.

But she, thoughtful Penelope, lay down
in her high rooms tasting neither food nor drink,
wondering if her son would escape death
or if he would be slain by the lawless suitors.   790
Just as a lion turns, fearful, in a throng
of men as they encircle him in a trap,
so her mind turned until sweet sleep took her.
Lying back, she slept, all her body relaxed.

Then the goddess, bright-eyed Athena, made
a phantom form in the shape of the woman
Iphthime, great-hearted Ikarios' child,
whom Eumelos wed in his home in Pherai.

She sent her to godlike Odysseus' home
to make the weeping, groaning Penelope   800
cease her tears, her weeping and her moaning.
She entered the room through the bolt's thong,*
stood by her head and said these words to her:

"Do you sleep, Penelope, your heart sad?
The gods who live at ease will not let you
grieve or mourn. Your son will yet come home
for he has in no way transgressed the gods."

Penelope, thoughtful, answered then,
slumbering sweetly at the gates of dreaming:

"Why have you come here sister? You have not come   810
often before since your house lies far away.
You bid me cease the pains and sorrows
that keep my heart and mind from rest.
Long ago my lion-hearted spouse died,
he who surpassed all Danaans in excellence,
that noble man wide-famed in Hellas and Argos.
Now my only child's gone in a hollow ship,
foolish, knowing nothing of work and gatherings
of men. I worry more about him than the other.
I tremble, fearing for him lest he suffer among   820
the people where he has gone, or on the sea
among the many men plotting against him,
bent on killing him before he reaches home."

The dark phantom, speaking, answered her:

"Take heart! Do not let fear enter your mind.
He has an escort with him that other men
would pray to have along, for she is strong,
Pallas Athena. She took pity on your weeping
and sent me here to tell you of these things."

Sensible Penelope replied at once: 830

"If you're a god indeed, or have heard a god's voice,
come, tell me of that other miserable one
if he yet lives and sees the light of Helios
or if he died and now is in Hades' house."

The dark phantom, speaking, answered her:

"Of that one I'll not tell you truly if he lives
or died. It's bad to speak words empty as air."

So speaking, she vanished instantly through the bolt
of the door like a breath of wind. Penelope
started up from sleep, her heart made warm   840
by this vivid dream that came in the dark night.

Their hearts plotting the murder of Telemakos,
the suitors boarded and sailed the vast seaway.
There's a rocky island midway in the sea,
small, between Ithaka and rugged Samos,
Asteris, with a double anchorage
where ships can hide. There the Akaians lay in wait.

BOOK FIVE

Council of the Gods
Odysseus and Kalypso; Odysseus departs
Poseidon's storm; Odysseus finds refuge on Skeria

Then Eos left noble Tithonos and their bed
to bring light for the deathless ones and mortal men.
The gods sat in council, high-thundering Zeus
the most powerful among them. Athena,
mindful of Odysseus' sufferings,
thought of him in that nymph's palace and said:

"Father Zeus and you ever-living gods,
let no scepter-bearing king be cheerful, nor good
and mild, nor know right thoughts in his heart!
No, let him be harsh and act unjustly   10
since no one now remembers King Odysseus
who ruled his people like a kindly father.
He's far away, ever suffering in the nymph's
island, in the halls of Kalypso who holds
him back. He cannot return to his homeland
for there's no ship ready for him, no oars, nor crew

to carry him across the sea's wide back.
And now there are those intending to kill his child
as he sails home, he who sailed for news of his father
to Pylos and to sacred Lakedaimonia.   20

Answering her, cloud-gathering Zeus spoke:

"My child, such words escape the fence of your teeth!
Did you yourself not devise this very plan
so that Odysseus might repay the suitors?
Telemakos you sent—your skill did this—
so that unharmed he might return to his own land
and those suitors sail back, nothing accomplished."

Thus he spoke, and then said to his son Hermes:

"Hermes, you in all things are our messenger.
Tell Kalypso my unchangeable plan.   30
Patient Odysseus shall start for home,
neither escorted by the gods nor mortal men,
but suffering alone on a rope-bound raft.
He'll reach fertile Skeria on the twentieth day,
the land of the Phaiakians, godlike men.
They will honor him dearly, like a god,
and they'll send him by ship to his native land
with gifts of bronze and gold and much good clothing,
gifts he would never have carried from Troy even
had he left unharmed with his booty share.   40
His fate is to return home and see his loved ones
and his great, high-roofed palace in his native land."

Thus he spoke. Then Hermes Argos-slayer did
as bid. On his feet he bound his sacred golden
sandals that carried him over the vast seas
and the boundless earth with a breath of wind.
He carried the staff that he used to charm men's eyes

or, when he wished, he roused those drowsing heads again.
He flew, staff in his hand, famed Argos-slayer.
He dropped from sky to Pieria then to the sea,   50
darting over the wave tops like a shearwater
searching in the deadly troughs of the waves in the barren
salt sea, hunting fish, feathers wet with brine.
Hermes was like to it, riding many waves.
But when he reached the faraway island,
he stepped on shore and left the deep blue sea.
He walked until he reached a large cave. The nymph,
the fair-haired one, lived there and he found her inside.

A large fire burned on the hearth with kindled thyme
and easily-split cedar whose scents carried across   60
the island. Inside she was singing prettily
while weaving, plying the loom's golden shuttle.
Trees grew thick around the cave: alder
and black poplar and sweet-scented cypress.
Birds with long wings roosted there: small horned owls
and hawks, and long-tongued cormorants, seabirds,
for all their feasting comes from the sea.
Just there, around the hollow cave, well-kept
vines were spreading, laden with clusters of grapes.
Four springs bubbled forth, flowing with clear water,   70
near each other but flowing in different directions.
And there were soft meadows teeming with violets
and wild parsley. Even a god coming here *
on seeing it would marvel, his heart well pleased.

Standing there, the Argos-slayer beheld the view.
When he had gazed at it to his heart's content,
he went straight into the broad cave. Nor did she fail
to know him, Kalypso, brightest of goddesses,
for the immortal gods are not unknown to one
another even if they live far away.   80

He did not find Odysseus there for he
sat weeping in his usual spot on the headland.
His heart was breaking as he, weeping with tears
and groans, gazed on the barren sea.

Then Kalypso, brightest of goddesses, asked Hermes,
having seated him in a polished chair:

"Why have you come holding your golden staff, Hermes?
I respect you, but you have never come here before.
Tell me what you have in mind and I will do it,
if I can and if it must come to pass.   90
First come with me so I can treat you as a guest."

Having spoken, she set a table by him, gave him
ambrosia and mixed red nectar for him.*
Argos-slayer, the messenger, then ate and drank.
When he had feasted and satisfied himself with food,
he answered her speaking these words:

"You ask, goddess, what brings me, a god, here.
I'll tell the truth to you, for you command it.
Zeus ordered me to come though I wished not to.
Who would willingly cross such a vast salt sea?   100
There's no town of mortals near, and no holy
offerings to the gods, no choice sacrifices.
It is not possible for any god to thwart
or to evade the will of aigis-bearing Zeus.
He says a man is here, most miserable of men,
one who fought nine years around Priam's city.
In the tenth year they sacked the citadel and
embarked for home. When leaving they outraged Athena
who raised a strong storm and tall waves against them.*
Then all his men perished, he alone survived,*   110
and those same winds and waves brought him here.
Now Zeus commands that you send him off at once!

His lot is not to die far from his loved ones. No,
his fate is to arrive home to his native land
and see his loved ones and his high-roofed palace."

Thus he spoke. The goddess Kalypso shivered
and addressed him, speaking with winged words:

"You gods are cruel, jealous far beyond others!
You envy goddesses when we openly
make a mortal our regular bedmate!   120
When pink-fingered Dawn chose Orion,
you gods in your easy life envied her,
until chaste Artemis slew him with her painless
arrows in the island of Ortygia.
Or when fair-haired Demeter yielded to
Iasion, mingling in love, making a bed
in fallow land thrice-plowed—but Zeus was told!*
He hurled his bright thunderbolt killing him.
So now the gods envy me for this mortal man!
I saved him when he was wrapped around the keel   130
alone, once Zeus had hurled his bright thunderbolt
into the purple sea splitting the swift ship.
There all his noble companions perished,
but wind and waves bore him near this land.
I loved and nourished him and I began to speak
of making him immortal and ageless through all time.
But it's not possible for any god to thwart
or to evade the will of aigis-bearing Zeus.
Let him die on the barren sea if Zeus urges,
nay orders it! But I will not send him away!   140
For there is no ship ready for him, no oars, no crew
who might carry him across the sea's wide back.
I will give him good advice, hiding nothing,
so he may return to his native land unharmed."

Messenger Argos-slayer answered her:

"Send him away now respectful of Zeus' wrath,
lest he hold a grudge and be angry with you."

Thus the Argos-slayer spoke and then he left.
The nymph went to find Odysseus,
for she had taken to heart the message of Zeus.   150
She found him sitting on the headland, his eyes
wet from tears, sweet life draining out of him,
wanting to leave since the nymph no longer pleased him.
He spent the nights beside her through necessity,
not wanting her though she wanted him.
By day he sat on the rocks and by the shore
rending his heart with tears and groans and woes,
ever looking over the barren sea, tears flowing.
The radiant goddess came near and said this:

"Miserable one, stop grieving! Don't waste your life this way!   160
For now with kindness I will send you on your way.
But come! With a bronze axe cut the tall trees
for a wide raft; build a half-deck on it
so it can bear you over the shadowy sea.
I shall give food and water and red wine,
enough that they will keep your hunger at bay!
I'll wrap you in clothes and send a following wind
so you may reach your native land unharmed,
if the gods who hold the wide sky wish it so,
for they are stronger both in knowing and doing."   170

Thus she spoke and much-enduring Odysseus
shivered and with these winged words began to speak:

"What are you planning, goddess? Not my return voyage
if you tell me to cross the sea's wide gulf by raft.
That's hard and terrible! Not even good swift ships

rejoicing in a following wind from Zeus could cross it!
I will not set foot on a raft without your favor,
goddess, unless you swear to me a strong oath
that you will plan no other evil thing for me."

Thus he spoke. The shining goddess Kalypso smiled;   180
her hands caressed him as she spoke his name and said:

"You are a rogue, but not without some knowledge
that you should come to say such words to me.
Be it known on earth and the wide sky above,
and the down-flowing stream of Styx, the greatest,
most terrible oath the happy gods have,
I do not plan any evil or pain for you.
What I have in mind, what I plan, is what
I would plan for myself were I in need.
I have a mind that's fair, and towards you   190
my heart is merciful, not made of iron."

Having spoken, the goddess led him away
swiftly and he followed in the god's foot tracks.
They reached her hollow cave, goddess and man.
Seating him on the same chair Hermes had just
sat on, the nymph placed good food beside him
to eat and drink, food mortal men eat.
Then she sat opposite godlike Odysseus.
Beside her, maids placed ambrosia and nectar.
They reached their hands out for the ready food.   200

But when they'd satisfied desire for food and drink,
Kalypso, bright goddess, began with these words:

"Zeus-born Laertes' son, artful Odysseus,
do you in fact wish to go homeward to your
native land now? If so, you can be happy!
If your heart knew what's in your destiny

before you reach your land, such pains will fill you!
But staying here with me you could guard this house,
become immortal, though you'd yearn to see
your bedmate, she whom you long for all your days.   210
In truth I claim to be no worse than her in form
or height since it is not likely for mortals
to vie with immortals in looks or shape."

Odysseus then spoke, answering her:

"Lady Kalypso, hold no anger at me! I know
that in all ways good Penelope
is less than you in both looks and form.
She is merely mortal, you deathless and ageless.
But what I wish for, long for all my days,
is home, to see the day of my return!   220
Though a god might shatter my ship in the dark sea,
I will endure it in my breast, patient in pain!
I have already suffered much in seas
and war. After those, let come what comes."

Thus he spoke. The sun set and night fell.
The two of them went to a corner in the cave
lying side by side, enjoying then their loving.

When early-born, pink-fingered Dawn appeared,
Odysseus put on his tunic and cloak.
The nymph dressed in an elegant, finely-woven   230
white robe, fastened a well-wrought golden belt around
her waist and draped a light shawl over her head.
Planning how Odysseus might leave, she handed
him a great bronze axe, both blades sharp-edged
and fitted for the hand. The well-carved haft
was made of fine-grained olive wood. And then
she gave him a well-polished adze and led him down
a path to the island's far side where ancient

trees grew tall: alder, black poplar, and sky-tall fir,
dry and well-seasoned to float him lightly on the sea. 240

Once she'd shown him where the tall trees grew,
Kalypso, shining goddess, went back to her palace.
Meanwhile he felled the timber, finishing quickly.
Twenty trees he felled and shaped them with his axe,
smoothing them with skill, making the timber straight.
Then Kalypso, shining goddess, brought an auger.
He drilled through the pieces and fit them each to each.
To hold the raft together, he pounded in pegs.
Just as a man trained in the skills of carpentry
shapes the wide bottom of a merchant ship, 250
just so did great Odysseus construct his raft.
Having set the boards, he fitted them with ribs
placed close. Then he added the long planks.
He stepped the mast and fit yardarms into it
and made the steering oar to sail the raft straight.
He caulked the raft throughout with reed matting
to make it watertight and piled in brush as ballast.
Kalypso, shining goddess, brought him cloth then
to make the sail, and he tied it with great care.
On the yardarms he tied reefing and sheeting ropes, 260
and then he levered the raft down to the sacred sea.

Four days he worked and then all was done.
Kalypso sent him off on the fifth day.
She'd dressed him in clean clothes that smelled of thyme.
She poured him a wineskin filled with dark wine
and a large skin of water. She gave him tasty well-
cooked food placed in a leather bag.
She sent him a mild but steady following wind.
Odysseus, glad, spread the sail to catch the wind.
With skill he set the steering oar straight, 270
and sat, but sleep did not fall on his eyelids.

He saw the Pleiades and the sinking Ploughman
and the She Bear, which they call the Wagon,
who forever turned, watches for Orion.
She alone does not bathe in Okeanos.*
Kalypso ordered him to keep the She Bear
to his left as he sailed across the sea.
Seventeen days he sailed on the wide sea.
On the eighteenth, shadowy mountains appeared,
Phaiakian land where it lay nearest to him.   280
A bright shield it seemed, flat in the murky sea.

Returning from the Aithiopians, from
the mountains of the Solymoi, Poseidon spied
him sailing on the sea. His heart was enraged!
He shook his head and then said to himself:

"While I was in Aithiopia, how can
the gods have changed my plans about Odysseus?
He's near Phaiakian land! Once he's there, his fate
is to escape the suffering he now endures.
But I'm still going to fill him with yet more pain!"   290

As he spoke he stirred up clouds and sea
with his trident. He stirred up a whirlwind,
all sorts of winds, and used the clouds to hide
the land and the dark sea as night dropped from the sky.
Winds from the east and south collided. The harsh west wind
and the sky-born north wind rolled up huge waves.

Odysseus' knees went slack, his heart froze.
Angry, he spoke to his ever-stalwart spirit:

"Oh miserable me! And what will happen now?
I fear the goddess spoke the truth to me   300
when she said that before I returned home
I'd be filled with pain; now that is coming true.

Zeus has filled full the wide sky with clouds
and stirred up the sea. The storm rages fiercely
with all sorts of winds. Certain death for me!
Thrice happier those Danaans, four times, those killed
in Troy's wide plains, a favor for Atreus' sons.
If only I had died there and there met my death
on that day near dead Peleus' son, when many*
Trojans hurled their bronze tipped spears at me!   310
That death would have brought me fame and funeral gifts!
Now a miserable death will be my lot!"

So speaking, huge waves crashed down on him,
terrible and swift, spinning the raft around.
He fell far from the raft, the steering oar
torn from his hands. The mast had broken in half.
The storm drove fiercely. Winds came from all directions!
The sail and yardarms plunged into the sea.
He was held long under water, nor could
he quickly surface from the onrush of such fierce waves.   320
The clothes Kalypso had given him weighed him down.
At last he broke the surface, his mouth spat out bitter
salt brine and it streamed down from his head.
Though weak, Odysseus did not forget the raft.
He made a dash for it in the waves and caught hold,
and he sat in the middle, dodging death's end.
Huge waves bore it down the current this way and that.
Just as when the north wind in late summer carries
thistles along the plain, the bunches sticking together,
so the winds carried the raft in the sea this way and that.   330
The south wind hurled it up, the north wind drove it back.
And the east wind made way for the west wind to chase it.

Ino Leukothea of the lovely ankles,
Kadmos' daughter, saw him. She once was mortal,
but now she was a goddess in the open sea.

She pitied Odysseus as he wandered in pain.
Like a shearwater in flight she rose from the brine
and sat down on the raft and said to him:

"Poor man! Why does Poseidon earth-shaker
hate you so terribly, causing you such pain?   340
He cannot kill you however much he wishes to.
So do what I say since you don't seem a fool.
Take off your clothes! Abandon your raft to the winds!
Use your strength and swim! Make for the land
of the Phaiakians! You will get free of danger!
Take this immortal shawl, spread it beneath your chest*
and have no fear that you will suffer or be killed.
But as soon as your hands feel dry land
untie it and throw it into the purple sea,
as far as you can, then turn your face away."   350

As she was speaking the goddess gave him the shawl,
and she dipped back into the surging sea
like a shearwater and the dark waves hid her.

Much enduring Odysseus again doubted,
and angry, he spoke to his own stalwart spirit:

"I fear one of the immortals weaves a trap
since she commands me to abandon my raft.
I will not do it yet, since far off with my
own eyes I saw land that looked like a refuge.
So this will I do and it seems best to me.   360
As long as the timbers stay in their fastenings,
that long I'll wait and endure, though suffering.
But should a giant wave smash through the raft
I will swim unless I think of something better."

While he pondered thus in his breast and mind,
Poseidon earth-shaker stirred up a frightening wave,

and, hanging over him, it drove down on the raft.
Just as the stormy wind blows through dry-parched
heaped-up chaff, then scatters it this way and that,
just so the raft's long timbers were scattered. But he   370
Odysseus rode one as a man rides a horse!
He peeled off the clothes Kalypso had given him.
At once he wrapped the shawl around his chest
and dropped into the sea face down, hands outstretched,
eager to swim. But lord Earth-shaker saw him
and shook his head, speaking to himself in anger:

"So! Now suffer much! Wander on the sea
until you should mingle with men, Zeus' children!
I hope you do not think I gave you too much pain!"

Having spoken, he whipped his long-maned horses   380
and arrived in Aigas, site of his splendid palace.
But Athena, maiden divine, had other plans.
She calmed the paths of all the other winds,
stopping them and ordering them to sleep.
She roused the north wind and broke the waves in front
of him so he might know the oar-loving
Phaiakians and thus avoid the doom of death.

Two nights and two days on the mighty wave
he drifted, feeling a foreboding of his death.
But when fair-haired Dawn brought the third morning,   390
the wind then dropped and all became calm
with the wind's pause. Lifted by a huge
wave, he saw very clearly land was near.
Just as a father's life appears to children
as he lies a long time wasting away, diseased
and in sharp pain—some evil god causing it—
then glad are they when the gods free him from doom,
just so Odysseus welcomed the land and woods.

He swam, eager to walk upon dry land.
But he was far away, well out of shouting range.
He heard the sea thudding against the sea-washed rocks.   400
The surf roared, crashing fiercely against the land,
a fearful noise and all was covered in briny foam.
There were no harbors or other shelter for ships,
only headlands jutting out and sea-washed crags.

Odysseus' knees went slack, his heart froze.
Angry, he spoke to his ever-stalwart spirit:

"Now that Zeus lets me see land I had not hoped for,
now that I have swum across this wide gulf,
still I see no way out from the gray salt water.   410
Just there the crags are sharp, waves roar around them.
And there the waves dash against sheer cliffs!
Close to the shore the sea's deep, no place for me
to stand on both feet to avoid this death!
If I try to climb out I fear a wave will seize me
and throw me hard against those sheer cliffs!
Any effort of mine would be useless here.
If I swim on seeking a bay or sheltered beach,
I fear a whirlwind may snatch me up again,
and carry me groaning back to the fish-full sea.   420
Or a god may set some huge sea monster on me
from the deep brine, one Amphitrite nourished,
for I well know how much the Earth-shaker hates me."

While he pondered this in his heart and mind
the great wave drove him on a jagged headland.
His skin would've been stripped off there, his bones smashed,
if bright-eyed Athena had not warned him!
With both hands he grabbed hold of the crag
and kept holding until the wave slipped past.
So he escaped though it rushed seaward again,   430

striking mightily and hurling him into the sea.
Just as when an octopus is dragged from its
own lair, its suckers clinging to some pebbles,
just so the rocks stripped away the skin
from both his hands and the huge wave engulfed him.
Odysseus would have died there—though not his fate—
had Athena not given him forewarning.
Having surfaced behind the waves roaring landward,
he swam along the shore, an eye on land, to find
some beach or bay sheltered from the sea.   440
As he swam, he came upon the mouth of a
swiftly flowing river. It seemed the best place,
free of rocks and sheltered from the wind.
At once he knew it for a river and prayed:

"Hear my prayers, god, whoever you are! I pray,
fleeing from the sea and great Poseidon's wrath!
You deathless gods are worthy of respect
from men who come wandering as I am now!
After such trials, I pray to you and to this stream!
Now, god, pity me your suppliant!"   450

Thus he spoke. The river god stopped the stream,
held back the wave, calmed the water and made him safe
in the river. His knees buckled, his strong hands dropped.
Even his heart had been battered by the salt sea.
His body was swelling and much seawater gushed
from his mouth and nose. He was breathless, voiceless.
He lay there weak, a dreadful fatigue subduing his heart.

When he had caught his breath and gathered his thoughts,
he loosened the shawl, freeing it from his chest.
Then he threw it in the ocean-flowing stream   460
and a wave bore it downstream where Ino took it
with her kind hands. Shaking, he turned from the river
and fell and kissed the wheat-growing land.

Angry, he spoke to his ever-stalwart spirit:

"What will I suffer now? How will this end?
If I stay by the river through the miserable night,
I fear a bad frost together with a moist dew
may make an end of me in my weak state,
when the cold wind blows from the river at dawn!
If I climb up the hill into the thick woods,   470
and lie down in the dense bushes, though free
from frost, worn out I'd fall into a heavy sleep.
I fear being hunted, a feast for some wild beast!"

Thinking of this, the latter seemed better to him.
He walked into the woods and found, near the water,
an open spot underneath two olive bushes
that grew from the same spot, one wild, one fruit-bearing.
There the force of the wet wind did not blow,
nor did the rays of the shining sun pierce,
nor did rain penetrate so thick the two grew,   480
branches overlapping. These Odysseus
crept under. He made a wide bed for himself,
scraping up a mass of fallen leaves,
enough to protect two or three men
in winter even if it blew very hard.
The sight of this made Odysseus glad. He heaped
a mound of leaves in the middle of his bed.
Just as one keeps an ember in black ashes
living in a lonely spot with no near neighbors
to save the spark of fire—no other place to find   490
a flame—just so Odysseus hid in the leaves.
Athena poured a sleep over his eyes that closed
his eyelids and ceased his heavy weariness.

BOOK SIX

Nausikaa and her maids at the river
Meeting of Odysseus and Nausikaa
Nausikaa leads Odysseus to town

So he slept, much-enduring Odysseus,
a weary, exhausted sleep. But Athena
entered the land and town of the Phaiakians
who once had lived in spacious Hypereia
near the Cyclopes, those arrogant men, stronger and
more powerful, who used to attack them.
Then godlike Nausithoös made them leave, led them
to Skeria, far from men who eat grain.
He drove the building of walls and houses, and then temples
for the gods, and then allotted tillable land.*   10
At last, taken by fate, he went to Hades' house.
Now Alkinoös ruled, skilled in the gods' ways.
To his house she went, bright-eyed Athena,
planning the homeward voyage for Odysseus.

She went to the richly wrought bedroom where
Nausikaa slept, Alkinoös' daughter,

her shape and form like to the immortal gods.*
Two maids were there, in beauty like to the Graces,
on each side of the doorposts. The polished door was shut.
Like a breath of wind she rushed to the girl's bed.   20
She stood at the head of the bed and spoke to her,
appearing as Dymas' daughter, he famed for ships;
she was of like age and had pleased her.
Having thus appeared, bright-eyed Athena said:

"Nausikaa, so messy? Does your mother know?
Your best clothes lie there neglected by you!
You're near the marrying age so you must dress well
and provide for those who will lead you away.
Do this and rumor will run among men,
and your father and lady mother will rejoice!   30
Let's go to wash these clothes when dawn first breaks!
I will go with you and help so the washing
will go faster! You won't be unmarried much longer!
Already the best of our people are courting you,
the best of all Phaiakians of your own race.
Rouse your father at dawn and have him prepare
the mules and a wagon to carry the clothes
and dresses, the robes and the good rugs, and you
yourself go in it, much better than by foot.
The good washing pools are far away from town."   40

Having spoken thus, bright-eyed Athena went
toward Olympos, the gods' ever-safe abode,
they say. Never is it blown by wind, nor soaked
by rain. Snow comes not near, but mild clear skies,
cloudless, dance there with a white radiance.
Here the happy gods rejoice all the days.
There she went, having spoken to the girl.

At once fair-throned Dawn came and woke

Nausikaa. Marveling at her dream, she went
quickly through the palace to tell her parents,   50
her dear father and mother. She found them inside.
Her mother sat by the hearth with her women
twisting sea-purple yarn. Coming through
the door, she met her father going to council.
The Phaiakian lords had bid him come.
Standing close, she began to ask her father:

"Papa, could you have the wagon prepared for me,
the high one with well-oiled wheels, so I can take
those dirty clothes piled there to wash them in
the river? And you yourself being foremost,   60
you must have spotless clothes to lead the council.
Five dear sons, you know, were born in these halls,
two are married, three unmarried in their prime.
They always wish to wear clothes newly washed
when they go dancing. It is my duty to do this."

Thus she spoke, too ashamed to speak of her
wedding day, but he understood and said:

"Of course you can take the mules and anything else.
Go! I'll have the men prepare a tall wagon
with good wheels and a fitted carrying basket."   70

So speaking, he gave the orders and the men obeyed.
They brought the mules to the side of the wagon,
led them under the yoke and hooked them to the wagon.
The girl carried the fine clothes from her bedroom
and piled the clothing in the well-polished wagon.
Her mother filled a chest with cooked meats and all
sorts of good food, and poured wine into
a goatskin wine bag. The girl climbed on the wagon.
Her mother gave her a golden flask with fine
olive oil so she and her maids could oil   80

their skin. Nausikaa set off with whip and reins,
lashing the mules to drive them. The wagon rattled on.
They ran at full stride, bearing the clothes and girl,
not alone, but with her maids following.

When they came to the clear current of the river
with washing troughs that never fail to flow—
water flowed under and cleansed the dirty clothes—
they unhooked the mules from the wagon
and drove them on along the eddying river
to graze the honey-sweet grass. From the wagon   90
they carried the clothes by hand to the pure water
and trod on them competing with each other.
When they had cleaned them and washed out all
the stains, they stretched them out along the shore
where the sea washed small pebbles onto the land.
Then they bathed and rubbed on fragrant olive oil
and lunched on the high ground by the river.
The clothes they left to dry in the sun's warm rays.
Once they'd enjoyed the food, the servants tossed
their veils off and began to play with a ball,   100
and white-armed Nausikaa led them in it.
When Artemis the Archer ranges the mountains,
on lofty Mount Taÿgetos or Erymanthos,
and delights in the boar and swift deer,
the nymphs and maids of aigis-bearing Zeus join her
to play in the wild. Then Leto's heart rejoices.
Artemis holds her head above them all.
Even among those beauties she is easily known:
just so the unwed maid stood out from her servants.

When they were just about to turn homeward,   110
about to yoke the mules and fold the clean clothes,
the goddess, bright-eyed Athena, decided
to rouse Odysseus to see this dazzling girl

who would lead him to the Phaiakian town.
Just then the princess tossed the ball to a servant
but she threw wild. The ball fell into a deep pool.
At this all the girls shrieked. Odysseus awoke.
Sitting up, he pondered in his mind and heart:

"Oh, no! Have I come to the land of some mortals?   120
And are they arrogant, wild, not civilized?
Or stranger-loving and their minds god-fearing?
It seems I'm surrounded by the high cries of girls,
of nymphs, those who dwell in the sheer peaks of mountains,
the source of rivers and the grassy meadows.
Or among those who speak with a human voice?
But get up! I should find this out for myself."

Odysseus crept from under the bushes.
His strong hands broke off a leafy sapling from the
dense growth and held it skin-close, shielding his manhood.   130
He set out as a mountain lion goes on his way,
strength-proud, through rain and wind, both eyes burning.
But when it comes upon oxen or sheep,
or upon some wild deer, its stomach rules
and it goes after the flock, even within a fold.
Just so Odysseus, stark naked, was about
to mingle with these well-groomed girls: need drove him.*
To them he looked frightful, disfigured from the sea.
They fled, scattering along the curving riverbank.
Alkinoös' daughter alone stood still.   140
Athena emboldened her heart, stripped away the fear.
She stood opposite him. Odysseus wondered
whether to beg, grasping the pretty girl's knees,*
or to stand back from her, speaking in honeyed words,
hoping she might point out the town and give him clothes.
It seemed to him better, more prudent, to plead
with honeyed words, standing far back from her

lest grasping her knees he offend the girl.
And so with crafted, honeyed words he spoke:

"O queen, I beg you. Are you goddess or mortal?   150
If one of the gods who hold the wide heavens,
I think you're Artemis, great Zeus' daughter!
You seem most like her in stature and form!
If you are mortal, of those who dwell on the earth,
thrice blessed are then your father and lady mother,
thrice blessed your brothers. Their hearts must be
always happy, gladdened as they are by you,
seeing such a young sprout going to a dance!
He whose bride price wins you, he beyond others
has the happiest heart and leads you to his home!   160
My eyes have never seen such a one as you,
not man nor woman! Beholding you, awe stuns me!

But once on Delos, by Apollo's altar,
I saw such a sapling of a palm tree growing.
Many of my men went there following me,
the expedition was hard and cost me much pain.
Just as I marveled then at that fine sapling—
since such a tree had never grown up from the earth—
thus woman, I marvel at you and fear, dreading
to grasp your knees though I am in dire need.   170
Just yesterday after twenty days did I
escape the dark sea! A rushing wave and violent
storm carried me from Ogygia. Some god cast me
here to suffer. I don't imagine it will stop,
but yet the gods in the past have done such things.
Queen, please pity me. I've suffered much and I
came to you first! I know no one and nothing of
the men who hold this land and its town.
Show where the town is, give me rags to wear,
if you brought some rags when you came here.   180

May the gods give you what your heart desires—
husband and home—and grant you harmony,
a noble thing. There's nothing better and stronger than this:
than when a man and woman live in harmony
and share a home, enjoying their lives. Their well-wishers
feel joy and those who hate them suffer much."

White-armed Nausikaa spoke in reply:

"Stranger, you seem neither a bad man nor foolish.
Zeus himself deals out fortune to all mankind,
to the good and the bad, to each one as   190
he wishes. And if he gave you these, you must endure.
Now since you have come to our land and town,
you will lack neither clothing nor other things
fit for a weary suppliant coming to us.
I shall show you the town, tell you our name.
Phaiakians hold and own this land and town.
I am daughter of great-hearted Alkinoös. On him
depend the strength and power of the Phaiakians."

Thus she spoke and bid her well-groomed handmaids:

"Stop now, girls. Why do you flee at seeing a man?   200
Surely you do not think he is hostile?
There is no mortal, nor will there ever be,
who can come to the land of the Phaiakians
bringing war because the gods watch over us.
We live at great distance in the far-surging sea,
isolated, and have no mixing with other mortals.
But this poor wanderer has come here to us;
now we must care for him, for all guests and beggars
are from Zeus, and kindness is a gift, small*
and dear. So give the guest meat and drink, my servants,   210
and bathe him in the river sheltered from the wind."

Her words stopped the maids. They called to one another
and sat Odysseus down in a sheltered spot
as Nausikaa, Alkinoös' daughter, had ordered.
They put clothes beside him, a tunic and a cloak,
and gave him the golden flask of olive oil,
telling him to wash in the river's current.

But then Odysseus addressed the servants:

"Handmaids, step away so I myself
may scrub the brine from my shoulders and rub myself   220
with olive oil. It's long since this skin has felt oil.
I am ashamed to wash myself in front of you
and be naked among such well-groomed girls."

So he spoke. They left and spoke to their lady.
In the river Odysseus washed off the caked brine
which completely covered his broad back and shoulders.
From his head he washed the salt from the barren sea.
When he had cleaned all and rubbed himself with rich oil,
he donned the clothes the unwed girl had given him.
Then Athena, born from Zeus, made him appear   230
taller and stronger, and down from his head
she let fall dark curls like a hyacinth blossom.
Just as a man hammers gold on silver with skill,
one taught all sorts of arts by Hephaistos and
Athena so that he makes finely crafted works,
just so the curls fell gracefully from head to shoulders.
Walking along the shore, he sat down alone,
dazzling in grace and handsome; the girl marveled at him.
Then she spoke to her well-groomed handmaids:

"Hear me white-armed girls! I'll tell you a strange thing!   240
This man's coming to meet the Phaiakians was not
against the gods' will, those who hold Olympos.
Earlier I thought him rather shabby,

but now he's like the gods who hold the wide sky.
If only such a man might be called my husband
and live here, and be content dwelling here!
Now girls, give this guest both meat and drink!"

So she spoke. They heard her clearly and obeyed,
putting the meat and drink beside Odysseus.
Noble Odysseus then ate and drank with zest—   250
it had been a long time since his last meal.

Then white-armed Nausikaa had a new thought.
She had them put the folded clothes into the wagon.
They yoked the strong-hoofed mules and she climbed up.
She roused Odysseus, calling and speaking these words:

"Up now, stranger, we're going to town! I will take you
to the halls of my father, skilled in peace. I think
you'll meet there all the best Phaiakians.
But do as I say—you don't seem foolish.
As long as we're among the tilled fields of men,   260
follow quickly behind the mules and wagon
with my servants and I will lead the way.
Then we'll reach the town. High towers surround it
and there's a pretty harbor on each side.
The entrance way is narrow, with ships drawn up along
the road and there's a slip for every ship.
The meeting place is there, with quarried stones embedded
on both sides, next to Poseidon's temple.
And there they store their gear for the black ships:
the cables and the sails and the sharp oars.   270
For the Phaiakians care not for bow and quiver,
but for sails, ship's oars and well-balanced ships
with which, exulting, they cross the vast sea.
I shun their rude speech lest they chide me later.
Among the people there are those who are arrogant.

Meeting us, one of the worst might speak thus:

'Who is this with Nausikaa, this big handsome
stranger? Where did she find him? Will he be her husband?
Or has she picked up some wanderer from off a ship,
from men far off, since there are none who dwell close by?   280
Or did some god at last answer her long prayers
and come down from the sky to keep her for all days?
It's better if she goes and finds a husband from
elsewhere for she insults those among our people
who court her, true Phaiakians and wellborn.'

Thus will they speak and I will feel their rebuke.
I would resent any other girl who might
do such a thing against her parents' will,
befriending some man before a public wedding.
So stranger, you must heed all my words so that   290
my father will give you escort to return home.
You'll come to Athena's poplar grove
near the road. A spring flows there within a meadow.
It's as far from the town as a shout carries.
Sit and wait there for a while. Give us time
to get within the town and reach my father's palace.
When you think we have arrived at the palace,
then go into the Phaiakian town and ask
for the home of my father, great Alkinoös.

It's well known, even a child could lead you.   300
No other Phaiakian home is built like it,
the palace of the warrior-king Alkinoös.
Once you are inside the courtyard and buildings
pass through the large halls until you reach
my mother. She sits by the hearth in firelight
spinning sea-purple yarn, a marvel to see, her chair
leaning against a pillar, a maid behind her.

My father's throne is near her and there he sits
and drinks his wine, just like some deathless one.
Walk past him and throw your hands around the knees   310
of my mother and you might learn your happy
return, and soon, though your land be far away.
If in her heart she thinks kind thoughts about you,
then you have hope of seeing your friends, reaching
your well-built home and seeing your native land."

Thus speaking, she lashed the mules with the
oiled whip and left the flowing river.
The mules galloped along with hoofs prancing.
She whipped the mules with cautious care so those on foot
could keep up, the maids and Odysseus.   320
The sun was setting when they reached the holy grove
sacred to Athena. Odysseus sat down there.
At once he prayed to the daughter of great Zeus:

"Atrytone, child of aigis-bearing Zeus,
hear me now, since when cast away before
you heard me not, when Poseidon wrecked my ship!
Let me seem to the Phaiakians a friend to pity!"

He spoke in prayer and Pallas Athena heard him,
but she did not appear to him, respecting
her father's brother who still raged furiously at   330
Odysseus till he should reach his native land.

BOOK SEVEN

Odysseus reaches the palace of King Alkinoös
Odysseus in the palace of the Phaiakian king
King Alkinoös agrees to convey Odysseus to Ithaka

Thus he prayed, much-enduring Odysseus,
as the strong mules bore the girl to the town.
When she arrived at her father's famous palace,
she paused by the gateway where both her brothers
stood like the deathless ones. They loosed the mules
from the wagon and carried the clothes within.
The girl went to her chamber. Her nurse had kindled a fire,
the old woman Eurymedousa from Apeire,
where she'd been seized, taken away on swift ships,
picked as Alkinoös' prize, for he ruled all   10
Phaiakians. They obeyed him as a god.
She'd raised white-armed Nausikaa in the halls.
Now she built the fire and prepared her dinner.

Odysseus then set out for the town. Athena,
caring for him, poured a dense mist about him
lest some fearless Phaiakians meet him

and taunt him with words, enquiring who he was.
But when he was about to enter the fair town,
there the goddess met him, bright-eyed Athena,
formed like a young maiden standing in front of him   20
holding a pitcher. Odysseus asked her:

"My child, won't you lead me to the house of the man
Alkinoös who rules this land, these men?
For I, a much-tried stranger, have come here from
a distant foreign land and thus I know no one
who lives in this town and works these choice fields."

To him in turn she spoke, bright-eyed Athena:

"Father stranger, the house that you ask me about
I'll show you since it's near where my good father lives.
But come in silence. I myself will show the way.   30
Do not look in men's eyes or ask them anything.
They do not tolerate strangers very well,
nor give friendly greetings to anyone who comes.
They only trust in their swift ships, nimbly crossing
vast seas. The Earth-shaker gave them these ships
and they fly as swiftly as feathers do or thoughts."

Having spoken, Pallas Athena quickly led
and he followed in the foot tracks of the god.
The Phaiakians famed for ships, did not
see him going through the town because fair-haired   40
Athena did not allow it. Caring for him,
she kept a divine mist densely over him.
The harbors and hollow ships amazed him,
the warriors' meeting spots, the long, lofty walls
with palisades on top, marvelous to see.

But when he reached the palace of the famous king
the goddess said these words to him, bright-eyed Athena:

"Father stranger, this is the house you asked me to
show you. There you will find kings dear to Zeus
taking their evening meal. Go now inside and have   50
no fear. A bold man proves to be best
in all things though he comes from far lands.
Go first to the lady mistress in the great halls,
Arete is her given name, and she was born
from the same stock as King Alkinoös.
Nausithoös was born of Poseidon
and lovely Periboia, best among women,
youngest daughter of heroic Eurymedon
who at one time ruled the arrogant Giants.*
He destroyed his people and destroyed himself.   60
Poseidon coupled with her and produced a child,
great-hearted Nausithoös, who ruled in Phaiakia.*
He fathered Rhexenor and Alkinoös.

Silver-bowed Apollo slew Rhexenor,
newly-wed and son-less, leaving only
a girl child, Arete, whom Alkinoös wed.
He honored her beyond all women on earth,
more than any who manages a man's home.
Thus she was—and is—honored in their hearts
by her loving children, by Alkinoös himself,   70
and by the people, who, seeing her, welcome her
like a god, cheering when she walks through town.
She lacks nothing in thought or nobleness.
She quells quarrels of those she respects, even men's.
And yes, if she thinks of you kindly in her heart,
you may then hope to see once more your dear friends
and high-roofed home and to reach your native land."

Speaking thus, bright-eyed Athena left, going
across the barren sea. She left fair Skeria,
and went to Marathon and to Athens' wide ways,   80

entering Erektheus' fine house. Odysseus
walked toward Alkinoös' famed palace; he kept
stopping and thinking until he reached the bronze threshold.

Light glowed from the high-roofed palace of great-hearted
Alkinoös like the light from the sun or moon.
Blue enameled walls of bronze enclosed all,
threshold to innermost nook. Golden doors
kept the well-fitted house secure. Silver
columns stood near the bronze threshold. The door
had a silver lintel and a handle of gold.   90
On either side were gold and silver dogs
which Hephaistos, crafting with skill, had made
to guard the palace of great-hearted Alkinoös,
deathless dogs, not aging for all days.
Chairs stood against the walls from the threshold
to innermost nook; they were covered in cloth,
thin and finely spun, woven by womenfolk.
The Phaiakian leaders were seated there, drinking
and eating—food and drink were abundant.
Boys made of gold stood on well-made plinth bases,   100
their hands holding burning torches for light,
shining for the feasters through the night.

Throughout the palace work fifty women servants,
some grinding apple-yellow grain in mills,
others plying looms or spinning yarn as they
sit, their fingers flickering like aspen leaves,
weaving cloth so fine olive oil runs off it.

Surpassing all men, the skilled Phaiakians
propel their swift ships across the seas, and their
women are wondrous with looms. Athena gave them   110
noble hearts and skill to craft marvelous things.
Outside the courtyard is a large orchard

in four parts, fenced in all around.
The tall trees there produce heavily:
pears, pomegranates, apples with splendid fruit,
trees with sweet figs and flourishing olive trees.
The fruit is never ruined by winter cold, nor spoiled
in heat but grows year round. The mild west wind
Zephyros brings some to bud and some to ripen.
Pear on the pear tree matures, apple on apple tree,   120
on top of grapes more grapes, on figs more figs.

There too lies the king's deep-rooted, fruit-laden vineyard;
in an open level place, grapes are drying
in the sun. Here they're gathering grapes
and there crushing them. There are some unripe grapes,
some budding out, others darkening.
There along the last vine row a bed of herbs
all flourishing, unfailing in their green sheen.
Two springs lie within, one flows through all
the orchard, the other flows near the courtyard gate,   130
toward the high house, where people fetch their water.
Such were the wondrous gifts the gods gave Alkinoös.

Standing there noble Odysseus marveled.
But when his heart had filled itself with wonder,
he quickly stepped across the palace threshold.
He found the Phaiakian lords and leaders pouring
libations from cups to keen-sighted Argos-slayer*
who had the last libation when they thought of sleeping.
Then much-enduring Odysseus crossed the hall
swathed in the mist with which Athena had hidden him   140
until he reached Arete and King Alkinoös.
Odysseus threw his hands around Arete's knees
and then the god's mist was taken from him.
When they saw him, silence engulfed the hall.
They marveled at him, but bold Odysseus begged:

"Arete, daughter of godlike Rhexenor,
I come to your knees, your spouse, and these guests,
having endured much! May the gods grant all
happy lives. May you bequeath to your children
your wealth and palaces and honors from your people.   150
But give me soon conveyance to my land
because I have long suffered far from my dear ones."

Thus he spoke and sat on the hearth in ashes
by the fire. All were silent, without a sound.
A long while after spoke hero Ekeneos,
born before all the Phaiakian men.
In words, knowledge and ancient lore he excelled.
With good sense he addressed them saying:

"Alkinoös, it's not good nor right a guest
sit on the ground among the ashes on the hearth.   160
These here are waiting! Do not hold your words back!
Come, make the guest stand up, have him sit
on a silver-studded chair. Bid the heralds
mix the wine for libations to Zeus who hurls
thunderbolts and kindly cares for suppliants.
Let the housekeeper bring food from the stores."

When mighty King Alkinoös heard this,*
he took the hand of battle-skilled Odysseus,
bade him rise from the hearth, sit on a chair
from which he bid his son stand up, Laodamas   170
who sat close to him, the son he loved the best.

A maid, carrying a lovely golden pitcher,
poured water over his hands into a silver bowl
so he could wash. She set a table alongside him.
The esteemed housekeeper brought in some food,
spread meat before him, freely given from the stores.
Odysseus, the much enduring, drank and ate.

And then Alkinoös addressed the herald:

"Pontonoös, mix the wine, pour it for all
so we may pour a libation to Zeus who hurls   180
thunderbolts and kindly cares for suppliants."

The herald mixed the wine—honey for the mind—
and to all he poured drops in the goblets.*
Libation made, they drank as much as they wished,
and Alkinoös began to address them saying:

"Hear me, lords and leaders of the Phaiakians
that I may tell you what my heart commands.
Having dined, take yourselves home now and sleep.
At dawn we'll summon many elders and entertain
this guest within my halls and to the gods we will   190
perform the holy rites. And then we'll think about
his passage home. With no distress or suffering,
he will reach his native land with our escort
and rejoice in our ship's speed, however far!
And let him suffer not while crossing the wide sea
before he walks on his own land. There he may
suffer whatever the Spinners of Fates have spun in*
the cord from his birth when his mother bore him.
If he be a deathless one down from the sky,
then the gods are planning something else here.   200
In the past the gods made themselves visible
to us when we performed the splendid sacrifices.
They dined with us, sitting down just where we were.
If one alone, a traveler, meets a god,
the god hides not, since we are very close to them,
as near as the Cyclopes and the fierce race of Giants."

Odysseus answering spoke with much craft:

"Alkinoös, do not worry, for I'm not like

the deathless ones who hold the wide sky,
not in form or size! I am a dying mortal.   210
There are men who endure many sorrows:
I liken myself to them in enduring pain.
And yet I could tell of things even worse, all
of which I endured caused by the gods' will.
But allow me now to eat though I'm sore troubled.
There's nothing more shameful or worse than the belly
for it commands: need makes us follow it.
Though in pain and holding sorrow in one's breast,
as I indeed hold sorrow, it always forces me
to eat and drink and it makes me forget   220
all I have suffered while ordering me to fill it.
But you must rouse yourselves when dawn appears
and convey my wretched self to my country,
though I suffer still. May I not die until I've seen
my lands, servants and great, high-roofed palace!"

So he spoke and all agreed with him, urging
that he send on the guest for what he said was right.
Once they'd poured a libation, each as his heart wished,
they went to their homes to lie down, each one.
Odysseus was left in the great hall. Beside   230
him sat Arete and godlike Alkinoös.
Maids cleared away the food and tables.
White-armed Arete began speaking with these words;
seeing the clothes, she knew both the cloak and tunic,
clothes she herself and her servants had made.
Addressing him with winged words she said:

"Guest, first of all I will ask you this,
Just who are you? Where from? Who gave you those clothes?
Do you not claim you came wandering on the sea?"

Artful Odysseus, answering her, spoke thus: 240

"Painful, queen, to continually declare
the woes that the sky gods have given me.
I will speak of what you ask, what you inquire.
Ogygia Island lies far off in the salt sea.
There Atlas' daughter wily Kalypso lives,
the fair-groomed, fierce goddess. None mingles
with her, neither god nor mortal man.
But some god drove me to that wretched isle alone
after Zeus split my swift ship with his bright
thunderbolt in the midst of the purple sea.   250
All of the others perished, my noble comrades,
but I grabbed hold of the keel with my arms.
Nine days I drifted. On the tenth, in black night
the gods brought me to Ogygia, to Kalypso,
the fair-groomed, fierce goddess. She took me up,
loved me kindly, nourished me, and kept saying
she'd make me deathless, not aging for all days.
But she convinced neither my head nor my heart.
I was there for seven years, my clothes ever
wet with my tears, the immortal clothes she gave me.   260
But when the eighth year came round, she urged me
to rouse myself, to ready for my return home.
Zeus' message it was that changed her mind.

She sent me on a cord-bound raft, gave me much,
food and sweet wine and immortal clothes to wear.
A fair following breeze she sent me, safe and warm.
I sailed seventeen long days crossing the sea.
The eighteenth day your land's shadowy mountains
appeared. My dear heart rejoiced seeing them!
But no, for much sorrow was next to come my way!   270
Earth-shaker Poseidon stirred up the sea:
he launched the winds and drove me from my path.
He roused terrible seas, nor did his battering waves
leave me aboard my raft even as I wept.

The storm suddenly scattered and left
me in the sea. I swam across a gulf
close to your land; wind and water bore me on.
But the waves there would have crushed me against the land,
hurled me against sharp rocks at a dangerous place.
Drawing back I swam again until I reached   280
a river that seemed to me the best spot,
free of rocks and sheltered from the winds. There
I fell on the shore. Fragrant night came on.
I climbed away from the god-swollen river
and in some bushes, drawing over me a blanket
of leaves, I slept. A god poured endless sleep on me.
There in the leaves my crushed, sorrowing heart
slept the whole night through, through dawn, through noon.
Toward evening as the sun declined sweet sleep left me.
Your daughter's maidens were playing on the beach.   290
She seemed a goddess among them. I approached,
a suppliant. Her noble heart did not fail.
You would not expect that in one so young, meeting
a stranger. Young ones always act so thoughtlessly.
But she gave me food and rich wine and she
washed me in the river, gave me clothes to wear.
Though it pains me to tell my tale, it is all true."

Then Alkinoös answered him and said:

"Guest, in truth my child did not act correctly
in this because she did not lead you straight to us   300
with her maidservants, and you her first suppliant."

Answering him, artful Odysseus spoke:

"Warrior, do not for that reproach the blameless girl.
She ordered me to follow her with the maids.
But I did not wish to lest I bring shame on her
or make your heart angry at seeing us—

for the race of men are ever quick to anger."

Speaking to him, Alkinoös answered:

"Guest, this heart of mine is not swift to anger
for no good reason; all in due measure is best.   310
Would that by father Zeus, Athena and Apollo,
being who you are and thinking as I do,
you could have my child and be my son-in-law.
If you stayed here I would give you lands, a home,
should you wish to stay, but no Phaiakian
will keep you here against your will: Zeus deems it so.
So that you may know, I will appoint an escort
tomorrow. But now you're overcome with sleep.
Lie down. My men will take you over the calm sea
to your country and home, to what is dear to you,   320
even if it is much farther than Euboia,
which our people who saw it say is most distant
of all lands. They took fair-haired Rhadamanthys
to visit Tityos, sprung of Gaia. They
arrived there and returned again back home without
toil—they did this in a single day! You will
see and know how far they surpass all others,
my ships and boys, oars tossing up the salt sea."

Thus he spoke. Odysseus rejoiced!
In prayer he spoke, saying these words, calling by name: 330

"Father Zeus, may Alkinoös perform all he
has said and over all the grain-giving ploughed lands
unquenchable be his fame! Let me reach home!"

So to one another they spoke about these things.

White-armed Arete ordered her maids to make
a bed under the portico with fine purple

blankets and stretched woolen cloaks over all
as coverings and all of them spread smooth.
The maids went through the hall, torches in their hands
and they made up the close-fitted bed quickly.   340
With these words they urged Odysseus to rise:

"Now stand and go lie down, be comforted in bed."

So they spoke and he was glad to lie down.
Thus did much-enduring Odysseus lie down
on the slatted bed in the echoing portico.
Alkinoös lay down in the inner chamber
by the mistress of the house, his bedmate.

BOOK EIGHT

The Phaiakians engage in athletic contests
The Phaiakians dance and the bard sings of Troy
King Alkinoös questions Odysseus

When early-born, pink-fingered Dawn appeared,
mighty King Alkinoös rose from his bed.
Odysseus, Zeus-born sacker of cities, rose too.
Then mighty Alkinoös led the Phaiakians
to the assembly ground built near the ships.
Arriving there they sat down close together on
the smooth stones. Athena went up through the town
appearing like the herald of Alkinoös,
ever planning Odysseus' homeward voyage.
Standing beside each man she said these words: 10

"Come here, lords and leaders of the Phaiakians.
In the assembly you'll hear about the guest
who came to Alkinoös, skilled in peace and war,
a wanderer from the sea, in stature like a god."

Her words roused the will and spirit of each.

The assembly place and seats were quickly filled
with mortals thronging together. Many marveled seeing
Laertes' son, skilled in peace and war. Athena
poured sweet grace over his head and shoulders.
She made him taller and stronger to look upon,   20
so the Phaiakians might see him with respect
as a friend, ready to perform in all
contests, all that they might try him with.
Once assembled, gathered in a crowd,
Alkinoös addressed them, speaking thus:

"Hear me lords and leaders of the Phaiakians
so I may tell what my heart bids me say.
This wandering guest came to my house from peoples of
the east or western lands. I know not who he is.
He wants conveyance home in a pledged voyage.   30
Let us encourage this escort as we've done before.
For no one arriving at my palace—none—waits long,
grieving, for lack of an escort. But come,
drag a black ship into the shining sea to make
its maiden voyage. Choose fifty-two young men from
the people, whomever are deemed the best, and bind
the oars well into the oar-locks and leave
the ship. Then quickly come to my house for
your meal. I will provide everything. These are
my orders for the young men. But you other   40
scepter-bearing kings, come to my great palace
and let us show ourselves friends to this guest.
Let none refuse. Summon the godlike bard
Demodokos; a god gave him the skill to please
surpassing all, whatever he is inclined to sing."

So he spoke. The scepter-bearing kings followed
him. The herald went to bring the godlike
bard. Fifty-two boys were chosen. They went

as ordered to the shore of the barren salt sea.
When they'd gone down to the ship and sea,   50
they hauled the black ship into the deep water.
They stepped the mast and readied the black ship's sails
and fixed the oars, binding them with leather thongs
in the right way and then they stretched the white sails taut.
They moored her in deep water, then went to the
palace of Alkinoös, skilled in peace and war.
So many came, both young and old, the halls
and portico were packed with men crowding in.
For them Alkinoös had twelve fat sheep slaughtered,
eight white-tusked boars and two rolling-gaited oxen.   60
They flayed them and prepared a sumptuous feast.

The herald returned leading the bard. The Muse loved him
above all others and gave him both good and bad:
she took his eyes from him but gave him sweet songs.
Pontonoös put him in the midst of the guests
in a silver-studded chair near a tall column.
The herald hung his resonant lyre on
a peg above him and showed him how to take it down.
On a table near the bard he put a basket
of bread and a wine goblet to drink as his heart bid.   70
The guests reached for the food set out for them.
When they had sated their desire for drink and food,
the Muse let him sing a song of the feats of men,
a song whose fame had reached the wide sky,
of strife between Odysseus and Akilleus.*
With violent words they quarreled at a rich feast
for the gods. The lord of men, Agamemnon,
rejoiced that the best of the Akaians quarreled.
For thus Apollo spoke in prophesy to him
when he crossed the marble threshold at Pytho,*   80
an oracle, and there began the woes
for Trojans and Danaans, all planned by great Zeus.

The famous bard sang of this. Odysseus,
grabbing the large purple cloak in his stout hands,
pulled it over his head and hid his handsome face,
ashamed that the Phaiakians might see his tears.
And when the godlike bard paused in his singing,
he pulled the cloak back and wiped his eyes,
seized his goblet, and poured libations to the gods.
And when the bard sang again, the Phaiakians   90
encouraged him, delighting in the song's words.
Odysseus groaned and hid his head.
He wept, escaping the notice of all the others.
But Alkinoös alone noticed him weeping.
He sat close and hearing him moan deeply
said at once to the oar-loving Phaiakians:

"Hear me lords and leaders of the Phaiakians!
Since we have satisfied our hearts both with the meal
and lyre, the companion of a fine feast,
let's go out to compete in athletic contests   100
so, when returning home, our guest might tell
his friends how much we surpass all others
in boxing, wrestling, jumping, and running."

Once he spoke these words they followed him.
The herald hung the lyre on the peg and took
Demodokos by the hands and led him from
the hall down the same path where all the best
Phaiakians went to watch the competitions.
They went to the meeting place, a great throng followed.
Many well-born youths stood to compete.   110
Akroneos, Okyalos and Elatreus rose,
Nauteus and Prumneus, Ankialos, Eretmeus,
Ponteus, Proreus, Thoön, Anabesineos,
Amphialos, son of Polyneos, Tekton's son.
Like to man-destroying Ares, Euryalos

stood, son of Naubolos, best of all
in looks and build after Laodamas.
And the three sons of Alkinoös stood:
Laodamas, Halios, and Klytoneos.

So they began by competing in foot racing.   120
Just for them the course had been lengthened. They flew
all together down the track raising dust.
The best by far was fair Klytoneos, leading by
as much as two mules can plow in a day.
He finished far in front. The rest struggled behind.
Next came wrestling, apt to cause pain.
And Euryalos surpassed all the rest in this.
In jumping Amphialos was the most skilled,
in discus throwing the strongest was Elatreus,
in boxing Laodamas, Alkinoös' child.   130
Once they had all enjoyed the competitions,
royal Laodamas addressed them thus:

"My friends, let us ask our guest if he knows
or learned any athletic feat. His build's not bad,
his thighs and lower legs and his strong hands
and the thick neck show great strength. Nor does
he lack for youth. But he's been broken by sore trials.
For I say there's nothing worse than the sea
to break a man, however strong he be."

Then in turn, Euryalos answered him: 140

"Laodamas, you speak very well and rightly!
Go, challenge him yourself and speak your thoughts."

Hearing this, the child of Alkinoös stood and
went to the center, addressing Odysseus:

"Come forth, father guest, and try a sport

if you have learned any. I'm sure you know some skill.
For there's no greater fame for man as long as he
may live than what he does with his own hands or feet.
So come. Try. Scatter those cares from your heart.
For your path is no longer so distant! Indeed   150
the ship's been hauled to the sea and the crew's ready!"

Answering him, artful Odysseus then spoke:

"Laodamas, why bid me to this mockingly?
My heart is filled with pain, not these contests.
Having suffered and endured many hardships,
I sit in your assembly now, craving my home,
begging this of your king and all the people!"

Euryalos answered, reproaching him:

"Guest, you are not like a man skilled in sports—
in any sports of the many there are for men—   160
but like to him who sails ships with many oarlocks.
A leader of sailors. A trader mindful of
your freight. A guardian of cargo, greedy
for profit. No, you are not like an athlete!" *

Scowling, Odysseus, ever artful, said:

"Stranger, you speak not well; you seem reckless.
The gods did not give out their grace to all men,
neither in stature, nor in heart, nor in speech.
For one man is worse in respect to beauty,
but a god crowns him with goodly speech, making   170
him pleasing to behold as he speaks fluently,
with modesty, standing out among his peers,
going through the town, appearing like a god.
Another man appears like the deathless ones,
but, when he speaks, no grace crowns his words.

Thus even though you seem distinguished—no god
could seem so more—yet your brain is useless.
You troubled this heart of mine when you spoke
such ill-considered words. I lack not skills in sports,
as you said, but I was ever among the first   180
as long as I could trust my youth and strong hands.
Now I'm held back by pain and suffering.
For I've endured men's wars and the trial of waves.
Even so, though suffering much, I'll try a sport,
for you angered me. Your words stung my heart."

Still in his cloak he sprang up and grabbed a discus,
larger and heavier and a little thicker
than the Phaiakians threw among themselves.
Whirling round, he hurled it from his strong hand.
The stone hummed and all crouched down to the ground,   190
the long-oared Phaiakians, famed for ships.
They ducked from the force. It flew beyond all marks
as from a god's hand. Athena marked where it landed,
appearing like a man. She spoke and called his name:

"Even a blind man, guest, feeling for the mark
could find this one. It's not among the others,
but the most distant! Take heart from this contest!
No Phaiakian will reach or surpass it."

So she spoke. Odysseus rejoiced,
glad to find a friend in the assembly.   200
With a light heart he addressed the Phaiakians:

"Match that young men and I will send another
that far, I think, or even farther yet.
Whatever your hearts want, command it of me.
I will try it here since you have angered me:
wrestling or boxing, or I even welcome running
against you all—except Laodamas.

He is my host. Who would quarrel with his friend?
Only a man who is a fool or worthless
would challenge his host in competitions   210
in a foreign land, reducing his guest gifts.

But of the others I spurn or reject no one,
though I want to face him and then try him.
For I'm not bad in such contests among men.
I know how to handle a well-polished bow:
I'd be the first to strike my man with arrows in
a hostile throng, even if many companions
stood near and loosed their arrows at those men.
Only Philoktetes surpassed me with a bow
among those Akaians at Troy shooting arrows.   220
I claim to be by far the best of the others,
the grain-eating mortals now upon the earth.
I would not wish to challenge men of former times,
not Herakles nor Oikalian Eurytos
who, with a bow, used to challenge the immortals.
So great Eurytos perished, nor did he reach old age
in his palace, for he angered Apollo who
slew him because Eurytos challenged him.
I'll throw a spear as far as others shoot an arrow.
But in running I fear lest some Phaiakian   230
overtake me. I am much weakened, damaged
from the many waves and when the ship's food
ran out. From this my legs have lost their strength."

So he spoke. They were without sound, silent.

Alkinoös alone spoke, answering him:

"Guest, these words you say to us are not ungracious.
You wish to show us your innate prowess
because this man of ours angered you. He did
insult you in a way no mortal would

who knew in his heart to speak sensibly.   240
But come, heed my words, so you may speak
of this to other heroes when you dine in your
palace alongside your bedmate and children,
remembering our excellence, what sorts of feats
Zeus bestowed on us since our fathers' time.

For we are not great boxers or wrestlers,
but we run very fast, and are the best with ships.
And we always love the feast, the lyre and dances,
freshly-changed clothes, warm baths, the marriage bed.
Come, you who are the best Phaiakian dancers.   250
Dance so that our guest on his return home
may tell his friends how far we surpass all
in seamanship, in running, dancing, and in song!
Let someone go at once and bring Demodokos
his resonant lyre that lies within our palace."

So spoke godlike Alkinoös. A herald went
to bring the resonant lyre from the palace.
All nine of the people's chosen stewards stood up,
each one well used to organizing a gathering.
They smoothed and widened a place for the dance.   260
The herald came bringing the resonant lyre
for Demodokos who went among the young men.
They stood around him in youth's prime, skilled dancers.
Then they danced, their flashing feet keeping the beat.
Odysseus watched their feet, his heart in awe.

The bard played on the lyre the beautiful song
of the love of Ares and fair-crowned Aphrodite,
when secretly in Hephaistos' home they first
mingled. Ares gave her gifts but shamed the bed*
of lord Hephaistos. At once a message came to him   270
from Helios who saw them making love.

Hephaistos, when he'd heard this heart-grieving message,
set out for his forge, his heart filled with dark thoughts.
He set his great anvil on its block and made
unbreakable chains so they would be bound forever.
So, in anger he built the trap for Ares.
He went to the bedroom where his own bed lay
and circled the chains all around the bedposts.
They draped down from the high roof beams just like
a fine spider web that no one could see,   280
not even the happy gods, so cunning was his trap.
But when he'd placed the trap all around the bed
he pretended to go to Lemnos, the well-built town,
the land he loved the most by far of all lands.

But Ares of the golden reins was keeping watch*
and saw Hephaistos, the famous craftsman, going away.
So he set out for Hephaistos' famous palace
eager with lust for fair-crowned Kythereia.
She was sitting there, just now returned from her
mighty father Zeus. Ares entered the palace   290
where he took her hands and said these words:

"Here, my love, let us lie down on the bed.
Hephaistos is not at home. He's likely reached
Lemnos by now and the barbarous Sinties."

So he spoke. She thought it good to sleep with him.
In bed they fell asleep. The cunningly-wrought chains
of wise Hephaistos fell all over them
and they could neither move nor raise a limb.
Then they knew there was no way of escaping.
That most famous lame one approached them,   300
for he'd turned back before he reached Lemnos:
Helios had kept watch and told him the story.
Grieving in his heart, he set out for his palace.

As he stood at the door fierce anger seized him.
All the gods heard him raging terribly:

"Father Zeus and all happy, deathless gods,
Come! See this laughable, intolerable act!
Since I am lame, Aphrodite, Zeus' daughter,
shames me always and loves Ares the destroyer
because he's handsome and sound of foot. But I 310
was born feeble. I was not to blame for this!
My two parents should not have given birth to me.
But you will see where those two lie down in love
in my bed! I cannot bear to see them there!
Yet I don't think they'll lie thus any longer,
though in love. Soon both will wish not to be found.
But my trap and my chains will hold them till
her father gives back to me all the great bride-price
which I gave him for that bitch-girl's sake.
The girl is beautiful but can't control her lust." 320

He spoke and the gods gathered in his bronze-floored house.
Poseidon, earth-embracer, came and helper Hermes.
And Apollo came, he who shoots from afar.
The goddesses, being women, from shame stayed home.
The gods, givers of good things, stood in the doorway.
These happy gods broke out in unquenchable laughter
seeing the great skill of artful Hephaistos.
In this way they spoke to one another:

"Bad never prospers! The slow captures the swift!
So Hephaistos, though slow, binds Ares, the swiftest 330
of the gods who hold Olympos, through his skill,
though lame! Ares owes the adulterer's fee."

Such things they were saying then to one another.
And then Apollo, Zeus' son, addressed Hermes:

"Hermes, messenger, giver of good things,
would you not be willing to find yourself pressed tight
in chains in bed alongside golden Aphrodite?"

The messenger, Argos-slayer, answered him:

"Would that such might happen lord Apollo!
Put three times such strong chains around us both,   340
so all you gods—and the goddesses—might see us
if only I could bed golden Aphrodite."

So he spoke. Laughter broke out among the gods.
Laughter held Poseidon, but he kept begging
for Hephaistos, famed for his work, to free Ares.
Speaking winged words he said to him:

"Free him! I pledge as you have bid to pay all
that's due according to the deathless gods."

The very famous lame one answered him:

"Do not command me Poseidon Earth-embracer!   350
Worthless the pledges pledged by the worthless!
How could I take you to task among the gods
if Ares, once freed, should leave and forget his debt?"

Then earth-shaking Poseidon answered him:

"Hephaistos! If Ares once freed should leave,
fleeing his debt, I myself will then pay it."

Then the very famous lame one answered him:

"I cannot and must not deny your word."

So speaking, Hephaistos with skill opened the chains.
And the lovers once freed from those strong chains,   360
immediately sprang up. He left for Thrace.

Laughter-loving Aphrodite went to Kypros,
to her altar in Paphos, fragrant with incense.
The Graces bathed her and rubbed her with immortal
olive oil which coats the skin of the gods
and dressed her in wondrously lovely robes.
So the bard sang his famous song and he,
Odysseus, was glad of heart hearing this.
So too were the Phaiakians, famous for ships.

Alkinoös bid Halios and Laodamas   370
to dance alone since no one could compete with them.
They grasped a beautiful dark red ball
with their hands—skilled Polybos made it—
and one tossed it toward the shadowy clouds
bending backwards. The other leapt from the ground,
catching it before his feet touched down.
When they'd done rounds throwing the ball straight up,
they danced on the nourishing earth, tossing it
back and forth frequently. The other young men
stood by beating time and a great din arose.   380

Odysseus then addressed Alkinoös:

"Lord Alkinoös, renowned of all the people,
you promised that these two dancers would dance the best
and that they have done. Seeing them, awe holds me!"

So he spoke and mighty Alkinoös rejoiced.
At once he spoke to the oar-loving Phaiakians:

"Hear me lords and leaders of the Phaiakians.
This guest seems to me to be very prudent.
So come now, let us give him guest-gifts as is fit.
Twelve kings reign over the people, all very   390
distinguished leaders. I myself am the thirteenth.
To honor him, let each leader bring for him

a well-washed tunic and a talent of precious gold.
Let us gather these at once, so our guest,
having these at hand, goes to dinner happy.
And let Euryalos himself make amends by word
and gift, since he spoke words not at all suiting."

So he spoke and all agreed and ordered it,
and each sent a herald to bring the gifts.

And then Euryalos, speaking, answered him: 400

"Lord Alkinoös, renowned of all the people,
I'll make the guest amends as you command.
I'll give him a sword, all brass, with a handle
of silver enclosed in a scabbard of new
cut ivory. It will be worth much for him."

Having spoken thus, he held out a sword
with silver studs and said, speaking with winged words:

"Farewell, oh father guest. If I spoke some bad words,
let a whirlwind seize them and carry them off. May
the gods let you arrive home and see your bedmate,   410
since you have suffered much, long away from friends."

Artful lord Odysseus answered him:

"And you, friend, farewell. May the gods make you happy.
And may you not wish to have this sword back
that you gave to me with such appeasing words!"

So he spoke and slung the sword over his shoulder.
The sun was setting and the guest-gifts had arrived.
The heralds had brought them to Alkinoös' palace.
The children of noble Alkinoös took them
and put them near their mother and the bard.   420
Then mighty King Alkinoös led them

into his palace and they sat on tall chairs.
Then King Alkinoös spoke to Arete:

"Woman, bring a large, well-made chest here,
the best. Put the cloaks and well-washed tunics in it.
Heat water in a bronze cauldron in the fire
so, once bathed and seeing all the gifts well stored,
gifts the noble Phaiakians have carried here,
he might enjoy the feast and hear the bard's song.
And I will give him my prized golden goblet   430
so he might think of me at home when he pours
the offerings to Zeus and to the other gods."

So he spoke. Arete told the maids
to heat at once the great tripod in the fire.
They set the washbasin in the blazing fire,
stoking it with kindling, and poured the water in.
The fire warmed the tripod, heating the water.
Meanwhile Arete brought out from her chamber
a well-made chest and filled it with the lovely gifts,
the gold and clothes which all had given him.   440
She laid inside the fine cloaks and tunics
and said to him, speaking winged words:

"Now look. Tie a cord around the lid so no
harm be done when you lie down in sweet sleep
as you travel on your way in our black ship."

When noble, much-enduring Odysseus heard this
he fit the lid on, tying a cord around with a
complex knot that cunning Kirke had taught him.
Straightaway the housekeeper bid him to bathe,
leading him to the washtub. His heart was glad   450
seeing the warm bath, since he had not had one
since he left the dwelling of fair-haired Kalypso
where he had always been cared for like a god.

When the maids had washed him and rubbed him with oil,
they dressed him in a tunic and in a fine cloak.
From the bath he walked toward the wine-drinking men.
Nausikaa, given beauty by the gods,
stood beside a column of the well-built house
and marveled when she saw Odysseus.
And she spoke to him, saying these winged words: 460

"Farewell, guest. Remember me even at home.
You came to me first and I saved your life."

Answering her, artful Odysseus then spoke:

"Nausikaa, daughter of lord Alkinoös,
may loud-thundering Zeus ordain that I
reach my home and see that day of homecoming!
Once there I would pray to you as a god
all my days. Maid, you gave me back my life!"

So he spoke and sat beside King Alkinoös.
Servants were now serving food and mixing wine.   470
The herald came near with the faithful bard,
honored Demodokos. He seated him in the
middle of the guests against a large pillar.
Artful Odysseus, who had just cut from the
white-tusked pig's back a piece of meat that had
rich oil around it, then spoke to the herald: *

"Herald, take this meat to Demodokos
so he may eat. Though grieving, I welcome him.
Bards partake of honor and respect among
all men who trod the earth because the Muse   480
taught them her songs. She loves the tribe of bards."

So he spoke. The herald took it to the bard
Demodokos who accepted it gladly.

Then all reached for the food lying ready at hand.
When they'd satisfied desire for food and drink,
artful Odysseus then said to Demodokos:

"Demodokos, I praise you beyond all mortals!
Either the Muse taught you or Apollo did.
You sing the fate of the Akaians in proper order,
what the Akaians did and suffered, what thy endured,   490
as if you were there or heard it from another.
But change themes now and sing of the wooden horse
that Epeios made with Athena's help.
Odysseus planned this trap, they pulled it in,
filled with men who then sacked Ilios.
If you can relate these things in the proper order,
I will at once affirm to all how a god
granted you this holy, inspiring song!"

So he spoke. The bard began, urged by the goddess,
taking up the song where the Argives sailed off   500
in their ships, arrows flaming the camp huts,
leaving behind those around Odysseus
sitting inside Troy, hiding in the horse.
For the Trojans had dragged the horse inside the walls.
So it stood there while they argued incessantly,
sitting around the horse. Three plans were put forth:
split the hollow wood open with ruthless bronze,
or drag it to the cliff and hurl it down,
or let it be, a great glory for the gods.
This last is what they finally settled on.   510
It was their fate to die once it had come inside
their walls, that wooden horse in which sat all the best
Argives bringing death and slaughter to the Trojans.
He sang how those Akaians destroyed the town,
dropping from the horse, leaving the hollow trap.
He sang how they utterly destroyed the city.

How, like to Ares, Odysseus went for
Deïphobos with godlike Menelaos.
He sang the fierce battle he won there,
Odysseus, with the help of Athena.   520

The bard sang of these famed events. Odysseus
wept, hot tears flowing down his cheeks.
Just as a woman weeps when her man has fallen,
slain fighting in front of his town and people,
holding back the pitiless day for his children,
she, seeing him gasping and dying,
embraces him, wailing loudly. From behind,
whipping her back and shoulders, they lead her off
into bondage where she'll endure toil and grief,
her cheeks consumed with the most pitiable anguish.   530
Just so Odysseus shed hot tears from his eyes.
His weeping escaped the notice of all the others.
But Alkinoös noticed and thought about it.
Sitting so near him, he also heard the deep groans.

Then he said to the oar-loving Phaiakians:

"Hear me, oh Phaiakians lords and leaders,
let Demodokos cease his resonant lyre,
for his singing does not find favor with all.
Since we were eating and the god urged the bard,
from that time our guest has not ceased tearful groaning. 540
Some strong grief encompasses his heart,
so cease the song so we can all feel equal joy,
guest and hosts, since it is better thus.
For this honored guest, we prepared all: the feast,
an escort, and good gifts that we as friends give him.
He who has his wits at all treats
a suppliant like a guest and like a brother.
Therefore no longer hide with cunning thoughts

what I ask you. Better it is for you to speak.
Tell me that name your mother and father named you,   550
and the others in your town who lived near you.
For no one of mankind is without a name,
neither the bad nor the good. At birth, parents
assign a name to all when a child is born.
Tell me your land, your people, your town,
so our ships can carry you there, ready in mind,
for although other ships have them there are no pilots,
nor steering rudder for the Phaiakians.
Our ships know the thoughts and hearts of men,
and know the towns of all, and the fertile lands   560
of men, and they speed over the depths of seas
concealed in mist and cloud. Nor is there any fear
of being harmed, nor of a ship's destruction.

But I heard my father Nausithoös say
Poseidon was angry at us because we give
all safe escort, no matter whom we carry.
So someday a well-made Phaiakian ship
would be crushed returning from an escort on
the sea, and a great mountain would encircle our town.   570
So the old man used to say. And this the god
may do or leave undone, as his heart bids.
But come now, tell me and recount truly
where you were forced to wander, what lands of men
you reached, of those fine towns they lived in,
as well as who were harmful, fierce and not just,
and who were guest-loving, who with minds god-fearing.
Tell me why you wept and wailed within your heart
hearing of the Argives, the doom of Ilios.
The gods made it happen. They spin the web of death
for men so there will yet be songs for those to come.   580
Did some kin of yours die at Ilios,
being noble: brother or father-in-law who

was most near by marriage after blood and family?
Or was it some noble friend who pleased you?
A friend, a companion, who is sensible—
such a man is worth as much as a brother."

BOOK NINE

Odysseus narrates his wanderings:
The raid on the Kikones; encountering the Lotus Eaters
In the cave of the Cyclops Polyphemos

Answering him, artful Odysseus then spoke:

"Lord Alkinoös, renowned of all people,
truly this is beautiful to hear: a voice
such as this bard's, a voice like to the gods!
For I say there is no more pleasing fulfillment
than when joy takes hold of all the people—
guests in the palace—listening to the bard,
sitting in rows alongside tables filled with food
and meat, the wine-pourer drawing the wine
from the mixing bowl and filling the goblets.   10
This seems to me in my heart most beautiful.
But your mind is set on learning of my sad troubles
so I may yet, grieving more, mourn more.
What shall I recount to you first? What last?
The gods of the sky gave me many pains.
First then, I will tell you my name, so that

you may know, and thus, should I not die, I may
be your guest-friend, though living far away.
I am Odysseus, Laertes' son. All men
know my stratagems. My fame reaches the sky.   20

I live in sunny Ithaka. Neritos,
a stately mountain, is there and trees with quaking leaves.
Around lie many islands very near each other:
Doulikion and Samos and wooded Zakynthos.
It's low-lying and farthest out in the salt sea
toward darkness. The others lie toward the morning sun.
Rugged it is but a good nourisher of young men.
There's nothing sweeter than to see one's own land!
That shining goddess Kalypso tried to keep me in
her hollow caves, wanting me to be her bedmate.   30
So too wily Kirke tried to hold me in
her palace on Aiaia, desiring me for bedmate,
but she did not persuade the heart within my chest.
For there is nothing sweeter than one's own land
and parents! Not even a rich home if it lies in
a foreign land, far from one's own parents.
But if you wish, let me tell the many troubles
of my return caused by Zeus when I left Troy.

The winds carried me to the Kikones, to Ismaros.
There I sacked the town, killing the men.   40
Outside the town we divided the women and spoils
so that no one might leave deprived of a fair share.
Then I ordered us to flee with nimble feet.
I ordered, but the great fools did not obey.
Much wine they drank there along the shore and ate
many sheep and shambling, spiral-horned oxen.
During that time, town Kikones called to Kikones
living in the hinterland—their neighbors
who were better fighters and knew how to use horses

while fighting men and how to fight on foot. 50
In early morning they came, like leaves or flowers
in spring. Zeus caused that evil fate that came
on us and doomed us to suffer many woes.
We stood fighting that battle alongside our swift ships,
hurling the bronze-tipped spears at each other.
Through dawn and all the while the day was growing,
we resisted and we held, though they were many.
But when the hour to bring the oxen in came near,
the Kikones overpowered the Akaians.
From each ship six of my well-armored men 60
perished; the others escaped death and fate.

Then we sailed onward, grieving in our hearts
for our comrades, though glad not to have died.
I did not let our curved ships sail on until
one of the crew cried out three times for each of those
who died: those cut down by the Kikones.
Cloud-gatherer Zeus stirred up the Boreal wind
for our ships—a furious storm which hid both land
and sea with clouds. And night dropped from the sky.
The ships were driven, plunging on, the wind's might 70
ripping the sails into three and four parts.
We lowered and stowed the tattered sails, fearing death,
and we rowed the ships toward land with all our strength.
Once there, we lay down for two days and nights,
fatigue and grief ever eating at our hearts.
Then on the third day fair-haired Dawn ended this.
We stepped the mast and raised the sails up high.
We sat oars ready but the wind steered our ships.
And now I would have arrived at my native land
but both wind and current pushed us away as we 80
rounded Maleia, away from Kythera.

Then for full nine days the deadly winds drove me

on the fish-full sea. We set foot on the tenth
in the land of Lotus Eaters whose food is flowers.
There we went forth on the land and drew water,
and my comrades took dinner by the swift ships.
When we'd satisfied desire for food and drink
I sent men forth exploring to find out what
kind of men lived in this land, what their food.
I picked two men and sent the herald to go with them.   90
They went at once to meet the lotus-eating men.
These Lotus Eaters planned no harm for these men
of ours but gave them lotus flowers to taste.
All who taste the honey-sweet food of the lotus
have no wish to come back nor sail on,
but prefer to be there with the Lotus Eaters,
to remain feeding on lotus, forgetting home.
I drove them weeping onto the ships by force
and bound them under a yoke to their oars.
I ordered all the other loyal comrades   100
to embark in the swift ships, moving quickly,
lest one who ate the lotus forget his own return.
They boarded the ships at once and sat at the oarlocks.
Seated in order, they beat the gray sea with the oars.

Then, grieving at heart, we sailed onward.
We came to the lawless land of arrogant
Cyclopes who, trusting in the deathless gods,
neither planted crops with their hands nor plowed.
Yet all things grew on their own, unsown, unplowed:
wheat and barley and vines with clusters of grapes   110
for wine, for there was always rain from Zeus.
They have no laws, no places for councils.
They live on the crags of lofty mountains
in hollow caves, each ruling over his children
and bedmate. Nor do they care about each other.

A wooded, fertile island stretches behind the harbor,
neither close nor far from the land of the
Cyclopes. Wild goats beyond number breed there.
There is no tread of men to keep them away,
no hunters there, struggling after them in woods,   120
nor chasing them on the bright mountain peaks.
Nor is it occupied with flocks or plowed fields
or men. It is unsown, unplowed all days.
And bleating goats graze there in the pastures.

The Cyclopes have no red-prowed ships
nor men skilled at ship building who would build
well-benched ships that could take them to every
town of men, as many towns as there are,
crossing the sea by ship as men are used to doing.
Craftsmen would make this land a good settlement.   130
The land is not poor but would bring forth all year.
There are meadows along the shore of the gray sea,
soft and well-watered. The vines would never lack fruit.
The plow land lies open, crops would grow dense,
reaped in season since the earth below is fertile.
The harbor has good mooring, no need to tie cables
or fasten the prow or to drop anchor stones.
Beached here, the crew can tarry until their hearts
urge them on and the winds are blowing fair.
At the harbor's end flows clear spring water   140
issuing from a cave with poplars growing round it.

We sailed to shore and some god drove us through
the dense dark, for nothing shone to see by.
There was a thick mist about the ship. The moon,
locked up by clouds, gave no light from the sky.
Then no one's eyes could make out the ships,
nor were we able to see the large waves
rolling landwards till the well-benched ships reached shore.

Beaching the ships, we took down all the sails
and we ourselves disembarked amid the surf.   150
There we fell asleep waiting for the dawn.

When early-born, pink-fingered Dawn appeared,
we roamed around the island, marveling at it.
Nymphs, daughters of aigis-bearing Zeus,
roused mountain-bred goats so my men might eat.
At once we grabbed our curved bows and long
goat-spears from the ships, and, in three ranks,
we struck. A god gave us a satisfying chase.
Twelve ships I brought with me. By lot nine goats
were given to each. For me alone they picked out ten.   160

That whole day until the sun was setting we sat
feasting on the boundless meat and rich wine.
But we did not consume all the rich, red wine
since much lay in the ships: my men took many
storage jars from the sacked Kikonian town.

So near were we to the Cyclopes' land, we saw
their smoke and heard the bleating of their sheep and goats.
When the sun had set and darkness had come on,
then we lay down beside the foaming surf and slept.
When early-born, pink-fingered Dawn appeared,   170
I called a meeting and I spoke to all thus:

'My loyal comrades: you must wait here for now
while I with my ship and my crew
will test those men to see who they are:
whether arrogant, unjust and fierce,
or whether guest-loving, god-fearing in their hearts.'

Speaking thus, I boarded and ordered my crew
to loose the hawsers and hoist them up on deck.
This they did at once and sat in their oar seats

in a row and beat the gray sea with their oars.   180
When we got to the near shore of the land, we saw
a cave there on the cliff above the sea,
high up and covered with laurels. Large flocks
of sheep and goats bedded down there. Around the pen
a high wall of quarried stone had been built
among tall pines trees and oaks dense with foliage.
At night the huge man—now away—slept there.
He tended the flock of sheep but exchanged nothing
with others and, being far off, lived lawless ways.
He was fashioned as a monstrous wonder, not like   190
grain-eating men, but like a wooded crag
on a tall peak that stands alone, far from others.

Then I ordered my trusty comrades to drag
the ship on shore and remain there beside it.
I chose twelve of the best of them and left.
I had the goatskin bag of dark, sweet wine
that Euanthes' son Maron gave me, the priest
of Apollo who had cared for Ismaros.
We had protected him, his woman and his child
out of respect. He dwelled in the tree-filled grove   200
of Phoibos Apollo and he brought me shining gifts.
He gave me seven talents of well-wrought gold,*
and mixing vessels of solid silver, and poured
it into twelve amphorae—rich unmixed wine,
divine drink. None of his male servants
or maids within his house knew of this,
only his bedmate and one housekeeper alone.
When he drank that sweet, red wine, he'd fill
one cup and pour it into twenty cups of water
and still the divinely sweet smell from the bowl   210
would fill the air, so pleasant no one would hold back.
I carried a large wineskin filled with this, and food
in my pack, for I thought in my heart we might

meet that man clothed in his fierce great strength,
knowing neither just laws nor right customs.

Quickly we climbed to the cave but found no one
inside. The fat flocks were grazing in the pasture.
Entering the cave, I looked at everything there:
baskets heavy with cheese, pens corralling lambs
and kids. Each group had been confined separately,   220
the first-year lambs away from second year ones,
the younglings apart. All the pails he used for milking
dripped with whey: the milk pails and the well-made bowls.

Inside, my men began to beg me, to urge me
to go back, taking the cheese and driving the kids
and lambs from their pens down to the swift ship,
and to set sail quickly on the briny sea.
But I did not agree. Far better if I had.
To get guest gifts I wished to see him. When he came,
he was nothing like a good host to my men.   230

We built a fire, sacrificed, took some cheese
and sat and ate. Then we waited for him inside
till he returned, driving his flocks. He carried
a huge load of dry wood to burn at dinner.
He threw it down in the cave—a great din!
In terror we darted back into a far corner.
He then drove all that needed milking from the large flocks
into the cave, leaving the males beyond the door,
the rams and billy goats outside in an enclosure.
Then lifting a huge door-block on high, he set it   240
mightily. Not twenty-two four-wheeled wagons—
good ones—could raise that stone from the earth,
such a towering boulder he set as a door block.
Sitting, he milked the sheep and bleating goats,
and put under each a newborn lamb or kid.

When the white milk had thickened, he drew
off half into woven baskets and half
he poured into a pail within his reach
to drink and have it at his own supper.
He worked quickly and finished all these tasks, 250
then he kindled a fire and saw us and he asked:

'Strangers, who are you? From which way did you sail?
Do you travel for trade? Or wander without plan
as pirates on the sea, risking your lives
to roam and harm those in foreign lands?'

Thus he spoke and my heart was shattered,
fearing the deep voice and the monster himself.
But even so, answering him, I said these words:

'We are Akaians forced by all the winds
to wander from Troy over the sea's great depth, 260
sailing home, but along a different path,
a different way. Thus it must be Zeus' plan.
We're proud to be Agamemnon's people.
His fame is greatest under the sky since
he sacked so great a city and thus slew
many people. But we came to your knees*
to see if you might give us guest-gifts or
some other gift customary for guests.
But, most powerful one, respect the gods: we are
your suppliants. Zeus protects suppliant-guests 270
and hosts who attend to guests with respect.'

So I spoke. His pitiless heart answered thus:

'You are foolish, stranger, or you've come from afar
to bid me either fear or flee the gods.
Cyclopes do not flee from aigis-bearing Zeus
or other blessed gods since we are much stronger.

Nor would I spare you or your men to avoid
the wrath of Zeus unless my heart bid it.
Tell me where you moored your well-made ship,
that I may know it. On the far shore or near by?'   280

So he tested us. But I knew this trick
and answered him with these deceitful words:

'Earth-shaker Poseidon shattered my ship,
throwing it on the rocks at your land's edge.
Carried by winds he dashed it on the headlands.
I with these few men escaped hard death.'

Thus I spoke but he said nothing. Instead
he sprang up, his hands reaching for my comrades.
Seizing two, he smashed them hard against the ground
like puppies. Their brains flowing wet the earth.   290
Cutting their limbs apart, he readied his dinner
and ate like a mountain lion, devouring all,
entrails and flesh and bones full of marrow.

Seeing this cruel act, our hearts helpless,
we wept and held our hands up to Zeus.
When the huge Cyclops had filled his belly
eating man-flesh and drinking uncurdled milk,
he stretched out in the cave alongside his flock.
I formed a plan for him in my great-hearted breast.
Going nearer, I took the sharp sword from my scabbard   300
to stab his chest where midriff meets the liver.
I aimed my hands there when a new thought stopped me:
for we would then die here, a grim death.
We could never push away that giant door-block
with our hands, so that huge boulder stopped escape.
Thus then, moaning, we waited for blessed Dawn.

When early-born, pink-fingered, Dawn appeared,

he built up a fire and milked his superb herd
all in order and put a new-born under each.
And when he had finished all his tasks,   310
he seized two more of my men to make his meal.
He ate, then drove the large flocks from the cave,
easily moving the huge door-block, and then
he put it back as if capping a quiver.
Whistling loudly, the Cyclops turned the flock
toward the mountains. Left behind, I pondered how
I might repay him should Athena grant my prayer.

This plan seemed the best that I could make:
the Cyclops' large club of green olive wood
lay by the pens. He had cut it to carry it   320
about once dry. Looking it over, we thought it like
a ship's mast, a black, twenty-oared ship,
a cargo carrier, or one made for deep seas.
It seemed of such a length and such thickness.
Standing near, I cut from it a six-foot length.
I bid my crew to make its point very sharp.
They smoothed it down and shaped a good, sharp point,
and then we hardened it in the hot fire.
To hide it well we buried it under dung,
of which there were ample piles in the cave.   330
Next I ordered them to choose by lot
who should help me raise the sharp stake
to grind it in his eye when sweet sleep took him.
The four I would have chosen won by lot
and I counted myself as the fifth.
As the wooly flock was grazing evening came.
He drove the large flocks into the broad cave,
nor did he leave any outside the deep cavern,
suspecting something or some god had bid him thus.

He lifted the huge door-block, putting it in place.   340

Sitting down, he milked the sheep and bleating goats
in the same order, put under each a new-born.
And when he had finished all his tasks,
he seized two more of my men to make his meal.
And then, standing near, I addressed the Cyclops
while holding a drinking cup of dark wine:

'Cyclops, since you eat man-flesh, drink this wine
so you may know what sort of drink we had
on board our ship. I brought it as a gift and hoped
you'd send us homeward. But you rage unbearably!   350
Why would any other of the tribe of men
come here, since you lack all sense of what's right?'

So I spoke. He drank the wine. Well did he like
drinking the rich wine. He bid a second cup.

'Give me a full cup more and tell me your name
so I may give you a host-gift that will please you.
For even the grain-giving land of the Cyclopes
bears clustered grapes for wine. Rain from Zeus makes
them grow. But this! This equals ambrosia or nectar!'

So he spoke and I poured more fiery wine.   360
Three times I filled it, three times he foolishly drank.
But when the wine had gone to his Cyclopean head
I spoke to him with these soothing words:

'Cyclops, you ask my famous name. I will tell you,
so you will give me the promised host-gift.
No One is my name. No One they call me—
my mother and father and so do all my friends.'

So I spoke. With no pity he replied:

'No One will I eat last, after his comrades.
These others first. Such will be my host-gift.'   370

And then he fell and lay on his back. And when
his thick neck twisted and all-subduing sleep
had seized him, out of his throat rushed the wine
and morsels of man-flesh in his wine-heavy vomit.
Then I drove the pole under the heap of ashes
to fire it. And with words I heartened my
companions, lest fear make any rise against me.
When the pole of olivewood neared the point
of catching fire, though green, it glowed most grimly.
Being nearer, I carried it from the fire, my men   380
standing close. A god breathed boldness into us.
They grabbed the olivewood pole near the point
and drove it into his eye while from above I leaned,
twisting it just as a man drills a hole
in ship wood, grabbing the leather strap on both sides
and pulling it so it runs even in the drill hole.
So we spun that fired pole deep into his eye
and so hot it was, his blood began to boil.

The fire singed all round his eyelid and eyebrow
and boiled his pupil and it sizzled in its roots.   390
Just as a blacksmith tempers an axe or adz
and dips it in cold water which hisses loudly—
for this is how to harden iron—so his eye
hissed and sizzled around the olivewood pole.
He shrieked, horrible to hear. The mountains echoed
and we, afraid, darted back. Out of his eye
he pulled that pole running red with dark wet blood.
Beside himself, he threw it from his hands.
Then this Cyclops bellowed loudly to all those
who lived around him in caves in the windy peaks.   400
They heard his shouts—different ones from different places.
Standing outside the cave they asked him what was wrong:

'Polyphemos what sort of pain makes you shout?

It keeps us from sleeping through the fragrant night.
Surely no mortal steals your flocks against your will?
No one could kill you, not by trick nor by strength!'

From his cave, strong Polyphemos answered:

'No One is killing me through tricks or by his strength.'

Speaking in winged words, they answered him:

'Since you are alone, no one is conquering you.   410
You can't avoid sickness sent from mighty Zeus,
so pray to your own father, lord Poseidon.'

Speaking thus, they went away. My heart laughed
since my name and my great cunning had tricked them.
The Cyclops, moaning and suffering great pain,
lifted with his hands the stone from the doorway
and sat himself there stretching his hands out
to grab anyone leaving with the sheep.
His foolish heart hoped it would happen thus.

But I thought about what might be far the best   420
for my comrades and me to help us all escape.
I tried to weave all my tricks and wiles together
since this meant life or death from this great evil.
Then finally this plan appeared best to me.
The male sheep were well-nourished, thick-fleeced,
beautiful and large, with dark-hued wool.
Silently I took the willow twigs the lawless
monster Cyclops used as a bed. I bound the sheep
three abreast and bound a man under the middle,
a ram on either side hiding and saving   430
my comrades. Each man carried by three sheep.
But I, grabbing the flock's best ram by far,
hung beneath in the fine thick wool of his

big gut. I twisted my hands deep into the thick
wool and held strongly with a patient heart.
And thus, moaning, we waited for noble Dawn.

When early-born, pink-fingered Dawn appeared,
the male sheep then rushed out to pasture but
the un-milked ewes bleated around the pens,
their udders ready to burst. Their distressed master,   440
in wicked pain, standing upright, felt the back
of each male. The fool did not know my men
were bound under the chests of the wooly sheep.
Last of the flock, the ram walked toward the door,
burdened with wool, with me and my dark thoughts.

Then mighty Polyphemos spoke, feeling the ram:

'Old ram, why did you go last of the flock
from my cave? Not your normal way, the sheep
leaving you behind! You're always first to graze
on tender flowers, first with long strides to stream's   450
current, first wanting to return home at evening.
But now you are the last. Do you mourn master's
eye, blinded by the bad man with his men
once they had tamed my spirit with strong wine? That
No One, whom I say has not yet escaped death.
If only you were like-minded and could talk,
telling me where he went, dodging my strength!
Then I'd smash his head all through the cave,
crushing him! That would console my heart and end
the evil that worthless No One brought me.'   460

So he spoke and sent the ram out the cave-mouth.
Going a little ways outside the cave and courtyard
I freed myself from the ram then freed my men.
With many a backward glance we drove the gathered
fat sheep quickly till we reached the ship.

Welcomed we were by our dear comrades. We had
escaped, but they began mourning for the dead.
But I did not let them mourn. Refusing them,
each one, I ordered them to load the ship quickly
with many sheep and to sail out on the salt sea.   470
Then they too boarded and sat at their oars,
all in order, and their oars beat the gray sea.

When I was as far out as a shout would carry,
I yelled at the Cyclops, taunting him thus:

'Cyclops, little did you know the man whose comrades
you chose to eat in your cave by strength and force!
But now, cruel one, you're learning that this foul deed—
dishonoring of guests in your home by eating
them—caused Zeus and other gods to take revenge!'

So I spoke. His heart filled with hard rage   480
and breaking off the crest of a great mountain,
he hurled it downward. It struck in front of the ship,
just barely failing to reach the high tiller.*
The sea from the boulder's plunge splashed high and
the wave drove our ship back toward the shore,
the surge carrying us from the sea back toward dry land.
Immediately my hands reached for a long pole
and I pushed from the ship's side, rousing my men.
Gesturing, I ordered them to row strongly
and thus escape our death. They fell to their oars.   490
When we'd rowed twice as far as before,
I shouted to the Cyclops. My comrades from every
side tried to stop me with soothing words:

'Hard-hearted man, why provoke that fierce monster?
What he threw drove our ship back from the sea
toward the land! We only just escaped dying!
If he should hear you speaking out or shouting,

he'd crush our heads and our wooden ship by hurling
jagged marble boulders, so far he throws!'

They spoke, but my great soul was not persuaded.   500
I shouted back to him from my anger:

'Cyclops, if ever anyone of mortal men
should ask about your maimed, blinded eye,
tell them Odysseus blinded you, sacker
of cities, Laertes' son, who lives in Ithaka.'

Thus I spoke. Crying out in grief, he yelled:

'Oh no! An ancient prophecy said this would come!
There used to be a seer here good and wise,
Telemos, who excelled in divination.
He grew old divining among the Cyclopes.   510
He told me all of this would happen: that I,
at Odysseus' hands, would lose my sight!
But I always expected some big, handsome mortal
to come here, a mighty man clothed in strength.
And now here's a small, worthless man, feeble,
who blinds my eye when he has conquered me with wine.
Come here, Odysseus. I'll give you a guest-gift:
I'll rouse the famed Earth-shaker to give you an escort!
I am his child and he boasts to be my father!
He himself will heal me if he wishes.   520
No other god or mortal man could do that.'

So he spoke and I, answering, said this:

'Would that I could send you to the house
of Hades, your life and soul stripped away,
so not even the Earth-shaker could heal you.'

So I spoke and he, stretching out his hands
to the starry sky, prayed to lord Poseidon:

'Hear me, dark-haired, earth-embracing Poseidon,
if I am your true son. You boast you fathered me.
Never let Odysseus, sacker of cities,   530
Laertes' son, reach his home in Ithaka!
But if it is his fate to see his dear ones,
reach his well-built home and native land,
let first a long time pass, his men all dead,
he on another's ship, his home embroiled in troubles!'

Thus he prayed and the dark-haired one heard him.
Then Cyclops lifted a huge stone, whirled it about,
hurled it, putting all his strength in it,
and it struck just behind the blue-prowed ship,
just barely failing to reach the high tiller.   540
The sea, splashing down, was dashed on the rocks.
The wave surge drove the ship away, off toward the island.

When we reached the island where the other
ships waited all together, their crews
sitting near, weeping as they waited for us,
we came and beached our ship in the sand
and we ourselves disembarked amid the surf.

We took the Cyclops' flock and shared them all among
the hollow ships: no one lacked his fair share.
My armored comrades gave the ram to me alone,   550
a special gift when they allotted the flock. To Zeus,
cloud-gathering son of Kronos, who rules all,
I burned the sacrificial thighbone. He ignored this,
since he was pondering how he might destroy
all my well-benched ships and loyal men.

The whole day until the sun set we sat
eating endless meat, drinking the rich wine.
When the sun had set and darkness come,
then we lay down beside the foaming surf and slept.

When early-born, pink-fingered Dawn appeared, 560
then, rousing my comrades, I ordered them
to board the ships and untie the mooring lines.
At once they boarded and sat at their oarlocks.
Sitting in order, their oars beat the gray sea.
And so we sailed onward, grieving in our hearts
for dear, slain comrades but glad to flee death."

BOOK TEN

Odysseus narrates his wanderings:
The winds of Aiolos; the Laistrygonian giants
Kirke the enchantress

"We came next to the floating isle Aiolia.
Aiolos, Hippotades' son, dear to the gods
lived there. Around the entire island stood a wall
of smooth stone and unbreakable bronze.
Twelve children had been born in that palace:
six daughters and six sons, all in their prime.
The daughters he gave to his sons as bedmates.
They always dined with their dear father and
loving mother with food before them in abundance.
The winds echoed throughout the fragrant house   10
all days. Nights they slept with their revered
bedmates under blankets on slatted beds.

To their town and beautiful home we came.
He feasted me a month asking about Troy,
and the Argives, the ships, the Akaians' returns:
in due order I recounted all this to him.

When I queried the route home, asked to leave,
he denied me not and, preparing our trip home,
gave me a bag from the hide of a nine-year ox.
Inside he bound the paths of all the howling winds,   20
for Zeus had made him keeper of the winds,
both to calm or to stir up as he wished.
With a shiny silver cord he bound the bag tight
so not even the smallest gust could escape.
And he sent Zephyros' breeze to blow
and drive the ships and us. But it was not to be.
Through our folly we ruined our own return.

For nine days and nine nights we sailed.
On the tenth we saw the tilled land of home
and, being near, saw men tending fires.   30
But then I wearied and sweet sleep came over me.
I ever held the tiller, gave it to no other,
so that we might reach our homeland more quickly.
My companions spoke among themselves:
they thought I had brought silver for myself
and gold, gifts of Hippotades' son Aiolos.
Thus one spoke, looking to another near by:

'Our loss! He is shown love and honor by
all men in whatever city or land he reaches.
And he brought much rich booty back from Troy,   40
treasures, but we, on the same journey as he,
come home with our hands holding empty air!
And now Aiolos has given him more in loving
friendship. Come, quick. Let's see what is in there.
How much gold and silver he has inside the bag.'

So he spoke: his evil words persuaded them.
They opened the bag and all the winds roared out.
At once a howling storm seized us and carried us out
to sea, away from our homeland. But I,

awake now, pondered in my noble heart   50
whether to jump in and perish in the sea
or to endure in silence, still among the living.
Waiting, I endured, lying hidden in
the ship. That evil gale of winds drove us
back to Aiolos' isle, my men wailing.

There we went ashore and got fresh water.
The men ate their meal by the swift ships.
When we had eaten of food and drunk wine,
I made the herald follow me with some men
and went to Aiolos' famous palace. I came   60
upon him dining with his woman and children.
Once at the palace, we sat on the threshold
by the doorpost. Their hearts surprised, they asked:

'You're back, Odysseus? A wicked spirit attacked you?
Kindly we sent you on that you might reach
your land and home and anywhere else dear to you.'

So he spoke and I, being grieved at heart, answered:

'My wicked crew and cruel sleep brought me to grief.
But hear me, friends, for yours is the power to help.'

So I spoke with sweet words. They all remained   70
silent. The father finally spoke with these words:

'Least of living things! Go from this land at once!
For him the happy gods hate we have
no duty to help or to send on his way!
Go, since you come here hated by the gods!'

So speaking he sent me from his halls moaning in
despair. And so we sailed away sore at heart.
The heavy rowing broke the spirit of my men:
rowing all morning with no following wind.

For six days we rowed on, night and day. The next   80
morning we reached the steep Laistrygonian towns,
Telepylos and Lamos, where a shepherd
called his flock homewards while another, driving
his out, heard him. A sleepless man could earn double
wages tending cattle by day and by night
pasturing sheep since night and day overlap.

We came to a harbor where lofty cliffs
rose straight up with no break on either side,
and two promontories faced each other,
joining at the mouth in a narrow passage.   90
All my other men steered their ships within.
Once in, the ships were moored close-packed in
the hollow bay. No wave arose inside that harbor,
neither large nor small, only a white calm.
But I alone moored my black ship outside
at the edge of it, tying cables to rocks.
I climbed up to a rugged lookout and stood.
There I saw neither the work of men nor beast,
but only saw some smoke rising from the land.
I sent men to investigate who these men   100
might be and if they ate grain from the land.
Choosing two men, I sent a herald as the third.

On shore, they walked a smooth road wagons used
to come down from high mountains carrying wood
to the town. They met a girl drawing water,
strong Antiphates' child, the Laistrygonian.
She had come down to the pretty flowing spring
Artakie. From there she carried the water home.
Approaching her they called out and asked who
was king there and who ruled over them.   110
She pointed out her father's high-roofed house.
They entered the shining palace where they found

his wife, big as a mountain crest and hideous.
She called her spouse King Antiphates in from
the courtyard: he planned a terrible death for them.
He seized one man and began to eat him.
The other two leapt up and ran back to my ship.
But the king shouted throughout the town. They came,
those strong Laistrygonians, gathering from all
parts, countless huge men, as big as giants.   120

From the cliffs they hurled boulders as heavy as
a man could lift. A fierce din came from the ships,
the sounds of men dying, ships being splintered.
Like fish they speared my men for a gruesome dinner!
While they killed those men in the deep harbor,
I drew my sharp sword hanging by my thigh
and cut the lines that moored the ship's blue prow.
Yelling to my companions, I roused them to make
their oars fly, churning the salt sea water
so that we might yet flee from those fateful cliffs.   130
To our relief my ship fled seaward from those over-
hanging rocks, but the others, trapped, died there.

And so we sailed away sore at heart. Well pleased
that we escaped, yet sorrowing to lose dear friends.
We came next to the isle of Aiaia where fair-
haired Kirke lives, dread goddess with a human voice.*
She is the sister of Aietes the destroyer,
both born of Helios, light-giver to mortals.
Perse is their mother, child of Okeanos.
There we silently brought our ship to shore   140
into a harbor haven, some god guiding us.
We went ashore and stayed two days there
and two nights, worn out, our hearts eaten by pain.

When fair-haired Dawn brought in the third day,
then, seizing my spear and sharp sword,

I quickly left the ships and climbed to a lookout,
hoping to see farm work and hear mortal voices.
Having climbed up to a rugged spot, I looked
over a wide area and I saw smoke
from Kirke's palace through dense shrubs and woods.   150
I was pondering in my heart and mind to leave
or go explore since I had seen smoke from a fire.
Thinking about this, it seemed to me best
to go back first to the seashore and swift ship
and give my crew food and then to go explore.
But while descending and nearing the curved ship,
some god, having pity for me being alone,
drove into my path a huge, high-antlered stag.
It was coming down from the high pastures
to drink. The great heat of Helios held him.   160

As he came out I struck him in the back, mid spine,
my bronze-tipped spear passing straight through.
He fell to earth with a cry, his spirit flying out.
My foot on him, I pulled my spear from his wound
and laid it down there on the ground. I tore
off green twigs and willow branches for a rope
some six feet long, plaited them, and bound
the feet of this huge beast tightly together.
With it across my back, tied to my spear—
it was too big to carry on my shoulder   170
with one hand—I went down to the black ship
and dropped it in front of the vessel. Waking my men,
I went up to each one, saying these soothing words:

'Friends! Though sore at heart we are not going down
to Hades' house until our destined day comes!
So look! As long as we yet have food and drink,
let's not forget to feast lest we die of hunger.'

So I spoke. They at once obeyed my words.

Uncovering their faces, they marveled at the stag *
on the barren seashore, for it was a huge beast.   180

Once their eyes had finished enjoying the sight,
they washed their hands and made a glorious meal.
So all day until the sun began to set
we sat feasting on boundless meat and rich wine.
When the sun had set and darkness come,
then we lay down beside the foaming surf and slept.

When early-born, pink-fingered Dawn appeared,
I brought them to assembly and spoke to them all:

'Hear my words my comrades, though you have suffered much!
My friends, we do not know where the darkness lies,
where Dawn comes from, where Helios the light-giver   190
goes under earth, nor where he rises! But let us think
if there's a way out for us now, though I see none.
Climbing up to the rugged lookout, I saw
this island circled by the boundless sea.
Though low-lying, I saw with my own eyes
smoke in the midst of dense shrubs and woods.'

So I spoke and their very hearts were shattered
recalling Laistrygonian Antiphates
and the man-eating, great-hearted Cyclops' strength.   200
They wept shrilly, letting big tears fall.
But they wept their tears to no avail.
I counted off all my well-armored men
into two groups and chose a leader for each.
I led one, the other brave Euryloxos.
And then we shook lots in a bronze helmet:
the lot of great-hearted Euryloxos fell out.
So he set off with his twenty-two men
all weeping. We, left behind, wailed too.
In a glen he found Kirke's palace, built   210

of smooth stone in a well-sited place.
Around it roamed mountain-bred wolves and lions
that she'd enchanted, giving them evil drugs.
Nor did they set on my men, but rather stood
on hind legs happily wagging their tails
just as dogs do around their master's home
when he returns from feasting always with some treats.
Just so round them the strong-limbed wolves and lions
pranced. My men feared greatly seeing such fierce beasts.
Standing in the doorway they heard Kirke,   220
the fair-haired goddess, singing with a fine voice.
She worked her divine loom on which the gods
weave their glittering, beautiful fine cloth.
Polites, that leader of men, closest to me
in kinship and most true, spoke thus to the men:

'My friends, someone is plying this great loom
and singing well! The stone floors echo her voice!
Goddess or woman, let's speak to her at once!'

So he spoke. They called out, greeting her.
She came at once, radiant. Opening the door   230
she bid them enter. Foolishly all followed her.
Euryloxos, sensing a trap, stayed behind.
She led them in, made them sit on chairs and benches.
She made a potion stirring cheese and barley
and golden honey into Pramnian wine. She added *
a dark drug that made them forget their homes.
Once she had offered it and they had drunk, just then
she struck them with a staff and penned them in a sty.*
They grew porcine heads, pig voices and bristles,
pig bodies, but their minds remained as before.   240
Penned up thus, they wailed, but Kirke only
tossed them acorns and fruit of the cornel tree
which hogs, wallowing in mud, always eat.

Euryloxos ran swiftly back to the black ship
to tell the bitter fate of his comrades.
Though set on speaking, he could utter no word.
His heart was stricken with great grief, his two
eyes filled with tears, his soul tried to wail.
Calling out, we all wondered at him
and then he told the death of the other men: 250

'We went to the woods as bid, Odysseus.
In the glen we found a fine palace built
of smooth stone in a well-sited place.
Inside she plied a great loom, singing clearly—
goddess or woman. Calling out we addressed her.
Coming at once, she opened the shining door
greeting us. In folly all followed her in.
But I stayed behind sensing a trap.
Then they were put out of sight. Not one of them
appeared. I sat, remaining on watch a long time.'   260

So he spoke. I strapped my silver-studded
sword and great bronze-tipped bow over my shoulders
and ordered him to lead me to the same path.
But grabbing both my knees, he begged me
and wailing said these winged words to me:

'Don't force me, for Zeus' sake, but leave me here!
I know that neither you yourself nor any of
the men will be safe. With these men let us
flee now! We can still escape this evil day!'

So he spoke. But answering him I said: 270

'Euryloxos, you stay here in this place,
eating and drinking by the hollow black ship,
but I am going: necessity drives me on.'

Speaking thus, I climbed from the ship and sea.
But when I was just entering the holy glen
to come to drug-skilled Kirke's great house,
Hermes of the golden staff met me,
coming to the house like a young man
in most beautiful youth with his first beard.
He put his hand on me, called my name and said: 280

'Unhappy one, why come alone to this hill
knowing not this place? Your men are locked in
at Kirke's like hogs held in a closed-packed hole.
Do you come to free them? I say you will
not return but will stay locked in with them.
But come! I will save you, free you from this evil.
Here! Take this drug and go in Kirke's house
for it is strong and will ward off this evil drug.
And I will tell you all of Kirke's wicked plans.
She will make a drink and stir in her drug,   290
but it will not enchant you. This good herb
will not allow it. I will tell you what to do.
When Kirke strikes you with her long staff,
draw then your sharp sword from your thigh
and rush upon her as if about to kill her.
Cowering in fear, she'll beg you to bed her.
Then you must not deny the bed of the goddess,
or she won't free your men nor wait on you.
But make her swear a great oath on the gods
not to devise any other traps for you,   300
nor make you weak, unmanning you when naked.'

So speaking, the Argos-slayer gave me the herb
he had pulled from the earth and showed me its nature.
It's root was black, the flower white as milk.
The gods call it moly. It's harmful for mortals*
to uproot, though the gods can do all.

Then Hermes left the wooded isle and returned
to happy Olympos. I went to Kirke's
palace, dark thoughts roiling in my heart.
I stood in the doorway of the fair-haired goddess.   310
Standing there I called the goddess who heard my voice.
Coming at once, she opened the shining door
and greeted me. With anxious heart I followed.
She made me sit, having led me to a lovely,
well-wrought, silver-studded chair with a footstool.
With evil in her heart she mixed a brew in a
gold cup with her drug in it for me to drink.
She gave it to me. I drank but it did not charm me.
Striking me with her staff, she called out saying:

'Now go to the pigsty, lie with your companions.'   320

So she spoke. But I drew my sword from my thigh
and sprang upon Kirke as if to kill her.
With a loud cry, she collapsed and grabbed
my knees, wailing with these winged words:

'Who among men are you? Where's your town, your parents?
Why did my drug not cast a spell on you?
For no other man could ever withstand my potion!
It always enchants whoever swallows it!
But your heart in your breast won't be charmed.
You must be shrewd Odysseus whom he said   330
would come, the Argos-slayer, he of the golden staff.
You came here from Troy in your swift, black ship.
Come, sheathe your sword, let the two of us
go to our bed and mingle in the sheets
in loving, and let us now trust one another.'

So she spoke. But answering her I said:

'Kirke, how can you bid me to be kind to you?

You changed my men to pigs in your palace
and now, planning more tricks, you bid me come
to your chamber and lie with you in your bed,   340
so that when naked you'll strip my courage and manhood!
I would not be unwilling to go to your bed
if you, goddess, would let yourself swear a great oath
not to devise any other traps for me.'

So I spoke. At once she swore as I had bid.
When she had sworn and completed her oath
I then climbed into Kirke's beautiful bed.

Four handmaids who were workers in her house
busied themselves throughout Kirke's palace.
They were born of the spring and sacred grove   350
and the holy river that flows seaward.
She had one maid cover the chairs with pretty rugs,
purple on top with linen underneath.
Another put silver tables by the chairs,
and on the tables she put golden goblets.
A third mixed rich, honeyed wine in a silver
mixing bowl and filled the golden goblets.
The fourth brought water and built a blazing fire
under the large tripod to heat the water.
When the water boiled in that bright, bronze pot,   360
she washed me in a tub, the hot water
mixed just right soothing my head and shoulders.
My limbs were freed of life-destroying weariness.

When she had washed and rubbed me with olive oil,
she wrapped me in a handsome cloak over a tunic
and had me sit in a well-wrought chair
with silver nails, a footstool underneath.
From a golden pitcher, a maid poured water
over my hands to wash them, a silver bowl

below. Beside me she put a smooth table.   370
The revered housekeeper brought food and laid it there
near at hand, favoring me with abundance.
She bid me eat, but my mind was not on eating.
I sat there with thoughts elsewhere, foreseeing troubles.

Kirke noticed that I sat, my hands not reaching
out for the food, a strong sorrow enfolding me.
Coming near she said these winged words:

'Odysseus, why do you sit thus speechless
touching neither food nor drink, your heart saddened?
Are you imagining another trap which you   380
need not fear? I forswore that with a strong oath.'

So she spoke. But answering her, I said:

'Oh Kirke, what man who is righteous could
endure to dine on food and drink before
seeing with his own eyes that his men were free?
If you wish me to eat and drink, free my trusty
comrades in advance so my own eyes see them.'

So I spoke. Kirke went out of the palace,
her staff in hand and opened the pigsty's gate.
Out she drove them, men like nine-year hogs.   390
They stood opposite her. She went among them,
rubbing each one with the salve of a drug.
Bristles that had grown from the first evil
drug Kirke had used started dropping off.
At once they became new men, as they had been
but far more handsome, much better to look at.

They became themselves and each grabbed my hands.
The deep wailing from all penetrated the palace,
echoing horribly. She too pitied them.
Kirke, shining goddess, stood near and said to me: 400

'Zeus-born Laertes' son, artful Odysseus,
go now to the seashore, to your swift ship.
First of all, drag your ship onto dry land,
carry all your goods and tools into the caves.
You yourself go now and lead your loyal men.'

So she spoke. Convinced in my manly heart,
I set out for the shore and the swift ship.
There I found my loyal men at the ship
weeping terribly, heavy tears falling.
Just like calves among a herd of field oxen   410
sated with grass, heading for the dung-heaped barn,
cavort among themselves—nor can a pen
hold them, endlessly running about, lowing
for their mothers—so they were when their eyes saw me.
Tears pouring down, their hearts seemed to me
as if they had arrived home to their town
on rugged Ithaka, where they were born and reared.

Wailing, they addressed these winged words to me:

'Zeus-born, we are glad you have come back to us,
glad as if we had returned to Ithaka!   420
But now tell us how our comrades died.'

So they spoke. With gentle words I answered them:

'First of all, let's drag our ship onto dry land,
and carry all our goods and tools into the caves.
Rouse yourselves and come along with me
to see your friends in Kirke's sacred house
eating and drinking with all in abundance.'

So I spoke. My words at once convinced them.
Euryloxos alone restrained my men
and addressed them, speaking these winged words: 430

'Fools! Why go there? Why look for worse trouble?
Going to Kirke's palace to be transformed
to pigs or worse? To become wolves or lions
where you will be forced to guard Kirke's palace?
Just like the Cyclopes captured our men when they
came to his cave following Odysseus?
Companions killed because of his reckless folly?'

So he spoke. Astonished in my heart,
I drew my sword from my stout thigh thinking
to cut his head off and roll it on the ground—   440
though he was close kin—when my men
restrained me with gentle words from all sides:

'Zeus-born, please permit this! If you so command,
let him remain by the ship to guard it
and you lead us to Kirke's sacred palace.'

So speaking, they started up from the ship and shore.
Nor would Euryloxos hold by the hollow ship
but followed, fearing my violent rebuke.

Meanwhile Kirke kindly freed those men
in her house, rubbing them with olive oil.   450
She dressed them in tunics and woolen cloaks.
And so we found them in the palace eating well
when we came and we pointed at one another.
Weeping, they shouted out, the house echoed their cries.
She, brilliant of goddesses, stood near and said:

'Zeus-born Laertes' son, artful Odysseus,
no longer stir up these heavy tears. I know
what pains you have suffered on the fish-full sea,
the horrible things men did to you on land.
But come now, eat meat and drink wine   460
until your heart in your chest becomes calm

such as when you left your native land,
rugged Ithaka. You're worn out, depressed,
ever mindful of the harsh sea, your heart
never glad since you have suffered so much.'

So she spoke, persuading my noble heart.
Then all the days until a year had passed
we sat, feasting on abundant meat, rich wine.
When a year had passed, the seasons changed,
months waning, our glad days brought full round,   470
then, calling out, my loyal men said:

'Infatuated man, think on your native earth!
If it is your true fate, then return safely
to your well-built home and to your fatherland.'

So they spoke and they convinced my noble heart.

So all day until the sun began to set
we sat feasting on boundless meat and rich wine.
When the sun had set and darkness come
throughout the dark palace, we lay down to sleep.
But I went to Kirke's lovely, well-wrought bed,   480
grasping her knees and begged, and the goddess
heard my voice as I spoke these winged words:

'Kirke, fulfill the promise you made to me:
send me home. My heart is eager and
the other men's, who voice their own hearts
lamenting to me when you are away from us.'

So I spoke. The shining goddess then replied:

'Zeus-born Laertes' son, artful Odysseus,
you stay not in my house against your will now.
But first you must complete another journey.   490
Go to the house of Hades and feared Persephone.

Consult the spirit of Theban Teiresias,
the blind seer, whose wits still remain.
To him alone, though dead, Persephone granted
reason. The others flit about, mere shades.'

So she spoke. But my own heart shattered.
Sitting down on her bed, I wept. My heart
no longer wished to live nor see sunlight.
When I had had my fill of weeping and pain,
then, with these chosen words, I answered her: 500

'Kirke, who will guide me on this journey?
No one has yet reached Hades in a black ship.'

So I spoke. The shining goddess then replied:

'Zeus-born Laertes' son, artful Odysseus,
don't let yearning for a guide bother you.
Raise the mast, stretch out the white sails
and sit: the breath of Boreas will drive your ship.
When you have passed through Okeanos, there is
a cliff, with rich earth and Persephone's sacred
grove—tall poplars, willow trees that lose their fruit.   510
There beach your ship far from deep Okeanos.
You yourself go to the moldy house of Hades.
There Pyriphlegethon flows into Akeron,
so too Kokytos, a branch of the river Styx.
The two streams meet crashing loudly against a rock.
Hero, when there, approach close. Do as I bid.
Dig a ditch this way and that, some six feet long.
There pour a drink-offering to all the dead.
Pour the honey first, and then rich wine,
and third, water; then sprinkle white barley on all.   520

Promise those strengthless heads of the dead that when you
return to Ithaka you'll kill the best, barren

ox and build a pyre piled with good things.
But promise to Teiresias alone
an all black ram, foremost in your flock.
And when you pray to the famed tribe of the dead,
sacrifice a ram and ewe, both all black
turning their heads to Erebos. But you turn
away, toward the river stream. Many souls
of the tribe of the dead will come to you there.   530

Then rouse your men and order them to flay
the slaughtered animals lying there
with bronze blades and burn them, praying to the gods:
mighty Hades and feared Persephone.
You yourself, unsheathe your sharp sword and sit.
Do not allow the strengthless heads of the dead
to near the blood until you hear Teiresias.
At once the seer will come to you as leader
to tell you of your journey, the trip's length
for your return, traveling on the fish-full sea.'   540

So she spoke. Then Dawn's golden throne arrived.
Kirke dressed me in garments, both cloak and tunic.
The nymph put on a silvery white mantle,
light and lovely, a beautiful golden belt
around her waist, a veil over her head.
I went throughout the palace rousing my men,
standing by each one saying these gentle words:

'Wake up now from your sweet sleep! Get up!
Let's go, for lady Kirke has told me the way.'

So I spoke. My noble heart persuaded them.   550

But I did not lead my men away unharmed.
One of the youngest, Elpenor, one not
well skilled in war nor well equipped in mind,

who, heavy with wine, seeking coolness, lay down
away from the men on the palace roof.
Hearing the noise and din of men moving around,
he suddenly leapt up, but his brain forgot
to climb down again, descending the long ladder.
He fell straight down from the roof, broke his neck,
shattering vertebrae. His soul fled down to Hades.   560

Ready to leave, I spoke a word among my men:

'Now you think that we are going homeward,
to our dear land, but Kirke told me that our path
is to the house of Hades and feared Persephone
to consult the spirit of Theban Teiresias.'

So I spoke. Now their hearts were truly shattered.
Weeping, they began to pull their hair out.
But this had no effect on me, this flood of tears.

Though grieving, we went down to the seashore
to our swift ship, heavy tears flowing down.   570
Meanwhile, going down to the black ship,
Kirke, moving lightly, brought us a ram and ewe,
both black. Whose eyes can see a god moving
here and there if the god does not wish it?"

BOOK ELEVEN

Odysseus narrates his wanderings:
His journey to the underworld and Teiresias' prophecy
His encounters with the souls of queens and heroes

"So we went down then to the ship and sea
and dragged the ship to the glittering brine,
stepping the mast and putting the sail on the black ship.
Seizing the animals, we loaded them on board,
and grieving, we boarded, heavy tears flowing.
She sent behind our ship with its blue prow
a fair wind like a comrade, filling the sail,
feared goddess, human-voiced, fair-haired Kirke.
Throughout the ship we stowed all our tackle,
then sat, the wind and pilot steering us.   10
Crossing the sea, the sails stretched out all day.
Then the sun set and all the pathways darkened.

The ship came to the limits of deep Okeanos.
The town and land of the Kimmerians lies there
shrouded in mist and clouds. Nor does Helios
ever look down on them with shining rays.

Nor does Helios go to the starry sky.
Nor does he turn back from the sky to earth.
Deadly night stretches over the luckless mortals.
Having come here, we beached the ship and took   20
the animals ashore. We came here, beyond
Okeanos, the place Kirke had described.

There Euryloxos and Perimedes held
the sacrificial animals. I drew my sword,
dug a ditch this way and that some six feet long.
Here I poured drink-offerings to all the dead,
first pouring the honey, after that rich wine,
and third, water. I sprinkled white barley on all.
I promised those strengthless heads of the dead that on
returning to Ithaka, I'd kill the best barren   30
ox and build a pyre piled with good things.
But I promised to Teiresias alone
an all black ram, the foremost in my flock.
Then I gave prayers to the famed tribe of the dead,
and grabbing the animals, I cut their throats.
Black pools of blood filled the ditch. They gathered
from under Erebos, those souls of the dead:
brides, unmarried boys, much-suffering old men,
young maidens with fresh sorrows in their hearts,
many men wounded with bronze spears of battle,   40
men battle-slain, gore-smeared, still in armor.
This throng flitted all about the ditch, a din
of shrieking. Pale-green fear began to seize me.

Then rousing my men, I ordered them to flay
with bronze blades the slaughtered animals
and burn them completely, praying to the gods,
mighty Hades and feared Persephone.
I myself drew my sharp sword and sat,
not allowing the strengthless heads of the dead

to near the blood until I heard Teiresias.   50

First came the soul of Elpenor, our companion,
who had not been buried under earth's wide paths.
We'd left his body behind at Kirke's palace,
unmourned, unburied. Another task drove us on.
Seeing him I wept, my heart pitying him.
Speaking to him, I said these winged words:

'Elpenor, how came you to this cloudy gloom,
you on foot and we in our black ship?'

So I spoke. Crying out, he answered me:

'Zeus-born Laertes' son, artful Odysseus,   60
an evil demon doomed me—and drinking too much wine!
At Kirke's I slept on the roof and, not thinking
to climb down again on the long ladder,
I fell straight down from the roof, broke my neck,
shattering vertebrae. My soul fled down to Hades.
I beg you now by those not present, those left behind,
by your bedmate and father who nourished you when little,
by him, Telemakos, whom you left alone,
for I know when you leave the house of Hades
your well-built ship will head for the isle of Aiaia.   70
When there, lord, remember me, I beg you!
Going back don't leave me unmourned, unburied,
abandoning me, lest I cause some god to curse you.
But burn me in my armor, all that I have.*
For this unfortunate man heap up a mound by
the gray sea's sands so those to come know of me.
Do this for me and stick an oar in my tomb,
the one I pulled alongside my companions.'

So he spoke. Replying, this is what I said:

'Unfortunate one, these I'll do and complete!'   80

Thus we sat talking in sad words, my drawn sword
on one side guarding the blood while the shadow
of my comrade talked long on the other side.

The spirit of my dead mother approached,
great-hearted Autolykos' daughter Antikleia
who lived yet when I left for sacred Ilios.
Seeing her, tears welled up, my heart ached.
Even so, I kept her from the blood
till I should hear Teiresias, though it grieved me.

Next came the spirit of Theban Teiresias   90
holding his golden scepter. He knew me and spoke:

'Zeus-born Laertes' son, artful Odysseus,
poor man, why came you here? You left sunlight
behind to see the dead in this most joyless place?
Step back from the ditch, hold off your sharp sword
so I may drink this blood and so speak truly.'

So he spoke. I stepped back and sheathed
my silver-studded sword. He drank of the black blood.
Then the noble seer addressed me with these words:

'Seek your sweet return shining Odysseus,   100
though a god will make it harsh. You did not
escape the Earth-shaker's notice. His heart's
ever angry since you blinded his dear son.

But you may yet reach home through much hardship,
if your heart wishes to find it, and your men too.
But when you first approach the isle Thrinakia,
turn your well-built ship! Flee to the deep-blue sea!
You'll find his oxen grazing there and large flocks.
Helios owns them, he who sees and hears all.

Think on your return. Harm none of them and you 110
may yet get to Ithaka, though suffering much.
But if you harm them, I foresee destruction,
both ship and men. If you yourself avoid this,
after a long, hard time you may return, though on
another's ship, your men all dead. You'll find
trouble at home: reckless men devouring your goods,
courting your godlike bedmate, giving dowry gifts.
But once there you will avenge their violence,
and when you kill these suitors in your palace
by deceit or openly with sharp bronze, 120
travel then, taking a well-balanced oar,
until you come to where men know nothing of
the sea, nor do they eat meat with salt.
They know nothing of ships with red prows
or well-balanced oars, the wings of ships.

Here's an easy sign to note; you won't miss it.
When you meet another traveler who says
you have a winnowing fan on your strong shoulder,
there stick your well-balanced oar in the earth.
Sacrifice pure animals to lord Poseidon: 130
a ram, a bull, a sow-mounting boar.
Then once home, sacrifice a hecatomb
to the deathless gods who hold the wide sky,
to each in due order. Your death will come far from
the sea, ever so gently, and it will bring you down
in hearty old age with your people prospering.
All these words I speak will surely come to pass.'

So he spoke. Answering him, I said:

'Teiresias, I think the gods themselves allot
these things. But come, say truly and tell me this: 140
I see my mother's soul among the dead.

She sits in silence near the blood, not trying
to speak, not even looking her son in the face.
Tell me, lord, how can I make her know me?'

So I spoke. Answering me he said:

'It's easy. I'll tell you how and lodge it in your mind.
Whichever one of the tribe of the dead you let
come near the blood, that one will tell the truth.
Whomever you refuse, that one goes back again.'

So speaking, the spirit of lord Teiresias,   150
after his prophecy, entered the house of Hades.
I waited there steadfast until my mother came.
She drank of the black blood. And at once she knew me,
and, lamenting, addressed these winged words to me:

'My child, how have you come to this murky darkness
being alive? It's hard for the living to see here.
There's a river with a fierce middle current,
the foremost of Okeanos, impossible
on foot if one does not come in a well-built ship.
Why here after years of wandering   160
by ship from Troy with your men? Did you not go
to Ithaka? Not see your bedmate in the palace?'

So she spoke. Answering her, I said:

'Mother, necessity drove me down to Hades
to hear the spirit of Theban Teiresias.
I never went near Akaia, nor did I step
onto our land, but wandered always in sorrow
from when I first followed noble Agamemnon
to Ilios, abounding in foals, to fight the Trojans.
But come, tell me this and tell it truly,   170
what fate laid you out with prostrating death?

A long disease? Did Artemis, shooter of arrows,
moving about, slay you with her gentle missiles?
What of my father, my son whom I left behind?
Are my prizes of honor still there? Or does
some other hold them, no longer thinking I'll return?
My wedded bedmate, what are her plans, her thoughts?
Waits she with our child, always guarding all?
Or has she married an Akaian, one of the best?'

So I spoke. She then, lady mother, replied: 180

'With an enduring heart she waits for you
in your palace. At night she is miserable,
wasting away, shedding tears through the days.
No one holds your beautiful prizes of honor.
Telemakos rules your land easily:
he eats with equals like a traveling judge,
for all invite him. Your father dwells on his
own farm, never going to the town. He has
no bed, no cloaks, no shining blankets. In winter
he sleeps where the servants do, in the house   190
in hearth dust near the fire, old clothes against his skin.
But in time of summer and autumn harvest,
wherever the garden slopes and vineyard blooms,
he sleeps on the ground on fallen beds of leaves.
He lies there grieving. Sorrow swells in his heart
longing for your return, harsh old age upon him.
For so I perished and pursued my fate.
Not in the palace did the sharp-eyed arrow shooter
approach and slay me with her gentle missiles.
Nor did some sickness befall me with hateful   200
wasting away, taking my heart from my limbs.
Longing for you, your counsels, shining Odysseus,
your honey-sweet gentleness, stole my spirit.'

So she spoke. But my heart willed me on:
I wanted to embrace my dead mother's spirit.
Three times I sprang up, my heart bidding me hug her.
Three times she fled my arms like a shadow
or a dream. Sharp grief grew strong in my heart,
and answering her, I said these winged words:

'Mother, why do not you wait for my embrace   210
so we may both enjoy wrapping our arms around
each other even in this house of icy wailing?
Or did noble Persephone stir up this likeness
so that I might yet mourn and lament more?'

So I spoke. My lady mother then replied:

'Ah me, my child, of all mortals most ill-fated.
Persephone, Zeus' daughter, does not deceive you.
This is the way of mortals when they die:
the tendons no longer bind flesh to bones.
Once the heart first leaves the white bones,   220
the burning fire's strength overcomes all
and the soul flies off as a dream flitters away.
So flee to the light quickly! Mind these things
so that you may tell your woman when you go back.'

With such words we talked together. But women
approached, stirred up by proud Persephone,
all of them the noblest bedmates and daughters.

They all thronged together around the black blood.
I had planned how I might speak to each one.
This plan is the one that seemed best to my heart.   230
Drawing my sharp sword from beside my thigh,
I did not let them drink of the black blood together.
Thus they came one by one and each declared
whose child she was. I questioned all of them.

First I saw Tyro, a noble father's daughter.
She said she was the child of brave Salmoneos
and mate to Kretheos, Aiolos' son.
She loved the river god Enipeus,
the most gorgeous river that shoots forth from the earth.
She used to travel on Enipeus' current.   240
Appearing like him, earth-embracing Poseidon
bedded her in the mouth of the eddying stream.
A purple wave surrounded them like a mountain,
curved, concealing the god and mortal woman.
He loosed her virgin belt and poured sleep on her.
But when the god had finished his love work,
he grabbed her hand and called her by her name:

'Rejoice in this love making, woman! After a year
revolves you'll bear splendid children, since the beds
of gods are never barren. Rear and care for them.   250
Now go home and take care not to name me
though I am indeed the Earth-shaker Poseidon.'

Speaking thus, he dove into the surging sea.
She, pregnant, bore Pelias and Neleus
who both became strong attendants of great Zeus.
In the open land of Iolkos Pelias dwelled,
rich in sheep, Neleus in sandy Pylos.
This queen of women bore with Kretheos these others:
Aison, Pheres, and chariot-man Amythaon.

Next I saw Antiope, Asopos' daughter.   260
She claimed she slept in the crook of Zeus' arm
and bore him two children, Amphion and Zethos.
They first built the city of seven-gated Thebes,
raised the walls, for in the open plain it could
not be lived in unwalled, strong though both were.

Amphytrion's mate, Alkmene, I saw next.

She gave birth to brave-spirited, lion-hearted
Herakles, after love in Zeus' bent arm,
and then Megara, Kreion's high-spirited daughter,
whom Amphytrion's mighty, tireless son possessed.*   270

I saw Oidipodes' mother, Epikaste.
Her monstrous act—though she was unaware—
marrying her own son. He'd killed his father
and married her. The gods let this be known to men.
He, though suffering, was lord of the Kadmeians
in much-loved Thebes through the gods' destructive plans.
She in sorrow went to Hades, the strong Gate-keeper:
she'd hanged herself with a lethal noose slung round
a high roof beam. She left behind many strong pains
for him: the Erinys fulfilled these for his mother.*   280

I saw lovely Kloris then whom Neleus wed
for her beauty after he had brought great gifts,
the youngest maid of Amphion, Iasion's son,
who ruled with might in Minyan Orkomenos.
She was queen in Pylos and bore him splendid sons:
Nestor, Kronios and Periklymenos.
After these sons, she bore beautiful Pero.
All nearby tried to court her, but Neleus *
would only wed her to who'd steal from Phylake
the broad-faced, spiral-horned oxen of Iphikles,   290
a hard task. The seer promised that only he
could drive them off, but a god's harsh fate held him:
the peasant herdsmen bound him in painful chains.
But when months and days had passed, the year
revolved and the season had come again,
then Iphikles freed him after he had spoken
all his prophecies, fulfilling the will of Zeus.

And I saw Leda, Tyndareos' mate,

who bore stout-hearted children to Tyndareos,
horse-tamer Kastor and Polydeukes the boxer.   300
Though they're alive, life-giving earth covers them.
Even below the earth they are honored by Zeus:
one day alive and the next dead again,
they alternate, though with honor equal to gods.*

Next came Iphimedeia, Aloeus' bedmate,
who used to claim she lay with Poseidon
and bore him two children, both short-lived:
far-renowned Ephialtes and godlike Otos.
The grain-giving land nourished them, the tallest
and most handsome after famous Orion.   310
When nine years old, they were nine cubits wide
and had indeed grown to nine fathoms tall.*
They even threatened to start the battle din
of war against the deathless ones on Olympos.
Ready they were to stack Mt. Ossa on Olympos,
wooded Pelion on Ossa to climb the sky*
and would have done so had they reached manhood.
But Zeus' son, whom fair-haired Leto bore, slew them*
both before down flowered below their temples,
before thick woolly beards covered their jaws.   320

Phaedra came, and Prokris, and lovely Ariadne,
destructive-minded Minos' maid whom Theseus
wanted to bring from Krete to sacred Athens' slopes,
but he had no joy of her. Artemis slew her
on sea-washed Dia on evidence from Dionysos.*

Maira, Klymene, and hated Eriphyle came,
she who had traded her bedmate for gold.*

I cannot name or mention all I saw—
many were bedmates of heroes or daughters—
before this sweet night slips away. But now's the time   330

to sleep down with the crew on the swift ship—
or here. You and the gods will take care of our leaving."

So he spoke. They all were still, in silence,
held in a spell within the shadowy hall.
White-armed Arete did address them thus at last:

"Phaiakians, how does this man appear to you
in form and height and balanced heart within?
He is my guest, but you each share in his honor.
Rush not to send him on nor cut short your own giving
of the gifts he wants. By the gods' will   340
you each have much wealth in your palaces."

Then the old hero Ekeneos spoke,
born before the other men of Phaiakia:

"My friends, our wise queen in her words did not
miss the mark of our own thoughts, so obey.
But now the word and deed depend on Alkinoös."

Speaking then, Alkinoös answered him:

"So let this be the word as long as I am king
and rule the oar-loving Phaiakians!
Guest, though wanting to return, endure more.   350
Stay until tomorrow when I shall complete all
gift-gathering. Your escort concerns all here, me most
of all since I hold the power in this land."

Then, answering him, artful Odysseus spoke:

"Lord Alkinoös, renowned of all people,
if you should bid me tarry here for a year
that you might plan an escort and give me great gifts,
I would wish this. It would be much better for me
to reach my native land with my hands filled.

It's much more awe-inspiring, more welcome to all men   360
who might witness my return to Ithaka."

Then again answered Alkinoös thus:

"Odysseus, looking at you we don't suppose
you are a cheat or thief. There are many whom
the dark earth feeds among the dispersed peoples,
preparing lies that no one could see through.
But you have a grace of words, a noble heart.
Your words are like those a bard with skill relates
of the sad cares of all Argives and of your own.
But come now, tell us truly if you saw any   370
of your godlike comrades who, along with you,
followed on to Ilios and met their fate there.
The night is unbearably long. Nor is it time
to sleep. So tell me of the wondrous deeds!
I could hold on till bright dawn in these halls
as long as you could bear telling your troubles."

Then, answering him, artful Odysseus spoke:

"Lord Alkinoös, renowned of all people,
a time there is for war tales, a time for sleep.
If you wish to hear more, I'll not hold back.   380
I will tell of these and more sorrowful tales,
those of my comrades who died earlier,
and the sad cries of those who escaped from Troy,
slain on return through a wicked woman's will.

When holy Persephone, most womanly of women,
had scattered those women's spirits here and there,
Agamemnon, Atreus' son's grieving spirit,
approached. Around him gathered others who'd died
in Aigisthos' palace where they met their fate.
That one knew me once he had drunk of the black blood.   390

He wept loudly, heavy tears falling down,
and reaching eagerly he stretched his hands toward me.
But he no longer had that might and strength,
the very sort that his bent arms once had.
Seeing his tears, I had compassion in my heart
and spoke to him with these winged words:

'Most glorious Agamemnon, lord of men,
what fate conquered you, laid you out in death?
Were you struck down in your ships by Poseidon
who stirred up terrible blasts of fierce winds?   400
Or did hostile men hurt you on land while out
raiding sheep or oxen from some rich herd,
or fighting near their town and their women?'

So I spoke. Answering me at once, he said:

'Zeus-born Laertes' son, artful Odysseus,
Poseidon did not strike me down in my ships,
having stirred up terrible blasts of fierce winds,
nor did hostile men hurt me on land while raiding.
Aigisthos planned my destiny and my death
with my accursed bedmate. Invited to his house,   410
while feasting, he slew me as one slays an ox at trough!
So I died a most pitiable death. My men
were all slaughtered just as white-toothed hogs
are butchered in a powerful man's wealthy home
for a wedding feast, outdoor meal or banquet.
You have seen the slaughter of many men
dying alone or in fierce battle, but seeing us,
especially there among the wine bowls and full tables,
you would have wept in your heart seeing how
we lay in the hall, the floor running with blood.   420
I heard Priam's daughter's voice, most pitiable
Kassandra's, whom Klytaimnestra slew standing

near me. Dying on the floor, a sword passing
straight through me, I pounded on the earth, cursing.
But she turned away. Nor did her hands—though I
was going to Hades—draw down my eyelids!
Nothing is wilder or more offensive than a woman
who puts such acts in her heart. That one alone
contrived this shameless act, having prepared
the slaughter of her wedded spouse. Truly,   430
just returned, I thought this a joyful welcome
for my children and servants, but wickedly
she poured shame down on all women, even those
yet to come, even those acting rightly.'

So he spoke. But answering him, I said:

'Strange how from the beginning far-seeing Zeus
hated the offspring of Atreus and
their scheming women. Many perished because of Helen.
With you away, Klytaimnestra planned this trap.'

So I spoke. And answering me, he said: 440

'So you also should not be gentle with your woman.
Don't tell her all your thoughts, which you well know,
but tell her some while some remain concealed.
Fear not death, Odysseus, from your bedmate,
for she is very smart, her heart keeps good counsel,
Ikarios' maid, thoughtful Penelope.
Behind we left her, a young, newly married bride
when we went to war. She had a young child
at her breast who now must sit among the men,
happy. That one will get to see his dear father,   450
and he will embrace his father, as is right.
My bedmate did not let my eyes be filled with my
dear son: she killed me before that could happen!
But I will tell you more and put it in your heart.

Once home, bring your ship secretly to land,
not openly, since there is no trust in women.
But come now, speak! And tell me truly if
you've heard that my child is among the living,
whether in Orkomenos or sandy Pylos,
or if alongside Menelaos in spacious Sparta.   460
For brilliant Orestes still walks the earth.'

So he spoke. Answering him, I said:

'Atreus' son, why ask this? I know not if
he lives. It's bad to speak words empty as air.'

So we two stood conversing in sorrowful words,
grieving, weeping, the flood of tears pouring down.

Then came Peleus's son Akilleus
and Patroklos and noble Antilokos,
and Aias: they were the best in form and build
of all the Danaans after Peleus' son.   470
The swift-footed descendant of Aiakos knew me.
Lamenting, he addressed these winged words to me:

'Zeus-born Laertes' son, artful Odysseus,
what plan of yours could surpass this trip to Hades?
How can you endure it down in Hades where
the strengthless dead abide, grieving phantoms of mortals?'

So he spoke. Answering him, I said:

'Brave Akilleus, far the strongest Akaian,
I came here needing Teiresias. He might tell me
of a way I might return to Ithaka.   480
For I've not come near Akaia, never trod
our earth, though I've always had troubles. But you,
Akilleus, are forever most blessed of men.
We Argives honored you living like to the gods.

Now, here, among the dead, you greatly surpass all.
Akilleus, do not thus grieve being dead.'

So I spoke. Answering me, he said:

'Console me not about death, Odysseus!
I'd rather be a hired day-laboring serf
for a landless man who has few goods—that   490
rather than lord over all these dead phantoms!
But come now, tell me of my illustrious son,
whether or not he leaps first into the fray.
And tell me of lord Peleus, if you know,
whether all the Myrmidons still honor him,
or if he's dishonored in Hellas and Phthia
because old age binds his hands and feet.
No longer can I aid him under the sun's glare
such as I did, killing the best fighters there,
defending the Argives in Troy's broad plains.   500
If I could go there to my father's house, though briefly,
I'd make that man hate my might and strong hands,
he who through brute force tries to dethrone him'

So he spoke. Answering him, I said:

'I learned nothing of King Peleus by inquiry,
but I will tell you truly of your son,
dear Neoptolemos, as you bid me,
since I myself brought him in my hollow ship
from Skyros to join the well-armored Akaians.
Whenever we talked of plans around the Trojan town,   510
he always spoke first and was not off the mark.
Only godlike Nestor and I surpassed him.
And when the Akaians fought on the plains of Troy,
he didn't wait in the throng or crowds of men,
but he ran far ahead, his might like no other,
and he slew many men in fierce combat.

I will not tell nor name the many he slew there
defending the army of the Akaians,
but he killed such a one as the son of Telephos,
the brave Eurypylos, and many Keteian men   520
around him fell because of a gift to a woman.*
He was the most handsome I saw after Memnon.
But when I climbed into that horse Epeios built
with the Akaian's best who'd been assigned to me,
both to open and close the tight trap,
there the other Danaan lords and leaders
wiped off tears while the limbs of each trembled.
I watched your son and saw all with my eyes:
his wondrous skin did not go pale, nor did he wipe
tears from his cheek. Many times he wished to be   530
sent out from the horse, fingering his sword hilt,
his bronze-tipped spear, eager for death for the Trojans.
But when we had sacked Priam's lofty city,
holding his portion of booty, he boarded the ship
unscathed, not struck by bronze sword, nor wounded
in hand to hand combat as many are in war
since Ares ever rages indiscriminately.'

So I spoke. Swift-footed Akilleus' spirit
strode down to the asphodel meadows
glad that I had told him of his son's renown.   540
The other spirits of the tribe of the dead
stood grieving, all asking about their own cares.
Only the spirit of Telemon's son Aias
stood aloof, still angry at my victory.
During the judgment by the ships, I won
Akilleus' armor. His noble mother set the prize.
Trojan youth gave judgment and Pallas Athena.
Would that I had not won in such a contest:
the earth now covers Aias for the sake
of armor, with such a body, in form and deeds   550

the best of all Danaans after Peleus' son.
Now I said to him these honey-smooth words:

'Aias, noble Telemon's child, will you not try
to cease your anger over Akilleus' cursed
armor? The gods poured trouble down on the Argives!
A tower we lost when you fell! We grieved
for you as for Peleus' son Akilleus,
ever mourning you. There is no one to blame
but Zeus who fiercely hated the Danaan army
of spearmen: he it was who etched your fate.   560
But come near, lord, that you might hear our words
and tales. Tame your anger and your manly pride.'

So I spoke, but he said nothing. He followed after
the other spirits to Hades and the tribe of the dead.
Still, though angry, he would have spoken or I
to him, but my own heart wished to see
other spirits of the tribe of the dead.

Then I did see Minos, Zeus' noble son,
holding a golden scepter, judging the dead.
The king inquired of the cases of those seated   570
or standing about in Hades' open-gated house.

Behind him I saw huge Orion netting wild beasts,
corralling them in the asphodel meadows,
those animals he'd slain in the lonely mountains,
his hard bronze club ready in his hands.

Then I saw Tityos, Gaia's son,
stretched on the ground over nine roods.*
Two vultures tore at his liver, their beaks
in bowels, his hands unable to ward them off.
For he had dragged off Leto, Zeus' glorious bedmate,   580
while going to Pytho by fair Panopeos.

Then I saw Tantalos in strong pain,
standing in a pool, water to his chin.
He looked thirsty but he could never drink.
Each time that raging old man bent to drink
the water went away, swallowed up, black earth
round his feet that a god had made dry.
Lofty trees laden with fruit top to bottom,
pear, mulberry and apple trees with splendid fruit,
and sweet fig trees and olive trees bloomed there.   590
Whenever the old man tried to reach the fruit
a wind would hurl them up to the shadowy clouds.

Next came Sisyphos, ever suffering,
his hands pushing a huge boulder uphill.
His feet scrambling, his strong hands ever straining,
he pushed the boulder to the crest. But just as he
reached the top, its heavy weight sent it back down.
Once back on the plain, the boulder careened along.
Then he, rousing his strength, would push it up, sweat
running down his arms, his head in swirling dust.   600

After him I saw mighty Herakles,
a phantom. He himself revels among the gods,
wed to Hebe of the fair ankles, Zeus' child—
the great god—and golden-sandaled Hera's.
The dead clamored around him on all sides
like birds wildly distraught. He, like dark night,
held his bow ready with arrow at bow-string,
fiercely peered around, and seemed ever about to shoot.
Around his chest a horrible belt of worked leather
and gold, where god-bidden acts were carved   610
of bears and wild boars and glaring-eyed lions,
of fighting and killing, and the slaughtering of men.
May whoever designed and wrought that belt with so
great skill never make another such again!

Herakles knew me when his eyes saw me
and lamenting, spoke these winged words to me:

'Zeus-born Laertes' son, artful Odysseus,
poor man! Some evil fate guided you here,
that same fate I endured under the sun's rays.
I am the child of Zeus, Kronos' son, but yet   620
unending sorrow holds me. For I was made to serve
a lesser man who gave me harsh labors.*
Once he made me bring the dog from here,
thinking this to be my hardest labor ever,
but I succeeded and drove the dog from Hades.
Hermes guided me and bright-eyed Athena.'

So speaking, he went back within Hades' house.
I waited on there hoping one of those heroes
who had perished in times long past might come.
I would have seen those ancient men I wished to see,   630
Theseus and Peirithoös, the gods' offspring,
but then a throng of the many dead flocked round
with frightful shrieks. Green fear began to seize me
that proud Persephone might send me some huge,
horrendous Gorgon-like head from Hades.

So then, going to the ship, I bid my men
to get themselves aboard and loose the mooring cables.
They boarded instantly and sat at the oarlocks.
A current bore the ship down Okeanos with us
bent rowing, and after came a fair following wind."   640

BOOK TWELVE

Odysseus narrates his wanderings:
The Sirens; Skylla and Karybdis
The cattle of the sun; the rescue of Odysseus by Kalypso

"Once the ship had left the flow of Okeanos,
she came to the swell of the wide seaways,
to the island of Aiaia, home of Dawn,
her dancing ground, the place of Helios' rising.
Having come there, we beached the ship in the sand
and we ourselves disembarked amid the surf.
And then we fell asleep, waiting for fragrant Dawn.

When early-born, pink-fingered Dawn appeared,
then I sent men to Kirke's house to bring
the corpse of Elpenor who had died there.   10
We cut dry wood, performed the rites where the cliff
juts farthest out, grieving, hot tears running down.
When his body and armor had been burned,
we made a mound and dragged a gravestone on it,
and then we planted his well-balanced oar on top.

Thus we arranged these things. Nor did Kirke fail
to notice our return from Hades' house. She made
things ready and came to us, her maids following
with bread, plentiful meat and fiery red wine.

Standing in our midst, the radiant goddess said: 20

'Rash men! While living you go down to Hades' house,
twice-dying, while other men die but once.
But come now, eat some food and drink wine
all day long. You shall, with the Dawn's coming,
sail on. I'll point you out the route, tell you
each thing so you won't feel pain, nor suffer
some painful mishap on the sea or on land.'

So she spoke. Our manly hearts were persuaded.
Thus for the entire day until sunset
we sat feasting on plenty: meat and red wine.   30
And when Helios had set and darkness come,
my men slept by the ship's mooring ropes.
But taking my hand, she led me far from my men,
bid me sit and, lying down, asked me all.
In due order I recounted everything to her.

Then lady Kirke spoke these words to me:

'All those things were well done. Now hear what I
tell you and a god himself will remind you.
You'll come first to the Sirens. They enchant all
the race of men, whoever sails within their reach.   40
Any who nears unwarned and hears the voices of
the Sirens, that man returns not home to his woman
and young children to crowd round him in greeting—
no, the Sirens clear song holds that man spellbound.
They sit in their meadow, while around them rots
a huge heap of men's bones, the skin decaying.

You must sail past, but plug your men's ears
with oil and kneaded wax so none may hear them.
If you yourself should wish to hear them, let your men
bind you upright hand and foot to the swift   50
ship's mast. From there, bound fast, you will be able
to hear and to delight in the Sirens' songs.
If you order your men to free you, or beg them,
let them bind you yet more tightly in the chains.

But when your men have rowed beyond the Sirens,
I will not tell you in detail which way to sail,
which of the two routes is the best. For that
you must decide for yourself. I'll tell you this:
one has overhanging rocks, where the huge waves
of dark-eyed Amphitrite smash against them.   60
The happy gods call these rocks the Wanderers.*
Neither flying things nor even the timid doves
that bring ambrosia to Father Zeus slip through
without the rocks taking at least one of them
though Father Zeus adds one back to keep the number.*
Whichever ship of men reaches them does not
escape, for sea waves and storms of deadly fire
carry off both ship planks and men's bodies.
Only one sea-traversing ship slipped past,
the Argo, known by all, sailing from Aietes.   70
Waves would have smashed it on the huge rocks
had not Hera's love for Iasion sent it through.*

The second route has two cliffs, one a sharp
peak in the sky; a dark-blue cloud surrounds it
and never draws back. The peak has no clear sky,
not in full summer and not in early fall.
Nor could a mortal man climb up and scale it,
not even if he had twenty hands and feet,
for the sheer cliff is slick as if it were polished.

In the middle of this cliff a murky cave   80
faces west toward Erebos. And you
will have to steer your ship past this, Odysseus.
But not even a strong man shooting arrows
from shipboard could reach up to that hollow cave.
Inside lives Skylla with her dire yelping.
The sound of Skylla is like a new-born puppy
but she is an evil monster. Not even
a god could ever be glad to see her.

Her twelve limbs are like tentacles.
Her six long necks stretch up and on each one   90
there is a fearful head with three rows of teeth,
close fitted and thick, all full of black death.
From her mid point down she's hidden in her cave.
But her heads reach outside the dread cave.
Peering about the cliff from her cave she fishes
for seals and dolphins where Amphitrite feeds
her thousands—or for whatever else she can catch.
There your bragging sailors will not sail by
unharmed. Each head of hers will carry off a man,
snatching them off your hollow, blue-prowed ship.   100

But the other cliff lies lower, Odysseus,
and near this cliff, an arrow's shot away,
a huge wild fig tree with abundant leaves grows.
Under it bright Karybdis gulps black water.
Three times each day she spouts, three times she gulps down
terribly. It's best not to be there when she swallows.
Nor could the Earth-shaker save you from that evil.
So drive your ship quickly past her and
instead approach Skylla's lookout. Better
to lose six of your crew than all die together.'   110

So she spoke. Answering her, I said:

'But come now, goddess, tell me truly, is there
a way to slip by deadly Karybdis and so
ward her off and protect my men from her?'

So I spoke. The divine goddess answered:

'Rash one. You think on warlike acts and deeds?
Will you not yield to the deathless gods?
She is not mortal; she is a deathless evil,
dreadful and painful, fierce and unconquerable.
There's no defense. Far better to flee from her.   120

If armed you linger alongside the rock, I fear
you might incite her to scoop down again with
her many heads and take many men away.
With all your might row on, praying to Krataiïs,
Skylla's mother, who bore this peril for mortals.
She'll stop her from attacking you again.

Next you'll come to the isle of Thrinakia.
Rich herds, the Sun's oxen, pasture there,
seven herds of oxen, seven flocks of sheep,
each fifty strong. But they bear no offspring,   130
nor do they ever die. Their shepherds, goddesses,
are fair-haired nymphs Phaesousa and Lampetia,
whom divine Neaira bore to Helios.
Their lady mother, having begot and raised them,
sent them to the distant isle of Thrinakia
to guard their father's herds of curved-horned oxen.
If you leave them unharmed, mindful of your return,
you might, though suffering much, still reach Ithaka.
If you harm them, I see destruction of your ship
and men. If you yourself avoid death, you will   140
return after a long, hard time, your men all lost.'

So she spoke. Then Dawn came on her golden throne.

Divine Kirke left, going across the island.
Boarding the ship, I quickly urged my men onward.
They boarded at once and loosed the mooring ropes,
and went at once to sit at their oarlocks.
Seated in order, their oars beat the gray salt sea
while behind our blue-prowed ship a fair wind blew
filling our sails, a noble friend sent by Kirke,
fair-haired, fierce goddess with a human voice.   150
Having stowed our tackle throughout the ship, we sat.
The helmsman and the wind steered our ship.

Aching in my heart, I then addressed the men:

'My friends, it is not right that only one knows what
Kirke, divine goddess, declared was god-ordained.
Thus I'll tell you so, fully informed, we might die
or by fleeing this risk, we might avoid death.
She bids us first avoid the Sirens' sound
and their flowery meadow. She ordered me alone
to listen to their song. But first bind me in chains,   160
though painful, so I'll wait upright, here, steadfast,
tied to the foot of the mast, bound there with chains.
If I beg you to free me—or order you—
you must keep sailing, binding me more tightly.

So speaking, I made these things known to each man.
Meanwhile, our well-built ship reached the island
of the Sirens, driven on by a fair wind.
The wind dropped and calm covered the sea,
the air still. Some god had made the waves sleep.
My men, standing, furled and stowed the sails   170
in the hollow ship. Sitting at the oarlocks
they beat the water white with oars of polished pine.
With my sharp bronze sword I cut small bits from a
great wheel of wax and kneaded it in my strong hands.
Quickly the wax softened since the Sun's great power

compelled it, the rays of lord Hyperion's son.
I plugged the ears of each of my men in order.
They tied my hands together and my feet and bound me
upright to the ship's mast, securing the chain.
Sitting, their oars beat the gray salt sea. 180

But when we were as far as a man's shout is heard,
though going swiftly, our fast ship did not slip by
unnoticed! We roused them! They readied their sweet song:

'Come here, oh praised Odysseus, Akaians' glory!
Stop your ship so you can hear our two voices!
For no one sails by in a black ship until
he's heard the honeyed melody from our mouths.
Then he goes home happy, knowing many things.
We know all that happened in spacious Troy,
how Argives and Trojans suffered the gods' will. 190
On this earth that feeds so many, we know all.'

So they spoke in their lovely voices and I
wanted to hear more. I ordered my men to free me
nodding my brow. They fell to their rowing.*
Rising, Perimedes and Euryloxos
bound me in more chains and pulled them tighter.
When the ship had slipped by them and I
no longer heard the Sirens' cries and songs,
then my trusty men took from their ears the wax
which I had put in and freed me from the chains. 200

When we had left the island, then at once I saw
smoke and a huge wave and I heard thunder.
From fear, they let the oars fly from their hands and
the oars banged the hull in the current. The ship
had stalled since no sharp-bladed oars drove her.
Moving through the ship, I encouraged the men
with soothing words, standing by each man:

'Friends! We knew about these terrible dangers.
This is no greater than when the Cyclops penned
us by his strength and might in his hollow cave.   210
Then my excellent plan and reasoning
let us escape. I think you do remember that.
Come now, as I said, let's all trust my plan.
Sit down and with your oars in their oarlocks beat
the sea's deep breakers! May Zeus grant that
we escape this, avoiding our destruction.
You, helmsman, I thus order you: put it
in your heart to steer our hollow ship's tiller!
Keep the ship far from the smoke and waves.
Steer you for the cliffs! Do not forget,   220
or heading wrong, you'll bring us greater danger!'

So I spoke. They straightaway obeyed my words.

I had not told of Skylla, that inescapable
horror, lest my trusty men afraid, stop
and no longer obey me and cower within the ship.
And I forgot Kirke's painful command to me
when she ordered me not to arm myself.
Instead I fastened on the famous armor, seized two
long spears with my hands and went on deck
to the prow. I thought she would appear there first,   230
Skylla, from her rock, bringing my men more pain.
But there was no way to see her. My eyes soon tired
of looking all about that mist enshrouded rock.

We rowed, all groaning, into the narrow strait.
Skylla on one side, opposite bright
Karybdis who swallowed the sea, frightful to witness.
Just as a cauldron in strong flames boils out all
that's stirred in, so she vomits up the foam
that spills down on either side of the high cliffs.

But whenever she gulps down the briny seawater,   240
what's within whirls round while the rocks roar
loudly and the sea floor's dark-blue sand appears
underneath. Yellow-green fear seized us all.
Fearing death, we all looked toward Skylla.
Just then from our hollow ship Skylla snatched
six men, the best in strength and best with their hands.
Looking back at my crew and swift ship,
I saw the snatched men's hands and feet high above me,
hoisted up. Crying out, they called my name,
their final sound, and my heart ached in pain for them.   250
Just as a man with fishing pole on a rocky
outcrop throws bait to trick the little fish and drops
the pointed horn of a field ox in the sea
and then pulls the writhing fish out of the water—
just so my men were tossed gasping on her rock.
Then in her cave she swallowed them, still screaming,
their hands reaching out to me in their death throes.
The most horrific thing my eyes have ever seen
in all my wandering on the wide sea was this.

Once we had escaped the rocks of fierce Skylla   260
and Karybdis, we came to the splendid isle
of the god. There were the lovely broad-faced oxen,
the many large herds of Helios the Sun.
While still at sea in the black ship I heard the penned
up oxen lowing and the bleating of the sheep.
And then the words of the blind seer, Theban
Teiresias, fell on my heart—and the words
of Kirke. They very strongly had ordered me
to flee the Sun's isle, he who delights mortals.

Anxious at heart, I spoke to my companions: 270

'Hear my words, my men, though greatly suffering,

and I'll tell you what seer Teiresias said
and Kirke. They very strongly ordered me
to flee the Sun's isle, he who delights mortals.
They said a most grim evil awaits us there.
So come, drive our black ship beyond this isle.'

So I spoke. Their very hearts were shattered.
Indeed Euryloxos answered with hateful words:

'You're cruel, Odysseus! Your might is beyond us.
Your limbs never tire! They are made of iron!   280
We would be well pleased with lying down to sleep,
but you won't let us land on this pleasant sea-washed
island where we might make a pleasant dinner.
Leave this island without delay, you bid us,
sail on to wander in the shrouded sea by night!
Hard winds blow at night, grief to ships.
How can one escape utter destruction
if suddenly, a storm of winds comes down,
Notos, or ill-blowing Zephyros. They most
of all shatter ships, despite the lordly gods.   290
Let us be persuaded by this black night!
Let's make our meal staying beside our swift ship.
At dawn we'll board, setting out in the wide sea.'

So spoke Euryloxos and the others agreed.
Then I knew some spirit planned this evil for us.
But I replied, speaking these winged words:

'Euryloxos, you could force me since I am but one.
But come now all of you, swear this strong oath.
If we find some herds of oxen or large flocks
of sheep, let no one through wicked folly   300
kill any ox or sheep. Restrain your appetite.
Eat only the food that deathless Kirke gave us.'

So I spoke. They swore to do as I had bid.
When they had sworn and their oath had been made,
we moored our well-built ship in a sheltered cove.
Nearby there was sweet water. The men disembarked
from the ship and skillfully prepared our meal.
When we'd satisfied desire for food and drink,
and remembering our dear companions, we wept,
those Skylla had seized and eaten from our hollow ship.   310
Sweet sleep finally came over my weeping men.

When night's third part had come and the stars traversed
the sky, cloud-gathering Zeus aroused a god-sent storm,
a mighty wind that then covered the land and sea
with clouds. A dark night dropped down from the sky.

When early-born, pink-fingered Dawn appeared,
we beached our ship and dragged it in a cave where nymphs
had chairs of carved rock, a lovely dancing ground.

Then I assembled my men and said these words:

'Friends, there's food and drink in our swift ship.   320
Let's leave the oxen alone lest we suffer for it,
for a fierce god owns these oxen and large flocks,
Helios, who looks on all, who hears all.'

So I spoke. Their manly hearts were persuaded.
But the south wind kept on blowing one full month,
no other wind came, only the east and south.
So long as they had food and red wine, so long
they left the oxen alone, longing to live.
But when the ship's food had been all consumed,
foraging through need, they tried to hunt wild game   330
and birds, and fish with bent fishhooks: whatever
came to their hands. But hunger wore out their bellies.
Then I climbed a hill alone that I might pray

to the gods, hoping one might guide me home.
I went across the island, avoiding my men.
I washed my hands, found shelter from the wind,
and prayed to all the gods who hold Olympos.
But they poured sweet sleep on my eyelids.

With bad counsel Euryloxos addressed the men:

'Friends, hear my words in your hard suffering!   340
Though we hapless mortals hate all ways of death,
far the worst is to die through hunger.
Let's seize the best of the Sun's oxen and sacrifice
them to the gods who hold the wide sky.
If we yet reach Ithaka, our land, we'll build
a rich shrine to Helios, Hyperion's son,
and there we'll give him many honorable goods.
If he is angry because of these high-horned oxen
and wants to smash the ship and other gods agree,
I'd rather die at once swallowing the waves   350
than slowly starving on a desolate island.'

So spoke Euryloxos. The other men agreed.
And they drove off the best of the Sun god's oxen:
those beautiful, spiral-horned, broad-faced oxen
pastured not far from our ship's blue prow.
The men stood around them and prayed to the gods.
Then they cut tender oak laves from the high branches
since no white barley remained in the well-benched ship.
When they had prayed, they slaughtered and flayed them,
cutting out thigh pieces, covering those with fat   360
folded double, placing the raw meat on top.
With no libation wine to sprinkle on the fat,
they used water on the blazing entrails.
Once the thigh pieces had cooked through, they tasted
the innards and cut the meat, fixing it on spits.

When that restful sleep had fled from my eyelids,
I set out for the shore and the swift ship.
But when I was approaching the curved ship,
the sweet savor of burnt fat enveloped me.
I shouted out in grief to the deathless gods: 370

'Father Zeus and all the ever-living gods,
you lay me down in ruthless sleep to ruin me!
My men, while waiting, planned a monstrous act!'

Lampetia went quickly in her flowing robes
to Helios about those oxen we had killed.
His angry heart called out to the deathless gods:

'Father Zeus and all the ever-living gods,
punish these men of Laertes' son Odysseus!
Lawlessly they killed my oxen. The ones
I rejoice in while traveling the starry sky   380
and when I turn again from the sky toward earth.
If they don't pay a price equal to my oxen,
I'll go to Hades' house and shine on the dead!'

Answering him, cloud-gathering Zeus spoke thus:

'Helios, you shine upon the deathless gods,
on dying mortals and on the grain-giving land.
Soon, hurling a bright thunderbolt, I'll cleave
that small ship in the midst of the purple sea!'

These things I later heard from fair-haired Kalypso.
She herself heard them from Hermes the guide.   390

When I had returned to the ship and sea,
I spoke angry words to each, one by one.
But we found no solution: the oxen were dead.
At once the gods wove a sign for them:
the hides began to crawl, the spitted meat lowed,

raw and roasted, as if in the speech of oxen.

For six days then, my loyal companions consumed
the slaughtered oxen, the best of the Sun god's herd.
But when Zeus counted out the seventh day,
then the wind ceased blowing incessant storms.   400
Boarding at once we put out into the broad sea,
stepping the mast, hoisting the white sails.

When we had left the island, nothing else
of land appeared, only the sea and sky.
Then the son of Kronos set dark clouds above
our hollow ship; the sea grew dark beneath her.
Our ship did not sail very long, for suddenly
a screeching blast of Zephyros blew up a storm.
The squall of winds broke both forestays of the mast.
The mast fell backwards. All our tackle was tossed   410
into the sloshing hold. The mast struck the helmsman
on the head, crushing the bones within his skull.
Like a diver, he fell down among the deck beams.
His manly spirit left his bones. At the same time
Zeus thundered and hurled his bolt at the prow.
The ship was whirled around. Dense sulfurous smoke
filled her, and my men were flung into the sea.
Like crows they were carried in the waves around
the black ship: the god denied them their return.

I moved about the ship until the keel broke free   420
from the sides and a wave carried it
away, the broken mast near the keel. On it
had been thrown a backstay of ox leather.
Keel and mast I lashed together with a cord.
Seated on these, the deadly winds carried me.

Then Zephyros ceased blowing up a storm
and Notos came quickly, bringing woe to me,

for I was borne back to deadly Karybdis.
It carried me all night. The sun rose as I reached
Skylla's cliff and terrible Karybdis.   430
Karybdis began swallowing the briny sea
but I reached up and grabbed the tall fig tree,
clinging to it like a bat. There was no way
I could secure my feet nor climb up on it,
the roots were far below. The overhanging branches,
long and large, cast a shadow over Karybdis.
I held on tight until she might vomit out
the mast and keel. I waited, hoping, and they came
late in the day. Just as a man who arbitrates
between young men comes late from the assembly   440
to dine, just so the timbers appeared from Karybdis.
I dropped my feet from the tree and leapt, landing
with a thud in the midst near the long timbers.
Scrambling on those, I paddled hard with my hands.
The father of gods did not let Skylla see me
or else I would not have escaped hard death.

For nine days I drifted. The night of the tenth
the gods carried me to Ogygia, fair-haired
Kalypso's home, fierce goddess with a human voice.
She loved and tended me. But why tell you of this?   450
Just yesterday I told this same tale to you
and your bedmate in your palace. It's hateful
to tell again things already clearly told."

BOOK THIRTEEN

Odysseus returns to Ithaka
The Phaiakian ship is turned to stone
Athena helps Odysseus guard his treasure

So he spoke. And all kept still, bound
in silent enchantment in the shadowy halls.
Alkinoös, speaking again, answered him:

"Odysseus, now that you've come to my high-roofed,
bronzed palace, I think you'll return home without
more troubles though you have suffered much indeed!
I lay this task on each of you men here,
you who come to drink my fiery wine
with the elders and hear songs in my palace.
Our guest has clothes in a well-crafted chest,   10
and well-wrought gold, and all the other gifts
the Phaiakian counselors brought to him here.
But come, let's give him a tripod and a cauldron,
each man of us. We'll recoup this by gathering it
from the people. It's hard for one to give so much."

So spoke Alkinoös. His words pleased them.
Then they went to lie down, each to his own house.

When early-born, pink-fingered Dawn appeared,
they hurried to the ship carrying bronze, man's joy.
Even mighty Alkinoös went down himself   20
to stow the gifts under the benches, lest they
hinder the men, speeding on with their oars.
Then they went to the palace and ate their meal.

Mighty Alkinoös sacrificed a bull
to storm-cloud Zeus, Kronos' son, who rules all.
Having burned the thigh parts, they feasted, enjoying
a glorious meal. Afterwards, the godlike bard
Demodokos sang to the people. Odysseus
kept turning his head toward the beaming sun, eager
for its setting, for he strongly yearned to leave.   30
Just as a man longs for dinner when, all day
stuck in the field, his dark brown oxen drag
the plough, so he welcomes the sinking light
to go home to dinner, though with weary knees—
just so Odysseus welcomed the sinking light.
At once he spoke to the Phaiakians, making
his thoughts known most to Alkinoös, saying:

"Lord Alkinoös, renowned of all people,
a libation. Then send me home safe and you
rejoice! For this was done as my heart wished: 40
an escort, fine gifts! The blessed gods of the wide sky
brought this about! May I find at my return
my noble bedmate at home, my loved ones safe!
And you, staying here, please your wedded women
and children and may the gods sow well-being in all
things and may no evil come among your people!"

So he spoke and all approved and urged the king

to convey the guest who spoke so properly.

And then Alkinoös addressed the herald:

"Pontonoös, mix wine in the bowl and pour it   50
for all in the hall. Praying to father Zeus,
let us send our guest home to his native land!"

So he spoke. Pontonoös mixed the mind-
delighting wine, pouring for each one. They poured
libations to the happy gods of the wide sky,
each from where he sat, but he, Odysseus,
stood and placed the goblet in Arete's hands.
Addressing her with winged words, he said:

"May good ever remain with you, oh Queen, though age
and death come to you. These come to all mortals.   60
Now I shall go. You, rejoice in your home,
your children, your people, and in King Alkinoös!"

So speaking, Odysseus crossed the threshold
and mighty Alkinoös sent the herald with him
to lead the way to the shore and the swift ship.
Arete sent her handmaids after them.
One carried down a well-washed cloak and tunic,
another provided a well-made chest,
yet another brought down food and red wine.

When all had been conveyed to the shore and ship,   70
the most illustrious crew, his escort, took them,
stowing them on board, all the meat and drink.
For brave Odysseus they spread rugs and cloth
on the half-deck at the hollow ship's stern
that he might sleep undisturbed. He boarded
and lay in silence. They sat at the oars in order
and freed the cable from the stone post.

As they leaned on their oars stirring up the sea,
a sweet, deep sleep fell over his eyelids,
a most pleasant sleep, still, almost like death.   80
Just as on a plain four yoked stallions
urged on by the whip's lash, pulling together,
bounding lightly, swiftly make their journey,
just so sped the ship, great waves surging behind
the stern, the loud-roaring sea seething.
The ship held safely and securely on course. No hawk,
though light and newly-fledged, could match her speed.
Thus the ship swiftly cleaved the sea waves
carrying this man, like to the gods in wise counsels,
who had suffered much pain deep in his heart   90
through the wars of men and the frightful waves.
He slept motionless, unmindful of past pains.

When the brightest of all the stars appeared,
the one that heralds the light of early-born Dawn,
then the sea-crossing ship neared the island.

Phorkys, the Old Man of the Sea, has a haven
on Ithaka's shore. Two rugged cliffs jut out
as though crouching toward the harbor, and these
shelter it from the great waves raised by storm winds.
Within it, well-benched ships may lie without   100
hawsers, arriving here to safe anchorage.
At the harbor's head, a long-leaved olive grows.
Near it lies a pleasing, misty cave sacred
to the Nymphs who are called Naiads there.
Inside are wine bowls and large jars made of
cave stone where the bees store their honey.*
And tall looms of stone that the Nymphs use
to weave sea-purple cloth—a marvel to behold!
And ever-flowing springs! Two entrances there are,
the one to the north is for men to descend,   110

the one to the south is sacred. No man
can pass. It's the way of the deathless ones.

Here they rowed in, knowing the place. The ship
plunged onto land, driving in half her length,
such was the hard-rowing force of the crew's hands.
Going from the well-benched ship onto dry land,
they took Odysseus, silently, still wrapped
in his blankets and rugs, and they placed him,
still overcome by sleep, on the sandy beach.
Next they brought the goods the noble Phaiakians   120
sent with him because of great-hearted Athena.
They stacked these at the foot of the olive tree,
off the path lest someone passing by
steal them before Odysseus awoke.
Then they left, homeward bound. But the
Earth-shaker did not forget the threats he'd made
to lord Odysseus and he told Zeus his plan:

"Father Zeus, I'll have no honor from the gods
nor from any mortals if the Phaiakians,
though bred from my family, honor me not.   130
I have always said he'd suffer terribly
till he reached home but his return I never stopped
since you first promised it, assenting with your nod.
They carried him sleeping on the swift ship,
landing him in Ithaka, with such gifts—
bronze and gold and plenty of woven clothes—
much more than he'd have brought from Troy if he'd
taken his booty with the army, leaving unharmed."

Cloud-gatherer Zeus then answered him, saying:

"Come now, mighty Earth-shaker, saying such things!   140
The gods dishonor you not! It would be hard
to throw insults at the eldest and the best!

If any man should yield to violence and strength
and dishonor you, take your revenge when you
wish to, as you wish to, whatever pleases you."

Poseidon Earth-shaker then answered him:

"I might do as you say at once, oh dark-cloud one,
but I avoid incurring your dread wrath.
Now I wish to strike the Phaiakians' fine ship
in the sea mists as they return from this escort,   150
to stop them, so that they cease conveying men!
And I'll encircle their city with a huge mountain!"

Cloud-gatherer Zeus then answered him, saying:

"Well, here's what seems best to my heart. When all
the town's people are watching as she drives home,
turn the swift wooden ship to a ship of stone
close to shore that men may marvel, but
do not hide the town under a mountain."

As soon as Poseidon Earth-shaker had heard this,
he set out for the Phaiakian land of Skeria   160
and waited. And when that sea-crossing ship came near,
driving swiftly, the Earth-shaker went out to her,
turned her to stone and drove her down with a flat hand,
rooting her there. Then he went far away.

The Phaiakians spoke winged words to each other,
men famous for their ships and long-bladed oars.
Thus one spoke having seen this at first hand:

"Oh no! Who has bound the swift ship in stone
as she drove home? All of us saw the ship!"

So one spoke but they knew not how this had happened.   170
Then addressing them, Alkinoös said:

"My friends, that ancient prophesy my father told
me of has come to pass. He said Poseidon would
envy us since we convey all who come.
He said he'd smash a beautiful Phaiakian ship
returning from conveyance on the shrouded sea,
and then encircle the city with a mountain.
So the old man said. Now it is happening.
But come now, let us all do as I say.
Let us cease to convey mortals, though one should   180
approach our town. And let's choose twelve bulls,
sacrifice them to the god so he'll take pity
and not encircle our city with a high mountain!"

So he spoke. Though afraid they readied the bulls.
Thus they prayed to lord Poseidon, the lords
and leaders of the Phaiakian people,
standing round the altar.

                 Odysseus awoke,
having slept in his own land, but gone so long
he recognized nothing. Pallas Athena poured
a divine mist over him so she could tell him   190
everything and disguise him completely,
lest his bedmate or friends and townsmen know him
before he repaid all the evils of the suitors.
For this reason she made all look strange to him:
the long footpaths, the harbors good for anchorage,
the high steep rocks, and even the leafy trees.
Springing up, he stood and looked at his own land.
He groaned and struck his thigh with the palm
of his hand and moaning, he said these words:

"Oh, no! Have I come to the land of some mortals?   200
And are they arrogant and savage, not civilized?
Or stranger-loving and their minds god-fearing?

How can I carry all this wealth? Where will I wander
next? Would that I'd stayed with the Phaiakians!
I could've gone to some other mighty king
who would have befriended me, sent me home.
Now I don't know where to put this wealth
nor how to hide it lest some others take it.
In truth the Phaiakian lords and leaders
were neither wise nor just when they brought me to   210
another land, though they told me they'd take me to
sunny Ithaka. But this they did not do!
May Zeus of the suppliants pay you! He watches
all men and punishes those who slight their duty!
I should go and count my wealth to know
if they took any while traveling in their ship."

So saying, he counted all the well-worked tripods
and cauldrons, the gold, and the lovely woven
clothes. Nothing was missing. But, longing for
his native land, he trudged along the loud seashore,   220
ever groaning. Athena approached him like to
a young man, a shepherd of sheep, but one most
delicate such as the children of chieftains are,
his shoulders wrapped in a well-made cloak,
sandals on his oiled feet, holding a spear.
Rejoicing in the sight, Odysseus approached,
then saying these winged words, addressed him:

"Friend, since you're the first I've met in this place,
hello to you and don't meet me with evil thoughts,
but save my things and save me! I pray to you   230
as to a god and I kneel down at your knees.
Tell me this and truly that I might know.
What land is this? What tribe? What men live here?
Is this some distinct island? Or the headland
sloping seaward of some fertile hinterland?"

Bright-eyed Athena answered him at once:

"You must be simple, stranger, or come from far away
if you need ask about this land. It is far from
nameless! A very great many know of it,
both those who live toward Eos and sunrise   240
and those who live there in the shadowy west.
It is a rugged land indeed, not fit for horses,
but it's not poor though it is not very wide.
In it abundant food grows and much wine,
for rain always comes, and dew is copious,
good for feeding goats and grazing oxen. It has
all kinds of forests and abundant pools of water.
So, friend, Ithaka's name reaches as far
as Troy they say, far from Akaian land."

So she spoke. And glad was he, much-enduring   250
Odysseus, in his own land, while Zeus' maid,
aigis-bearing Pallas Athena told him the truth.
Answering her, he said these winged words,
but holding back. He did not speak the truth,
for in his breast he always dealt out shrewd thoughts:

"I'd learned of Ithaka even in wide Krete,
far off over the sea. And now I've come here
with these goods though I left my sons with more.
I fled because I'd killed Idomeneus' son
Orsilokos, swift of foot, who beat in racing   260
all grain-eating men in the wide land of Krete,
because he wished to rob me of all the spoils
of Troy. I'd suffered much for these in the war
of men, and in the sea, pierced with pain.
And all because I would not serve his father
in the Trojan fight but led my own men.
Waiting with my men by the path, I struck him

with my bronze-tipped spear as he came from the fields.
A deep dark night fell from the sky and no man knew
of us nor noticed when I took his life away.   270
But after I'd slain him with the sharp bronze spear,
I boarded a Phoinikan ship. I begged for passage
and gave treasure enough to satisfy them.
I urged them to put out for Pylos and land me there,
or to Elis where the Epeians rule in strength.

But the winds' strength pushed them back from there
against their will. They didn't wish to deceive me.
From there we wandered till we reached here at night.
Rowing, we struggled into the cove, and no one took
his dinner though we all strongly craved it.   280
We landed as we were and we all lay down.
Then, exhausted, sweet sleep came over me
and they took all my goods from the hollow ship,
and put them beside me here on the sandy shore.
Then they boarded and headed for well-peopled
Sidonia, leaving me here, sore of heart."

So he spoke. But bright-eyed Athena smiled,
caressing his hand. She changed from man to woman,
tall and beautiful, skilled in wonderful crafts,
and, addressing him with winged words, she said: 290

"Clever and tricky he must be who can surpass
you in deceits, even if you meet with a god!
Stubborn one, ingenious, lover of tricks, you can't
even stop your deceitful words and tricks
in your own land! You love them with all your heart!
Come, let's not speak of this. Both of us
are wily: you of all mortals far best in plans
and words and I of all the gods am most famous
for counsel and tricks. But you did not recognize

Pallas Athena, Zeus' maid, though I always   300
stand beside you and guard you in your toils.
I made all the Phaiakians befriend you.
Now I've come here to weave you a plan
to hide your goods, all that the lordly Phaiakians
sent home with you through my plans and thoughts.
And to tell you of the great portion of pain
you'll find in your well-built house. You must endure.
Do not reveal to anyone—no man no woman,
no one—that you've come back from wandering. Keep silent.
Though suffering much, accept the violence of men."   310

Answering her, artful Odysseus then said:

"Goddess, it's hard for a mortal to know a god,
wise though he be, for you assume the form of all.
But I know this, you were always kind to me
when we Akaian sons were fighting in Troy.
But since we sacked Priam's steep citadel
and sailed for home, a god scattered the Akaians,
and I have not seen or sensed you, child of Zeus,
on my ship when you might have kept me from pain.
I wandered, my heart in my breast shredded,   320
until the gods freed me from this evil, until
that time in rich Phaiakian lands, encouraged
by your words, then you led me into their town.
Now I beg you by my father, for I don't think
I'm in sunny Ithaka, but in some land,
some most confusing place! I think you're taunting me,
telling me this, deceiving me once again.
So tell me truly: have I come to my own land?"

Then bright-eyed Athena answered him:

"This is the way your mind works, always the same,   330
and so I cannot leave you in your misery,

for you are kind, sensible, ready of wit.
Another man, coming home from wandering,
would gladly rush to see his children and bedmate.
But you are eager to inquire and learn until
you have tested your bedmate. Yet she indeed
sits in misery in the palace night after
night, and days too, pouring out her tears.
But I never doubted in my heart that you
would return though all your men had perished.   340
However I wanted no fight with lord Poseidon,
my father's brother who holds a grudge in his heart,
and is angry that you blinded his dear son.*
But come, I'll let the land of Ithaka persuade you.
The Old Man of the Sea, Phorkys, has a cove here.
At the cove's head is a long-leaved olive tree.
Near it lies a lovely, misty cave, haunt
of the Nymphs here who are called Naiads.
This is the high-roofed cave where you offered
many sacrifices to the Nymphs, and this   350
mountain covered with woods is Neritos."

So speaking, she dissolved the mist. The land appeared.
Rejoicing, much-enduring, brave Odysseus,
glad in his land, kissed the tilled, grain-giving earth.
At once, raising his hands, he prayed thus to the Nymphs:

"Nymphs, Naiads, Zeus' daughters! I did not hope
to see you! But now I welcome you with kind prayers!
We'll give you gifts as before if Zeus's child,
the warrior goddess Athena, should allow me
to live and to bring my son to full manhood!"   360

Bright-eyed Athena answered him at once:

"Take heart lest all this wealth becomes a care to you.
Let's put your goods in some nook of the Nymphs' cave

at once. Yes now, so that they stay there safe for you.
Then let's take thought how things might come out far the best."

So saying, the goddess plunged into the misty cave
to find a nook within, while brave Odysseus
carried it all nearer, the gold and hardened bronze,
the well-made clothes—all the Phaiakians had given.
When he had put them in the recess, Zeus's child,   370
Pallas Athena, placed a boulder as a barrier.
Then sitting beneath the holy olive tree,
she told him how to kill the arrogant suitors.

Bright-eyed Athena began with these words:

"Zeus-born Laertes' son, artful Odysseus,
think how you might lay hands on these shameless wooers
who've lorded it in your palace for three years now,
courting your godlike bedmate, giving her bride-gifts.
But she, with heart ever grieving for your return,
gives hope to all, promises each man something,   380
sends words, but her mind longs for other things."

Answering her, artful Odysseus then said:

"So then, I would have died in my palace,
Agamemnon's terrible fate, if you,
goddess, had not told me of these things!
Come, weave me the plan of my revenge!
Stand you by me! Imbue me with your steely strength
as when we tore down Troy's diadem of towers!
If now, as you once eagerly stood by me then,
bright-eyed one, I would fight three hundred men   390
if you, mighty goddess, tell me you'll come to help!"

The goddess, bright-eyed Athena, answered then:

"Yes, I'll be beside you, nor will you be free

of me when we do these things. I know that some
of those who wolf down your wealth will splatter
your palace floor, their blood and brains defiling it.
But come, I will make you unknown to all men.
I will wither up the skin on your curved limbs,
shear that fair hair on your head and dress
you shabbily, making you ugly in front of men,   400
dim those eyes that were so beautiful before.
You will seem ill-favored to all those suitors,
to your child and bedmate you left in the palace.
Now you go first to the swineherd who watches
over your pigs. He has kind thoughts of you,
and he loves your son and wise Penelope.
You'll find him sitting among the swine. They feed
by Raven's Rock near Arethousa spring,
where they eat acorns and drink the still water.
These nourish and make them grow abundantly fat.   410
Wait there, sitting beside him, and ask him anything
while I go to Sparta, land of fair women,
to summon back your son Telemakos from
Lakedaimonia's wide lands. He has gone
to seek news, whether or not you still lived."

Answering her, artful Odysseus then said:

"But why did you not tell him, you who know all things?
Was it so he might suffer too, wandering on
the barren sea while others were eating his wealth?"

The goddess, bright-eyed Athena, answered then: 420

"Let your heart not be so burdened for him!
I guided him there that he might win fame
by going. He's not toiling now, but sitting at ease
in Menelaus' palace amid boundless goods.
The suitors in their black ship plan a trap. They

were sent to kill him before he arrives home.
But I think this will not happen. Sooner will those
wooers be covered in earth, those who eat your wealth."

Speaking thus, Athena struck him with her staff.
His skin withered, his arms and legs curved in age.   430
His fair hair was gone from his head, his skin
on all his limbs was made that of an old man.
His once so beautiful eyes became dim.
She threw on him a terrible cloak, a tunic
filthy and torn, soiled badly by smoke.
Over him she wrapped a large, worn skin
of a swift deer, gave him a staff and an old
pouch full of holes with a braided strap.

So having made their plans, they parted. She went
to Sparta to bring back Odysseus' son.   440

BOOK FOURTEEN

Odysseus is disguised as a beggar
Odysseus and the swineherd Eumaios
Odysseus tells Eumaios a false story of his life

Odysseus left the cove, climbing
the stony path through densely wooded hills
to where Athena said he'd find his best slave
guarding his livelihood, the godlike swineherd.

The swineherd sat on the stoop of the hut
within a high enclosure cleared all around,
a long, wide view to all sides. He'd built
it for the swine of his lord, long-gone
now from his lady and old Laertes. He'd made
it from quarried stone topped with wild pear wood.   10
He'd hammered stakes around the outside here and there,
close packed, stakes he had cut from dark heartwood.
Inside he'd made twelve sties near each other
for the pigs to bed in. In each were kept
fifty pigs sleeping on the ground, sows
for breeding and the boars slept outside

at night. There were far fewer for the arrogant suitors'
feasting had shrunk their number. And he always
sent them those well fed, fattest, the best of all.
Now there were but three hundred and sixty left.   20

Four dogs, wild as beasts, always passed the night
with them. The swineherd, chief of men, had reared them.
He himself was cutting a good ox hide, making
sandals for his feet. Three of his men
were tending the gathered herds of swine.
The fourth he had to send with a boar to town
for the arrogant suitors so they
could kill it and satisfy their hearts with meat.

Seeing Odysseus, the dogs began barking.
They ran at him growling, but Odysseus   30
wisely sat down. His hand let fall his staff.
He might have suffered pain there on his own land
but the swineherd quickly ran toward them
through the gate letting the hide drop from his hands.
Shouting and throwing stones, he drove them away
from the man. Then he addressed the stranger:

"Old man, these dogs would have hurt you sorely
and quickly and you'd have brought much shame on me.
But the gods gave me other pains and sorrows.
I sit lamenting, sorrowing for my godlike lord.   40
I have raised these fattened hogs for others to eat,
while he, lacking all provisions, wanders among
the lands and towns of foreign-speaking men—
if somehow he yet lives and sees sunlight.
But follow me, old man, come to my hut so you
may eat and drink to your heart's content
and tell me who you are and what you've suffered."

So speaking, the noble swineherd brought him to

his hut, leading him in, and spread twigs to sit on
and smoothed the shaggy hide of a wild goat, his own   50
large thick bedcover. Odysseus rejoiced
at being so welcomed and he said these words:

"May Zeus and other deathless gods give you, stranger,
what you most wish since you have thus received me!"

Then you, Eumaios the swineherd, answered him, saying:*

"Stranger, it is not right, not for one worse off
than you, for me not to respect a stranger! All strangers
and beggars are from Zeus. What we can give is small
but kind. For this is the way of servants, always
fearful, especially when the masters are young.   60
The gods have blocked the return of that man
who always loved me kindly, who gave me all my wealth:
a house and plot of land, a sought-after woman.
Such things a kindly lord gives a servant
who toils hard for him. A god makes his work prosper
as mine has prospered here, so here I stay. So would
my lord have helped me had he grown old here. But he
perished. May Helen's tribe perish utterly
since she loosed the knees of so many men,*
even of him who went to horse-rich Ilios   70
for Agamemnon's honor, to fight the Trojans!"

So speaking, he quickly tightened his tunic with
his belt and set off for the sty where the young pigs
were penned. Seizing two, he killed them both,
singed them, cut them up, spitting them on skewers.
Once roasted and hot on skewers, he carried them to
Odysseus. He sprinkled them with white barley,
mixed honey-sweet wine in a wooden bowl,
then sat opposite. Urging him on he said:

"Eat now, my guest, these young pigs the servants eat.   80
The suitors feast on fattened hogs and sows,
no pity in their hearts, no thought of the gods watching.
For the happy gods love not reckless deeds.
They honor custom and the honest work of men.
Even hostile, evil-acting raiders who plunder lands
of others, though Zeus may grant them booty, as they board
their ships returning homeward, a strong fear
of the gods watching them fills their hearts.

They must know of this from some god-sent rumor
of his mournful death. Hence they don't wish to woo   90
following custom, nor go to their own homes, but linger
arrogantly devouring his wealth, sparing nothing.
In these nights and days that come from Zeus they do
not stop at killing one beast or even two!
They pour his wine recklessly, wasting it!
Though his wealth was measureless, none among
the heroes nor those living on the fertile mainland,
nor on Ithaka itself—not twenty men
had such abundance. But let me tell you of it.
The mainland feeds twelve herds of oxen, vast herds of sheep,   100
great herds of swine, herds of wide-ranging goats.
His own shepherds and other men watch over them.
Here, far and wide, eleven herds of goats *
feed beyond the fields, watched over by righteous men.
Each man leads one each day to the suitors,
a well-fattened goat, whichever seems best to him.
But I guard these swine, protect them, and choose
the best of these boars and send it off to them."

So he spoke. The stranger gratefully devoured
the meat and wine in silence, planning the wooers harm.   110
Once he had eaten, his spirit sustained with food,
the swineherd filled the bowl with wine, the one he used,

and gave it to the stranger, who took it, his heart glad.
And speaking with winged words said to him:

"Friend, who bought you with his wealth? Was he
so rich and powerful as you say he was?
You were saying he died for Agamemnon's honor.
Tell me if I might know of such a man, for Zeus
knows and the other deathless gods, that if
I'd seen him, I might bring news for I have wandered much."   120

Then the swineherd, leader of men, answered him:

"Old man, no traveler coming here with news
of him could persuade his woman and dear son.
Other wanderers in need of help claim this
and lie. They never wish to speak the truth.
Whoever wandering comes here to Ithaka
goes to my mistress and tells lying tales.
And she befriends him well, asking searchingly
after him, lamenting, tears falling from her eyes,
the way of woman when her mate dies elsewhere.   130
And you, old man, might quickly fashion thus your words,
so she might give you clothes, a tunic and a cloak.
By now dogs and swift birds must have stripped
the skin from his bones, his soul having left,
or fish devoured him in the sea, his bones,
washed up on some far shore, buried in deep beach sand.
So he died and those he loved will long suffer
from what has happened, me most of all.
For I'll not find another lord so kind, go where
I might, not even in my parents' home   140
should I return where I was born, where I was raised.
But it is not for this I mourn, though I long
for them and my eyes yearn to see my native land.
Yet most I miss Odysseus who's lost to me.

Stranger I am awestruck to name him since he is
not here. He loved me, cared for me in his heart,
and I call him my master though he has not returned."

Much-enduring Odysseus answered him:

"Friend, though you will not hear of it and you think
in your ever-untrusting heart he will not come,   150
I will tell no traveler's tales, so hear my oath.
Odysseus will return. For now let there
be no reward but when he does arrive home,
then dress me in fine clothes, a cloak and a tunic.
Until then, though my need is great, nothing.
For as I hate Hades' double gates, so hate
I him who citing poverty speaks in lies!
By Zeus, first of the gods for guests and offerings,
by good Odysseus' hearth where I've arrived,
all these things I say will come to pass!   160
Odysseus will come here in this very month
with the waning moon, when the new moon rises.
He will return home. He will repay any
who honored not his bedmate and his glorious son!"

Then you, Eumaios the swineherd, answered him, saying: *

"Old man, I will pay you no reward,
nor will Odysseus return home. But be
at ease. Drink. Let's reminisce apart from this.
Remind me not of him. My heart aches in my breast
when I think about the suffering of my master.   170
And your oath? Let's let it be. I do wish
Odysseus might come such as you say, as do
Penelope, Laertes and Telemakos.
Now I mourn that child Odysseus sired,
Telemakos. The gods raised him from a sprout.
And I tell you he is in manhood no less than

his dear father in form and to be wondered at.
But some deathless one has swayed his mind's balance
or some man. Seeking news of his father
he went to holy Pylos, but the suitors plan   180
to ambush him coming home, to make nameless*
godlike Arkeisios' tribe from Ithaka.
But let us let it be. Either the boy's captured
or he escaped. It's under Zeus' protective hands.
But come now, ancient one, tell me of your pains
and tell me this and tell me truly so I might know.
What man are you? From where? From what town and parents?
You came on what sort of ship? How did the sailors
bring you to Ithaka? Who do they claim to be?
For I hardly think you came here on foot." *   190

Answering him, artful Odysseus then said:

"Well then, I'll tell you these things very precisely.
If there were both food and pleasant wine, we two
for a while might eat inside here undisturbed,
while others keep following their workday tasks.
Easily then I could pass through one year entire
without telling all the pains of my heart,
so much I've suffered by the will of the gods.
I am, you see, of the tribe of Krete's broad land,
a rich man's son. And many other sons he had   200
and raised within his halls, lawful sons of his
bedmate. Though the mother who bore me was bought,
a slave, he honored me as a lawful son.
I say I'm of the tribe of Kastor, Hylax's son,
who's honored in the land of Krete as a god
in happiness, in wealth, and in his renowned sons.
But the fates of death carried him off
to Hades' house. Then his wanton sons
split up his wealth, throwing lots for their shares.

To me they gave a dwelling and little more.   210
But I won a woman of means from her family
through my skill, for I was no kind of fool
nor a coward in battle. Now that is all gone.
I think you see what crop I'm from, though I am but
a reaped stalk now, having suffered much.
Ares and Athena gave me courage and
the strength to scatter men. When I chose the best
men for a trap, sowing evil for our foes,
never did my manly heart imagine death,
I it was who jumped up first and seized the nearest   220
of our enemies not as fast as I.

Such I was in war. Work was not for me,
chores that help to raise good children.
No, my love was ever ships fitted with oars,
and battles and well-crafted spears and arrows—
evil fortune—things that make others shudder.
These things I liked. Some god put them in my heart:
different men rejoice in different labors.
Before the Akaian sons set out for Troy,
nine times I led my men and swift-moving ships   230
against foreign men. And fortune gave me booty.
I chose what pleased me, more came my way by lot.
My household wealth grew quickly, and so both fear
and a certain awe arose among the Kretans.
And when far-seeing Zeus planned that hateful siege
where the knees of many men were loosed,
they pressed me and far-famed Idomeneus
to lead our ships to Ilios. There was no means
of refusing. The people's voice pressed harshly.
There Akaian sons waged war for nine long years.   240
In the tenth, we sacked Priam's city and left
by ship for home but a god scattered us all.
And Zeus, the counselor, planned evil for me.

I stayed home enjoying my children, my wealth
and wedded bedmate only a month, for then
my heart led me to sail for Egypt after I
had readied my ships and gathered my godlike crew.
Nine ships were prepared. Crewmen gathered quickly.
Six days my loyal men sat and feasted,
and I brought them many sacred animals   250
to sacrifice to the gods and to feast on.
On the seventh, we boarded and sailed from broad Krete
easily, the north wind blowing fair and strong
as if on a stream. Thus none of the ships met
any harm, but safe and sound we sat,
the wind and steersmen guiding us along.

On the fifth day we came to Egypt's watery land
and moored the curved ships in Egypt's river.
Then I ordered my companions to stay
there by the shore and guard well our ships,   260
and I sent lookouts to good watching places.
But my men gave way to their pride and plundered
the Egyptians' rich fields of grain and carried
off the women and little children and killed
the men. The alarm spread quickly to the town.
They heard the shouts and they came as dawn broke.
The plain was filled with foot soldiers and chariots,
the flash of bronze. Zeus the thunderbolt hurler
sent my men into headlong flight, none stayed
to face the foe. Disaster came from every quarter.   270
Their sharp bronze killed many of us there.
They led those yet living away to do forced labor.
Then Zeus put a thought in my heart. Oh! Rather
had I died and met my fate just there
in Egypt, for much more pain was yet set for me.
I took the helmet off my head, the shield from
my shoulder and tossed the spear from my hands.

I went to the king's chariot and kissed
his knees. He pitied me, and, shedding tears,
he drew me up, seated me, and carried me home.   280
Many men approached with bronze-tipped ash spears,
eager to kill me—and exceedingly angry—
but he withdrew, respecting the wrath of Zeus,
god of strangers who hates greatly such evil acts.

I stayed there seven years and gathered up
great wealth that the Egyptian men gave me.
In the eighth year a wily Phoinikan came,
a scheming trafficker well skilled in deceit
who had already done much harm to others.
He swayed me then to go to Phoinika   290
with him where his homes and wealth lay.
There I stayed with him for one full year.
And when the months and days were completed,
the old year passing and new seasons coming,
he put me on a ship to cross to Libya.
And lying, sent me on to help him get the cargo,
so thus he might sell me, getting a huge price.
With misgivings I followed him onboard his ship.
She sped on with a north wind blowing strong
beyond Krete, but Zeus planned death for these men.   300
When we had left Krete behind, no other land
appeared, only the sky and sea. Then Zeus,
Kronos' son, stirred up a dark storm cloud
over the hollow ship, shrouding her in darkness.
Lightning flashed as Zeus hurled his thunderbolts.
The ship was whirled around. Dense sulfurous smoke
filled her, and my men were thrown into the sea.
Like crows they were carried in the waves around
the black ship: the god denied them their return.
But Zeus himself, though he kept my heart in pain,   310
put the dark-prowed ship's tall mast in my hands

so that I might yet escape my death.
Holding tightly, the deadly winds bore me along.
Nine days I was carried. In the tenth black night
a great rolling wave brought me to Thesprotia.
There King Pheidon took care of me
without payment, for his own son had found me
shivering cold and overwhelmingly weary.
He took my hand and led me to his father's palace
where he dressed me in clothes: tunic and cloak.   320

Odysseus I learned of there. The king said he
had welcomed and befriended him on his way
back home, and he showed me Odysseus' wealth:
the bronze and gold and the well-worked iron,
enough to feed his family ten generations.
Great was his wealth that lay there in the palace.
The king said he had gone to Dodona to hear *
Zeus' plan from his sacred oak tree:
whether to go openly to Ithaka's
rich land, or secretly, being so long absent.   330
The king swore to me, poured libations to
the gods, that a ship and crew stood ready
to carry him to his own dear native land.
But he sent me away on a Thesprotian ship
which was moored there, bound for grain-rich Doulikion.

Kindly he bid them take me to King Akastos,
but an evil plan for me pleased their hearts
so that I might feel more pain and misery.
When, crossing the sea, the ship was far from land,
at once they made it my day of slavery.   340
They stripped off my fine clothes, both cloak and tunic,
and threw on me other mean rags: this old
torn tunic that your eyes now see me in.
In the evening they came to sunny Ithaka.

They bound me fast with twisted rope in their
well-benched ship and stepped down on the shore
and there hurriedly took their evening meal.
But the gods easily loosened my bonds.
Wrapping the rags about my head, I slid
down the hewn loading plank into the sea   350
breast-high and struck out swimming with both arms.
Soon I was on dry land away from them.
I climbed up to a thicket of blooming branches,
crouching for concealment. They went back and forth
with loud groans but it was not worth it to them
to keep looking for me, so they went back again
to their ship. The gods had hid me easily
and led me here to this place, to a wise man.
And so for now it is my lot to keep on living."

Answering him, the swineherd Eumaios said: 360

"Wretched stranger! You stirred my heart greatly telling
these things of how much you have suffered and wandered!
But you spoke not true of those things about
Odysseus. Being the man you are
why did you need to lie? I know very well
of my lord's return. The gods hate him!
Why did they not kill him among the Trojans?
Or in his friends' arms when the war wound down?
All Akaians would have heaped a mound for him
and brought great glory down to his son.   370
But now, far away storms have snatched him up.
Among the swine, I have turned away from men
and go not to the town unless Penelope
asks me to when news comes from somewhere.

Then they sit beside me asking of each thing,
both those who mourn our long absent lord and those

who enjoy his wealth and feast without paying.
But I have not liked such asking or inquiring
since that Aitolian man's tale deceived me.
He'd killed a man and roamed through many lands   380
before he came here and I welcomed him.
He claimed he saw my lord with Idomeneus
in Krete, repairing his storm-battered ships.
He'd said he'd come in summer or late harvest time
bringing much booty and his godlike men.
And you, much-suffering old man, a god brought you
to me. But tell no lies. Do not deceive me!
It's not for this I honor you and befriend you,
but fearing Zeus of Guests. Also, I pity you."

Answering him, artful Odysseus then said: 390

"Indeed the heart in your breast is untrusting
if my oath won't change your mind or persuade you.
But come now, let's agree before the gods
who hold Olympos as witnesses for us.
If your lord does return to his home,
dress me in a tunic and cloak and send me to
Doulikion where my heart rejoices.
But if your lord does not come as I say,
urge your slaves to hurl me down on those great rocks
so any other beggar will shun deceiving you."   400

Answering him, the noble swineherd said:

"And what honor and good repute, oh guest,
might all men give me both now and in the future
when I sheltered you—gave you gifts too—
if I should kill you and take away your life
and then sit and pray to Zeus, Kronos' son?
Hah! It's time to eat. Soon my men will come.
Let's set for them a tasty meal in my hut."

Thus they spoke to each other about these things.
The sows came near with their swineherds following.   410
They shut the sows in their accustomed places.
Ungodly noises arose from them as they were penned,
but the noble swineherd called to his men:

"Bring the best boar! I'll kill it for our guest
from far away and we too will enjoy it,
we who work hard for the white-tusked swine
while those others eat our work without paying."

So he spoke and split some wood with his bronze axe,
and they led in a very fat five-year boar.
They stood it on the hearth, nor did the swineherd   420
forget the deathless ones in his good heart.
He began by throwing into the fire bristles
from the boar's head, praying to all the gods
that brave Odysseus might return one day.
Standing, he struck the whited-tusked boar with an oak log
and life left the boar. They flayed it and singed it,
and cut it up. The swineherd wrapped raw meat
from every limb in the rich fat and threw it
into the fire, sprinkling it with barley corn.
Then they cut off pieces and skewered them,   430
roasting them skillfully. They drew the meat
off and tossed it on platters. The swineherd
stood and carved the meat. He did it fairly.
Dividing it, he made seven portions, and one
portion he set aside praying for the nymphs
and Maia's son Hermes. The rest he gave to each.
He gave the white-tusked boar's long back to him,*
Odysseus, an honor that pleased his heart.

Addressing him artful Odysseus said:

"I wish, Eumaios, father Zeus would honor you   440 as you greatly honor such a one as me."

Answering him, the swineherd Eumaios said:

"Eat, ill-starred stranger, enjoy these things
we have here. God gives this, withholds that,
as his heart desires, for he can do all things."

He burnt offerings to the ever-living gods
and mixing the fiery wine, he put it in the hands
of city-sacking Odysseus then sat to eat.
The bread was served by Mesaulios whom
Eumaios had purchased on his own, his lord being   450
gone, with no help from his mistress or old Laertes.
He bought him from the Taphians as his own.
They reached for the food made ready before them.
When they'd satisfied desire for food and drink,
Mesaulios put the food away. They longed
to go to bed, well sated with their dinner.
The night came on, foul, dark, moonless. Zeus brought
rain the whole night and a strong, wet, westerly wind.
Odysseus spoke then, testing the swineherd,
if he might strip off his cloak and give him it   460
for his great need, or urge one of his men to:

"Hear me now, Eumaios and all you others,
I'll tell you what I'm wishing for since the wine
makes me foolish like it makes the wise man sing
and laugh feebly, and stand up and dance,
and put in words what's better left unsaid.
But since I have begun to speak, I won't stop now.
Would I had the strength and vigor I used to
when at Troy we planned and led an ambush.
Odysseus and Menelaos led the group   470
with me as the third leader: they commanded me.
When we came to the city and the steep walls,

we hid around the city among the thick bushes,
in reeds on marshland, crouching under our armor.
When night came, a foul north wind fell on us,
icy cold. And snow fell on us like a frost,
cold, with ice crystals enveloping our shields.
All the others had cloaks and tunics and they
slept comfortably, shields covering their shoulders.
Foolishly, I'd left my cloak with my men.   480
In any case I didn't think I'd feel the cold,
but I followed with shield only and leather breechcloth.
When the night's third part came and stars had moved,
being near I nudged Odysseus with my
elbow and spoke. He immediately gave ear:

"Zeus-born Laertes' son, artful Odysseus,
count me no more among the living, for the cold
is killing me. I have no cloak! A god beguiled me
to come half-dressed. Now there's no way out."

So I spoke and he had a thought in mind   490
since he was always ready to plan or fight.
He spoke to me softly and used these words:

"Be silent lest any of the Akaians hear."

And, his head propped on his bent arm, he called:

"Friends, hear! While sleeping a god-bourn dream came.
We've come far from our ships, but one must go to speak
to Atreus' son Agamemnon, shepherd
of the host, to urge for more men from the ships."

So he spoke. Thoas, Andraimonos' son,
stood up. He threw off his purple blanket   500
and set out to run to the ships. I welcomed his
blanket and slept as golden-throned Dawn appeared.

If I still had the strength and vigor I used to have,
one of the swineherds would give me a cloak,
both from friendship and respect for a warrior.
But they don't respect me in these foul clothes."

Answering him, the swineherd Eumaios said:

"Old man, it is a noble tale you tell and you
spoke not a word amiss or unprofitable.
Here you shall not lack clothing or other things   510
fit for a much-tried suppliant from his host.
But tomorrow you'll be in your old rags again.
There are no changes of cloaks or tunics here
to dress in. Each man has just one set.
But when Odysseus' own son comes next,
he'll give you clothes himself, a cloak and tunic,
and send you where your heart and mind should bid."

So saying he stood and placed near the fire a bed
for him and tossed on it skins of sheep and goats.
Odysseus lay down there. The swineherd placed   520
a thick cloak on him, one he kept for change
of clothing when some winter storm came near.

And thus Odysseus slept. Alongside him
the young men slept. But the swineherd was not pleased
with a bed here, sleeping far from the swine, so he
made ready to go. And Odysseus was glad
his goods were being cared for in his absence.
First Eumaios put his sharp sword over his
strong shoulders, wrapped a thick, wind-breaking cloak on top
and the dense fleece of a large, well-fed goat,   530
and carried a sharp spear to ward off dogs and men.
He went to where the white-tusked boars bedded, under
the hollow crags, sheltered from the north wind.

BOOK FIFTEEN

Telemakos leaves Sparta
Eumaios tells his story
Telemakos returns safely to Ithaka

Pallas Athena then went to the broad plains
of Lakedaimonia to remind the son of brave
Odysseus to return, to urge him on.
She found Telemakos and Nestor's glorious son
in bed in the forecourt of Menelaos' palace.
Here Nestor's son was bound in soft sleep,
but sleep came not to Telemakos. All through
the fragrant night concern for his father kept him
awake. Standing near, bright-eyed Athena said:

"Telemakos, no longer wander far from home,   10
leaving your goods and those men in your palace,
so arrogant, devouring all, dividing up
your wealth, lest this journey prove a mistake.
Urge warrior Menelaos to send you off
quickly so you might reach your mother still at home.
Her father and her brothers order her to wed

Eurymakos, for he surpasses all suitors
in good bride gifts and adds to the bride price.*
Take care lest she seize your wealth against your will.
You know the heart in a woman's breast is thus.   20
She plans to swell the house of him who weds her,
no longer mindful of her dear lawful spouse
now dead, nor remembering their children.
But you, go home and turn your things over
to the handmaid who seems the best to you
until the gods show you a lusty bedmate.

Another word I'll tell you, understand it well.
The leaders of the suitors have set a trap in
the channel between rugged Ithaka and Samos.
They want to kill you before you reach home,   30
but I don't think this will happen. Sooner will
the wooers who eat your wealth be covered in earth.
But hold your well-built ship far off the islands
and sail by night. The deathless ones will send
a following wind to guard you and to drive you on.
When you reach the first bluffs of Ithaka,
urge the crew to take the ship to the town,
but you yourself go first up to the swineherd,
the swine's protector, well disposed and kind.
Sleep the night there and send a message   40
to the town telling thoughtful Penelope
that you are safe and have returned from Pylos."

Having spoken, she went up to high Olympos.
Then he roused Nestor's son from pleasant sleep,
urging him with a kick, and spoke these words:

"Up, Nestor's son Peisistratos. Yoke
the horses to the chariot so we can go!"

Nestor's son Peisistratos replied to him:

"Telemakos, though you're eager, there's no way
to drive this road in the dark. Dawn's almost here.   50
So wait until Atreus' son, hero
Menelaos, known for spears, brings gifts
to the chariot and speeds us with kind words.
For that's the man a guest remembers all
his days—the host who shows him true friendship."

So he spoke and golden-throned Dawn arrived.
Menelaos of the great war cry approached them,
just up from bed beside the bright-haired Helen.
But when Odysseus' son saw him
he quickly pulled his bright tunic over his skin,   60
threw his cloak over his sturdy shoulders,
and stood by the door. There Telemakos,
godlike Odysseus' own son, said:

"Atreus' son, Zeus-nourished Menelaos,
leader of the people, send me now to my
own land for my heart longs for home once more."

Then Menelaos of the great war cry replied:

"Telemakos, I will not keep you long here
since you yearn for home. I'd not approve of
a host excessive in friendship or excessive   70
in hatred: all in due measure is better.
It's bad both to urge on a guest unwilling
to go or to detain one hurrying to leave.
Best befriend who comes, dispatch him when he wishes.
Before I load my gifts on your chariot,
which you'll see with your eyes, I'll tell my women
to make a meal in the hall from my abundance.
There is both praise and honor—and benefit—
in eating before going far across dry land.
If you wish to go toward Hellas or Argos,   80

I myself shall follow. I'll yoke your horses,
lead you to towns of men, nor shall any
send us away without bearing some gifts,
some well-made bronze tripods or cauldrons, or
perhaps two mules, or goblets all of gold."

Then shrewd Telemakos answered him:

"Atreus' son, Zeus-nourished Menelaos,
leader of the people, I wish to go home.
Coming here I left no one to guard my wealth.
While looking for my father, I might ruin myself,   90
or a great heirloom be stolen from my home."

When Menelaos of the war cry heard this,
he called at once to his bedmate and slaves
to make a meal in the hall from his abundance.

Boethois' son Eteoneus came near him,
just out of bed, for he lived very near.
Menelaos of the great war cry bid him
roast the meat. He understood and obeyed.
Menelaos went down to his sweet-smelling storeroom
and Helen and Megapenthes went with him.   100
When they had reached the room where lay his treasures,
Menelaos chose a two-handled cup
and told Megapenthes to take a silver bowl.
Helen stood beside a chest in which
lay much finely woven cloth that she had made.
From these she, noblest of women, took one,
the prettiest and best, with scenes woven in.
Bright as a star, it lay at the bottom.
They went back through the house and reached Telemakos,
and there fair-haired Menelaos said to him: 110

"Telemakos, your wished-for return home,

may loud-thundering Zeus, Hera's spouse, grant it!
But of the gifts that lie treasured in my house
I will give you the best and most honorable.
I will give you a mixing bowl wrought of
pure silver, the rim finished off with gold,
Hephaistos' work. Warrior Phaidimos gave
it to me, Sidonia's king, when he sheltered me
on my return. I wish you to take this."

So speaking, warrior Atreus' son put the   120
two-handled cup in his hands and Megapenthes,
carrying the shining silver bowl, placed it in front
of him. Fair-cheeked Helen stood beside them
holding a bolt of cloth. Naming him, she said:

"I give this gift to you, dear child, a memento
of Helen's hands for the lovely time of
your wedding, to give to your bedmate. For now let it
lie in the hall by your mother. I wish you joy
returning to your well-built house in your own land."

So speaking, she put it in his hands. He took it gladly.   130
Taking everything, young Peisistratos put
all in a wicker trunk, and marveled at the gifts.
Then fair-haired Menelaos led them to the palace
and the two youths sat down on chairs and benches.
A maid brought a pretty, golden water jar
and filled a silver basin to wash their hands.
Next she placed a smooth table alongside them.
Then the respected housekeeper brought bread for them
and much food, bounteous and generous.
Boethois' son carved the meat, giving them slices.   140
The son of renowned Menelaos poured the wine.
They reached their hands out for the ready food.
When they'd satisfied desire for food and drink,

Telemakos and Nestor's splendid son yoked
the horses and climbed on the inlaid chariot,
driving from the echoing portico and gate.
Atreus' son, fair-haired Menelaos, followed,
holding mind-pleasing wine in his right hand
in a gold cup, a libation for their safe trip.
He toasted them standing in front of the horses: 150

"Farewell you two and greet Nestor, the people's
shepherd. He was like a kind father to me
when we Akaian sons fought there at Troy."

Then shrewd Telemakos answered him:

"We will tell him, Zeus-nourished one, all you have said
of these things when we arrive. But would that I
find brave Odysseus at home in Ithaka!
I'd tell him how I won your friendship when I came here
and brought home many splendid, noble treasures!"

Just then a bird flew overhead on the right,   160
an eagle grasping a white goose in its talons,
large and tame, from the courtyard. Women
and men followed it shouting, but it rushed by
near them on the right in front of the horses.
Seeing it they were glad, their hearts rejoicing.
Nestor's son Peisistratos said this to them:

"Tell us, Menelaos, leader of the people,
did a god make this sign for us or you?"

So he spoke, and Menelaos, dear to Ares,
pondered, wondering how to read this sign.   170
But long-robed Helen answered, speaking thus:

"Hear me! I'll prophesize. The deathless ones sent this
thought to me and I think it will be fulfilled.

The eagle, coming from the mountains where it was
born and raised, snatched up the barnyard goose. Just so
Odysseus with hard suffering and far
wandering will return home to take revenge—
or is home now planning ruin for all the suitors."

Then shrewd Telemakos answered her:

"Let Zeus, Hera's loud-thundering spouse, make it so.   180
Then at home I'd pray to you as to a goddess!"

And so he put the lash to the horses and they,
wanting open land, flew swiftly through the town.
All day long both horses made the yoke shake.
Then the sun set and all the pathways darkened.
They came to Pherai, to the house of Diokles,
Ortilokos' son, sired by Alpheios.
There, treated as guests, they spent the night.

When early-born, pink-fingered Dawn appeared,
they yoked the horses, climbed on the inlaid chariot,   190
and drove from the echoing portico and gate.
They whipped them on and unconstrained they sped.
Soon they reached Pylos' steep citadel.
Telemakos then called to Nestor's son:

"Nestor's son, can you take and fulfill
my request? Through our fathers' friendship
we claim to be guest-friends. We are of the same age.
This trip has made us more and more like-minded.
Zeus-nourished one, don't drive me past my ship
but leave me there so Nestor won't keep me as guest   200
against my will since I must hurry homewards."

So he spoke. Nestor's son understood
and promised he'd fulfill this properly,

for this appeared to be the better way.
He turned the horses toward the shore and the swift ship
and, at the ship's stern, unloaded the lovely gifts,
the clothes, the gold—all Menelaos had given him.
Urging him on, he said these winged words:

"Quickly now, board and tell your men to board
before I reach home and tell the old man.   210
For I know well both in my heart and mind
how headstrong is his heart. He would not let
you leave. He himself would summon you here.
Nor would he bid in vain or he'd be very angry."

So speaking, he drove the horses with fine manes
back to Pylos quickly reaching his home.
Telemakos roused his men and ordered thus:

"Stow the gear, friends, and ready the black ship.
Let us all board her and speed on our way home!"

So he spoke. Hearing him, they did his bidding,   220
quickly embarking and sitting at their oars.

While he worked and prayed and offered to Athena
at the ship's stern, a man approached him from
far off, a seer, fleeing Argos because he'd killed
a man. He was descended from Melampous *
who used to live in Pylos, famous for flocks, and he
was rich, his house far better than the Pylians.
But he went to another country, fleeing his land
and great-hearted Neleus, noblest of men,
who had seized his great wealth by force for the course   230
of a year. Meanwhile, he was bound in painful chains
in Phylakos' palace, suffering greatly because
of Neleus' daughter and the dire god-blindness
the avenging, house-destroying Erinys put on him.

But he escaped, drove the loud-bellowing oxen
from Phylake to Pylos, avenging the shameless deeds
of godlike Neleus. He brought the girl home
for his brother. But he himself left for
horse-pasturing Argos since it was now his fate
to live there, ruling over the many Argives.   240
There he wed and built a high-roofed palace,
and sired Antiphates and Mantios, strong sons.
Antiphates sired great-hearted Oïkles
who sired Amphiaraos, rouser of men,
whom aigis-bearing Zeus loved well as did
Apollo. He did not reach old age's threshold
but perished at Thebes because of bribes to his bedmate.
His sons were Alkmaios and Amphilokos.
Mantios sired Polypheides and Kleitos.
Kleitos was taken by golden-throned Dawn   250
because of his beauty to live among the gods.
Apollo made headstrong Polypheides a seer,
far best among mortals once Amphiaraos died.
Angry at his sire, he moved to Hyperesia
where he lived and was seer for all mortals.

It was his son, called Theoklymenos,
who approached Telemakos, reaching him
as he made the libation by the swift, black ship,
and addressing him with winged words he said:

"Friend, since I reach you in this place praying,   260
tell me, by your prayers and offerings, your heart,
and by your men: who are you? Tell me truly
and do not lie. Who are you among men?
Where is your town? And who are your parents?"

Then shrewd Telemakos answered him:

"Well then, stranger, I'll tell you very truly.

From Ithaka—that race—Odysseus my father,
should he still live. He might've perished a painful death.
Now I'm come with my men and black ship
to find out news of my father, gone so long." 270

Then godlike Theoklymenos answered him:

"I too have left my land. I killed a man
of my tribe. He has many brothers and kin.
Their might rules the Akaians in horse-pasturing Argos.
Avoiding them, I escaped my end, black death.
Now it is my fate to wander among men.
Seat me on your ship so they won't kill me since
I think they're following me. I come a suppliant."

Then shrewd Telemakos answered him:

"If you so wish, I won't keep you from the ship. 280
Board now and there we'll treat you as a friend."

So speaking, he took the man's bronze-tipped spear from him
and laid it on the half deck of the curved ship.
Then he himself boarded the sea-cleaving ship.

He sat at the stern, bidding Theoklymenos
sit beside him. The crew freed the mooring lines.
Urging them, he ordered his men to fasten
the tackle and they were quickly persuaded.
Having attached the grooved tie beams they stepped
the fir mast and bound the forestays tightly down, 290
hoisting the white sails with well-braided ox cords.
Bright-eyed Athena sent a following wind
blowing strongly from the sky to speed
the ship on its crossing over the salty sea.
They ran beside Krounoi and fair-streamed Kalkida.

Then the sun set, and the lands and seas grew dark.

The ship, driven by Zeus' wind, sped toward Pheai,
then past shining Elis where Epeians ruled.
Then, as he steered for the jagged islands,
he wondered if he would be killed or captured.   300

Meanwhile, Odysseus and the noble swineherd
ate dinner in the hut; the other men ate too.
When they'd satisfied desire for food and drink,
Odysseus spoke to them, to test the swineherd
and see if he would treat him kindly and bid him
stay there or urge him on to the town:

"Hear now, Eumaios, and you other men.
In the morning I plan to go to the town
to beg so not to burden you and your men.
But give me good advice and send a worthy man   310
to guide me there. I'll wander through the town to see
if any might give me food from the abundance.
And going to brave Odysseus' palace,
I might tell thoughtful Penelope a message
and mix with the arrogant suitors to see
if any might give me a meal, since there's so much.
I might do some quick service that they wish.
For I will tell you and you should hear and understand:
by the favor of Hermes Messenger, who grants
grace and praise to the works of all men,   320
in household work, no mortal can compare with me:
in building a good fire, in splitting firewood,
in roasting and carving meat, in pouring wine—
in all things where the lesser serve their betters."

Angry, the swineherd Eumaios answered him:

"My guest, why do you have this thought in your mind?
Or do you wish utter destruction on the spot?
So it will be, mixing in the throng of suitors

whose strong hubris stretches to the iron sky.
For their servants are not like you. They are young,   330
dressed in fine tunics and cloaks, their hair
always oiled, their faces beautiful. Such are
their servants. The well-made tables are laden
with food and meat and good wine. But come now,
for there is nothing for you to worry about
from me or any of my men, for they are mine.
But if Odysseus's son should arrive,
he will dress you in clothes—a cloak and tunic—
and send you on when your heart shall bid it."

Much-suffering Odysseus then replied: 340

"Eumaios, would that Zeus held you as dear
as I do! You ended my wanderings, my dire troubles.
The worst thing for mortals is wandering. Because
of fierce bellies, men endure terrible pain,
the suffering and misery which wandering brings.
But since you keep me here and bid me wait,
now tell me of godlike Odysseus' mother
and father, whether within the threshold of old age
they are yet living under the light of Helios,
or if they have died and gone to Hades' house."   350

Then the swineherd, leader of men, answered him:

"Well then, my guest, I will tell you very truly.
Laertes yet lives but he's always praying to Zeus
for his spirit to leave his limbs within his home.
He grieves strongly for his long absent son and for
his wedded bedmate, a skillful lady whom he mourns
the most. These aged him before his time.
She died mourning her glorious son who died
so sad a death that I would not wish any friend
living nor any acting kindly to die so.   360

So long as she lived—though sorrow filled her life—
it gave me pleasure to ask and question her about
long-robed Ktimene, her comely daughter and *
the youngest child she bore. Her she nursed with me.
I was raised with her, only a bit less honored.

But when we both came to our much-desired prime,
her they gave away in Same with many bride gifts.
But she gave me a cloak and tunic and dressed me in
lovely clothes and strapped sandals for my feet.
She sent me to the fields though she loved me deeply.   370
I miss these things now, but the happy gods make all
prosper. I do my work and abide here.
I eat and drink and give to those who are in need.
From my mistress I have heard nothing pleasing,
neither in word nor deed. Evil has fallen on
the house, and godless men. The servants long to speak
before their mistress, to learn the news, to eat
and drink, and then take something back to
the fields, which always warms the servants' hearts.

Answering him, artful Odysseus then said: 380

"You, while very young, swineherd Eumaios,
were led far from your father and ancestors.
But come now, tell me this and tell me truly,
was the town of wide streets destroyed where
your father and lady mother were living?
Or alone among the sheep and oxen, did
hostile men take you in their ships to sell
to the house of some man who paid their price?"

Then the swineherd, leader of men, answered him:

"Stranger, since you inquire, asking of this,   390
sit and listen now in silence. Enjoy and drink

some wine. These winter nights are endless. You
can sleep or listen in pleasure. You need do nothing
until it's time to sleep. And too much sleep is bad.

As for you others, any whose mind and heart bids
may sleep outside and eat when dawn appears.
Then you shall tend to our master's swine.
But we two will drink and feast in the hut
finding comfort in the past sorrows of each other
as we recall them. After suffering, a man   400
finds comfort in his past pains and wanderings.
These I'll tell you since you ask and inquire.

An island, Syria, you may have heard of it,
lies beyond Ortygia where the sun turns,
not so very much peopled but good land,
fine pastures. Sheep, wine and grain abound.
Famine never enters the land, nor does any
terrible illness come upon poor mortals.
When the tribe of men grows old in the town,
Apollo with his silver bow and Artemis   410
approach, killing with their gentle arrows.*
There lie two towns and they share the island.
They both were ruled by my father Ktesios,
Ormenios' son, a man like to the gods.

Phoinikan men, famous for ships, came there,
traffickers with many trinkets in their black ship.
A Phoinikan woman worked in my father's house,
tall and pretty and skilled in fine handicrafts.
But the crafty Phoinikans deceived her.
When at the washing basins by the ship,   420
one bedded her in love. This may beguile the heart
of even a respectable woman.
He asked her then who she was, and where from.

She quickly pointed out my father's high-roofed house:

'I declare myself to be from Sidon, famous
for bronze. I am the child of wealthy Arybas.
But Taphian men, pirates, snatched me up
coming from the fields. They brought me to
this man's house a slave and he paid their price.'

And then the one who lay with her in secret said: 430

'Would you go back again with us to our home
to see the high-roofed house of your father and mother,
and them too? They live yet and are called rich.'

The woman then answered him with these words:

'This could be so if you sailors were willing
to swear with an oath to take me home unharmed.'

So she spoke, and they all swore as she bid.
When they had sworn, the oath being complete,
the woman spoke again to them in these words:

'Silence now, and let none of your men   440
speak a word to me should we meet in the road
or by the spring. Someone might go to the palace
and tell the old man who might suspect and bind me
in harsh chains and devise some death for you.
Keep these words in your heart and hurry your
trading. When the ship is full with your cargo,
swiftly send me a message to the palace.
I'll take what gold is there at hand and bring
willingly yet more to give for my passage.
In the palace I care for the good man's child,   450
a clever boy who goes with me everywhere.
I'll bring him on your ship. You will get a good price
when you sell him to some strange-speaking men.'

So speaking, she went back to the well-built palace.
They tarried there among us for a year, trading,
amassing a huge cargo in their hollow ship.
When their laden ship was ready to sail,
they sent a messenger with news to the woman.
A shrewd man arrived at my father's palace
holding a gold necklace strung with amber beads.   460
The maids in the hall and my lady mother
touched it and admired it and
they bargained while he nodded to my nurse in silence.
So nodding, he went back aboard the hollow ship,
and she seized my hand and pulled me outdoors.
She found in the forecourt both cups and tables of
the guests who had gone to attend my father:
they had gone to the people's gathering.
Quickly hiding three gold goblets in her gown,
she left and foolishly I followed her.   470

Then the sun set and all the pathways darkened.
Going quickly, we came to the famous harbor
where the swift ship of the Phoinikans was moored.
They boarded and set sail on the watery way,
we two aboard. And Zeus sent down the wind.
For six days we sailed on, night and day.
When at last lord Zeus brought on the seventh day,
then Artemis with her arrows slew that woman.
She fell into the hold, a sound like a tern's splash.
They threw her overboard to meet the seals and fish.*   480
But I was left alone there, my heart grieving.
The wind and current bore them on to Ithaka.
There Laertes bought me as his property.
Thus I first saw this land with my own eyes."

Zeus-born Odysseus answered him thus:

"Eumaios, you've stirred the heart in my breast greatly
telling me these things, the pain your heart has suffered.
But with all this evil, Zeus did do some good
for you came to the house of a worthy man
who gave you meat and drink in kindness, and you   490
live a good life. But I come here having
wandered through many towns of mortals."

So they spoke of these things to each other
and fell asleep, not long, but for a short time.
Soon well-throned Dawn came.

                    Meanwhile they neared
the shore, Telemakos' men, furling the sails.
Quickly dropping the mast, they rowed into
the anchorage, dropped mooring stones, tied the stern
and they themselves disembarked amid the surf.
They readied their meal, mixed the sparkling wine.   500
When they had sent desire for food and wine from them,
shrewd Telemakos spoke these words to them:

"Go you now. Take the black ship to the town
and I will go to my fields and herdsmen.
Having seen my lands, I'll come to the town
in the evening. At dawn, I'll treat you as reward
to a meal of good meat and sweet wine."

Godlike Theoklymenos answered him:

"In what way shall I go, dear child? Shall I go to
the house of men who rule rocky Ithaka?   510
Or to the house of your mother, your house?"

Then shrewd Telemakos answered him:

"If things were different, I would urge you to go
to my house for we have all a good host needs.

But it may go badly for you with me away.
My mother will not see you. She does not appear
when the suitors are there, but stays upstairs
weaving. There's another man you may turn to,
Eurymakos, skilled Polybos' son,
who seems to be a god to the Ithakans.   520
By far he's the best man and most eager to wed
my mother and take Odysseus' kingship.
But Zeus, who lives in Olympos, knows these things,
whether their doom will come before the wedding day."

As he spoke a bird flew by on the right side,
a hawk, Apollo's swift messenger. It plucked
feathers from the dove its talons held. They fell
midway between Telemakos and the ship.
Theoklymenos drew him apart, alone,
held his hand tightly and spoke, naming him: 530

"Telemakos, this bird flew on the right, but not
without god's will. Seeing it I knew it was
a sign. No other clan in Ithaka is as
kingly. Yours will always be the strongest."

Then shrewd Telemakos answered him, saying:

"Would that these words should come to pass, stranger.
You'd quickly know my friendship and have my gifts.
Anyone meeting you would know you lucky!"

He called Peiraios, a trusted man:

"Peiraios, Klytios' son, you think most   540
like me of my friends who followed me to Pylos.
Now take this stranger to your house for me
and treat him with friendship and honor till I come."

Peiraios, famous spearman, answered him:

"Telemakos, though you might stay away long,
I'll care for him. He'll lack nothing due a guest."

So he spoke. Then he boarded and called the men
to board and to free the mooring ropes.
They boarded quickly and sat down at their oars.
Telemakos bound his sandals on his feet   550
and from the deck grabbed his strong spear, sharp-edged
with bronze. The men freed the mooring lines
and rowed to sea, just as Telemakos
had bid, that son of brave, godlike Odysseus.
His feet carried him swiftly up until he reached
the clearing with the large herd of pigs where
the noble swineherd slept, loyal to his lord.

BOOK SIXTEEN

Telemakos visits Eumaios
Odysseus reveals his identity to Telemakos
The suitors learn of Telemakos' escape

At dawn, Odysseus and the noble swineherd
kindled the fire, prepared breakfast within the hut
and sent the herdsmen out with the herd of swine.
The dogs, usually barking, wagged their tails around
Telemakos but didn't bark. Odysseus
noted the dogs' fawning and the sound of footsteps.
He spoke at once to Eumaios with winged words:

"Eumaios, one of your men is coming here,
or someone else well known since the dogs aren't barking.
They're wagging their tails and I hear footsteps."   10

No word was said before his own son arrived
at the doorway. Surprised, the swineherd started up
and the mixing bowl for the gleaming wine
fell from his hands. He went up to his master,
kissed him on the head, both shining eyes and then

both hands. Hot tears fell from his eyes.
Just as a father shows his son affection after
returning from ten years in a far land, his only
dear son for whom he has suffered much,
just so did the noble swineherd cover godlike   20
Telemakos with kisses as though he'd cheated death
and in tears, addressed him with these winged words:

"Telemakos, you've come! Sweet light! I thought I would
never see you again once you'd left for Pylos.
But come now, come inside, my child, you make my heart
glad seeing you here just back from afar.
But you do not often visit the herdsmen and fields.
You stay in town, for it pleases you more
to watch that destructive throng of wooing men."

Then shrewd Telemakos answered him: 30

"For that I've come here now to you, uncle,
to see with my own eyes, to hear your words
whether my mother yet waits in the palace or if
some man has wed her, and if Odysseus' bed
lacks occupants, unused, covered in foul cobwebs."

That leader of men, the swineherd, then replied:

"Truly that one waits with steadfast heart
in the palace. She mourns for him always,
pining at night, her days filled with heavy tears."

So he spoke and grasped his bronze-tipped spear.   40
Then they both entered, crossing the stone threshold.
As he neared the seat Odysseus withdrew,
but wise Telemakos restrained him, saying:

"Sit, stranger. We can find another seat
in our hut. There's a man who'll set it up."

So he spoke. Odysseus sat back down.
The swineherd spread green branches, put a fleece on top,
and the son of brave Odysseus sat down.

Then the swineherd placed platters of roasted meat
for them, leftovers of what they had eaten before.   50
He quickly put bread into a reed basket
and mixed honey-sweet wine in a wooden bowl.
Then he sat down facing Odysseus.
They reached their hands out for the ready made food.
When they'd satisfied desire for food and drink,
Telemakos then addressed the noble swineherd:

"Uncle, where is this stranger from? Why did sailors *
lead him to Ithaka? Who does he claim
to be? For I do not think he came here on foot." *

Answering him, Eumaios the swineherd said: 60

"Well, I'll tell you all, child, and the truth.
He claims to be of the tribe of wide Krete
and says he has roamed through many towns,
wandering, for thus some god spun his fate.
Making his escape from a Thresprotian ship
he came here. Now I put him in your hands.
Do as you wish. He claims to be a suppliant."

Then shrewd Telemakos answered him:

"Eumaios, these words you speak do distress me.
How can I receive a stranger in my house?   70
I am young and do not trust my hands to ward
off some man when he becomes violent.
My mother's heart is pulled in two directions:
whether to stay with me and care for the house,
honoring her lord's bed and what people

say, or to follow the Akaian's best man,
the man who woos her and offers her the most.
As for this stranger who has come to your hut,
I will clothe him in fine clothes, cloak and tunic,
give him a two-edged sword and sandals for his feet   80
and send him where his heart and mind command.
Or if you wish, keep him on your farm.
I'll send clothes here and food to eat
so that he'll be no burden to your men.
But I will not allow him to go there among
the wooers—those men are full of reckless arrogance—
lest they mock him. That's difficult to bear.
Among so many it's certain harm will result
even for a strong man for they are far the stronger."

Then he, Odysseus, the much-enduring, said: 90

"Friend, surely it is right for me to speak.
Hearing this devours my heart. Do you
say these wicked acts are planned by wooers
in your halls and they are there against your will?
Tell me, are you restrained by them, or do those in
your land hate you, a god's voice plying them?
Or do you blame your brothers in whom a man
should trust when fighting should a great feud arise?
If I were young and angered as I now am,
were I Odysseus' child or he himself   100
who had returned from wandering—there is yet room
for hope. May some foreigner cut off my head
if I would not cause the ruin of those within
the halls of lord Laertes' son Odysseus!

And should that throng slay me if I fought alone,
I'd willingly be killed there in the palace and die,
rather than see these outrageous acts:

strangers struck, women and handmaids dragged
in shame throughout the beautiful palace,
wine poured out continuously, bread devoured   110
idly—with no end to these actions!"

Then shrewd Telemakos answered him:

"Well then, stranger, I will tell it to you truly.
Neither do the people scorn nor hate me,
nor do I blame any brothers in whom a man
should trust when fighting should a great feud arise.
For Kronos' son thus made ours a one-son tribe:
Arkeisios had but one son, Laertes.
And Laertes had but one, Odysseus,
who sired me and left me in the halls alone.   120
Now in my house there's a hostile crowd
of lords who rule over nearby islands:
Doulikion, Same and wooded Zakynthos,
and those who rule over rocky Ithaka.
They all court my mother as they devour my house.
She cannot refuse the loathed wedding nor bring
it to completion. So they eat, devouring
my wealth. Soon they will bring me to ruin.
But these things are in the hands of the gods.
So you, uncle, go now to wise Penelope,*   130
tell her I am safe and have returned from Pylos.
I'll wait here till you return. But tell her
when she's alone. I trust none of the Akaians
since many of them are plotting against me."

Answering him Eumaios the swineherd said:

"I know. I see. You bid, knowing I understand.
But come now, tell me and tell me truly.
Should I go on the same path with news for poor
Laertes who grieves greatly for brave Odysseus?

He used to tend his fields and eat with his servants   140
in his house. He ate and drank as his heart bid him.
But now since the time your ship left for Pylos
they say he neither eats nor drinks like before,
nor keeps watch over his fields. He sits groaning,
and weeps and wails, the flesh wasting from his bones."

Then shrewd Telemakos answered him:

"It's sad, but we must let it be, though we grieve.
And if we mortals could choose anything,
let's first choose the day of my father's return.
You tell her and come back at once. Do not   150
go looking in the fields for him but tell my mother
to urge a maid or housekeeper to go quickly
in secret bearing this news to the old man."

The swineherd stood and took up his sandals, bound
them on his feet, then set out for the town.
But his departure did not escape Athena.
She came near seeming a tall, lovely woman,
noble, skilled in crafts. Revealing herself,
she stood facing Odysseus' sleeping place.
Telemakos neither saw nor noticed her,   160
for the gods do not reveal themselves to all.
Odysseus saw, the dogs too but barked not.
They whimpered, retreating to the shelter's far side.
She signaled brave Odysseus with her eyebrows
to go outside to the courtyard wall.
He stood before her and Athena said to him:

"Zeus-born Laertes' son, artful Odysseus,
tell now your tale to your son, do not hide it.
Plan now with him the ruin and death of the suitors.
Then go to your well-known town. I will not   170
be long away, for I am eager to fight them."

Athena touched him with her golden staff.
She wrapped a well-washed tunic and cloak about
his chest and put youthful vigor in his frame.
His skin darkened, his jaw became more forceful,
the gray beard grew darker on his face.
Having done this she left. Then Odysseus
went back into the hut and his son marveled,
and fearful, looked away lest this be some god.
Speaking winged words to him he said:

"You seem different to me, stranger, younger than   180
before. Your skin has changed. You wear other clothes!
Are you some god of those who hold the wide sky?
Be gracious that we might honor you and give
golden well-crafted gifts, but harm us not!"

Odysseus, the much-enduring, then said:

"I'm not some god. Why do you liken me to them?
I am your father. Because of me you weep
and suffer pain, endure men's violence."

So speaking he kissed his son and his tears fell
to the ground: till now he'd always held them back.   190
Telemakos did not believe this was his father,
so he spoke once more, responding with these words:

"You're not Odysseus, my father, but some
spirit enchanting me that I might suffer more!
No mortal man could plan these things in his
own mind unless a god himself came to him,
easily willing to make him young or old.
Just now you were an old man dressed in rags,
now you're like the gods who hold the wide sky!"

Answering him, artful Odysseus then said: 200

"Telemakos, it's not right that you marvel
or wonder so at your father's being here.
No other Odysseus will come here.
But this is me, after hard suffering and
long wandering, back home after twenty years.
This is the work of Athena, bearer of booty,
she makes me thus as she wills, for she can.
Now like a beggar. Now like a man in his prime,
handsome, with good clothes against his skin.
It's easy for the gods who hold the wide sky   210
both to honor mortals and to harm them."

So speaking he sat down. And then Telemakos
embraced his father and wept, tears pouring down.
A longing to weep arose in both of them
and they wailed shrilly and thickly, as birds do,
like vultures or eagles with curved talons,
when country folk seize their unfledged young.
Just so, piteous tears fell from their eyes.
The sunlight would have gone as they wept
but then Telemakos abruptly asked him: 220

"What ship and sailors, father, brought you here
to Ithaka? Who did they claim they were?
For I do not think you came here on foot."*

Odysseus, the much-enduring, then said:

"Well then, I will tell you, and tell you truly:
The Phaiakians, famous for ships, carried me here,
as they have brought others, whoever comes to them.
I kept sleeping on the voyage and when they set
me in Ithaka and unloaded my gifts:
much bronze and gold and the piles of woven cloth.   230
These things now lie in caves entrusted to the gods.
Now I'm here through Athena's inspiration

so we can plan the killing of our foes.
But come now, number the suitors and tell me so
I know how many and which men they are.
I will ponder this in my unerring mind
and decide whether we two can set against them
alone, without others, or if we must find help."

Then shrewd Telemakos answered him:

"Father, I always heard of your great fame,   240
in the strength of your hands, your wise counsel.
But you speak what cannot be! Wonder holds me!
Never could two men fight so many warriors!
There are not just ten suitors, or twice ten,
but many more! Hear me count the number!
From Doulikion came fifty-two superb
young men with six servants to attend them.
From Same there are twenty-four young men.
From Zakynthos twenty Akaian youths.
From Ithaka itself twelve, all noble,   250
in addition Medon the herald and the bard,
and two retainers, men skilled at carving meat.
Were we to meet them all inside, your coming
would be bitter! Ruinous! A failed revenge!
If you can think of any to help us, tell me,
any who would defend us with eager hearts."

Odysseus, the much-enduring, then said:

"Well, I will tell you. So listen and mark my words
and think if we, Athena and Zeus aiding us,
will do or if I should seek some other help."   260

Then shrewd Telemakos answered him:

"Noble protectors are those you speak of!

They sit aloft in the clouds, and these
two rule both men and the deathless gods."

Odysseus, the much-enduring, then said:

"Those two will not keep long from the fierce din
once our combat, the strong trial of Ares,*
begins in my palace between the suitors and us.
But you must go home with the shining dawn
and mingle with those arrogant suitors.   270
The swineherd will lead me to town later,
disguised like an old miserable beggar.
If they insult me in the palace, let the heart
in your breast endure it though I suffer badly,
though they drag me by the feet out of the house,
beat me or throw things. Watch but accept it.
Then you should bid them cease their folly, speaking
soothing words, though they will in no way
be persuaded, for their allotted day has come.
I will tell you this and guard it in your heart: 280
when Athena, wise in counsel, puts it in
my mind, I will nod my head. When you see this,
take all the weapons lying in the halls
and put them in the corner of the upper
chamber, all of them. Speak these soft words
to the suitors should they ask or miss them:

'I moved them from the smoke since they are not
as they were when Odysseus left for Troy
but are marred where the fire's heat reached them.
Some spirit put this more important thought in mind.   290
When you are drinking, some quarrel might arise
and wounding one another, you shame the feast
and the wooing, for iron attracts men.' *

Now for the two of us, leave behind two swords,

two spears and two bull-hide shields ready at hand
so that, rushing over we might grab them. Athena
and wise Zeus will enthrall the suitors.
I tell you this and guard it in your heart:
if you are my son and are of my blood
let no one learn Odysseus is here inside! 300
So do not let Laertes know, nor the swineherd,
nor any others, not even Penelope herself.
You and I will test the temper of the women,
and we will test the men of the household,
to know who honors us, holds us in awe,
and who heeds you not, holds no regard for you."

So answering, his noble son then said:

"Father, I think you shall learn of my mettle.
A lack of good sense does not shackle me.
But I don't think your plan is a good idea 310
for either of us. I beg you to reconsider.
It would take you long to test each man,
farm by farm while they, in arrogant ease,
devour your wealth, sparing nothing in the palace.
But I bid you learn of the women, who
of them has dishonored you, who is guiltless.
Of the men, I would not be willing to test them
by going to their farmsteads. Do that later if
you have some sign from aigis-bearing Zeus."

So they spoke, one to the other, about these things. 320

Meanwhile the well-built ship arrived in Ithaka,
the ship that had carried Telemakos to Pylos.
When the crew had come into the deep harbor,
they dragged the black ship onto dry land.
High-spirited servants carried their gear away
and took the beautiful gifts to Klytios' house.

Then they sent a herald ahead to the palace
giving a message to wise Penelope
that Telemakos was in the country but
had bid the ship sail to the town, lest the queen,   330
her heart fearful for him, let fall her soft tears.
So then the herald and the noble swineherd met
with the same message to give to the woman.
And when they'd come to the godlike king's palace,
the herald, standing among the handmaids, then spoke:

"Indeed, my queen, your own son has returned."

And the swineherd, standing near Penelope,
told her all her son had bade him tell her.
When he had told all as he had been bid, he set
off to his swine, leaving the courtyard and the palace.   340
The suitors, quiet, were troubled in their hearts.
From the halls they went outside by the great wall
of the courtyard and sat in front of the gates.
Polybos' son Eurymakos then spoke:

"Friends, this boy's journey has been made! A deed
too bold! Telemakos! We said he could not!
But come, let's drag a black ship, the best one,
then gather rowing seamen and have them quickly
take a message to our friends to return now."

He'd not finished speaking when Amphinomos,   350
turning, saw the ship in the deep harbor,
the crew furling the sail, oars in their hands.
Laughing heartily, he said to the others:

"Let's not urge on a messenger for they are here.
Either a god told them of this or they
themselves saw the ship go by but could not catch her."

So he spoke. They stood and went down to the shore.
Quickly they dragged the black ship onto dry land
and high-spirited servants carried the gear away.
They went in a throng to the meeting place,   360
letting no other man, young or old, sit there.
Eupeithes' son Antinoös spoke to them:

"Damn! The gods kept this youth from destruction!
We kept watch, one by one, sitting on
the windy heights by day. When Helios went down
we didn't sleep at night on land but sailed on
the sea in our fast ship, awaiting bright Dawn
to waylay Telemakos, to seize and kill him.
But in the meantime, some spirit conveyed him home.
So let us now devise a wretched death here   370
for Telemakos. He must not live! For while
he lives I think our plans will not succeed.

He is shrewd in planning and in thinking,
and the people here no longer favor us.
But come, before he calls the Akaians
to assembly. I do not think he will be idle,
but angry. He will stand and tell them all
how we devised a plan of murder but did not
catch him. And they won't praise us for that evil scheme.
I fear lest they do us harm and drive us from   380
our lands so we must go to another land.
Let's seize and kill him in the fields, away from town,
or on the road. We'll take his goods and wealth and
divide them by lots among us, but we will give
the palace to his mother and to whom she weds.
If this plan does not please you and you wish him
to live and have all his patrimony, let us
no longer devour his wealth in merriment gathered
here. Rather each from his own home should woo,

paying the bride price. Let her choose him   390
who offers most, he who is destined for her."

So he spoke. All kept still, bound in silence.
But Amphinomos spoke and addressed them.
He was the son of Nisos, Aretios' son,
who came to woo from grassy Doulikion,
rich in wheat. He pleased Penelope the best
with his words for he had a good heart.
With good intent, he spoke to them, saying this:

"Friends, I do not wish to kill Telemakos.
It's terrible to kill one of kingly stock.   400
But first let us ask the will of the gods.
If the oracle of great Zeus concurs,
I myself will slay him and bid others to.
But if the gods deny this, I will bid you stop."

So spoke Amphinomos and his words pleased them.
They stood and entered the house of brave Odysseus,
and there they sat down on the polished chairs.

Then sensible Penelope thought to show
herself to the wantonly proud suitors.
She knew of the planned murder of her child at home,   410
for the herald Medon had overheard the plot.
She went down to the halls with her handmaids.
When she reached the suitors, she stood among her maids
by a column supporting the well-built roof,
and holding her shining veil before her face,
she rebuked Antinoös, naming him, saying:

"Antinoös, arrogant man, plotter of evil!
They say you are the best of your Ithakan peers
in plans and words. But you are not such a one!
Madman! Why do you plot Telemakos' fate   420

and death with no care for suppliants whom Zeus
protects? It is not right to plot against others!
Don't you remember when your father fled, coming
to us, fearing his people? They were very angry
because he joined the Taphian robbers and harried
the Thesprotians who were our friends.
They wanted to kill him, to tear out his heart,
devour his wealth that once was enormous.
But lord Odysseus stopped them though they were eager.
Now you freely devour his house, court his woman,   430
plot to slay his son causing me most grief!
I urge you to stop and order the others to stop!"

Polybos' son Eurymakos answered:

"Ikarios' maid, wise Penelope,
take courage! Don't let these things be a care for you.
No man alive or unborn—or to be born—
shall lay hands on your son Telemakos
while I have sight and live on this earth.
For I will say, and it will truly come to pass,
that man's black blood at once shall gush around   440
my spear. For Odysseus, sacker of cities,
often put me on his knees, put roast meat
in my hands and offered me red wine. Thus of
all men Telemakos is most dear to me,
so I bid him not tremble fearing death from
the suitors, but from the gods no one can escape it."

Thus boldly he spoke though plotting the boy's death.
Then she went upstairs in silence to weep for lord
Odysseus her spouse and the bright-eyed goddess
Athena poured sweet sleep over her eyelids.   450

That same evening, the noble swineherd returned home.
Odysseus and his son prepared the meal:

a sacrificed, year-old sow. But Athena
stood near Laertes' son Odysseus, tapped
him with her rod and made him old again,
foul clothes against his skin, lest the swineherd
see him face to face, know him and rush the news—
not keeping the secret—to Penelope.

Telemakos spoke first with these words:

"You've come, good Eumaios. What's new from town?   460
Are the manly suitors there back from their ambush?
Or do they yet lie waiting for my homeward trip?"

Eumaios, the swineherd, answering him said:

"Going about the town asking and inquiring,
this did not concern me. My heart bid me
to speak my message and return here quickly.
But I met a messenger from those men,
the herald, who gave the news to your mother first.
I know other news, for my eyes saw it.
Above the town, at the crest of Hermes' hill,   470
as I was coming back, I saw a swift ship
enter our harbor with many men aboard.
It was heavy with shields and double-pointed spears.
I thought it might be them but I do not know."

So he spoke. God-protected Telemakos
smiled at his father. The swineherd did not see.

When they had finished preparations for their meal,
they ate and their hearts did not lack a fair portion.
When they'd satisfied desire for food and drink,
they thought of bed and seized the gift of sleep.   480

BOOK SEVENTEEN

Telemakos returns to the palace
Eumaios leads Odysseus to the palace
Odysseus begs from all the suitors

When early-born, pink-fingered Dawn appeared,
Telemakos, godlike Odysseus's son,
bound his well-made sandals to his feet,
seized his strong spear which fit in his palm,
and eager for town, he said to the swineherd:

"Uncle, I'm going to the town so my mother
may see me, for I think she will not stop wailing
or bitter weeping with her teary eyes
until she sees me. But I charge you with this:
lead this miserable stranger to town   10
so he may beg his meal there. Let who wishes give
him bread and a cup. I can't take care of all
men while I have such pain in my heart.
If this stranger gets angry, then so be it!
For me, I like to speak the simple truth."

Artful Odysseus, answering him, then said:

"Friend, I do not wish to be kept here.
As a beggar it is better to be in town
than countryside to beg. They'll give what they wish.
I am not so old yet to stay on the farm   20
obeying some overseer in his commands.
So come, let this man lead me as you urge,
but let me warm myself in the fire's heat
lest the frost take me. These old clothes I have
are very thin. They say the town is far."

So he spoke. Noble Telemakos set out
with swift strides planning evil for the suitors.
When he reached the comfortable palace,
he stood his spear against a high column
and, crossing the stone threshold, went in.   30

His nurse Eurykleia saw him first while she
was spreading fleece on the embellished chair.
Tearfully, she went straight to him; other maids
of big-hearted Odysseus gathered round,
kissing him in joy on his head and shoulders.

Wise Penelope came from her chamber
resembling Artemis or golden Aphrodite.
Crying, she threw her arms around her child,
kissed his head and both his shining eyes.
Sobbing, she addressed these winged words to him: 40

"You have come back, Telemakos, sweet light! I thought
I'd never again see you, since you sailed against
my will in stealth to Pylos for news of your father.
But come, tell me who you met with, what you saw."

Then shrewd Telemakos answered her:

"Mother, don't urge your heart to weep lest you trouble
the heart in my breast, though I did escape sheer death.
But bathe yourself, put on fresh clean clothes,
go up to your rooms with your women servants.
Promise the gods to sacrifice a hecatomb   50
that Zeus might one day bring about revenge.
I'll go to the gathering place to bid a stranger
come to our house; he followed me from Pylos.
I sent him on before me with my godlike men
and ordered Peiraios to take him in, to treat
him kindly, honoring him till I might come."

So he spoke. His words lodged in her heart.
She bathed herself and put on fresh clean clothes
and promised the gods to sacrifice a hecatomb
that Zeus might one day bring about revenge.   60

Telemakos traversed the halls and left,
taking his spear. His two swift dogs followed him.
Athena poured a divine grace over him,
and all those who came upon him marveled.
The manly suitors gathered all about him,
speaking nobly but with dark plans in their hearts.
But he shunned this great throng of them and went
where sat Mentor, and Antiphos and Halitherses,
all were companions of his father from of old.
He sat and they asked him about everything.   70
Then Peiraios, famed spearman, came near:
he led the stranger to the town's assembly.
Seeing them, Telemakos stood up.

Peiraios was the first to speak, saying:

"Telemakos, send your women to my house
so I can send the gifts Menelaos gave you."

Then shrewd Telemakos answered him:

"Peiraios, we don't know how things will turn out.
If the proud suitors kill me in my home
treacherously, they will divide my father's treasures.   80
Rather than them, I'd wish that you enjoy them.
But if I should cause their death and slaughter,
then, rejoicing, bring them to me and I'll be glad."

So speaking, he led home his much-suffering guest.
Once they reached the comfortable palace,
they placed their clothes on couches and chairs and went
to the polished bathtubs where they bathed.
When the maids had washed them and rubbed them with
fine oil, and dressed them in thick tunics and cloaks,
they left the bathing area and sat on couches.   90
A handmaid brought water in a golden jug
and poured it into silver washbasins to wash
their hands and placed polished tables beside them.
Bringing bread, the honored housekeeper gave it
to them, and other goodly food from her pantry.
His mother sat opposite, beside a column,
reclining on a couch, spinning fine wool thread.
They reached their hands for the ready food.
But when their desire for food and wine was sated,
Penelope began speaking to them these words: 100

"Telemakos, I will go up to my quarters
and lie in my bed, that bed of sorrows,
always wet with my tears since Odysseus
went with the sons of Atreus
to Ilios. But you did not have the heart,
before the suitors returned, to tell me plainly
of your father, if you heard anything."

Then shrewd Telemakos answered her:

"Well then, Mother, I will tell you truly now.
We came to Pylos, to Nestor, the people's shepherd.
He kindly befriended me, receiving me in   110
his high-roofed palace. As a father welcomes his son
after a long time back from afar,
so he took care of me with his renowned sons.
But of Odysseus he could not say, whether
he lives or died, having heard no word from anyone.
But in a fine chariot he sent me to
the palace of Menelaos famed for spears.
There I saw Helen for whom many Argives
and Trojans suffered through the will of the gods.

Then Menelaos, good at the war cry, asked me   120
what brought me to rich Lakedaimonia.
I told him everything truthfully.
And he responded saying these words to me:

'See now how these weak men wish to use
his very bed, the bed of a strong-hearted man!
As when a doe leaves in a mighty lion's lair
both her suckling, newborn fawns to sleep while she
searches the mountain spur and grassy hollows for
a place to feed, the lion, returning to his lair,
then sends those two fawns to their hard fate—just so   130
Odysseus will send those men to their hard fate.
By father Zeus, by Athena and Apollo,
would he were as he was when in well-built Lesbos!
Because of a quarrel, he wrestled Philomeleïdes,
and threw him down hard. Glad were the Akaians!
So may Odysseus come among the wooers!
They'd enjoy an early death, a bitter wedding.

You beg and ask these things, and I will not
swerve from the telling nor deceive you but will tell

you truly as the Old Man of the Sea told me.   140
I will hide nothing, hold back nothing.
He said he had seen him suffering strong pains
in the nymph Kalypso's palace. She held him
by force so he could not return to his own land.
For there was no ship ready for him, no oars, nor crew
to carry him across the sea's wide back.'

So spoke Menelaos, famous spearman.
My task completed, I returned. The deathless ones
gave me a fair wind, speeding me to my own land."

So he spoke and stirred the heart in her breast.   150
Then godlike Theoklymenos said to them:

"Honored woman of Laertes' son Odysseus,
hear my words for he did not understand.
I'll prophesy for you truly, concealing nothing.
By Zeus, first of the gods, by this welcome table
and hearth of lord Odysseus where I have come,
Odysseus is now here in his land!
Sitting or walking, he's learning of their evil acts,
and he plots revenge on all the suitors!
Such was the omen I saw on the well-benched ship.   160
I prophesied this and I told Telemakos."

He spoke, but sensible Penelope then said:

"If your words might be thus fulfilled, stranger,
you'd quickly know my friendship and have such gifts
that any you should meet would name you blessed."

And thus they sat speaking among themselves.

Meanwhile the suitors in front of the king's palace,
enjoyed hurling goat-spears and discus throwing on
the leveled terrace with their usual arrogance.

When it was time for eating and the flocks   170
came from the fields, the usual shepherds leading them,
then Medon spoke. For of the heralds, he pleased
them most and he attended them in their feasting:

"Young men, since you have cheered your hearts with sports,
now come to the palace so we may ready a feast.
For it is not wrong to lay hands on food at meal time."

So he spoke. They went, persuaded by his words.
When they reached the comfortable palace,
they put their cloaks down on couches and chairs,
then killed a large ram, succulent goats,   180
fattened hogs and an ox from the herd,
readying the feast. And now Odysseus
and the swineherd prepared to leave for town.
The swineherd, leader of men, began speaking these words:

"Stranger, you wish to go to town today
as my lord bids, but my advice for you would be
to stay and act as guardian of this farm.
I honor my lord and fear him lest in anger later
he blames me. The anger of one's master is serious.
So now let's go, for the day is going quickly,   190
and the cold of evening will come soon."

Answering him, artful Odysseus then said:

"I know. I see. You bid me knowing I understand.
So let's go, you lead the way directly there.
But give me a staff to lean on if there's one
ready cut, for you say the path is rough."

Over his shoulders he slung his shabby bag,
full of holes, held by a twisted strap,
and Eumaios gave him a staff that pleased his heart.

The two set out. The other shepherds and the dogs   200
remained, guarding the farm. To town he led
his lord who looked like a wretched old beggar
leaning on his staff, dressed in worn rags.

As they climbed the rugged path and neared town,
they reached a sweet-flowing spring of hewn stone
where the people came for water. Ithakos
built it with Neritos and Polyktor. Round it
grew a grove of black poplars which grow by water,
all in a circle, the cold water flowing down
from high rocks. An altar to the Nymphs had been   210
built where all wayfarers made an offering.
Dolios' son, Melanthios, met them there
leading goats selected from the herd
for the suitors feast. Two shepherds followed him.
Seeing them, Melanthios rebuked them with ugly,
nasty words stirring Odysseus' heart:

"It's always thus, the bad lead the bad!
So always a god brings together like to like!
Where do you lead this wretch, you miserable
swineherd, this troublesome, plate-licking beggar?   220
Many doorposts will he rub his shoulders on,
begging food scraps, never sword or cauldron.*
If you'd give him to me to guard my farm,
to clean my barn and give green food to kids,
he'd put meat mass on his thighs drinking the whey.
But since he's learned bad ways he doesn't wish to do
real work! He'd rather wander the land begging
to fill his ever-insatiable belly.
But I will tell you this and thus it shall be:
if he comes to lord Odysseus' palace,   230
his head and ribs will be shattered from footstools
hurled by the hands of men throughout the palace."

So speaking, he foolishly kicked Odysseus
in the hip as he was passing by but did
not move him off the path. Odysseus pondered
whether to rush him and kill him with his staff,
or seizing his waist, bash his head on the earth.
But he endured, his temper contained. Eumaios cursed
the other to his face. Raising his hands, he prayed:

"Nymphs of the spring, Zeus' maids, if ever   240
Odysseus burned to you wrapped, fat-rich thighbones
of lamb or kid, grant now this wish for me!
Grant that my lord return, led by some god,
that he might scatter those with swaggering ways,
such as you have, always arrogant throughout
the town while bad herding destroys your flocks."

Melanthios, herder of goats, answered him:

"How the old man speaks with a dog's malice!
Someday I'll lead him on a well-benched ship
far from Ithaka and sell him for my gain.   250
If only silver-bowed Apollo would slay
Telemakos today or the suitors kill him!
Odysseus perished far off. He won't come back!"

So speaking, he left. They walked on slowly but
Melanthios strode fast till he reached the palace.
He went inside and sat among the suitors
next to Eurymakos whom he liked the best.
The servants set slices of meat by them
and the honored housekeeper brought bread to eat.
Odysseus and Eumaios arrived and moved   260
in close, hearing the sound of a hollow lyre.
The bard Phemios was just beginning to sing.
Putting his hand on the swineherd Odysseus said:

"Eumaios, these must be Odysseus' lovely halls,
noticeably standing out from others.
Hall upon hall it has and courtyard walls
finished off with fine coping and those strong
double gates! No man could build them better!
I see that many men are feasting now inside
and I smell roasting meat. And the lyre   270
is sounding, which the gods made companion to feasts."

Then swineherd Eumaios, you answered him: *

"You see quickly and lack not sense in other things.
But come, let's think how these things will work out.
Either you go first into the stately palace
and go among the suitors while I wait here.
Or wait here if you wish while I go in.
But do not wait long lest someone see you and strike
you or drive you off. I bid you think on this."

Then lord Odysseus the much-enduring, said: 280

"I know. I see. You bid me, knowing I understand.
You go first. I will wait here outside,
for I am not unused to blows or missiles.
My heart endures since I have suffered much
at sea and in war. Let these add to those.
But no man can hide his hungry belly.
It's ruinous and brings men much evil.
It's for the belly that well-benched ships sail
the barren sea bringing ruin to our foes."

So they spoke of these things to each other.   290
A dog sleeping near raised its head, ears alert—
Argos, the dog Odysseus himself had reared
but had no joy of, for he had to leave
for holy Ilios. Young men used to take him

hunting for wild goats, deer and hare, but now,
his master long absent, he lay neglected
on the deep dung of mules and oxen piled
in heaps before the gates, until his master's
servants carried it out to enrich their fields.
There Argos lay, covered with fleas and ticks.   300
But being near he knew Odysseus
and wagged his tail letting his ears droop down.
He was too old to rise and go to his master.
Odysseus, seeing him, wiped away
a tear—Eumaios didn't see—and said to him:

"Eumaios, this is puzzling, this dog lying
in dung! His build is good, but I don't clearly know
if he runs swiftly to match his fine build
or if he's one of those dogs kept by the table
whose masters keep them as an adornment."   310

Then swineherd Eumaios, you answered him: *

"This dog belongs to a man who died far away.
If he were still in form and deed as he was then
when brave Odysseus went to pillage Troy,
you would marvel seeing his speed and strength.
No wild thing that took flight deep in the dark woods
could escape him for he knew well their tracks.
He's ill kept now, neglected, his lord dead in a
far land. The women do not care for him.
Slaves, when their lord no longer rules them,   320
no longer wish to work as is their duty.
Loud-thundering Zeus takes half the good from a man
on the day when he's taken as a slave."

So he spoke and going into the stately palace,
he went straight to the hall where the suitors were.
Then having seen Odysseus once again,

after twenty years, death took old Argos.

As the swineherd came into the palace
godlike Telemakos saw him and waved
him to approach. The swineherd saw a stool   330
the carver used when slicing up meat
for the suitors who were feasting in the halls.
This he took and set it by Telemakos
and sat down there. The herald brought meat and bread
from a wicker basket, setting them before him.

Right behind him Odysseus entered the palace,
like to a sad beggar, an old man,
leaning on a staff, rags against his skin.
He sat on the ash threshold inside the doors,
leaning against a skillfully hewn and smoothed   340
cypress column that had been set straight and true.
Taking a whole loaf from the well-made basket
and as much meat as his hands could hold
Telemakos called the swineherd and said to him:

"Take these and give them to the stranger. Bid him
approach all the suitors and beg of them as well.
Shame is not good for a man in need."

So he spoke. Hearing his words, the swineherd went
and standing near the beggar spoke these winged words:

"Telemakos gives you these things and bids you   350
approach all the suitors and beg of them as well.
He said that shame is not good in a beggar."

Answering him, artful Odysseus said:

"Oh Zeus, make Telemakos most blessed of men
and grant him all his heart most desires!"

He took the food in both hands and set
it on the tattered bag in front of his feet
and ate while the bard was singing in the hall.
He'd finished his meal when the godlike bard ceased
and the suitors grew loud in the palace.   360
But Athena, standing near Odysseus,
urged him to beg loaves of bread from the suitors
so he might know who was righteous and who not.
But not one was destined to ward off his own ruin.
He set off begging from each man left to right,
reaching his hands to all like a practiced beggar.
They took pity and gave and marveled at him,
wondering who he was and from whence.

Then goatherd Melanthios said to them:

"Hear me, suitors of the famous queen,   370
I know of this stranger! Earlier I saw
the swineherd leading him straight here but I
know nothing of him or who he claims to be."

So he spoke. Antinoös rebuked Eumaios:

"Foolish swineherd! Why did you lead this man
into town? Aren't there enough crowds of other
wanderers begging, ruining our feasting?
Is it right that they come to eat your lord's wealth,
gathering here, but you must bring yet one more?"

Then swineherd Eumaios, you answered him: *   380

"Antinoös, though noble, you speak not well.
Who would bid a stranger from another land
come here unless they were of the hired workers,*
seers or healers of the sick, or carpenters,
or god-inspired bards whose singing brings us joy?

These are invited across the boundless earth.
But no one burdens himself inviting a beggar.
Of the suitors, you are the one who is harsh
on Odysseus' servants, especially me.
But I care not as long as good Penelope   390
lives in the palace, and godlike Telemakos."

Then shrewd Telemakos answered him:

"Keep silent. Don't answer him with many words.
Antinoös often speaks with harsh words,
evilly, and he urges others to."

Then he spoke these winged words to Antinoös:

"Antinoös, your kind concern for me, as father
to son, urges me to drive this stranger off
with hard words—may Zeus not bring this to pass!
Give him something. I will bear you no ill will,   400
so give. Let not respect for my mother or
the servants in Odysseus' palace stop you!
But this is not the thought within your heart. You
yourself would rather eat than give to another!"

Then Antinoös, answering him, said:

"Telemakos, braggart! How daring in what you say!
If all suitors would give him what I give,
we would keep him far from here for three months!"

So he spoke and picked up his footstool as if
to throw it and then rested his feet on it and feasted.   410
All the others gave to the beggar, filling his bag
with bread and meat. Having tested the Akaians
with no reaction, Odysseus, about to go
to the threshold, stood by Antinoös and said:

"Give something, friend, for you don't seem to be the worst
of the Akaians, but the best, like to a king.
So you should give me better food and I
will speak your fame throughout this boundless land.
I once lived in a house among men, blessed,
wealthy, and I gave to many wanderers,   420
whoever they claimed to be, wherever from.
I had a great number of slaves and such things
as men have who live well and are called wealthy.
But Kronos' son ruined me, for so he wished.
He sent me with some men, far-ranging pirates,
to holy Egypt, a long trip, that I might die.
I moored the curved ships in Egypt's river.
Then I ordered my loyal shipmates to stay
there with the ships and to guard them,
and I sent men off to scout the land.   430

But they gave way to their pride and plundered
the rich fields of the Egyptians and carried off
the women and small children. And they killed
the men. The word spread quickly to the city.
Having heard the shouts, they came as dawn broke.
The plain filled with foot soldiers and chariots,
the flash of bronze. Zeus, hurler of thunderbolts,
sent my men into headlong flight. None stayed
to face the foe. Disaster came from every quarter.
There they killed many of us with sharp bronze   440
and led those yet living away to forced labor.
They bound me to a passing stranger from Kypros,
Iasos' son Dmetor, who ruled Kypros with might.
That's how I've come here, suffering many pains."

Speaking up, Antinoös answered him:

"What spirit brought this fool, troubling our feast?

Stand away, in the middle, far from my table
lest you quickly reach a bitter Egypt and Kypros.*
So daring a one and you a shameless beggar!
One by one, all of them give to you   450
thoughtlessly since no one restrains their pity,
giving what's not theirs, each keeping his own plenty."

Drawing back, artful Odysseus then said:

"See now! Your heart is not like your outward form!
Even at home, you would not offer a bit of salt!
Sitting at another's table, you won't give me
a single piece of bread although there's plenty here!"

So he spoke. Antinoös angered quickly
and scowling at him, said these winged words:

"And now you won't be able to leave this palace   460
so easily since you speak such foul abuse!"

So speaking, he grabbed the footstool and hurled it,
hitting him in the shoulder. Odysseus
stood rock still; the thrown footstool did not fell him.
In silence, he shook his head, black plans in his heart.
He went back to the threshold and sat down, spreading
his full bag out and, speaking to the suitors, said:

"Hear me, suitors of the famous queen:
I say what my heart in my breast bids!
There's no pain in the heart or sorrow when   470
a man is hit fighting for his possessions,
for his oxen or for his white sheep. But he,
Antinoös, struck me because of my belly,
this belly that gives such destructive ruin to men!
But if there is a god or revenge for beggars,
may death reach Antinoös ere his wedding!"

Eupeithes' son Antinoös spoke back:

"Eat at ease, stranger, sitting, or go elsewhere,
lest the young men drag you through the halls by hands
or feet, shredding your skin for what you have just said!"   480

So he spoke. But all felt more righteous and just,
and one of the young men spoke thus in pride:

"Antinoös, it's not wise to strike a poor
vagrant, your ruin if he's some sky-dwelling god.
For gods appear as foreigners, strangers,
appearing in all shapes, and they visit cities
of men, observing the arrogant and the good."

So spoke a suitor but Antinoös heard not his words.
Telemakos felt great pain for the beggar
who was struck but his eyes let fall no tears.   490
In silence he shook his head, planning evil in secret.

But wise Penelope heard about the beggar
struck by the stool and spoke among her servants:

"So may Apollo's bow strike you who threw the stool!"

The housekeeper Eurynome said these words:

"May our prayers reach their just completion
that none of these men see Dawn's splendor!"

Then sensible Penelope answered her:

"Good mother, since they plan evil, all are hateful,
but Antinoös most of all is black as death.   500
A poor stranger wanders through the hall,
begging of men since his own need compels him.
All gave to him, filled his bag, but Antinoös
struck him with a footstool on the right shoulder!"

So she spoke to her women upstairs in
her chamber while Odysseus ate below.
She then summoned the swineherd and said to him:

"Go, Eumaios, approach the stranger and bid
him come that I might speak to him and ask if he
knows anything of long-enduring Odysseus   510
or has laid eyes on him, for he looks much traveled."

Then swineherd Eumaios, you answered her:

"Would that these Akaians kept their silence, my Queen!
The tales he has told me enchanted my own heart!
I had him for three nights, and kept him in my hut
three days—escaping from a ship, he reached me first—
but he had not completed his tales of suffering.
Just as a man beholds a bard who has learned
his singing from the gods, ever charming mortals
who wish to listen insatiably when he sings,   520
so he who now sits in the hall charmed me.
He says his father and Odysseus' were friends.
He lives in Krete where the tribe of Minos lives.
He has come here now though suffering much pain,
wandering endlessly. He claims he's heard he lives:
Odysseus is near, among Thesprotians
in their rich land and brings much wealth home."

Then sensible Penelope answered him:

"Go. Bid him here so I can talk to him in person.
Let the rest amuse themselves sitting by   530
the door or in the house since their hearts are merry.
Their wealth lies in their houses untouched, their bread
and sweet wine, their household feeds on these.
But they do come and go in our house daily,
sacrificing oxen, sheep, our fattest goats,

reveling in recklessly drinking the shining wine.
They are consuming everything. For there's no man
such as Odysseus was to save our goods.
Were Odysseus to come, reach his own land,
he would with his strength and son repay these men!"   540

So she spoke. Telemakos sneezed loudly,
echoing through the palace, Penelope laughed.
Straightaway she told Eumaios these winged words:

"Go and summon the stranger here before me.
See you not how my son sneezes at my words? *
Death will come to all the suitors here;
none shall escape death and dark fate.
I'll tell you more but guard it in your heart.
If I perceive he tells everything with truth,
I'll dress him in fine clothes, a cloak and tunic."   550

So she spoke. Having heard her, the swineherd went,
stood near Odysseus and said these winged words:

"Old man, she calls you, wise Penelope,
Telemakos' mother. Her heart bids her ask you
about her husband though it make her suffer.
If she perceives you tell everything with truth,
she'll dress you in cloak and tunic—you stand
in great need. And you will feed your belly begging
food throughout the land. Let him give who will."

Then lord Odysseus, the long-enduring, said: 560

"Eumaios, at once I'll tell everything with truth
to Ikarios' child, wise Penelope,
for I know well of him. We suffered the same pain.
But I fear this throng of harsh suitors
whose arrogance and power reach the iron sky.

Even now when I was going through the hall
doing nothing bad, a man struck me, hurt me.
Nor did Telemakos nor another prevent it.
Now bid Penelope wait in the hall,
curbing her impatience till Helios sets.   570
Then let her ask me of his return, her spouse,
seating me close to the fire, for the clothes
I wear are bad. You know this for I came first to you.”

So he spoke. The swineherd left once he had heard him.
And when he crossed her threshold, Penelope said:

“Eumaios, why did you not bring him? What does this mean?
Does the wanderer fear something here? Is he
ashamed here? For shame is bad in a wanderer.”

Then swineherd Eumaios, you answered her:

“He speaks rightly, as anyone might,   580
who shuns the arrogance of overbearing men.
He bids you wait till Helios has set.
And for you yourself this will be better, my Queen,
to speak to him alone and hear his tale.”

Then sensible Penelope answered him:

“He is not stupid, that stranger, whatever he predicts,
for there have never been among mortals any
men so arrogant and reckless as these.”

So she spoke. The swineherd went down to
the throng of suitors once he had told her everything.   590
And then he told Telemakos these winged words,
standing near his head so others might not hear:

“Friend, I now leave to guard swine and farm,
your livelihood and mine. You mind all here.

Save yourself first and stay on guard
lest you suffer. These Akaians have evil thoughts.
May Zeus destroy them ere they bring us pain!"

Then shrewd Telemakos answered him:

"Let it be so, uncle. Have your meal and go.
At dawn drive down the sacrificial animals.   600
I—and the deathless ones—will mind all here."

So he spoke. Eumaios sat on the polished
stool and, having had his fill of food and drink,
left for his swine, leaving the hall and courtyard
filled with revelers. They were enjoying song
and dance now, for evening had come upon them.

BOOK EIGHTEEN

Odysseus fights and defeats the beggar Iros
Odysseus begs in his own palace
Penelope appears before the suitors

A wandering beggar arrived used to begging
in Ithaka town, known for his raging belly
continuously needing food and drink. He had
no strength or vigor but was huge to look on.
His name was Arnaios, for his mother gave
that at birth, but he was called by the young men
Iros because he carried messages when bid.*
Now he was driving brave Odysseus from his
own house and, wrangling, spoke these winged words:

"Move from the door, old man, lest I drag you away   10
by your foot! Don't you see how they make signs,
urging me to drag you? Still I'd rather not.
So up! Quickly! Lest our quarrel bring us to blows!"

Looking grim, artful Odysseus then said:

"How so? I do you no harm, nor speak any,
and I don't care if they give you of their abundance.
This threshold will hold us both. You do not need
to be concerned with others. You seem to be
a wanderer like me: the gods grant fortune as
they wish. Don't challenge me with fists lest you rouse   20
my wrath. I'm not so old I couldn't bloody your lips
and chest. Yet it would give me more peace tomorrow,
for I think you'd not come a second time
to the palace of Laertes' son Odysseus."

The beggar Iros answered him angrily:

"For shame! How this swine speaks so glibly,
like an old woman cooking! I'll show him harm,
hitting both his cheeks until his teeth drop from
his jaw as I'd drive out a crop-consuming hog!
Tuck your clothes up so all will see and know of our   30
fighting. How can you fight with a younger man?"

Thus, on the polished threshold in front of
the lofty doors the two quarreled most bitterly.
Princely Antinoös urging them on
to fight, burst out laughing and addressed the suitors:

"My friends, there's never been so rare a sight as this!
Such a delight the gods have brought to this palace!
The stranger and Iros are ready to have
a fistfight so let's drive them together quickly!"

So he spoke and they all sprang up, laughing   40
as they gathered round the ill-clad beggars.

Eupeithes' son Antinoös said this:

"Listen, manly suitors, to what I say to you:
on the fire lie goat-belly sausages

being grilled for dinner, full of fat and blood.
Of these two, whoever proves better and wins,
let him choose which sausages he wants
and let him always eat here among us. And we'll
allow no other beggar to beg in here."

So spoke Antinoös and his words pleased them.   50
But brave Odysseus spoke to them cunningly:

"My friends, an old man worn out with pain
cannot fight a younger man, but though I will
be beaten, my belly wickedly urges me on.
So come now and all swear me a strong oath
that no one wickedly taking Iros' side
strike me a low blow so I'm brought down by him."

So he spoke and all swore as he had bid.
But when they'd sworn and completed the oath,
God-protected Telemakos spoke to them: 60

"Stranger, if your heart and mind urge you to fend off
this one, fear none of the other Akaians
since he would fight more than you alone.
I am your host and these two lords agree with me,
Eurymakos and Antinoös, both sensible."

So he spoke and all applauded. Odysseus
tucked his rags about his loins, thus showing his
great thighs, his wide shoulders, his chest and his
strong arms. For Athena, standing near him,
had broadened the limbs of the people's shepherd.   70
All the arrogant suitors were amazed
and one said turning to another near him:

"Iros will lose, though he brought this about,
such thigh muscles the old one shows beneath his rags!"

So he spoke and Iros' heart was badly shaken.
The servants readied him and led him out by force.
He was afraid and his flabby flesh trembled.

Antinoös scolded him saying these words:

"Would that you weren't here nor ever born, braggart,
if you tremble at this one and fear him so,   80
this old man so worn by what has come to him!
I will tell you this and it will come to pass:
if this one wins over you and is the better,
I'll send you in a black ship to the mainland,
to King Eketos, murderer of mortals, so he *
with ruthless bronze will cut your nose and ears off,
slice off your genitals and give them raw to his dogs."

So he spoke. More trembling seized the braggart's limbs.
They led him to the center and both raised their fists.
Artful Odysseus pondered whether   90
to drive him hard so that, falling, his life might leave him,
or to drive him lightly and knock him down.
Thinking on it, this seemed better to him,
a light blow lest the Akaians suspect him.
Their fists up, Iros drove at his right shoulder
but Odysseus hit his neck, crushing
the bone. At once red blood gushed from his mouth.
He fell howling to the dust, smashing his teeth,
his feet kicking the ground. The noble suitors
threw up their hands in laughter. Odysseus   100
dragged him by the foot through the doorway till
he reached the courtyard gates. Leaning him up against
the courtyard wall, he thrust his own staff in his hand
and speaking, said these winged words to him:

"Now sit here and keep the pigs and dogs away!
Don't try to be king of strangers and beggars,

you wretch, or you will win worse trouble."

He slung over his shoulders his shabby bag,
rife with holes, held by a twisted strap.
He then went back to the threshold and sat down.   110
Laughing, toasting him, the suitors entered saying:

"Stranger, may Zeus and the other deathless gods
give you what you most wish, dearest to your heart,
since you have stopped this glutton from wandering in
this town. We'll take him straightaway to the mainland,
to King Eketos, murderer of mortals."

So they spoke. Odysseus rejoiced at this.
Antinoös gave him a goat-belly sausage
full of fat and blood. Amphinomos,
from a basket of reeds gave him two loaves   120
and, toasting him with his golden goblet, said:

"Welcome, old man! May you have joy in times
to come though now you suffer many troubles!"

Artful Odysseus, answering him, then said:

"Amphinomos, you seem to be very wise.
Such was your father. His fame made him noble.
Nisos of Doulikion was brave and wealthy.
You are his son they say, and you seem courteous.
I will tell you and mind my words and hear them:
of all that breathes or walks upon the land   130
the earth nourishes none weaker than a man.
He thinks he'll suffer no trouble in the future.
While gods give him prosperity his knees have spring.
But when the happy gods bring him grief, he carries
on unwillingly but his heart endures.
Such is the mind of men who tread the earth, taking

daily what the father of gods and men gives.
I used to be happy among men, but I
did wicked things, driven by my strength and might,
and trusted in my father and my brothers.   140
Let no man be wholly without the sense of law,
but keep gods' gifts, whatever they give, in silence.
Such I see here: suitors planning wanton acts,
devouring a man's wealth, dishonoring
his mate, and he, I say, will not be long away
from friends and home but is very near. So may
a spirit lead you home lest you meet him
when he returns here to his own native land.
For when he's in the palace, I think his reckoning
with the suitors will not lack for bloodshed."   150

So he spoke. He poured a libation, then drank
the rich wine and handed the goblet back to him.
Amphinomos walked back, his heart sad, his head
bowed, for he had forebodings of evil.
But he could not escape his death, for Athena
bound him to fall under Telemakos' spear.
He sat back down in the chair he'd risen from.

The goddess, bright-eyed Athena, put it in her,
Ikarios' child, wise Penelope,
to show herself before the suitors and make their hearts   160
soar and that she might be honored more
by her spouse and by her son who were there.*
With a forced laugh, she said to good Eurynome:

"Eurynome, my heart longs as never before
to show myself to the suitors though I hate them.
I'll speak a word to my son for his own good.
He should not mix with those reckless suitors.
They speak well but plan evil behind his back."

The housekeeper, Eurynome, responded thus:

"Yes truly child, you speak these things as is fit.   170
Go to your son and speak, concealing nothing.
But wash your face first and anoint your cheeks.
Don't go with these tears traced on your countenance.
It's bad to grieve so unceasingly.
Your child has such an age as you prayed for
to the deathless ones: to see him grow a beard."

Then sensible Penelope answered her:

"Eurynome, though you're distressed, don't ask me
to wash this skin and rub on soothing oils.
My beauty? The gods who hold high Olympos   180
destroyed that when he left in the hollow ships.
Bid come Autonoë and Hippodameia
so they can stand beside me in the hall.
It's unseemly to go alone among those men."

So she spoke and the old woman went from the room
straight to the maids and told them, urging them to go.

But bright-eyed Athena thought otherwise.
She poured sweet sleep on Ikarios' child
who leaned back and slept on the couch, all
her joints relaxed. The goddess gave to her immortal   190
gifts to make the Akaians marvel at her.
She first enhanced her face's beauty with a balm
ambrosial that fair-garlanded Kythereia
herself uses for the Graces' lovely dance.
She made her seem taller and more imposing
and whiter than newly-hewn ivory.
Having completed this, the shining goddess left.
The white-armed maids darted into the room
chattering and sweet sleep was lifted from her.

Rubbing her cheeks with her hands, she said: 200

"Though suffering, a soft sleep enveloped me.
If only Artemis might bring so soft a death
even now that I not waste my life, my heart
sorrowing, longing for my own dear spouse
who in all ways was far the best of the Akaians."

Speaking thus, she went down from her bright room
but not alone, her two maids followed her.
And when in her splendor she reached the suitors,
she stood by a thick, roof-supporting column
holding a bright veil in front of her cheeks.   210
A loyal maid stood on either side of her.
The suitors knees were loosened, their hearts enflamed
with desire, all praying to lie in her bed.
But she spoke to her own son, Telemakos:

"Telemakos, no longer are your heart and mind
steadfast. As a child your wits were much better,
but now that you are bigger and near manhood—
even though to someone from afar you seem
in size and looks to be a wealthy man's son—
your heart and mind are no longer right.   220
Such things have happened in these halls that you've
allowed, treating a stranger so disgracefully!
What if some stranger sitting in our house
so roughly treated should come to harm? Such shame
and such disgrace you would have among men!"

Then shrewd Telemakos answered her:

"Mother mine, I'm not troubled that you are angry,
since now I think in my mind and know things
both good and base. Before I was just a child.
But I cannot yet think through all things so wisely.   230

These men sit on either side and drive me crazy
with their evil thoughts and I with none to aid me.
Yet this contest of Iros and the stranger did not
suit the suitors since the stranger proved the stronger.
Would that father Zeus, Athena and Apollo
crush these suitors always here in our halls
and make their heads droop in the courtyard
or inside the halls, loosing the limbs of each
as the stranger did to Iros who now sits with
his head drooping as though he were wine-drunk!   240
Nor can he stand straight on his feet nor go home,
wherever that might be, since his limbs are loosed."

Thus they spoke these things to each other.
Eurymakos then said this to wise Penelope:

"Ikarios' child, wise Penelope,
if all the Akaians of Argos could see you,
there would be more suitors feasting in your house
from morning on, since you surpass all women
in shape and stature, and you have a sound mind."

Sensible Penelope replied thus: 250

"Eurymakos, the deathless ones destroyed my spirit,
my shape and my stature when the Argives went
to Troy and brave Odysseus, my spouse, went too.
If he comes back and takes care of me, my life
would have a better and more splendid repute.
But now I grieve. An evil god heaped this on me.
When that man went, leaving his native land,
taking my right hand by the wrist, he said:

'My lady, I don't think the well-armored Akaians
will all return safe and unharmed from Troy,   260
for they say that the Trojan men are warriors,

both spearmen and shooters of arrows, and riders
of swift, horse-drawn chariots which quickly
decide a great fight in the leveling of war.
I don't know if some god will restore me here
or if I'll fall in Troy. So guard all things here.
Be mindful of my father and mother in
the palace, both now and more so when I'm far away.
But when you see our child growing a beard,
marry whom you wish and leave your home.'   270

Thus he spoke. Now all this is coming to pass.
The night will come when that hateful marriage comes
to ill-fated me and Zeus robs me of joy.
But this wooing brings my heart an acrid ache:
for this is not the way for suitors to act!
They who wish to woo a good woman, a daughter
of wealth, and who wish to vie with others for her,
must bring oxen and fat sheep to feast the friends
of the bride and give her splendid gifts. They don't
devour a man's wealth without recompense!"   280

So she spoke. Odysseus the much-enduring
rejoiced because she gained gifts by deceiving
them with sweet words, though not her intention.

Then Antinoös, Eupeithes' son, addressed her:

"Ikarios' child, sensible Penelope,
let any of the Akaians who wish bring gifts.
Accept them. It is not good to refuse a gift.
But we'll not go to our farms nor elsewhere
until you wed that Akaian you find the best."

Thus spoke Antinoös and his words pleased them.   290
Each sent his herald home to bring back gifts.
Antinoös' man brought a gown, well woven,

many colored. It had twelve golden pins
fitted with twisted clasps to fasten it.
Eurymakos' man brought a well-wrought necklace
of gold strung with sun-bright amber beads.
Earrings were brought by Eurydamas' two men,
like mulberries in three clusters, shining in beauty.
From the house of lord Peisandros, Polyktor's son,
a man brought a neckpiece, a glorious delight.   300
So each of the Akaians brought a wondrous gift.
She then went upstairs, most divine of women,
and her maids carried up her exquisite gifts.

The suitors turned to the delights of dancing and
singing and were happy, waiting for evening to come.
And darkness came while they were enjoying themselves.
Then they set up three braziers in the vast halls
for light and piled beside them good firewood,
long dry, well-seasoned, newly split by a bronze ax,
and kindling too. Noble Odysseus' maids   310
kept the lights burning. But he himself, Zeus-born,
artful Odysseus, addressed the maids:

"Maids of lord Odysseus who has been long
away, go to the chambers of your honored queen.
There twist the clean wool, cheer the lady up,
sit in her rooms and comb the raw wool by hand.
I will keep the light burning for all these men.
If they wish to wait for Dawn's golden throne,
they will not wear me out: I can endure much."

So he spoke. The maids laughing, looked at each other,   320
lovely-cheeked Melantho rebuked him.
Good Penelope had taken in this child
of Dolios, given her things that pleased her,
but her heart had no love for her queen

and she loved and slept with lord Eurymakos.
She rebuked Odysseus with these words:

"Wretched man, you have had your wits knocked out.
Don't you want to go sleep at the blacksmith's? *
Or some public place? Do you stay here speaking
boldly among these many men with no fear   330
in your heart? Either the wine holds your head,
or this is always your way, babbling vainly.
Are you puffed up from beating that cur Iros?
Beware or one better might stand up soon who will
bash your head with strong fists, fouling you
with much blood and driving you from this great house!"

Scowling at her, artful Odysseus spoke:

"I think I will now tell Telemakos what
you said, bitch, so he can cut your limbs apart!"

Speaking thus, he scared the women with his words.   340
They scattered in the halls, the limbs of each
loosed with fear, for his words rang true to them.
But he stood by the braziers keeping them burning,
watching the suitors, and all the while pondering
in his mind things that should not be left unfinished.

Athena did not wholly restrain the proud wooers
from their grievous outrage so that Laertes' son
Odysseus might feel yet more pain in his heart.
Polybos' child Eurymakos spoke thus,
taunting Odysseus, spreading laughter in the halls.   350

"Hear me, suitors of the famous queen,
while I speak what my heart bids. This man
did not come to Odysseus' house without
the gods' will. Surely the fire's glow is from
his head since he is bald, without a single hair!"

Then he called Odysseus, sacker of cities:

"Man, if I hired you, would you do day-work
on a remote farm for guaranteed pay
gathering stones for walls, planting trees
to grow tall? I would give you food enough   360
and clothes and sturdy sandals for your feet.
But since you've learned bad ways, you have no wish to do
real work but prefer to beg throughout the land,
begging to fill your ever-insatiable belly."

Answering him, artful Odysseus then said:

"Eurymakos, would that there were a match
between us in summer when the days are long
in the fields, I wielding a well-made sickle,
and you one too, that we might try ourselves in farm
labor with grass to cut, fasting till evening.   370
Or if there were oxen to drive, the best,
healthy and large, both well-fed on grass,
of like age and size, their strength hard to tax.
On four acres where soil would yield to plough,
there you'd see me cut a furrow to the end.
Or if Zeus were to stir up war anywhere,
that day, if I had two spears and a shield
and a helmet of bronze that fit my temples,
there you'd see me with the first in battle,
nor would you say a word of blame about my belly.   380
You're very haughty and have a mind that's harsh.
You think yourself some great and powerful man
because you mix with so few and none strong men.
But were Odysseus to come, arriving home,
immediately those gates, though they are wide,
would prove too narrow for escape from the palace!"

So he spoke. Eurymakos grew very angry

and, scowling at him, said these winged words:

"Wretch, I'll deal with you soon for speaking so
boldly among this crowd of men with no fear   390
in your heart. Either the wine holds your head
or this is always your way, babbling vainly.
Are you puffed up from beating that cur, Iros?"

So speaking, he seized a stool. Odysseus
sat down at the knees of Amphinomos,
fearing Eurymakos. The blow struck the wine-bearer
in the right hand. The wine bowl hit the floor with
a crash and groaning, he fell on his back amid
the dust. The suitors made a din in the halls
and one spoke to another sitting nearby: 400

"Would that this wandering stranger had died elsewhere
before coming here. He's caused such a ruckus!
Now we wrangle over beggars and there's no good
in our fine feast since such vile things prevail!"

Then god-protected Telemakos spoke thus:

"Fools, are you so mad that you forget the food,
the drink you've had? Some spirit must have unhinged you.
But now, well fed, go home to your own beds.
But go whenever you wish. I drive no man out."

So he spoke. Biting their lips, they all   410
marveled at Telemakos who spoke so boldly.

Amphinomos, famous son of Nisos—
himself the son of lord Aretios—then spoke:

"Friends, with what is fairly spoken let no man
get angry, answering with wrangling words.
Let no one mistreat the stranger or other

servants in the home of brave Odysseus.
Come, wine-bearer, pour drops in our cups and
we'll make a libation, then home to our beds.
Let's leave Telemakos to deal with the stranger   420
who has come to Odysseus' house."

So he spoke. His words pleased the hearts of all.
The warrior Moulios mixed the wine for them,
Doulikion's herald, where Amphinomos ruled.
He poured the wine to each in order. They poured
to the happy gods and drank the rich wine.
When they had offered and drunk as they each wished,
they left, each going to his own home to sleep.

BOOK NINETEEN

Penelope and Odysseus talk
The nurse Eurykleia recognizes Odysseus' scar
Penelope plans the challenge of the bow

But lord Odysseus remained in the hall
with Athena, pondering the slaughter of the suitors.
Then he addressed Telemakos with winged words:

"Telemakos, you must put all the battle weapons
within, but speak to the suitors with soft words
when, missing them, they ask about them:
'I moved them from the smoke since they are not
as they were when Odysseus left for Troy,
but are marred where the fire's heat reached them.
Some spirit put this more important thought in mind.   10
When you are drinking, some quarrel might arise
and wounding one another, you might shame the feast
and the wooing, for iron attracts men.'"

So he spoke and Telemakos obeyed.
Summoning nurse Eurykleia, he said to her:

"Good mother, come and shut the women in their chambers
so I can move father's good weapons into safety.
They've been neglected and are marred with smoke since
my father left when I was a child. But now
I want to put them where the fire's heat won't reach."   20

Then his nurse Eurykleia replied to him:

"Yes indeed, my child, you are wise to take
good care of the house and guard all its wealth.
But come, who would then bring light for you
since you won't let the maids be here to help you?"

Then shrewd Telemakos answered her:

"This stranger. For I will not let anyone be lazy
who draws a ration here, though coming from afar."

So he spoke. His words lodged in her heart.
She bolted the door of the comfortable palace.   30
Odysseus and his splendid son sprang up
and carried in the helmets, the studded shields,
the sharp-pointed spears. Pallas Athena went
first with a gold lamp casting a lovely light.
Telemakos suddenly called to his father:

"Father, I see a great marvel with my eyes!
I see the palace walls, the column supports,
the fir beams, the columns that hold the upper part,
glowing before my eyes as if they were burning!
Some god is here of those who hold the wide sky!"   40

Artful Odysseus answered him thus:

"Keep silence in your mind and question not.
This is the way of the gods who hold Olympos.
But go you to bed now, I will remain here

so I can test the maids and your mother.
Though weeping, she'll ask me about everything."

So he spoke. Telemakos went through the halls
under the shining torch, going straight to his room
where he usually rested when sweet sleep reached him.
There he lay down awaiting bright Dawn.   50
But he, Odysseus, remained in the hall
with Athena, pondering the slaughter of the suitors.

Sensible Penelope came from her chamber,
like to Artemis or golden Aphrodite.
There was a chair by the fire, her usual place,
inlaid with spirals of ivory and silver. It was
made by the wood-worker Ikmalios. A footstool
seemed to grow from it covered with a fleece.
Sensible Penelope sat down on this
and the white-armed maids came out from the halls.   60

They took the abundant food, the tables, and the cups
that the nobles had been drinking from.
They tossed the brazier's embers on the ground
and piled in wood for light and heat. Melantho then
upbraided brave Odysseus yet again:

"Old man, are you still bothering us during the night,
wandering through the house and ogling the maids?
Out the door, wretch, and savor what you've had,
or you'll be driven out with fire brands thrown at you!"

Scowling at her, artful Odysseus replied: 70

"Mad woman! Why does your heart resent me so?
Because I am dirty? Bad clothes cover my skin?
That I beg throughout the town? Need compels me.
This is the way of beggars and wandering men.

I once lived in a house among men, wealthy
and blessed, and I gave to many wanderers,
whoever they claimed to be, wherever from.
I had a great number of slaves and such things
as men have who live well and are called wealthy.
But Kronos' son ruined me for so he wished.   80
So beware, woman, lest you lose that beauty
you have which excels that of the other servants.
Your mistress might grow angry and harsh with you.
Or brave Odysseus may come—there's room for hope.
But if he perished and there's no return for him,
there is his very son under Apollo's favor,
Telemakos, who's not one to ignore reckless
women in the halls, for he's a child no more."

So he spoke. Wise Penelope heard him
and calling her, said these words to the maid: 90

"Insolent, bold bitch! I saw what you were doing!
You will be wiping this off your own head! *
You know well since you yourself heard me say
how I would question this stranger in the halls
about my spouse since I'm always grieving for him!"

Then she spoke these words to good Eurynome:

"Eurynome, bring a chair here and a fleece
so this stranger may sit down there and speak
his tale and he may hear me, for I will ask much."

So she spoke. The housekeeper quickly brought   100
a well-fashioned chair and spread a fleece on it.
And so Odysseus the much-enduring sat down.

Then sensible Penelope said these words:

"Stranger, I will begin with these things first.

Among men who are you? Whence from? What parents?"

Artful Odysseus then answered her:

"Oh lady, what mortal on the boundless land
might fault you? Your fame reaches the wide sky
like that of a wise king who is god-fearing
and rules many men—and powerful ones—   110
upholding good ways. For him the black earth bears
wheat and barley, the trees are heavy with good fruit,
his flocks bear endless young, seas teem with fish
from his good rule and people thrive under him.
Here in your house ask me any other thing,
but don't ask me my tribe and native land,
for you will fill my heart with yet more pain.
If I think of them, I am filled with grief.
It is not right to sit lamenting in a house
not my own. It's bad to mourn so endlessly.   120
I'd not have any of your maids, or you yourself,
think I weep because my mind is thick with wine."

Then sensible Penelope answered him:

"Stranger, the deathless ones destroyed my spirit,
my shape and stature, when the Argives went
to Troy and brave Odysseus, my spouse, went too.
If he comes back and cares for me, this my life
would have a better and more splendid repute.
But I now grieve. An evil spirit heaped this on me.
The noble lords who rule over these islands—   130
Doulikion, Same, and wooded Zakynthos
and those who rule over rocky Ithaka—
these men are wooing me now, devouring this house.
So now I pay no heed to strangers who come,
not even to heralds who come on public business.
My whole heart keeps yearning for Odysseus.

The suitors urge marriage but I pulled off a trick.
Some spirit first gave me the thought: a shroud.
I had a large loom built in my rooms to weave on
with long fine thread and then I spoke to them: 140

'You, my suitors, since noble Odysseus is dead,
though eager for my marriage, wait till this shroud
is finished, lest my weaving count for nothing.
It's for hero Laertes' burial when his
terrible time shall come, when he's laid low by death.
Let no Akaian women be angry with me that
I let a wealthy man lie without a shroud.'

So I spoke, and their brave hearts were thus convinced.
By day I sat weaving at the great loom.
Nights, with torch placed near, I undid the thread.   150
For three years this trick convinced the Akaians,
but as the hours passed and the fourth year came,
moon after moon waned, the days marched on.
Then, through my maids—those careless, heedless bitches—
they caught me and rebuked me with hard words.
Thus, not wanting to, I had to finish it.
I cannot now avoid marriage nor can I find
another path. My parents urge me to marry;
my child's distressed knowing the suitors devour
his wealth. Indeed, he's now a man who can care for   160
his own house, for Zeus has given him renown.
But now, tell me of your tribe, where you're from.
For you are not from some ancient oak or rock." *

Artful Odysseus then answered her:

"Good woman of Laertes' son Odysseus,
will you not stop asking me my parentage?
Well, I will tell you though it adds more pain to what
I have. For this is how it is for a man

so long away from his homeland as I am now,
drifting through many towns of men, suffering much. 170
But I will tell you what you ask and seek from me.
There's a land, Krete, in the purple sea,
lovely and rich, circled by water. There live
many people, numberless, in ninety towns.
Languages mix with languages. Akaians
live there, great-hearted Eteokretans, Kydonians,
the three Dorian tribes, the noble Pelasgians.
There's a great city there, Knossos, where Minos rules.
Every nine years he goes to speak with great Zeus.*
Minos fathered Deukalion, who fathered 180
both me and Idomeneus the king
who went to Ilion in the curved ships
with Atreus' sons. He named me glorious Aithon,
the younger born. My brother was first, more warlike.
I saw Odysseus there, made him my guest.
The winds' force drove him towards Krete as he went
past Maleia toward Troy but was blown off course.
He moored at Amnisos near Eileithyia's cave,
a bad harbor. He'd struggled to escape the storm.

He went to the city seeking Idomeneus, 190
claiming to be his guest, a friend and honored.
Ten or twelve Dawns had come since he'd sailed,
going in curved ships to Troy. I led him,
Odysseus, to my house, receiving him
kindly like a friend as we were well supplied.
And for his men who followed him, I collected
from the people barley and fiery wine,
oxen to sacrifice to satisfy their hearts.
Those noble Akaians waited there twelve days.
A fierce North wind held them and it would not let them 200
go: some harsh spirit had stirred it up. Then, on
the thirteenth day, the wind dropped and they left."

His many lies took on the form of truth,
and hearing him, she melted, tears flowing down.
Just as the snow on lofty mountains melts
when the east wind melts what the west wind laid down,*
the rivers running full with the snowy water,
just so her melting tears flowed down her lovely cheeks
while she mourned him who sat beside her. And he,
Odysseus? His heart pitied this weeping woman   210
but his two eyes were fixed in his eyelids as if
made of horn or iron, his tears hid by deceit.

When she had had her fill of tearful weeping,
she answered him again, speaking these words:

"Now indeed, stranger, I think to test you to see
if you hosted my husband with his godlike men
there in your own halls as you have claimed.
Tell me of what sort were the clothes he wore?
What was he like? And the men who followed him?"

Answering her, artful Odysseus then said: 220

"Good woman, after such a time it's difficult
to say, for it is now the twentieth year
since he set out from there, leaving from my country.
But I will tell you how my heart pictures him.
A mauve cloak, doubled, lord Odysseus wore,
woolen, fastened with a golden clasp with two
pin sheaves. Its facing was artfully wrought:
a dog holds in its forepaws a spotted fawn,
his jaws choking it. All marveled seeing this
clasp made of gold, the dog strangling, the fawn   230
struggling the while, trying to escape.
His tunic, I noticed, glistened against his skin,
fine-woven, fitted like a dried onionskin.
Very soft it was, radiant like the sun,

and many women indeed marveled at it.
But I will tell you this and mark it in your heart:
I do not know if he wore this against his skin
when he left home or if one of his men gave it
to him on the swift ships, or if some stranger did,
for many liked him. Few Akaians had such friends.   240

I gave him a bronze sword, a thick purple cloak,
a goodly one, and a fringed tunic, and in
his well-benched ships I sent him on with due honor.
A herald went with him, a small man, a bit older
than he. I'll tell you what kind of man he was.
He had bent shoulders and dark skin with curly hair,
Eurybates was his name. Odysseus
prized him as they both were of like mind."

Thus he spoke and yet more longing for tears arose
for she knew well the certain signs he had described.   250
When she had had her fill of tearful weeping,
she answered him again, speaking these words:

"Indeed, stranger, though I pitied you before,
now you are my friend and honored in my halls.
Those clothes that you describe, I myself gave them
to my husband, brought them folded from our room,
and that clasp, to please him. But no more will I see him
coming home, back to his dear native land.
It was bad fate when on those ships Odysseus
went to that ruinous, not-to-be named Ilios."   260

Answering her, artful Odysseus then said:

"Good woman of Laertes' son Odysseus,
no more destroy your lovely skin, nor let
your heart melt away. Nor do I blame you.
Any woman would weep losing her wedded man

to whom she bore a child, mingling in love, though not
so like the gods as your Odysseus.
But pause in your weeping and hear my words,
for I will tell you the truth, withholding nothing.
I've heard of the return of lord Odysseus.   270
It's soon. He's in the rich Thesprotian land,
alive and bringing much worthy wealth
he's gathering from the people. But his loyal men
perished, his ship sank in the purple sea
when leaving Thrinakia. Zeus and Helios
were angry: his men had killed the Sun's oxen.
For this his crew were killed in the storming sea.

But he rode the ship's keel and a wave cast him
onto Phaiakian land, that race near to the gods.
They honored him in their hearts as a god   280
and gave him much. They wanted to send
him homeward unharmed. He could have been back here
before but it seemed best to him in his mind
to go about the land gathering wealth.
Odysseus knows more about gathering wealth
than other mortal men. None living can match him.
Such did the Thesprotian King Pheidon, tell me.
He swore me this himself pouring a libation.
He'd had a ship hauled down and a ready crew
to take him home to his beloved native land.   290
But he sent me away first. A Thesprotian ship
happened to be there, going to grain-rich Doulikion.
And he showed me the wealth Odysseus had gathered,
enough to feed his family for ten generations.
Such was Odysseus' wealth in the palace.

The king said he had gone to Dodona to hear *
the plan of Zeus from the high-branched oak,
whether, being so long absent, to return

to Ithaka's rich land in secret or openly.
So he is safe and he will come and soon, 300
for he is near to his well-loved native soil,
though long absent. I'll gladly swear an oath
before Zeus first, highest and best of the gods,
then by Odysseus' hearth where I have come:
all these things that I say will come to pass.
Odysseus will come here in this very month
with the waning moon, when the new moon stands."

Then sensible Penelope answered him:

"If it did happen according to your words, stranger,
then you would quickly know friendship and have gifts 310
from me that you'd seem blessed to any meeting you.
But I feel otherwise and thus it will turn out:
Odysseus will not come home, nor will you find
your home since this house has no master among men
such as Odysseus—if he ever lived—
to welcome honored guests and send them on their way.
But come, maids. Wash his feet. Make up a bed
on a bedstead. Place cloaks and shining rugs so he'll
be well warmed when Dawn's golden throne arrives.

At first light, bathe him and then rub him with oil. 320
He'll eat in the hall sitting with Telemakos.
Worse for any who would show malice
toward him or annoy him beyond the limit.
His wooing will come to nothing, despite his fierce anger.
How would you think of me, stranger, comparing me
to other women in sense and in wise counsel
if I let you dine in the hall thus dirty
and wrapped in rags? All men are short-lived.
Whoever is mean and hard and knows mean thoughts,
all mortals will invoke pain and curses on him 330

while he lives, and when he's dead, they will mock him.
But he in himself who is righteous with righteous thoughts,
strangers will repeat his fame widely
among all men and many will call him noble."

Answering her, artful Odysseus then said:

"Good woman of Laertes' son Odysseus,
cloaks and shining rugs please me not since first
I left from Krete's snowy mountains, setting off
in my long-oared ship. I will lie down now as
I'm used to lying down to pass a sleepless night.   340
I have passed many nights in wretched beds,
lying there, waiting for Dawn's golden throne.
Nor does it please my heart to have my feet washed.
I will not let any woman touch my foot,
any who are servants in your hall,
unless there is an old one, long in years, skilled,
trusty, who's suffered in her heart as I have.
The washing of my feet by her would not annoy me."

Then sensible Penelope answered him:

"Friend, for there is not any man so shrewd,   350
a stranger, come from his far land to my house
as you who always speak wisely and clearly.
There is here one old woman with a wise heart.
She nourished and reared him, that wretched man.
She took him in her hands when his mother bore him.
Though she is feeble now she will wash your feet.
But come now, stand up wise Eurykleia.
Wash this one who's the age of Odysseus.
His feet and hands must be much like these.
All too quickly do mortals age in hard times."   360

So she spoke, but the old woman held her hands

before her weeping face, hot tears falling, and said:

"Alas that I cannot help you, child! Zeus *
must hate you, though you are god-fearing, above all people!
To Zeus who delights in thunder, no mortal
burned such fat thighs nor such choice hecatombs
as you gave him, praying that you might reach
a gentle old age and rear your shining son.
But you alone were robbed of your day of return!
How women must have mocked him in strange   370
far off lands, when he entered their famous homes,
as these all mock you here shameless as dogs!
But now you shun such outrages and bitter shame
and don't let them wash you. But I am not unwilling
to do as this dear child, Penelope, bids me.
So I will wash your feet for her and
for you, for my heart within has been stirred
with pity. But mark my words when I speak:
many long-suffering strangers have come here, but
none have I seen as like to him in form, in voice—   380
and in feet—as you to Odysseus."

Answering her, artful Odysseus then said:

"Old woman, they do say, those who have seen both
of us, that we do seem like each other.
So what you say is very well-observed."

So he spoke. The old woman took the shining
basin she used to wash feet, poured in much cold
water, then added hot water. Odysseus
sat on the hearth, then suddenly turned away
from the light, struck by the thought that washing him,   390
she might recognize the scar and reveal him.
Coming to him, she began washing his feet.
At once she knew the scar a boar's white tusk had cut

in Parnassos when he was with Autolykos
and his sons. Autolykos, father of
his mother, surpassed all men in thievery and oaths,*
a gift from Hermes, for whom he burned thighbones of lambs
and kids. Hermes himself granted him these favors.
Going to Ithaka's rich land, Autolykos
was presented with his daughter's child.   400
Eurykleia placed him on his knees
after dinner and said these words, naming him:

"Autolykos, you must find a name to give
your child's child, for he has long been prayed for."

Autolykos answered her saying this:

"Daughter and son-in-law, take this name I give you.
I've arrived at this stage angry at many,*
both men and women, on this life-giving earth.
So give him this name, Odysseus, and I,
when's he's grown and comes to his mother's home,   410
Parnassos, where my wealth and goods all are,
I will give him gifts and send him back happy."

And so he went there to bring back splendid gifts.
Autolykos and his sons welcomed him
in their arms with warm words. His mother's mother,
Amphithea, embraced Odysseus
and kissed his head and both his shining eyes.
Autolykos ordered his sons to make ready
a feast. They heard him and were urged on.
They brought an ox, a male, five years old,   420
flayed it all round and cut the joints.
Then they cut it up, skewering it with skill.
They roasted it well and divided the parts.
So they feasted the whole day till the sun had set,
nor did the heart of any lack his due share.

When Helios had set and darkness come,
they lay down and the gift of sleep took them.

When early-born, pink-fingered Dawn appeared,
they set out for the hunt, the hounds and the sons
of Autolykos and young Odysseus.   430
They went to Parnassos, that steep mountain
covered in forests, and soon reached its windy uplands.
The sun's rays had just reached the fields, up from
Okeanos' softly flowing, deep currents,
when the beaters reached a glen into which
the hounds dashed following tracks. Behind them came
Autolykos' sons, Odysseus with them
wielding his long spear near the hounds.
A huge boar's lair lay there in a dense thicket
that neither the ever-blowing wind's damp force   440
nor Helios' bright rays ever reached.
No storm had ever pierced through it, so dense
it was and filled with a deep mass of leaves.
The din of the men's feet and hounds reached it
as the beaters came on. In front of its lair,
hair bristling and its eyes filled with fire,
it stood at bay. Rushing up, Odysseus
was first, raising his strong spear in his hand,
eager to strike but the boar was first, striking
above the knee, ripping much flesh with its tusks,   450
darting sideways—but it did not reach the bone.
Odysseus wounded it in the right shoulder,
the point of his strong spear piercing straight through.
The boar fell in the dust and its life went out.

Autolykos' children skillfully bound
the wound of godlike, brave Odysseus
and staunched the black blood with an incantation.*
They took him back to their father's house.

And when Autolykos and his sons
had well healed him, they sent him home rejoicing   460
to his land, to Ithaka. His father and
mother welcomed him and each asked what had
happened, how he had received his wound.
He described the hunt in great detail.
How the boar had driven his white tusks in him
in Parnassos with Autolykos' sons.

Washing this scar, the old woman knew it
at once, and she let go of his foot.
His leg fell in the basin, the bronze clattered, tipped
on its side, and water poured onto the ground.   470
Joy and pain seized her heart, her eyes filled
with tears, her voice caught inside her chest.
Touching Odysseus' chin, she said:

"You are Odysseus. But I, I knew it not
until I touched the flesh of you, my lord."

She looked Penelope in the eyes,
wishing to point out that her spouse was here.
Penelope could neither gaze at her nor talk:
Athena turned her thoughts away. Odysseus
seized the old woman's throat with his right hand   480
and pulling her close with his left, he whispered:

"Nurse, why do you wish to kill me? You yourself
fed me at your breast. Now, having suffered much,
I've come back to my homeland after twenty years.
Some god put it in your heart that you knew me,
but keep silent so no one else may learn.
For if not, for so I say and so it will be,
if through me a god should slay these suitors,
though you reared me, I will not spare you when
I slay the other women, the maids in the palace."   490

But sensible Eurykleia answered him:

"My child, what words escape the barrier of your teeth?
You know my mind is firm and it does not yield,
I will hold as strong as stone or iron.
But I will tell you this and mark it in your heart.
If through you a god should slay these suitors,
I will tell you of these women in the palace,
those who dishonored you, those innocent."

Answering her, artful Odysseus said:

"Nurse, why speak of them? There is no need to.   500
I myself will note them and come to know each one.
But hold your words in silence. Leave it to the gods."

So he spoke. The old woman went from the hall
for water for his feet—the first had all spilled out.
When she had washed his feet and rubbed them with oil,
Odysseus moved a stool near the fire
to warm himself, hiding his wound under his rags.

Sensible Penelope spoke first, saying:

"Stranger, I'll ask you this small thing, for it is near
the pleasant hour of rest when sweet sleep   510
may take one, even one who has suffered much.
Some spirit has brought me this immense grief.
By day my joy is in my weeping, lamenting
while I do housework and see to the maids.
But when night comes and sleep has taken others,
I lie in my bed and keen cares crush my heart
and sharp sorrows keep me ever from rest.

As the greenwood nightingale, Pandareos'
child, with lovely song when spring stands newly fresh,*
perches in the close-packed leaves of a tree,   520

with frequent trilling in her many-toned song,
mourning Itylos, lord Zethos' son—
her own child she foolishly killed with bronze—
so my heart is divided, urged here and there.
Should I wait with my son, firm, guarding
my wealth, my maids, and my high-roofed palace,
honoring my husband and the people's voice,
or follow him who is the best of the Akaians
wooing me here, he who brings a boundless bride price?
When my son was foolish, young, light of thought,   530
he wouldn't let me marry or leave my husband's house.
But now that he is older and has reached manhood,
he prays that I leave, abandon this palace,
worried about the suitors devouring his wealth.
But hear my dream and interpret it for me.
Away from water the twenty geese from my house
eat my grain, and I am glad watching them.
A huge, hooked-beak eagle comes from the mountains killing
all, breaking their necks, huddled in a mass
in the halls. The eagle flies off in the bright sky.   540
I am weeping and wailing within this dream.
The fair-haired Akaian maids gather round me
moaning in pity because the eagle killed my geese.
But the eagle comes back and, perched on a roof beam,
his human voice stops my weeping and he says:

'Be glad, child of famed Ikarios. No dream
this, but a noble vision of what will be.
The geese are the suitors, but I, the dream's eagle,
am now your husband having returned home.
I will bring a fierce death on all the suitors.'   550

So he spoke and sweet sleep released me.
I looked around and saw the geese feeding
on wheat from the trough where they usually eat."

Answering her, artful Odysseus then said:

"Good woman, in no way can this dream be bent
to another meaning. Odysseus himself
showed you what he will do. All the suitors' deaths
are shown, nor does one escape his destruction."

Then sensible Penelope answered him:

"Stranger, dreams are difficult to know,   560
unclear, nor are all in them fulfilled for men.
There are two gates for such fantastic dreams,
one made of horn, the other of ivory.
Those that come through the gates of hewn ivory
deceive, carrying words not to be fulfilled.
But those that come through the doors of hewn horn
they are fulfilled, if a mortal can see them.
But my fierce dream did not come through this one,
though welcome to me and my son if it had.

I will tell you this, and mark it in your heart.   570
The dreaded dawn will make me depart from
Odysseus' palace. I will hold a contest
with axes. Those that lie in the halls
set up in a row, on props, all twelve, as he
used to prop them up to shoot an arrow through.*

I will tell the suitors of this contest then.
Who bends the bow in his hands with most ease
and shoots an arrow through all twelve axes,
him will I follow, quitting my marriage home—
so very beautiful, teeming with life—   580
and I will remember this as in a dream."

Answering her, artful Odysseus then said:

"Good woman of Laertes' son Odysseus,

put off this contest in your palace no longer.
Brave Odysseus will be here well
before any of them touches the polished bow,
pulls taut the string, or shoots through the iron."

Then sensible Penelope answered him:

"If you wish, stranger, to stay here charming me,
sleep would not be poured on my eyelids.   590
But none of us mortals can be always sleepless:
for the deathless gods have given to each thing
its due portion on this our grain-giving earth.
So now I myself will go up to my quarters
and lie in my bed, that bed of sorrows,
always wet with my tears since Odysseus
went to that ruinous, not-to-be named Ilios.
I will lie down there. You lie here in the house,
on the ground or I will have a bed made up."

So speaking, she went to her upper chamber,   600
not alone, but all her maids went with her.
When she'd gone up with all her women helpers,
she wept for her husband Odysseus until
Athena poured sweet sleep on her eyelids.

BOOK TWENTY

The suitors gather and feast
The suitors insult Odysseus
Dark omens appear as the suitors feast

In the forecourt artful Odysseus lay down.
He stretched out an untanned ox hide and added
fleeces of sheep sacrificed by the Akaians
and Eurynome covered him with a blanket.
Lying sleepless, Odysseus was planning doom
for the suitors as the women left the palace
to bed down with the suitors as they usually did,
with merriment, laughing among themselves.
But his very heart stirred in his breast as he
weighed these things deep in his mind and heart: 10
should he rush out and deal death to each girl?
Or let them bed those arrogant suitors again
one final time? The heart within him growled
as a dog standing over her helpless pups
growls, eager to fight, seeing an unknown man,
so his heart growled, riled by such shameful acts.

He struck his heart, rebuking it with these words:

"Endure heart, for you've endured more dog-like acts.
That day when the Cyclops with his immense might
ate my brave men, you endured, though expecting   20
to die, and then your plan led you from that cave."

And so he spoke addressing his own heart,
and his heart remained bound to endure,
steadfast. But he himself tossed back and forth,
just as a man turns back and forth a spitted sausage
filled with fat and blood in a fire's blaze,
longing for it to be quickly cooked through,
just so back and forth did he toss, thinking
how he might take on the shameless suitors,
he alone, they so many. But Athena,   30
nearby, stepped down from the sky in a womanly form,
and leaned over his head saying these words to him:

"Why are you yet awake, most wretched of mortals?
You have your home, your woman within your home,
your child whom anyone would long to call his son."

Answering her, artful Odysseus then said:

"Indeed, goddess, all these things you say are true.
But this heart in my breast keeps pondering
how I might lay my hands on the shameless suitors,
being but one while they're always in a group.   40
And this other, bigger thing I ponder too:
if by grace of Zeus and you I should kill them,
can I escape their families? Tell me this."

Then she, bright-eyed Athena, said to him:

"Stubborn one! Any lesser man, though mortal,
could convince you, though ignorant of what I know.

But I am a goddess and I will guard you through
all your troubles. And I will tell you this plainly:
if fifty bands of armed men were to surround us,
and Ares made them eager to murder us,   50
still you'd drive off all their oxen and their sheep.*
But now let sleep take you. It's bad to lie awake
the whole night. You will get through these troubles."

So she spoke, pouring sleep over his eyelids.
And she, bright goddess, then went up to Olympos.

All care slipped from his mind when sleep took him,
loosing his limbs but his true bedmate awoke.
Lying in her soft bed, she cried. But when
her heart had had its fill of crying, then she,
brightest of women, prayed first of all to Artemis: 60

"Mistress goddess, Artemis, Zeus' child,
shoot your arrows in my heart, take my life now! *
Or let a storm pick me up so that
I might be carried down the shrouded path
into the mouth of Okeanos' backflow.*
Thus were Pandareos' daughters taken up.
The gods killed their parents and they were orphaned
in the palace, but Aphrodite nourished them
with cheese, with sweet honey and good wine.
Hera gave them wisdom above all women,   70
and beauty; chaste Artemis gave them stature;
Athena taught them to perform their work with skill.
So Aphrodite went back to high Olympos
requesting fruitful weddings for the girls—
for all is known to thunder-hurling Zeus,
the good and the bad that comes to mortal men—
but meanwhile the storm winds snatched up the girls
and gave them to the dreaded Erinys.*

So may those on Olympos make me disappear
or Artemis shoot me, that with Odysseus   80
in mind I go under the cold, hateful earth
and never gladden the heart of a lesser man.
Thus terrible things can be borne though one
might weep by day with a sorely grieving heart
if by night sleep holds us, for sleep makes us
forget all, good and bad, when it enfolds
our eyelids. But a spirit sends me such bad dreams!
This very night one like him lay beside me,
just as he was when he went with the army. My heart
was glad! I thought this no dream but real indeed!"   90

So she spoke as golden-throned Dawn arrived.
Noble Odysseus heard her voice weeping
and pondered this, for it seemed to his heart
that she was near, standing by his head.
He gathered the blankets and fleece he had slept in,
put them on a chair, and took the ox-hide
out the door. Raising his hands, he prayed to Zeus:

"Father Zeus, if you gods led me across
earth and sea, home to my land, suffering so,
let someone now awake indoors tell me an omen,   100
and outside may Zeus send me a sign as well!"

So he prayed. Counselor Zeus heard him and
immediately thundered from bright Olympos.
Odysseus heard him and rejoiced.
Nearby, a slave girl at a quern spoke an omen.
The mills of the lord's palace lay there
where twelve women in all worked grinding
the barley and wheat flour, marrow of men.
The others were sleeping, having finished their grinding.
She alone, the weakest grinder, had not finished.   110

Stopping the mill, she spoke the sign to her lord:

"Father Zeus who rules over gods and men,
this great thunder from the starry sky where no
clouds are, you show this as a sign to someone.
Grant even wretched me this blessing I ask:
for the last time may the suitors eat
the rich food in lord Odysseus' palace!
They have broken me in hard toil
grinding barley. Let this now be their last feast!"

So she spoke. Odysseus welcomed her words   120
and Zeus' thunder. He would indeed punish the wooers.

The other maids, gathering in Odysseus'
fine house, built up the hearth's ever-blazing fire.
Telemakos rose from his bed, a godlike man,
pulled on his clothes, put his sharp sword over
his shoulder, bound his sturdy sandals to his feet
and took up his sharp bronze-tipped spear.
Going to the threshold he said to Eurykleia:

"Dear nurse, did you honor the stranger in the house
with bed and food? Or did you leave him uncared for?   130
Such is my mother, though being wise, she will honor
one who is among the worst of men and then
dishonor one who's better, sending him away."

Then wise Eurykleia replied to him:

"Child, do not accuse your mother. She is blameless.
Sitting, he drank some wine, as much as he desired.
When she asked him he said he had no hunger for food.
But when he remembered about a bed and sleep,
she bid him lie down on a bed in the house,
but he, being the most wretched, ill-starred of all,   140

wanted not to sleep in a bed with bedclothes,
but on an untanned ox hide with fleeces of sheep. He slept
in the forecourt and we covered him with blankets."

So she spoke. Telemakos went through the halls
holding his spear, two swift dogs following him.
He went to the assembly of well-armored Akaians.
But she, brightest of women, Eurykleia,
child of Ops, Peisenor's son, summoned the maids:

"Come! Get busy! Sweep the halls and sprinkle
the floors. Cover these well-wrought chairs with   150
the purple rugs. Some of you wipe all these tables
with sponges. Clean the bowls, get the two-handled
wine cups ready. You others bring water from
the spring and be quick about it! For
the suitors are away from the palace for now
but will be back early since it's a public feast day." *

So she spoke. They heard her and obeyed.
Twenty maids went to the spring for black water,*
the others worked hard and well in the palace.

The proud serving men came inside. Toiling   160
skillfully they split firewood while the women
returned from the spring. The swineherd came
leading three fat hogs, the best of them all,
and he let them feed grazing near the fence.
He himself addressed Odysseus gently:

"Stranger, do the Akaians now treat you better?
Or do they still dishonor you as before?"

Answering him, artful Odysseus then said:

"Indeed, Eumaios, would that the gods might avenge
their monstrous deeds! And they plan their wicked acts   170

in another's house. Their hearts have no shame."

So they spoke about these things to each other
as the goatherd Melanthios drew near.
He was leading goats selected from the herd
for the suitors' feast. Two goatherds followed him.
He tied the goats under the echoing portico
while saying jeering words to brave Odysseus:

"Stranger, are you still here stirring men up throughout
the house with begging? Why don't you leave this place?
I think we two will not be separated until   180
we test our fists since you beg beyond all bounds!
You know there are other Akaian feasts elsewhere."

So he spoke. Odysseus did not reply,
but shook his head silently, pondering evil.

A third man joined them, Philoitios, leader of men,
driving an un-bred ox cow and fat goats.
They were brought by ferrymen who speed *
other men on their way, whomever comes.
He tethered these under the echoing portico,
and then, standing near the swineherd, he asked him: 190

"Swineherd, who is this stranger newly come
to our house? What men does he claim to be from?
Where is his tribe and his family's plowed land?
Wretched man, though he's built like a king or lord.
But the gods wrap wandering men in pain,
though they be kings, when they spin threads of sorrow."

And indeed, reaching his right hand forward,
he greeted him and said these winged words:

"Welcome, old man! May you have joy in times
to come though now you suffer many troubles!   200

Oh Father Zeus, you punish more than other gods!
You sired our race but do not pity us,
mixing evil things for us with sorrowful pains.
I sweated when I saw this one, my eyes broke out *
in tears remembering Odysseus. I think
he too is in rags wandering among men,
if he yet lives and sees the light of Helios.
But if he is dead and in the house of Hades,
alas for him! He who set me when yet young
over his oxen in Kephallenia.*   210
Now they're beyond count. For none other would those
broad-faced oxen multiply like grains of corn!
These strangers urge me to drive the oxen away
for them to eat! Nor do they care about the child
of the house nor fear the gods. They long
to divide the wealth of our long-absent lord.
When I turn these thoughts over in my heart,
it's very bad, the son yet in the house, to drive
his oxen to another's land, to a land
of foreigners! But it's worse to stay here,   220
suffering pain, sitting among another's oxen.
And long ago I would have fled to some land
of mighty kings since it is hard to bear here.
But yet I think of him, if he should come back,
and make a scattering of the suitors in his house."

Answering him, artful Odysseus then said:

"Herdsman, you do not seem bad or lacking sense.
I myself know you have a discreet mind.
So I will tell you and make a solemn oath:
by Zeus, first of the gods, by this guest table   230
of brave Odysseus' hearth where I am now,
while you're here in this house Odysseus will come!
If you should wish, your own eyes will witness

the slaying of the suitors who so lord it here."

The shepherd of the oxen answered him:

"Stranger, if Kronos' son fulfills your words,
you will know what strength my two hands yet have!"

So also did Eumaios pray to all the gods
that lord Odysseus come back to his own home.
So they spoke about these things to each other.   240

Meanwhile the suitors were plotting Telemakos'
doom and death when an eagle flew from the left,
high up, clutching a timid dove in its talons.
Then Amphinomos addressed them and he said:

"My friends, our plan to kill Telemakos will not
end well. So it's better to go into the feast."

So spoke Amphinomos and his words pleased them.

Going to brave Odysseus' palace,
they put their cloaks down on couches and chairs,
then killed a large ram, succulent goats,   250
fattened hogs and an ox from the herd.
They roasted the innards and gave them out and mixed
the wine in the bowl. The swineherd gave them cups.
Philoitios gave them bread from a reed basket
while Melanthios poured them their wine.
The men stretched their hands out over the readied feast.

But Telemakos, thinking ahead, seated
Odysseus in the hall by the stone threshold
and put an old stool and tiny table there.
He dished a portion of innards for him, poured wine   260
into a cup of gold and spoke these words to him:

"Be seated here and drink your wine among these men.
I myself will ward off blows or ridicule
from the suitors since this is no public place
but lord Odysseus' house and I'm his heir.
And you, suitors, free your minds from abuse
and blows or you'll stir up strife and anger."

So he spoke. Biting their lips, they all
marveled at Telemakos who spoke so boldly.
Eupeithes' son Antinoös then spoke: 270

"Though hard, Akaians, we must accept these words
of bold Telemakos who uses such strong threats.
Kronos' son Zeus did not permit our plan
to stop forever his lucid words in these halls."

So he spoke. But Telemakos ignored him.
Heralds were leading holy hecatombs up from
the town while the long-haired Akaians gathered
in far-shooting Apollo's shady grove.

Once they had roasted the outer meat and pulled it off
the spits, they shared it, enjoying the glorious feast.   280
The servers set an equal portion for
Odysseus as for themselves, for so demanded
Telemakos, Odysseus' godlike son.

But yet Athena did not keep the wooers from
their grievous outrage so that Laertes' son
Odysseus might feel yet more pain in his heart.
There was one among the suitors, reckless in acts,
Ktesippos his name, who dwelled in Same.
His abundant wealth persuaded him
to woo the spouse of long-absent Odysseus.   290
He then addressed the arrogant suitors:

"Hear me, heroic suitors, listen to what I say.
For awhile this 'guest' has had his portion equal
to ours, for it's not good or just to spurn a guest
of Telemakos, whoever comes to the house.
Look, I'll give a 'guest' gift so that he might give
it to the old woman who pours his bath or to
any slave of godlike brave Odysseus."

So speaking, with his fat hand he grabbed an ox
hoof from the basket and threw it, but Odysseus,   300
bending his head, dodged it and in his heart he smiled
bitterly. The hoof bounced off the thick wall.

Telemakos then said this to Ktesippos:

"Ktesippos, it's better for your life that you
missed the stranger—he dodged your thrown ox hoof—
or I'd have struck you in the gut with my sharp spear
and, in place of a wedding, your father would have
provided for a funeral. Let there be no
more abuses seen here. Now I see and know
these things, the good and bad. Before I was a child.   310
Still we see these things and must tolerate them:
the slaughter of our sheep, the wine consumed,
the bread. It's hard for one man to restrain many.
But come, show me no more hostile acts.
If you yet wish to kill me with bronze swords
I would choose that, for it is much better to die,
better that than always seeing outrageous acts,
strangers struck, women and handmaids dragged
in shame throughout this beautiful palace."

So he spoke. All kept still, bound in silence.   320
At last Damastor's son Agelaos spoke up:

"Friends, let no one be angry at this just speech

nor challenge him with harsh fighting words.
Let no one strike this stranger nor any of
the maids throughout godlike Odysseus' palace.
I offer Telemakos and his mother
these gentle words to please both their hearts.
As long as your hearts had cause to hope that he,
artful Odysseus, might return to his house,
so long could none blame you for waiting and   330
holding back the suitors, since this was best
if he, on his return, had come back to his house.
But now it's clear that there will be no return.
So come now, sit beside your mother and tell her
to wed the man who's best and gives the most bride gifts.
Then you'll be glad, enjoying your patrimony,
eating and drinking, while she keeps another's house."

Then wise Telemakos replied to him:

"No, by Zeus and by my father's suffering
who has died far from Ithaka—or wanders yet!   340
I don't hold back my mother's wedding but tell her to
wed whom she wishes and I'll give boundless gifts!
But it shames me to drive her from the palace,
forcing her away. May god prevent that!"

So spoke Telemakos. Then Athena urged
the suitors to senseless laughter, their minds straying.
They kept laughing as though their jaws weren't their own,
the meat they ate was blood-splattered, their eyes
filled with tears, their minds with thoughts of wailing.
Then godlike Theoklymenos addressed them: *   350

"Wretched ones! What evil do you suffer? Your heads,
your faces, your knees below are shrouded in darkness.
Your wails come bursting out, your cheeks are tear soaked,
the walls and column bases are splattered with blood.

Dead spirits fill the doorway and the courtyard, rushing
to the nether dark in Erebos. The sun
is blotted from the sky, a black mist covers all!"

So he spoke but they all laughed at him.
Then Polybos' son Eurymakos replied:

"He's mad, this stranger newly come from abroad.   360
Quickly men, take him out the door to the
open ground since he sees only darkness here."

Then godlike Theoklymenos answered him:

"Eurymakos, there's no need for an escort.
I have my eyes, my ears and two feet,
and in me, my mind is in working order.
With these, I leave you through the door since I know well
evil is coming and not one of you suitors
will escape here in Odysseus' palace
where you've abused men and planned shameless acts!"   370

So speaking, he left the well-sited house and went
to Peiraios' home and there was well received.
The suitors looked from one to another and,
mocking the strangers, they taunted Telemakos.
One of the young arrogant ones spoke thus:

"Telemakos, who is more unlucky in guests?
You have this one, this wanderer brought here to you
who needs food and wine, who has no skills in work
and no strength, a burden on good farmland!
And that other who stands up to prophesize!   380
But if you might hear me, this would be better:
toss these strangers in a large ship, send them to
the Sikels. You'll get a good price there for them!"

So spoke a suitor. Telemakos ignored him,

quietly watching his father, ever waiting
to lay his hands on the shameless suitors.

Then she moved a well-wrought lovely chair,
wise Penelope, Ikarios' child,
so she could hear the words of each in the hall.
Having their dinner they laughed, for there was much   390
good food and they had sacrificed many beasts.
But there would be a bitter meal that a goddess
and a brave man planned for them soon, for these
men who first began the shameless evil acts.

BOOK TWENTY-ONE

The challenge of the bow
The suitors fail to string the bow
Odysseus succeeds and completes the challenge

Bright-eyed Athena put this in the mind of wise
Penelope, Ikarios' daughter,
to place at hand in Odysseus' palace
the bow and gray iron: contest and slaughter's start.*
She went up the high stairs to her rooms
and took in her firm hands the curved key,
a key of fine bronze with an ivory handle.
She went to the innermost storeroom with
her handmaids. There were kept her lord's treasures,
bronze and gold and hard to work iron.   10
His recurve bow lay there and the quiver
filled with many grief-causing arrows.

These were his guest-gift in Lakedaimonia
from Eurytos' son, godlike Iphitos.
The two met each other by chance in Messene,
in wise Ortilokos' house. Odysseus

came to collect a debt owed by all the people.
From Ithaka they had stolen three hundred sheep
and their shepherds, carrying them off in their swift ships.
Still a boy, Odysseus came far on this   20
mission, sent by his father and the elders.
Iphitos was looking for his twelve mares
and hard-working suckling mules stolen from him.*
Soon these mares would bring about his death
when he went to Zeus' strong-hearted son,
mighty Herakles, doer of great deeds.
Though a guest in his house Herakles killed him.
Cruel man, no awe for gods nor the guest table
placed before him! He killed him there and kept
the horses for himself in his palace. Searching   30
for these, Iphitos met Odysseus and gave
him the bow that Eurytos once carried. On
his death he'd left it to his child in his palace.
Odysseus gave him a sword and a strong spear.
This began their guest friendship, but they would never host
the tables of each other. Zeus' son slew
Eurytos' son, godlike Iphitos
who gave Odysseus the bow. He never took
the bow when going to war in the black ships, but kept
it in his house, a remembrance of his friend.   40
When at home, he used to take it hunting.

When she reached the room with her women, she stepped
on the oak threshold. The expert carpenter
had hewn and shaved it, set it straight and true
and fitted it with doorposts to hold the polished doors.
She pulled the leather strap from the door handle,
pushed the key straight in and threw back
the bolt: it bellowed like a bull feeding
in a meadow. So sounded the polished doors when
struck by the key and they swung quickly open.   50

She went to the high platform where stood
the chests filled with incense-laden clothes.
She reached up and from a peg took the bow
in its fine case, the polished cover protecting it.
Weeping bitterly, the case across her knees,
she sat and took the master's bow from its case.

When she had had enough of tearful grieving,
she set out for the hall and the proud suitors,
the bow in her hands and the quiver
filled with many grief-causing arrows.   60
Her maids carried down the box with the axe heads
and bronze-tipped arrows—tools for the contest.
And when she in her splendor reached the suitors,
she stood by a thick, roof-supporting column,
and held a bright veil in front of her cheeks.
A loyal maid stood on either side of her.
She then addressed the suitors in these words:

"Hear me, proud suitors who abuse this house
by ever eating and drinking here
while its lord has been long absent. You have not   70
been able to give me any other cause for this
than to wed me, making me your woman.
So come, suitors, for this is your challenge. I have
put here the great bow of godlike Odysseus.
Whoever with his hands strings it with ease
and shoots an arrow straight through all twelve axe heads,
with him I will go, leaving my bridal house,
a home most fair, full of wealth, which I think
I will ever remember, though in dreams."

So she spoke and bid the swineherd Eumaios   80
place the bow and gray iron before the suitors.
Weeping, Eumaios took it, setting it down in front.

The other herdsman cried out seeing the master's bow.

But Antinoös rebuked them, speaking with these words:

"Country hicks! Thinking only of today!
Wretches! Why do you shed tears and stir up
the heart in the lady's breast? Her heart is steeped
in other pains because her bedmate was killed.
Sit and eat in silence, or go out of doors.
Weep there. But leave the bow here, the challenge,   90
decisive for the suitors. For I think it will not
be easy this, to string his well-polished bow.
No, there is not a man among us all
such as Odysseus was. I saw him once
and I remember still though I was a young child."

So he spoke, but he hoped in his heart
to string the bow and shoot a shaft through the axe heads.
But he was doomed to taste the first arrow from
Odysseus' hands—who sat in the hall—
for he'd dishonored him and urged the suitors on.   100

God-protected Telemakos addressed them thus:

"How strange! Kronos' son Zeus has taken my wits!
My dear mother, though she is wise, now says
she will leave this house with another man
while I wear an idiot's grin and laugh!
But come, suitors, your prize stands before you,
for there's not such a woman in Akaian lands,
not in holy Pylos, Argos or Mykene,
not even in Ithaka or the dark mainland!
But you all know this. What need have I to praise her?   110
Come now, no more excuses, nor shall we turn
away from this bow so long unstrung. Let's see!
I myself might give that bow a try.

If I should string it and shoot through the axes,
my lady mother would not depart with another
leaving me grieving, for I'd be still be here as one
able to assume my father's mantle and prizes!"

Standing up, he took his deep red cloak from
his shoulders and unslung his sharp sword.
Digging a trench first, he stood the axes up,   120
all in one long row—a rule made it straight—
tamping the earth around them. All were held in awe.
He stood them straight though he had not seen them before.
Standing up, he went to the bow and tried it.
Three times, longing to string it, he made it quiver.
Three times his strength let go, though he still held hopes
to string the bow and shoot through the iron axes.
And now, on the fourth try, he would have strung it but
Odysseus shook his head, halting his effort.

To them god-protected Telemakos spoke thus: 130

"So be it! I will always be weak and unmanly,
or I am too young yet and cannot trust my hands
to ward off a man who has begun a quarrel.
But come now, you who are stronger than I,
try the bow and let us end this contest."

So he spoke and set the bow on the ground,
leaning it against the well-made, polished door
and against it he propped the swift arrow.
Then he sat down in the chair he'd risen from.

Eupeithes' son Antinoös addressed them: 140

"All rise, let's do this in order, right to left,
beginning from there where the wine is poured."

So spoke Antinoös and his words pleased them.

Oinopos' son Leodes stood up first.
A sort of seer, he sat in the far corner among
the wine bowls. To him alone were reckless acts
hateful and he resented all the suitors.
He was first to take the bow and swift arrow.
Going to the threshold, he tried the bow
but could not string it. His hands soft, unused   150
to work, soon tired and he said to the suitors:

"Friends, I cannot string it. Let another take it.
This bow will rob the life and mind of many
of the best. But it is better to die than live
failing in our quest as we gather here,
ever expectant, waiting day after day.
Some of you hope in your hearts and yearn
to wed Odysseus' bedmate Penelope.
But when you've tried the bow and seen what comes,
then woo some other fair-robed Akaian maid   160
with bride gifts. But let Penelope wed who brings
the most and whom she is destined to marry."

So he spoke and set the bow on the ground,
leaning it against the well-made, polished door
and against it he propped the swift arrow.
Then he sat down in the chair he'd risen from.

But Antinoös rebuked him, speaking these words:

"Leodes, such words escaped the fence of your teeth,
terrible and painful! Hearing them I'm angered!
This bow will rob the life and mind of many   170
of the best? Since you cannot string it?
Your mother did not make a son with such strength
to string this, nor to be an archer.
One of these proud suitors will string it soon."

So he spoke and summoned Melanthios the goatherd:

"Melanthios, come. Start a fire in the halls
and place a stool with a fleece on top
and a big cake of hard fat nearby so we
young men might warm the bow, rubbing it with fat,
and then we'll try to string it and end the contest."   180

So he spoke. Melanthios built up the fire
and placed in front a stool with a fleece on top
and a big cake of hard fat nearby so that
the young men could warm the bow. But none could string it.
They were not nearly strong enough, not one. Only
Antinoös and Eurymakos held back,
the suitors' leaders and far the best in skill.

Then the two left the hall, exiting together,
the oxherd and godlike Odysseus' swineherd,
and Odysseus himself left after them.   190
When they had gone outside, well beyond the door,
he spoke, uttering these soft words to them:

"Oxherd, and you, swineherd, should I say a word
to you or hold back? My heart bids me speak.
Would you be men fighting for Odysseus
if he returned at once, some god leading him?
Would you fight for the suitors or Odysseus?
Tell me as your heart and mind direct you to."

Then he who watches over the oxen answered:

"Father Zeus, may this wish come to pass!   200
Grant that he will return led by some god!
You will know what strength my hands yet have!"

So also did Eumaios pray to all the gods
that wise Odysseus come back to his own home.

And when he knew the true minds of them both,
he answered them then, speaking these words:

"I am he, here, having suffered much.
After twenty years I've come back to my land.
I know you two alone of my servants
have yearned for my coming. I've heard no others   210
praying for my return, for my homecoming.
To you I will tell the truth, how it shall be.
If some god allows me to subdue the suitors,
I will bring you both bedmates and give you wealth,
and build you homes near mine, and you shall be
my comrades and as brothers to Telemakos.
But come, I'll show you something else, a clear sign
that you will know well and trust me in your hearts:
the scar that the white-tusked boar gave me in
Parnassos when I went with Autolykos' sons."   220

So speaking, he showed the large scar beneath the rags.
When they had seen it and examined it closely,
they cried and threw their arms around Odysseus
and kept kissing his head and shoulders happily.
And brave Odysseus kissed their heads and hands.
And thus Helios' light would have sunk
had lord Odysseus not restrained them, saying:

"Cease these wails and weeping or someone coming
from the hall might tell of it back inside.
One by one go inside, but not together.   230
I will go first, then you. And let this be your sign:
all the others, as great as these suitors are,
will not let me be given the bow and quiver.
But you good Eumaios, carry the bow through
the house and put it in my hands. Tell the women
to bolt their hall's tightly-fitted doors.

If any hear the noise and din of men within,
let them not peek through the doors but stay
inside, silent, and keeping at their work.
And you, good Philoitios, I charge to bolt   240
the courtyard gates and tie a chain to hold them."

So speaking he went back inside the stately house.
He sat down on the stool he had risen from.
Separately the two servants entered the palace.

Meanwhile Eurymakos held the bow,
turning it to warm it in the fire's flames.
But he could not string it and moaned in his heart.
Angrily he spoke and addressed them all:

"Oh no! I am in pain for me and all of you!
I grieve not for this wedding though that is painful.   250
There are many other Akaian women here
in sea-washed Ithaka and in other towns.
No, I grieve because we need the strength of him,
godlike Odysseus! We cannot string his bow!
Thus will those yet to be born know our shame."

Eupeithes' son Antinoös then answered him:

"Eurymakos, it won't be so and you know it!
For throughout the land this is the holy feast
of the god! Who could string a bow? So put
it down. We can leave the axes still standing   260
for I don't think anyone coming to
the palace of Odysseus will steal them!
But come wine-bearer pour some wine in our cups,
a libation, that we might set the curved bow down.
At daybreak bid that goatherd Melanthios
bring she goats, the best of all the goat herd, and we
will give thigh pieces to Apollo, famed Archer.

Then we'll try the bow and end this contest."

So spoke Antinoös and his words pleased them.
The heralds poured water over their hands.   270
The servants filled the wine bowls with wine for drinking
and with this wine they filled every cup. After
the offering, they drank as much as they wished.

With a plan, artful Odysseus addressed them:

"Hear me you suitors of the famous queen
while I tell you what my heart and mind bid.
I pray most to Eurymakos and then to godlike
Antinoös who spoke those very proper words.
Cease with the bow for now, leave it to the gods.
At daybreak may god give strength to whom he wishes.   280
But come, give me the polished bow that I here
among you might try the strength and vigor of my hands,
if any yet remains such as I had when young,
or if wandering and lack of care has ruined me."

So he spoke and all the suitors were furious
for fear that he might somehow string the bow.

But Antinoös rebuked him, speaking these words:

"Miserable man, you have no sense! Not even a jot!
Are you not pleased to feast at ease with well-born men,
not lacking your share, listening to our words   290
and conversations? For no other hears
our talks, neither guest nor beggar hears us.
The sweet wine has wounded you as it has wounded
others who gulp it down, not drinking wisely.
Wine blinded famous Eurytion the Kentaur
in the palace of great-hearted Peirithoös
when he went to the Lapiths. His mind blind

with wine he raged, doing harm throughout the house.
In anger the Lapith heroes sprang up, seized him
and dragged him out through the door and gates.   300
They cut his ears and nose off with pitiless bronze.
Thus damaged he went about with blinded mind, witless.
The feud between Kentaurs and men began through this.
Eurytion learned the harm of wine-drunkenness.
And so I say it will be a great pain for you
should you string the bow. You'll meet no kindness
from us. No, we'll send you in a black ship
to King Eketos, murderer of mortals,*
nor will you escape him unhurt. So drink
at ease here and no fights with younger men."   310

Then sensible Penelope answered him:

"Antinoös, it's neither good nor just to abuse
Telemakos' guest, whoever comes here.
Do you think this stranger might string the great bow of
Odysseus? That his hands have such might and force?
That he might lead me home? Set me as his bedmate?
He himself, in his heart, expects this not!
Let none of you feasting here worry in
your hearts at this—it will never happen!"

Polybos' son Eurymakos answered her: 320

"Ikarios' maid, wise Penelope,
we do not think he'd lead you off—that's not right.
We dread the shame from talk of men and women
if some base man should say among the Akaians:
'Far weaker men are wooing the bedmate of a
noble man. And they could not string the bow!
But some wandering man, a beggar, came and strung
it easily and shot an arrow through the axes!'
So they'd speak and yes, that would disgrace us all."

Then sensible Penelope answered him: 330

"Eurymakos, there can be no honor in this
land for those dishonoring and eating away
a better man's wealth. So why be concerned?
This stranger's big and well-built and he says
he is the son of a good father, of good stock.
So come, give him the polished bow that we might see.
For this I say and so it will come to be:
if he should string it and Apollo give him glory,
I will give him a cloak and tunic, fine clothes,
and a sharp spear to ward off dogs and men,   340
a two-edged sword, and sandals for his feet,
and send him wherever his heart and mind should bid!"

Then wise Telemakos replied to her:

"Mother, of the Akaians none has more right
over the bow than me to give or to withhold,
not those who lord it in rocky Ithaka
nor those who rule in horse-pasturing Elis.
No man will prevent me if I wish to give
the bow to the stranger, a gift, to carry off!
But go up to your rooms, busy yourself at   350
the distaff or the loom and bid your maids finish
their own work. Leave the bow to the men,
to all, and to me—for I am master here!"

Stunned, she turned at once toward her rooms,
her son's serious words sitting in her heart.
Up in her rooms with all her women helpers
she wept for her husband Odysseus until
Athena poured sweet sleep on her eyelids.

The noble swineherd took the bow and carried it,
but the suitors in the hall all cried out.   360

One of the young arrogant ones spoke thus:

"Where are you taking the curved bow, wretched swineherd?
Are you mad? Soon your dogs will feast on you,
alone among your pigs—dogs you reared—if lord
Apollo and the deathless gods grant us this!"

Such was their speech. Eumaios put the bow back,
afraid because of the shouting in the hall.

Across the hall Telemakos called out a threat:

"Old man, pick up the bow! You can't listen to
everyone! Though young, I will drive you away,   370
throwing stones since I am stronger than you!
Would that I were stronger than all these suitors
in my house, mightier with my hands,
so I could quickly—hatefully—drive any from
our house who are planning wicked acts."

So he spoke and all the suitors laughed at him,
and they relaxed, freed from their harsh anger at
Telemakos. The swineherd carried the bow through
the hall and put it in Odysseus' hands.

From there, calling Eurykleia, Eumaios said: 380

"Telemakos bids you, oh wise Eurykleia,
to bolt your hall's tightly-fitted doors.
If any hear the noise and din of men within,
let them not peek through the doors but stay
inside, silent, and keeping at their work."

So he spoke. His words lodged in her heart
and she closed and bolted the doors of the great hall.

In silence, Philoitios went through the door

and barred the gates of the well-walled courtyard.
In the yard lay a ship's cable of reeds.   390
With this he bound the gates then went back in
and sat on the stool he had risen from.
He watched Odysseus, who handled the bow
turning it, trying it this way and that,
checking the horn for worm-damage in his long absence.*

Then one man spoke to another nearby:

"A man who knows what a bow's about!
Perhaps he has one lying about at home
or wants to construct one, so much his hands turn it
this way and that, this wanderer skilled in deceit!"   400

Another of the young, arrogant ones said:

"May he reap all the success he well deserves
as he attempts to string Odysseus' bow!"

So they spoke. But then artful Odysseus
lifted the bow, examining it well,
and, as one who knows lyre and song stretches
easily a new string on the peg, attaching
the flexible sheep gut at both ends, just so
without effort Odysseus strung the bow.
With his right hand he tried the taut bowstring.   410
It sang out sweetly like a sparrow's song.
The suitors felt a great pain and their faces
went pale—and Zeus thundered with a great flash.
And noble, much-enduring Odysseus rejoiced
that devious Kronos' son had sent a sign.
At once he picked up the arrow that lay loose
by the table—the others lay in the quiver
and the Akaians were destined to know these well.
He fitted it on the bow, notch to string.

From there, sitting on the stool, taking aim,   420
he shot the heavy, bronze-tipped arrow straight through all
the axes, from the first hole right through to
the last one, then addressed Telemakos:

"Telemakos, the stranger sitting in the hall
did not shame you, nor did he miss the mark
and wasn't long stringing the bow. I yet have strength
in spite of what the suitors, mocking me, have said.
But now's the hour for the Akaians' feasting
while it is still daylight, and then for entertainment,
let's cap the feast with dancing and with lyre."   430

Odysseus nodded at Telemakos,
his godlike son who put his sharp sword on,
and closed his hand around his spear and stood close to
his chair with his shining bronze weapons.

BOOK TWENTY-TWO

The slaughter of the suitors
The treachery of some servants
The punishment of the maids and Melanthios

Odysseus stripped off his rags and sprang to the
threshold, holding the bow and the full quiver.
He quickly poured the arrows out on the ground
around his feet and called then to the suitors:

"Thus this contest has been decided. But there's
another target no man has struck which I will try,
if it may be and if Apollo grants my prayer."

He then aimed the feathered arrow at Antinoös
who was just then lifting a beautiful, two-handled
goblet of gold. He had it in his hands   10
to drink some wine with no thought of death in
his mind. For among so many men feasting,
how could one alone, strong though he be,
bring death to him, an evil and dark doom?
Odysseus aimed and shot at his throat.

The arrow tip went straight through his tender neck.

He fell to one side, the cup thrown from his hands,
a thick jet of blood spurting from his nose.
At the same time he thrust the table away,
kicking with his foot, food falling to the ground,   20
the bread and roast meat fouled. The suitors raised
a din throughout the house when they saw him falling.
Alarmed they jumped up from their chairs and searched
the well-built walls, looking every which way,
but there was neither shield nor strong spear to seize.
They shouted angry words at lord Odysseus:

"Stranger, your arrow evilly struck this man.
No more contests for you! Now your death is sure!
Now you have killed a man by far the best of
the youths in Ithaka! Vultures will eat you now!" *   30

Each man assumed the stranger had not wanted
to kill the man. Fools! They did not understand
that the chains of death now bound them all.

In anger, artful Odysseus then said:

"You dogs! You thought I'd never come back to my high-
roofed house, home from Troy! So you stripped my house,
took and slept with my women servants by force,
secretly courted my bedmate—with me alive—
fearing not the gods who hold the wide sky,
nor any vengeance from men in the future!   40
Now the chains of death bind you all!"

So he spoke and all turned green with fear,
each man thinking how to flee sheer death.

Eurymakos alone spoke, answering him:

"If you are Ithakan Odysseus come home,
you're right. The Akaians have done many wanton
acts in the halls, many in the land. But he
who lies there is to blame for everything,
Antinoös. He instigated all these acts,
not that he craved or needed the marriage,   50
but for other reasons that Zeus did not fulfill.
He wanted to ambush and kill your son
and rule the settled land of Ithaka himself.
Now he is slain, so you should protect us, your own
people. We'll pay you back, and do it in public,
for what we've drunk and eaten in the halls,
each man bringing you the worth of twenty oxen!*
We'll give you bronze and gold until your heart
is softened. Until then, no one could blame your wrath."

In anger, artful Odysseus then said: 60

"Eurymakos, not if you should give me all
your father's wealth and all you could ever gather,
not even then would I withhold my hands from slaughter
till I've repaid the wrongs of all the wanton suitors!
Now it's your choice either to fight me here
or flee—if any can escape this death and doom!
But I predict none will escape sheer death!"

So he spoke. Their knees loosened, their hearts froze.

Eurymakos spoke to them a second time:

"My friends, this man will not hold back his mighty hands,   70
but will use his polished bow and shafts to shoot
from the smooth threshold until he's killed us all!
Remember your battle fury! Draw your swords
and use the tables to stop the swift-killing
arrows! Let's all go at him in a crowd at once

and drive him from the threshold and the doors
so that we can run through the town and raise the call.
Then this man will have shot for the last time!"

So speaking, he drew the sharp double-edged sword
of bronze and leapt forward shouting a fierce   80
war cry, but brave Odysseus at the same time
let fly an arrow that struck him near a nipple.
The swift arrow drove into his liver. The sword
fell from his hand. He sprawled on a table
bent double, and the food and wine goblet
fell to the ground. His forehead struck the earth
in great pain. Kicking with both his feet,
he shook the chair, a mist clouding his eyes.
Then Amphinomos charged far-famed Odysseus
with sharp sword drawn. Dashing right at him,   90
he thought to drive him from the doors. But then came
Telemakos from behind and hurled the spear
between his shoulders, driving through his chest.
He fell with a thud, his brow striking the ground.
Telemakos sprang back, leaving the long spear
in Amphinomos. He feared that one of
the Akaians might stab him with a sword while he
was stooped down pulling the long spear out.
He quickly dashed over to his father
and standing near he said these winged words: 100

"Father, I'll bring you a shield and two spears,
and a bronze helmet to cover your temples.
I'll get armor for myself and for the swineherd
and the oxherd for it's better to wear armor."

Answering him, artful Odysseus then said:

"Run! Bring them while these arrows keep them back,
or they might drive me from the doors when I'm alone."

So he spoke. Telemakos obeyed his father
and went to the room where the prized arms lay.
There he chose for them four shields, eight spears,   110
and four bronze helmets topped with bristling horsehair,
and rushed back quickly to where his father was fighting.
First he put the armor on himself
and then gave the armor to the two slaves who stood
on either side of battle-skilled Odysseus.

And he, as long as he had his arrows at hand,
kept aiming and shooting the suitors in his palace.
He always hit them and they fell thick together.
But when the lord archer ran out of arrows,
he leaned the bow on a strong column in the hall,   120
left it standing against the bright inner walls,
and put the four-layered shield over his shoulders.
On his head he put the well-made helmet,
the terrifying horsehair crest waving above,
and picked up two strong spears tipped with bronze.

There was a postern door in the well-built wall
of the stately hall, far from the threshold,
a passage to the road barred by wooden doors.
Odysseus, pointing, told the noble swineherd
to guard it—there was only room for one to rush it.   130

Agelaos spoke, saying these words to all:

"Friends, is there no one to go up there
and tell the people and quickly raise the cry?
Then this man would soon have shot his last."

The goatherd, Melanthios, answered him:

"There is no way, Zeus-born Agelaos.
The passage is steep and near the front gates.

One man might stop us all if he were bold.
But come, I'll bring you weapons from the storeroom.
I think they are inside since there's no other place   140
for Odysseus and his son to put them."

So speaking, the goatherd Melanthios dashed up
the stairway in the hall to the storeroom.
There he seized twelve shields, as many spears,
and also twelve helmets with horsehair plumes.
Returning quickly he gave these to the suitors.
Odysseus' knees went loose, his heart froze,
as he saw them arming themselves, wielding the long
spears in their hands. His task now looked enormous.

He said these winged words to Telemakos: 150

"Telemakos, a woman in the halls has urged
war on us, or it's that bad Melanthios."

Then wise Telemakos answered him:

"Father, I myself failed in this. No one
else is at fault. I left the storeroom's doors
wide open. A suitor spotted this before I did.
Go, Eumaios, close the storeroom's doors
and see if one of the women did this or
Dolios' son Melanthios whom I suspect."

So they spoke among themselves just as   160
Melanthios went back again to the storeroom
for more weapons. The swineherd saw him and he said
at once to lord Odysseus for he was near:

"Zeus-born Laertes' son, artful Odysseus,
as we ourselves all thought, that evil man
is going to the storeroom. Tell me what you want.
Shall I kill him if I am indeed the stronger?

Or shall I bring him here that he may repay
the many wrongs he planned against your house?"

Answering him artful Odysseus then said: 170

"Telemakos and I will hold these suitors here
in the hall though they strive against us.
You two go upstairs, tie his hands and feet,
and throw him in the storeroom. With braided cord
strap his back to a board and hoist him up
to the roof beam near the column to dangle
alive there, suffering long in agony!"

So he spoke. They heard him and obeyed.
They went up to the room. He was inside
in the far corner looking for more weapons.   180
The two waited, one on each side of the door.
When the goatherd Melanthios crossed the threshold
he was carrying a good helmet in one hand
and in the other an ancient broad shield with dry rot
that the hero Laertes carried when he was young.
So long had it lain there that seams were coming apart.
The two rushed him, dragged him inside by the hair
and threw him on the floor where he lay in terror.
They bound his hands and feet with painful cord
and twisted them behind his back as they'd been told   190
by Laertes' son, artful Odysseus.
They strapped him to a board, hoisted him up to
the roof beam near the column to dangle there.

Then in scorn the swineherd Eumaios said:

"And now Melanthios, watch the whole night
lying in this soft bed you so well deserve.
Nor shall you miss early Dawn coming from
the sea-waves on her golden chair at the hour

when you drive goats here to make the suitors' feast."

There he was left, bound in his terrible cords.   200
Then the two donned armor and closed the polished door
and went to battle-skilled warrior Odysseus.
On the threshold the four stood, fired with fury,
the suitors in the halls were still numerous.
Zeus' daughter, Athena, came near them.
In shape and voice she seemed like Mentor.

Seeing her, Odysseus was glad and said:

"Mentor, fight off our ruin! Remember me, your friend!
I did much good for you! We've been friends since childhood!"

So he spoke, knowing Athena the warrior goddess.   210
But the suitors across the hall called out.
The first with rebukes was Agelaos:

"Mentor, don't let Odysseus persuade you
to fight the suitors with you defending him!
This is our plan and this is how it will end:
when we have killed them both, father and son,
then we will kill you. Whatever you hope to do
in the hall, you'll pay the price with your head.
When our bronze has taken the lives of all of you,
we'll take your goods—home, wealth and land—and mix   220
them with Odysseus' goods! Your sons will not
be left alive in your halls nor your daughters,
nor will your loving bedmate remain in Ithaka!"

So he spoke. But Athena got very angry
and she scolded Odysseus with harsh words:

"Odysseus, have you lost that might and strength
you had when fighting ceaselessly for white-armed
Helen with Trojan men those nine long years?

There you slew many in fierce battle-strife!
Priam's broad-wayed city fell through your plan!   230
Now that you've come back to your home and goods,
your strength wanes and you wail before the suitors?
But come now friend, stand by me and see my deeds
so you will know how Alkimos' son Mentor
repays your past goodness fighting these hostile men!"

So she spoke but would not give him victory yet,
for she wanted to test the strength and prowess
of both Odysseus and his famous son.
She flew to the roof beam of the smoke-darkened hall
and perched there, a swallow to all appearances.   240

But Agelaos, Eurynomos, Amphimedon,
Demoptolemos, Polyktor's son Peisandros
and wise Polybos urged on the suitors—
for these were the best of the suitors still
alive in battle bravery, ready to fight.
Thick-falling arrows had felled the strength of the rest.

Agelaos spoke, saying these words to all:

"My friends, this man will not hold back his mighty hands,
and look, Mentor has left with his empty boasts
leaving them alone in front of the door!   250
So don't throw all your long spears at once!
Come! You six throw first! If Zeus grants us
to hit Odysseus we'll win our fame!
Don't mind the others once that one has fallen!"

So he spoke. The six all hurled their spears as bid,
sending them off. But Athena made them useless.
One struck a pillar of the well-built hall
while another hit the close-fitted door,
and one heavy ash spear lodged in the wall.

Having avoided the suitors' spears, he began   260
to speak, brave, much-suffering Odysseus:

"My friends, I say now that we should hurl our spears
into the throng of suitors, for they—on top
of their viciousness—wish to kill us now!"

So he spoke. Aiming straight, all threw their spears:
Odysseus felled Demoptolemos,
Telemakos hit Euryades, the swineherd
killed Elatos, the oxherd Peisandros.
They all fell at once, teeth biting the bitter dirt.
The suitors backed into a corner of the hall.   270
The four rushed in, seizing spears from the corpses.

The suitors again all hurled their spears as bid,
sending them off. But Athena made them useless:
one struck a pillar of the well-built hall
while another hit the close-fitted door,
and one heavy ash spear lodged in the wall.
But Amphimedon hit Telemakos' wrist,
a graze, bronze breaking the topmost skin.
Ktesippos grazed Eumaios' shield shoulder;
the spear flew over and fell to the ground.   280
Again skillful warrior Odysseus and
his men hurled spears into the throng of suitors.
Warrior Odysseus slew Eurydamas,
Telemakos Amphimedon, the swineherd
Polybos. The oxherd struck Ktesippos
in the chest and boasting, he cried out:

"Polytherses' son, mocker of men, no more
give way to folly and to boasting! Let
the gods have their way since they are much the stronger!
Take this for your guest-gift of the ox hoof that *   290
you sent Odysseus while begging in his house!"

Thus spoke the herder of oxen. Then in close
combat Odysseus speared Agelaos.
Telemakos pierced Leokritos,
his spear driving through his belly's center.
He fell prone, forehead striking the floor. Only
then did Athena in the roof beams raise
the slaying aigis. The suitors were all terrified.*
They fled down the hall like a herd of oxen
as though driven by an angry darting gadfly   300
in the season of spring when the days grow long.

Just as hooked-beak eagles with sharp talons
come from the mountains and dive below the clouds
to swoop down on birds that scatter on the plain
as they attack and kill them, no hope of aid
nor of escape—the country folk enjoy the sight—
just so they rushed down the hall toward the suitors
striking them this way and that. Horrible groans
came from wounded heads. Blood covered the broad floor.
Leodes, rushing up, grabbed the knees of lord   310
Odysseus, begging him with winged words:

"I beg you, Odysseus! Respect me! Spare me!
I tell you I neither spoke nor did wrongs
to any of the women in the palace.
I tried to stop the suitors who did such things,
but they would not hold their hands from viciousness,
and from these wicked deeds they have met their fate!
But I, their seer, will lie dead having done nothing!
Are there no thanks in future times for good deeds?"

In anger, artful Odysseus then said: 320

"Being the seer and praying among them, you must
have often prayed in my hall for this result:
to keep my sweet return beyond my grasp!

You hoped for my bedmate to bear your children!
You will not escape here a bitter death!"

So speaking, in his strong hand he took a sword
that lay there—Agelaos had dropped it to the ground
when he was killed—and drove it through his neck.
His head was still talking as it fell in the dust.

Terpias' son Phemios, forced to sing   330
among the suitors, was fleeing from black death.
Near the postern door he held the clear-toned lyre
in his hands. He stopped between two thoughts,
whether to leave the hall and go to the temple
of great Zeus where Odysseus used
to burn thigh pieces of oxen for the god,
or grasp Odysseus' knees pleading for
his life. Pondering this it seemed better
to grasp the knees of Laertes' son Odysseus.
He lay his hollow lyre down on the floor   340
between the mixing bowl and silver-studded chair
and rushed to grasp Odysseus' knees
and pleading, said these winged words to him:

"I beg you Odysseus! Respect me! Spare me!
How bad it would be in the future if you kill
a bard—I sing for the gods and for men!
I am self-taught but a god planted song-craft
of every sort in me. I'm fit to sing to you
as to a god! Do not wish to cut my throat!
Telemakos, your own son, will tell you this.   350
I came not willingly to your house nor did
I crave to sing so often at their feasts.
Being many and stronger, they forced me there!"

So he spoke. God-protected Telemakos
heard him and said quickly to his father:

"Hold back lest you wound with bronze this faultless man!
And let us save Medon the herald who always cared
for me when I was a child in our house,
unless Philoitios or the swineherd has killed him,
or you met him when raging through the halls!"   360

So he spoke and wise Medon heard him.
Having fallen, he lay under a chair covered
with a bloody ox hide, escaping black death.
Crawling out quickly and discarding the ox hide,
he rushed to Telemakos and grasped his knees.
Pleading he said these winged words to him:

"My friend! I'm here! Stop your father! Tell him
so in his strength he won't hurt me with sharp bronze
while in wrath at the suitors who ate the wealth
of his house and then dishonored you!"   370

Artful Odysseus smiled and said:

"Take heart! He has protected you and saved you
so that your heart may know and may tell others
how far better good deeds are than bad deeds.
Go from the halls outside and sit in the courtyard
away from the slaughter, you and the song-filled bard,
so I might do the work inside that I must do."

So he spoke and the two left the hall,
and there they sat near the altar of great Zeus,
looking around them, still expecting their murder.   380

Odysseus looked around the hall to see
if any yet lived, hiding to avoid black death.
He saw that all of them had fallen in blood
and dust, all. When a fisherman has dragged his catch
from the curving shore of the gray sea

with his large-holed net, the fish long for the sea
as they lie there, poured out on the sandy shore
where the beating sun takes their lives away.
Just so the suitors lay one atop another.

At last Odysseus spoke to Telemakos: 390

"Telemakos, bid nurse Eurykleia come
that I may say these words I have in my mind."

So he spoke. Telemakos obeying him,
pounded on the door and said to nurse Eurykleia:

"Rise, come here ancient woman, you
who watch over the women slaves in our great house.
Come! My father wants you. He will tell you why."

So he spoke. His words lodged in her heart.
She unlocked the door of the great hall
and entered with Telemakos leading her.   400
She saw Odysseus among the slain bodies,
splattered with blood and gore. Just as a lion
coming from feeding on a field-dwelling ox,
its chest is bloody and warm blood on both
its cheeks, terrible to look upon, just so
Odysseus was bloody from feet to hands.
Seeing the bodies and the boundless blood,
she began a triumphant cry at the great deed.*
But then Odysseus stopped her, restrained
her cry, and spoke these winged words to her: 410

"Be glad in your heart, old woman, but hold your cry!
It's not right to boast over these slain men.
The gods' laws and their bad acts brought them down.
They honored not a man who walked the earth,
be he bad or noble. They honored none they met!

Their recklessness brought them this shameful death!
But come, tell me of the women in the palace,
who has dishonored me and who guiltless?"

Then Eurykleia the dear nurse replied to him:

"Well then I will tell you child, and truthfully.   420
There are fifty slaves in the halls, housemaids.
We taught them all how to do the housework,
to comb wool and to bear being a slave.
Of them all, twelve took the shameful path,
shaming me and even her, Penelope!
Telemakos is only recently grown up.
His mother would not let him rule the women slaves.
But come, let me go to the bright upper room
to tell your bedmate—some god put her to sleep."

Answering her artful Odysseus then said: 430

"Don't wake her yet! Go tell those twelve women
who plotted shamefully to come before me here!"

So he spoke. And she went straight to the women
telling what had happened, ordering them to come.
Bidding Telemakos, the oxherd and the swineherd
come to him, Odysseus spoke winged words:

"Start carrying out the dead. Have the women help.
Then have them scrub and clean the well-used tables
and chairs with water and porous sponges.
When the whole house has been set in order,   440
lead the twelve slaves out of our great hall,
put them between the round-house and the courtyard wall.
Kill them with your long swords until their life
is gone and they forget Aphrodite
who had them bed beneath the suitors in secret lust!"

So he spoke. The twelve came huddled together,
crying in dread, tears falling heavily.
First they carried the slain bodies out,
put them beneath the portico against the wall,
propping one against the other. Odysseus   450
gave the orders, kept them working—they had no choice.
They were made to wash the well-used tables
and chairs with water and porous sponges.
Telemakos, the oxherd and the swineherd
scraped the floor of the well-built house with shovels,
and the twelve slaves carried the scrapings out.
When the whole house had been set in order,
they led the twelve out of the well-built hall,
put them between the round-house and courtyard wall,
and shut them in so there was no way of escape.   460

Then wise Telemakos began addressing them:

"Let me not make the death of them a clean one!
They have long heaped on me and on my mother
their abusive words while they bedded the suitors!"

So he spoke. And from a dark-prowed ship they took
a rope, stretched it from a column and the round-house,
and tied it high so their feet would clear the ground.
Just as when long-winged thrushes or doves fly
into a hidden net set up in a thicket
where they seek a roost—they get a terrible sleep—   470
just so their heads were held all in a row,
noose about the neck to kill them horribly.
They struggled, their feet moving a little but not for long.*

Then out they led Melanthios to the courtyard.
They hacked his nose and ears off with pitiless bronze,
then tore his genitals off and fed them raw to dogs.
Raging in their hearts they lopped his hands and feet off.

Then, having washed their hands and feet, they went inside
to lord Odysseus, their work accomplished.

Odysseus then said to nurse, Eurykleia: 480

"Bring sulfur, old woman—the cure for evil—and
bring fire so I can cleanse the hall. And then bid come
Penelope, and with her, all her handmaidens.
And tell the other women throughout the house to come.

Then the old nurse Eurykleia answered him:

"All things you have spoken are correct, my child.
Come, let me dress you in clothes, tunic and cloak.
That's not the way to stand in the halls, your shoulders
covered in rags! That would be a great disgrace!"

Ingenious Odysseus then answered her: 490

"First let there be a fire in the hall."

So he spoke and she did not disobey.
She brought sulfur and fire. Odysseus
fumigated the hall, house and courtyard.
She went up through Odysseus' great house
telling what had happened, telling the women to come.
They came to the hall, torches in their hands.
They crowded round Odysseus and welcomed him
and kissed his head and shoulders with love, and held
his hands. A sweet longing for weeping and for tears 500
seized him, for he knew the hearts of them all.

BOOK TWENTY-THREE

The secret sign of the bed
Odysseus and Penelope reunite
Odysseus goes to Laertes' farm

The old woman hurried upstairs—glad she was
to tell her lady that her bedmate was in the house.
Her knees climbed quickly but her feet were unsteady.
Leaning over the bed, she spoke these words to her:

"Awake, Penelope! See with your own eyes
what you have so long been longing for! He's home!
Odysseus has come, though late in his coming!
He killed the proud suitors who were ruining his
palace and wealth, devouring his child's livelihood!"

Sensible Penelope then answered her: 10

"Good nurse, the gods have made you mad, for they can make
one witless, even one so sensible as you,
or lead the silly ones to walk towards wisdom.
The gods did this. You always were of sound mind.

When I have such sadness in my heart, why do
you mock me with a wild tale that wakes me
from the sweet sleep that bound me, enfolding my eyelids?
I have not slept thus since Odysseus
went to that ruinous, not-to-be named Ilios.
But now go back down to the hall again. 20
If any other of the women whom I have here
had come with this wild tale and awakened me,
quickly would I have sent her back to the hall
with a scolding! Thus your great age helps you now!"

The good nurse Eurykleia answered her:

"I don't mock you, my child! In truth Odysseus
has arrived at the palace as I told you!
He is the stranger whom all kept dishonoring.
Telemakos knew him before he came back here,
but he was sensible and hid his father's plan 30
to punish those reckless men for their violence!"

So she spoke. Her mistress rejoiced and, springing from
the bed, hugged the nurse, her eyes weeping hot tears.
Speaking, she said these winged words to her:

"Come now, good nurse, and tell me truly if
he's really come back home as you have said
and how, being alone, he lay his hands upon
the shameless suitors who always stay in a group."

The good nurse Eurykleia answered her:

"I didn't see and wasn't told but heard such groans 40
of the dying! We huddled in terror in a corner
of the storage room, held in by fitted doors
until your son Telemakos bid me come
to the hall. His father sent him to call me.

There I found Odysseus standing among
the bodies. They lay in heaps, one atop another,
covering the ground. Seeing him thus like
a gore-splattered lion would have warmed your heart!

They're all now in a heap near the courtyard gate.
He fumigated the great hall of the palace   50
and lit a fire. And he sent me to bid you come.
Follow me so your two hearts might have
some joy; you both have suffered many trials.
Now has come what you have so longed for!
He has come to his own hearth alive and found
you and your child in the palace! And on the suitors
who treated him badly he's had his full revenge!"

Then sensible Penelope answered her:

"Good nurse, do not rejoice over these men!
You know the great welcome he would have in this hall   60
from all, most from me and from the son I bore.
But these words that you speak are not true.
One of the gods killed these high-born men,
offended by their violence, their evil acts.
They honored not a man who walked the earth,
be he bad or noble. They honored none they met!
Their recklessness brought them down. Odysseus
lost his homecoming far away and lost his life."

The good nurse, Eurykleia, answered her:

"My child, such words escaped the fence of your teeth!   70
You say your bedmate will never come home though he
is here now at the hearth! Yet your heart trusts not!
But come, I'll tell you of another clear sign:
that scar that the white-tusked boar left him with!
I noticed it washing his feet and wished to tell

you then but he gripped my mouth with his hands
and in his mind's wisdom would not let me tell you.
Now follow me. I'll stake my own life on this.
If I deceive you, kill me with a horrible death!

Then sensible Penelope answered her: 80

"Good nurse, hard it is to know the ways
of the ever-living gods, wise though you be.
Nevertheless I will go to my child and see
the slain suitors and who it was who slew them."

So speaking, she left her upper room, her heart split
whether to hold back and question her bedmate,
or go near and kiss his head and hold his hands.
Thus she went in, crossing the stone threshold,
and sat by the far wall facing the man in the
firelight. Odysseus was sitting near a tall   90
column looking down, waiting to see if his
bedmate might speak when her eyes beheld him.
But she sat long in silence, awe seizing her heart.
At last she looked him in the face, but she
failed to know him with the rags he was wearing.

Telemakos rebuked her saying these words:

"My mother, my hard mother with a hard heart!
Why do you shrink back from my father in this way
not sitting by him, asking, learning from his words?
No other woman would stand thus apart from his   100
enduring heart! He's suffered many evil things
and come back after twenty years to his own land!
But your heart was always hard, as hard as stone!"

Then sensible Penelope answered him:

"My child, the heart in my breast is struck with awe.

I cannot speak a word nor ask anything,
nor look him in the face. If this is truly
Odysseus come home, we shall know each other
much better soon, for there are signs we have which we
alone know but are hidden from all others."   110

So she spoke. Noble Odysseus smiled
and said these winged words to Telemakos:

"Telemakos, let your mother test me
in the hall. Soon she will see more clearly.
I'm filthy and wear rags against my skin,
so she dishonors me and won't say I am he.
But we must think what's far the best to do.
Even he who kills but one man in a land,
though a man who had not many to support him,
he still will flee, leaving kin and town behind.   120
We slew all the best young men of Ithaka:
this is what I think you should consider well."

Then wise Telemakos replied, saying to him:

"You look to this, my father, for they say
you are the best at planning among men and no
other man upon the earth can challenge you.
We'll follow you eagerly! None will say
we lack in valor as long as our strength holds."

Answering him, artful Odysseus then said:

First, all bathe and put on clean tunics.   130
And have the maids in the hall put on clean clothes.
Then bring the godlike bard in with his clear-toned lyre
to lead us in a joyful dance, so any man
who hears might say there's a wedding here,
whether a stranger passing by or a local.

There must be no report in the town of the
suitors' slaughter until we are out of the town
and at the tree-filled farm. Once there we'll see
what plan of action the Olympian grants us."

So he spoke. They heard him clearly and obeyed.   140
First they bathed and put on clean tunics and made
the women do so. Then they brought the godlike bard
with his hollow lyre inside. He roused in them
longing for a sweet song and a fitting dance.
The lordly house resounded with the sound of feet,
men sporting like children, women's dresses flowing.
Someone outside the house, hearing the sounds, might say:

"Someone has wed the much-courted queen.
How cruel, not waiting for her wedded mate,
not keeping the lordly house until the lord comes back!"   150

So one might say not knowing what had really happened.

Meanwhile the housekeeper Eurynome washed him,
great-hearted Odysseus, and rubbed him with oil
and she dressed him in a fine cloak and tunic.
Athena then made him appear more handsome
and taller than he was, and stronger. And she put
his hair in curls like the flower, the hyacinth.
Just as a man pours gold on silver skillfully,
one taught by Hephaistos and Pallas Athena,
and with artful hands completes his wondrous work,   160
just so she poured grace on his head and shoulders.
Thus from his bath he strode like to the deathless ones.
Quickly he sat on that chair he'd arisen from
opposite his bedmate and said these words to her:

"Strange lady, those who live on Olympos gave you
a heart harder than that of all other women.

No other woman would stand apart from a man's
enduring heart who's suffered many evil things
and come back to his land after twenty years!
Come nurse, make me a bed that I might sleep   170
alone, for the heart in her breast is iron hard!"

Then sensible Penelope answered him:

"Strange man, I am not proud, nor do I mock you.
I'm not amazed. But I know well how you looked
when you left Ithaka in the long-oared ship.
But come Eurykleia, move the hand-made bedstead
outside my chamber, the one the master himself built.
There put out some bedding for the bedstead,
some fleeces and some cloaks and clean blankets."

So she spoke, testing her mate. Odysseus   180
burst out in anger at his trusty, knowing bedmate:

"Oh woman! The words you speak cut my heart!
Who could move that bed elsewhere? It would be hard
even for the best workman, unless helped by
a god who could move it outside with ease!
Though in his prime no living mortal man
could move it! With art a unique feature was built
into the bed. For I and none other built it!
An olive tree grew in the walled courtyard,
a full grown tree, its trunk as thick as a column.*   190
I built a room around it there with stones
close-fitted. I covered it well with a roof
and I added tight-fitting jointed doors.
Then I cut the branches from that olive tree.
With a bronze adz I smoothed the trunk from the root up,
well and skillfully, straight as a plumb line,
and drilled it with an auger. I had my bedpost!
With this beginning I built my bed, finishing it

with artful gold, silver and ivory inlays
and bright purple cords of ox leather.   200
Thus I show you a clear sign but I don't know
if the bed is yet tied to the earth, or if
it has been moved elsewhere, the olive tree felled."

So he spoke. Her knees loosened; her heart froze.
Odysseus knew well the earth-rooted sign!
Tears flooded down. She ran to him, threw her hands
about his neck, kissed his head and said:

"Do not be angry Odysseus since you
in other things are wisest among men. The gods
sent us sorrow. While young they kept joy from us,   210
and still they do as we near the edge of old age.
But do not be angry or hold it against me
that when I first saw you I did not greet you.
In my heart I was in constant fear of some
man coming to deceive me with his words,
for there are many with evil in their counsels.
Argive Helen Zeus' child would not have slept
with a foreigner in love and in his bed
if she had known the best Akaian sons would come,
destined to lead her back to her native land.   220
A goddess urged her to this shameless act
and that is when she knew the disastrous madness
of her deed. From that madness came all our pain!
Now that you have told the sure sign of our bed
that no other mortal has ever laid eyes on,
the sign you and I know—and one maid,
the one my father gave me when I came, Aktoris,
she who guarded the doors of our snug bedroom.
Now you have convinced my heart, hard though it is!"

So she spoke, rousing in him a longing to weep.   230

He cried holding his lovely, warm-hearted bedmate.
Just as those mariners rejoice seeing
land—their strong ship shattered by fierce winds
and strong waves, the crew scattered in the sea,
Poseidon's work, a few surviving and swimming
landward, their skin incrusted with brine—when they reach
dry land, dangers passed, those mariners rejoice!
Just so did she rejoice beholding her spouse,
nor could she unwrap her white arms from his neck!

While they wept, Dawn's pink fingers would have come   240
had bright-eyed Athena not had other plans.
She held back night, making it longer, held back
Dawn's golden-cart on Okeanos. Nor did she let
her yoke the horses to bring light to men, Lampos
and Phaethon, those foals who pull Dawn's chariot.

And then Odysseus said this to his bedmate:

"Woman, not yet have we come to the end of these
troubles, for there is much immense hard work ahead.
I must complete it all to bring this to an end.
The spirit of Teiresias foretold this to me   250
that day when I went down to Hades' house
seeking a return home for my men and myself.
But come, let's go to bed woman, so we two might
enjoy ourselves lulled into a most sweet sleep."

Then sensible Penelope answered him:

"Your bed awaits when your heart desires it,
because the gods brought this about, your return
to your well-built house and native land. But since
you say it and some god put it into your mind,
come, tell me the trouble. I think I'll learn of it   260
one day, so hearing now cannot be any worse."

Artful Odysseus then answered her:

"Strange lady! Why do you urge me to tell you?
Very well, I will tell you, hiding nothing.
Your heart will not be glad nor will I rejoice.
Teiresias bid me go through many towns
of mortals holding in my hands a balanced oar
till I should come where men know nothing
of the sea nor do they eat meat with salt.
They know nothing of ships with red prows   270
or well-balanced oars, the wings of ships.
He gave me a sure sign that I won't hide from you.
When I should meet another traveler who says
I have a winnowing fan on my strong shoulder,
there I am to bury the oar in the earth,
sacrifice pure animals to Lord Poseidon:
a ram, a bull, a sow-mounting boar.
Then once home, sacrifice a hecatomb
to the deathless gods who hold the wide sky,
to each in proper order. Then my death will come   280
far from the sea, ever so gentle, and it will bring
me down in hearty old age, my people prospering.
All these words he said will surely come to pass."

Then sensible Penelope answered him:

"If the gods should grant a happy old age,
there's hope that you'll escape from all your troubles."

Thus they spoke about these things. Meanwhile
Eurynome and the nurse lay the bed
with soft bedding by the light of burning lamps.
When they had finished making the bed comfortable,   290
the old woman went to her rooms to lie down.
Eurynome, the chambermaid, led their way
to bed, the torch in her hands a light for them.

She then went back to her own room. Odysseus
and Penelope rejoiced in their own bed.

Telemakos, the oxherd and the swineherd then
from dancing stilled their feet, the women's too,
and all went to their beds in the darkening palace.

After enjoying their exquisite lovemaking
they talked happily, telling everything: 300
she, how she had endured among her women,
looking at the throng of shameless suitors who ate
many oxen and fat sheep because of her,
and drank all day emptying many wine casks.
Zeus-born Odysseus, of the troubles he gave
his men, how he himself had suffered—he told
her everything and she listened rapt, and sleep
touched not her eyelids till she had heard his tale.

He began with the pillage of the Kikones,
then how they came to the Lotus Eaters'   310
tilled land. Then what the Cyclops did and how he paid
him back for his strong men eaten without pity.
Then how he came to Aiolos, how received
and how sent off, how fate did not let him come to
his land because a storm snatched him, carried him
on the deep-groaning fish-full sea until they came
to Laistrygonian Telepylos,
where his ships and companions were all destroyed.
Of the black ships, Odysseus' alone escaped.
Then he told of Kirke's wiles and tricks,   320
and how he came to the dank home of Hades
in his well-benched ship, to Teiresias' spirit,
that golden Theban, and how he saw all his men,
his mother, she who bore him and reared him.
And how he heard the Sirens lovely song. How he

came to the woeful Wanderer Rocks, then of Skylla
and Karybdis, from whom none had ever escaped.
How his remaining men ate the Sun-god's oxen.
How high-thundering Zeus sent a smoking bolt,
shattering his ship, killing all his noble men   330
while he alone escaped that dark fate.
How he came to the nymph Kalypso's island,
Ogygia. She kept him there—though he pined for
his spouse—in hollow caves, caring for him and said
she'd make him deathless and ageless all his days.
But she did not convince the heart within his breast.
After much grief, he reached the Phaiakians,
who honored him as if a god, and they
carried him back in their ship to his own land
and gave him piles of bronze and of gold.   340
As soon as he had said these words, sweet sleep—
limb loosening—poured down, freeing his anxious heart.

But bright-eyed Athena was making new plans.
When she thought brave Odysseus had in his heart
enjoyed his bed, bedmate and sleep enough,
she urged from Okeanos golden-throned Dawn
to bring light to mortals. Odysseus arose
from the soft bed saying this to his bedmate:

"Woman, we have had our fill of too much strife,
both of us, you wailing over my return   350
while Zeus and the other gods sent me pain
and held me back from the earth of my forefathers.
But now we've both come to our own beloved bed.
You look after the wealth yet within this palace,
I the flocks those arrogant suitors consumed.
Some I'll get from raiding and the Akaians
will give me others till my folds are full again.
Now I am going to my well-forested farm

to see my noble father who grieves for me.
But you, careful as always, watch things here,   360
for word is going about with the rising sun
of those men, the suitors I killed in the palace.
Go up to your rooms with your handmaids now
and sit there. See no one and ask nothing."

He then slung armor over his shoulder and stirred
Telemakos, the swineherd and the oxherd,
telling them to take up their battle weapons.
They did not disobey and armed themselves with bronze.
Odysseus leading, they opened the gates and left.
Though light was on the land, Athena cloaked them   370
in darkness, leading them swiftly from the town.

BOOK TWENTY-FOUR

The souls of the suitors in the underworld
The final battle with the suitors' families
Athena imposes peace

Kyllenian Hermes summoned the souls of *
the suitors with the lustrous golden staff
in his hand. With this at will he charmed
the eyes of men to sleep or woke those entranced.
The souls came shrieking and followed him.
Just as in the recesses of a huge cavern
bats shriek, flying about when one falls from
their chain where they all hold each other up,
just so the shrieking souls followed the healing god
Hermes who led them down that moldering path.   10
They went past river Okeanos and the White Rock,
on past the gates of Helios, past the land
of dreams, until they reached the fields of asphodels
where stay the souls, those shapes of worn out men.

They found the souls of Akilleus, Peleus' son,
and Patroklos and brave Antilokos,

and Aias, being the best in form and shape
of the Danaans after lord Akilleus.

These stood with Akilleus. Then the soul
of Agamemnon, Atreus' son, approached, lamenting.   20
Around him gathered other souls, those who had died
and met their fate in the house of Aigisthos.*

Akilleus' spirit was first to speak to him:

"Atreus' son, we deemed you of all the heroes
to be dear to thunder-loving Zeus all
your days because you ruled many strong men in the
land of Troy where we Akaians suffered much.
But it was your fate to meet untimely death.
No man born will escape that ending.
Would that you had delighted in honor   30
as lord and died at Troy, meeting your fate there!
Then all Akaians would have heaped a mound for you
and you'd have won great fame hereafter for your child.
But now you have met a terrible death!"

The soul of Atreus' son spoke to him:

"Happy Peleus' son, godlike Akilleus!
You died at Troy far from Argos. The best sons
of Trojans and Akaians died around you,
fighting over you. You lay in swirling dust,
in death still strong as you were strong in life, horse skill   40
forgotten. We fought all day nor would we have stopped
the fight if Zeus had not stopped it with a storm.
Then we bore you from the battle to the ships
and laid you on a bier, washed your lovely skin
with water and warm oil. For you the Danaans
wept many hot tears and cut their flowing hair.
Your mother when she heard came from the salt sea

with her sea nymphs. A god-grief cry sounded over
the sea and all the Akaians began to tremble.
And then they would have run to the ships to flee   50
had a man who knew many ancient things
not stopped them—Nestor—who always gave the best counsel.

Nestor spoke, addressing them with kindly words:

'Restrain yourselves, Argives! Flee not, Akaian youths!
His mother has come from the sea with her deathless
sea nymphs to be with her child who has been killed!'

So he spoke. The noble Akaians ceased fleeing.
These daughters of the Old Man of the Sea wept
for you and wrapped you in immortal robes.
All nine Muses sang the antiphonal dirge with sweet   60
voices. No Argive would you have seen tearless,
such did the clear-voiced Muses move them all.
Likewise for fully seventeen nights and days
we wept for you, both deathless gods and mortal men.
On the eighteenth day we gave you up to fire
and slew many goats and curved-horn oxen.
You burned in robes from the gods, with much oil
and sweet honey. Many Akaian heroes danced
ritually in armor around the burning pyre,
on foot and on horseback. A huge din arose.   70
When Hephaistos' flames had finished you,
at dawn we laid your white bones, Akilleus,
in unmixed wine and unguents. Your mother gave
a two-handled golden jar; she said it was
a gift from Dionysos, the work of Hephaistos.
In it lie your own white bones mixed with
Menoitios' son, dead Patroklos.
Apart lay Antilokos' bones, whom you esteemed
above all other men after dead Patroklos.

And over the bones we heaped up a huge mound,   80
we, the sacred host of Argive warriors, on
a cliff projecting toward the wide Hellespont,
easy to see for men traveling on the sea,
both for those now living and those to come.

Begging the gods for wondrous prizes, your mother placed
them before the gathering of the best Akaians.
You've seen the funerals of many heroes and
how at a king's death the young prepare
themselves for sport in order to win the prizes.
But seeing those prizes you would have been amazed at heart.   90
For you the goddess silver-footed Thetis offered
most wondrous prizes! You were dear to the gods!
Though dead you've not lost your name. All men
will know forever your noble fame, Akilleus!
For me, what joy remained when that war wound down?
On my return Zeus planned for me a vile death
by the hands of Aigisthos and my cruel bedmate."

So they spoke of things to each other until
the messenger Argos-slayer came near leading
the suitors' souls, those slain by brave Odysseus.   100
The two, amazed at seeing them, approached. The soul
of Atreus' son Agamemnon perceived
famous Amphimedon, Melaneos' child,
who lived in Ithaka and who had been his host.

Agamemnon's spirit addressed him first:

"Amphimedon, what happened that you sink in the
dark earth, all chosen men of like age? No one
could choose better men from the town.
But did Poseidon overwhelm your ship,
stirring up his howling winds and giant waves?   110
Or did men do you harm on dry land while you

were raiding their oxen and flocks of sheep?
Or fighting round their town for their women?
So tell me this. I beg you as a guest-friend.
Or do you not remember when I came there
to your house with godlike Menelaos to urge
Odysseus to follow our ships to Troy?
One full month we sailed crossing the wide seas
to win over city-sacking Odysseus."

The soul of Amphimedon answered him: 120

"Atreus' son, most honored Agamemnon,
lord of men, I well remember these things you speak of.
So I will tell you all, and truly, how it was
brought about, our end in death, a bad one.
We were courting long-absent Odysseus' spouse.
She neither refused marriage nor made it happen
while she planned death for us, a black fate.
She had planned some tricks for us such as this:
she stood in front of a large loom in her chambers
weaving with long threads and said these words to us: 130

'My young suitors, since Odysseus is dead,
wait and do not press marriage on me until
I weave this cloth, lest my weaving be lost.
It is a shroud for hero Laertes when he
should meet his dark fate, lying in woe.
I would not have any Akaian women rebuke me
if he, with such wealth, should have no shroud.'

So she spoke; our brave hearts were convinced.
By day she kept weaving at the great loom.
Nights, with torches near, she unwove the thread.   140
For three years this trick convinced the Akaians.
But as the hours passed, the fourth year arrived,
moon after moon waned, the days marched on,

then one of her women spoke out and plainly.
So we surprised her undoing the fine loom work.
Thus, she had to finish though not wanting to.

Once finished, she washed and showed the cloth woven on
the great loom. It was bright like the sun or moon.
Then a bad spirit led Odysseus from the
far edge of his land where his swineherd dwelled.   150
And the son of godlike brave Odysseus
came back in a black ship from sandy Pylos.
The two planned the dark death of the suitors.
Telemakos came first to the famous town
and then Odysseus came as well.
The swineherd brought him dressed as a poor beggar,
foul rags against his skin. He seemed an old man
leaning on a staff. His rags were tattered looking.
When he so suddenly appeared none of us
knew who he was, not even the oldest of us.   160
We cursed him with bad words and threw things at him.
Though in his own palace, he endured it long:
the things we threw, the words vile to his heart.
But when the mind of aigis-bearing Zeus roused him,
he, with Telemakos, took the well-made weapons
and put them in a storeroom, barring the door.
With great craft he bid his bedmate put
his bow before the suitors and the gray iron,
our doom—the contest and slaughter were beginning.
Not one of us could stretch taut the bowstring   170
of that strong bow, falling far short of it.
When that great bow came to Odysseus' hands,
we all called out together not to give the bow
to him whatever he might say to us,
but Telemakos urged him to take it up.

Godlike Odysseus took it in his hands.

His might strung it with ease. He shot straight through
the irons, walked to the threshold and poured the arrows out.
With a fierce look he loosed at prince Antinoös.
Then he loosed the terrible arrows at others.   180
With his strong sure aim they dropped dead in heaps.
Then it was clear some god was helping him.
Wielding their might, turning this way and that,
they slew us throughout the halls, with horrible groans
from heads falling, all the floor flowing with blood.
Thus Agamemnon, we died and now our bodies
still lie uncared for in Odysseus' halls.
Our kin in our own houses know nothing of this.
There is no one to wash the black gore from our wounds
and weeping, to lay us out, the last honor of death."   190

The spirit of Atreus' son answered him:

"Happy child of Laertes, most artful
Odysseus who won an excellent bedmate,
right-thinking, sensible Penelope,
Ikarios' maid. She held to her wedded
man Odysseus! The fame of her virtue
will never die! The gods will make a song on earth
of graceful, sensible Penelope! Not so
Tyndareos' maid who planned such wicked acts,*
slaying her wedded bedmate! Hated will be that song   200
among men! Harsh the infamy following
all womankind, even those acting rightly!"

So they spoke of these things while standing
in Hades' house in the depths of the earth.

Meanwhile, Odysseus and the three left town *
and went to the well-tilled farm made by Laertes.
He had cleared the land himself through hard work.
His house was there, surrounded by outbuildings

in which would sit and eat and sleep the slaves
he owned who did all the heavy farm work.   210
There was an old Sikel woman who looked after *
the old man on that far distant farm.

Odysseus then said to his son and herdsmen:

"You all should go now into the well-built house
and sacrifice one of the best hogs for your meal.
As for me I'm going to test our father to see
if he observes and knows me with his eyes, or if
he fails to know me since so much time has passed."

So speaking, he gave his fighting gear to the slaves.
They quickly entered the house. But lord Odysseus   220
went toward the fruit-rich orchard to make his test.
Among the trees he did not find Dolios
nor his sons or other slaves. They had gone
to gather stones to repair the orchard walls
and they were being led by old Dolios. *
He found his father all alone in the orchard,
digging round a plant, dressed in badly-sewn
dirty clothes. Patched leather leggings wrapped
around his calves to help prevent scratches.
He wore gloves on his hands because of thorns and on   230
his head a goatskin cap. These clothes helped feed his grief.

Long-suffering Odysseus saw him worn out
with age. His heart felt a great pain as he stood there
under a tall pear tree, his tears welling out.
He pondered then in his mind and heart whether
to kiss and hug his father, tell him everything,
his wanderings and return to his own land,
or if to ask about things first, thus testing him.
It seemed to him that it would be better if he
should begin to test him first with bantering words.   240

With this in mind, noble Odysseus went straight
to his father whose head was bent down hoeing.

Standing near, his shining son said this to him:

"Old man, you don't lack skill in tending an orchard.
All is well cared for. There is nothing, not
a plant, not a fig tree, grapevine or olive tree,
not a pear or plant bed that lacks your care!
But I'll tell you—don't hold anger in your heart—
you yourself are not well cared for. You are in
a squalid old age dressed in shameful rags.   250

Clearly it's not through sloth that your lord does not
take care of you. Nor do you seem to be a slave.
By your form and size you are more like a king.
You seem like one who should wash and eat,
and sleep in a soft bed. It's what is due old age.
But come tell me, and please tell me truly.
What man's slave are you? Whose orchard do you tend?
And tell me truly this so that I may know well.
Have I really come to Ithaka? That man
over there I met as I came here says so.   260
He was not sharp of mind and did not wait
to listen to me. I wanted to know about
a guest I'd had, whether he lives still somewhere
or has died and gone to the house of Hades.
I will tell you and you mark it and listen.
He was a guest once in my own land when
he came and never was a man from far lands
as dear to me as he was in my home.
He claimed to be Ithakan and said
Arkeisios' son Laertes was his father.   270

I brought him to my house, received him well,
with true friendship and of the wealth in my house

I gave him many gifts, those due a guest.
I gave him seven talents of well-wrought gold,
a mixing bowl all of silver adorned with flowers,
twelve light cloaks, as many blankets and
as many bolts of cloth, and as many tunics,
and more: four fair women, all hard working
and well-skilled. He picked them out himself."

Then his father, tears falling, answered him: 280

"Stranger, you have indeed come to that land you asked
about, but arrogant, wanton men hold it.
Those many gifts you spoke of were in vain.
If you had found him still alive in Ithaka,
he would have sent you home with gifts in kind,
received you well as is right, as good hosts do.
But come now, tell me this, and tell me truly.
How many years has it been since you received
that wretched man, my ill-fated son—if
ever he lived. Far from his friends and native earth   290
the fishes fattened on him. Or on dry land he was
the spoils for beasts and birds of prey. His mother
could not wrap his shroud and weep, nor his father.
We gave him birth. Nor did his bedmate, wooed with gifts,
Penelope, wail over the bier of her mate,
closing his eyes in death, the due of the dead.
Now tell me this and tell me truly so I might know.
Who are you among men? From what town
and parents? Where did you moor your swift ship?
And where are your godlike crewmen? Or did   300
a ship sailing onwards leave you here?"

Ingenious Odysseus answered him:

"So I will tell you all and tell it truly.
I'm from Alybas where I dwell in a fine house,

son of Apheidas, lord Polypemon's son.*
My name is Eperitos. A god drove me here *
from Sikania. I came not wishing to.
My ship stands off the farmland away from the town.
As for Odysseus it's five years now since he
left there, departing from my fatherland.   310
Ill-fated! But bird signs were good, on the right
as he went. I rejoiced at the good omens.
He left happy. In our hearts we hoped to share
again in guest meetings exchanging goodly gifts."

So he spoke. A cloud of grief shrouded Laertes.
With both hands he scooped black dirt up and poured it
over his gray head, groaning ceaselessly.
This stirred Odysseus' heart and a sharp pain
welled up through his nose seeing his father thus.
Springing on him he kissed him all over and said: 320

"I am that man, the one you ask about, father.
After twenty years I have indeed come home.
But hold back now your weeping, the groans and tears,
I'll tell you all, but we must hurry now!
I have killed the suitors in our palace, punished
their heart-wrenching outrages and evil acts."

Laertes answered then and said to him:

"If you're my son Odysseus home at last,
convince me now by giving me a clear sign."

Ingenious Odysseus answered him: 330

"First then this scar, examine it with your eyes.*
A boar's white tusk charged into me while I
was in Parnassos. You and mother sent me there
to my mother's father Autolykos so I

once there might have the gifts he promised me.
Let me tell you of the trees in your orchard
that you gave me. As a child I asked about
each tree, trailing you as we went through the orchard.
You named them, telling me what each one was.
You gave me thirteen pear trees, ten apple trees,   340
and forty fig. You named fifty rows of grapes
ripening at different times that you would give me.
All had grape clusters at different stages
as the seasons of Zeus fell down upon them."

So he spoke. The old man's knees loosened, his heart
froze, knowing these signs Odysseus gave him.
He threw his arms around his son and then noble,
enduring Odysseus held him as he fainted.
When he'd come to his senses and his spirit rallied,
then he answered his own son, saying these words: 350

"Oh Zeus! The gods yet live on high Olympos if
it's true the suitors have paid for their violence!
But I fear in my heart that now all men
of Ithaka will attack us and send out
messages to all Kephallenian towns!"*

Ingenious Odysseus answered him:

"Take heart! Do not let these things worry you!
Let us go quickly to your house near the orchard
where I sent Telemakos, the swineherd and
the oxherd to make a quick meal for us."   360

So speaking, the two went toward the well-built house.
When they arrived at that comfortable dwelling,
they found Telemakos, the swineherd and the oxherd
carving slabs of pork and mixing the red wine.

As soon as great-hearted Laertes entered his house,
his maid, the Sikelan, bathed him and rubbed in oil
and threw a fine cloak on him. But Athena
stood near and she strengthened the old man's limbs
and made him taller and stronger to look upon.
As he came from his bath his own son was in awe,   370
seeing him as if a deathless god were there.

He spoke these winged words to his father:

"Father, one of the ever-living gods has made
you seem both bigger and better to look upon!"

Then wise Laertes answered him saying:

"By Zeus, Athena and Apollo! If only
I were as when I led the Kephallenians!
I captured well-built Nerikos, the mainland town!
Then I would have donned armor on my shoulders
yesterday in our house to stand and fight   380
those suitors! I'd have loosed the knees of many
in the halls and made the heart within you glad!"

So they spoke to each other about these things.
Having prepared the meal the others ceased their work
and sat down in order on chairs and couches.
All were about to set hands to the meal when the
old man Dolios, worn out from fieldwork, approached
with his sons. Their mother had summoned them,
the old Sikelan woman who kindly fed and cared
for Laertes once age had overtaken him.   390
They were amazed seeing Odysseus!
They stood there in the hallway marveling!

Odysseus then said these soothing words to them:

"Old man, sit down. Eat and forget your surprise.

Though eager, we have been waiting awhile for you
in the house, ever ready for you to join us."

So he spoke. But Dolios with arms outstretched
went straight to him and took his hand and kissed his wrist.

Then he said these winged words to him:

"Master, you have come back! We longed for this   400
but long ago stopped hoping! The gods themselves led you!
Most welcome home! May the gods give you happiness!
Now tell me this truly that I might know.
Does sensible Penelope know clearly
that you have come back or should we send a message?"

Artful Odysseus then answered him:

"Old man, she knows. Don't worry about this."

So he spoke. And Dolios sat down then.
His sons welcomed and greeted famous Odysseus,
speaking to him and taking his hand in theirs.   410
Then they sat down near their father Dolios.
Thus they went about their meal in the house.

But rumor, the messenger, sped quickly through the town
speaking of the suitors' moans, their deaths and fate.
From this way and that people gathered with moans
and groans before the house of brave Odysseus.
They carried the bodies out, performing the last rites.
They sent those from another town each to his home.
The rest they gave to sailors in swift ships.
Sore at heart they went to the assembly ground.   420
When they had assembled and come together,
Eupeithes then stood up and addressed them.
Unceasing grief for his son lay on his heart,
Antinoös, the first Odysseus had killed.

With tears falling he thus addressed them saying:

"Friends, this man did us a most terrible deed.
Some, many and noble, he led out in his ships.
He lost those hollow ships and lost those good men!
Returning, he killed the best Kephallenians!
But go quickly before he leaves for Pylos   430
or to Elis where the Epeians rule.
Let us go now or else we will be shamed forever!
For this outrage will carry into the future
if we do not avenge the murder of our sons
and brothers! For me to live would lose it sweetness!
I would rather die and dwell among the dead!
But come or they will flee now, escaping across the sea!"

Thus he spoke and pity seized the Akaians.
But freed from sleep, Medon and the godlike bard
left the halls of brave Odysseus and approached   440
and stood in the middle. Wonder seized each man.

Then wise Medon addressed all with these words:

"Hear me now, Ithakans! Odysseus
did not do this deed against the will of the gods!
I myself saw an immortal god who took
the form of Mentor stand next to brave Odysseus.
The deathless god was seen now with Odysseus
urging him on, now darting through the hall
panicking the suitors. And they fell in heaps."

So he spoke and all were turning green with fear.   450
To them spoke old hero Halitherses, the son
of Mastor: he who saw both in front and what's behind.*
He then addressed them with kind words, saying:

"Listen now, Ithakans, to what I say:

your wickedness brought these bad deeds about!
You listened not to me nor Mentor, the shepherd
of the people, to stop your children's folly!
Their 'great deed' was one of wanton wickedness,
devouring the wealth, dishonoring the bedmate
of a great lord. They said he would never come home!   460
So now let it be thus! Hear what I have to say!
Go not or you will bring evil on yourselves!"

So he spoke. Some stayed where they were, but more
than half sprang up with a loud battle cry.
The seer's words had not convinced them. They listened to
Eupeithes and quickly went for their weapons.
Once they had prepared themselves with flashing bronze,
they gathered in a crowd before the spacious town.
Eupeithes took command of them in their folly.
He thought he would avenge his son's murder, but he   470
would not return. He would meet his own dark fate.

Athena then spoke to Zeus, son of Kronos:

"Our father Kronos' son, highest lord,
I'm asking you to tell me what thought you have
in mind? More war and dread battle cries?
Or will you bring to pass a pact between them?"

Cloud-gatherer Zeus answered her saying:

"My child, why do you ask and question so?
Did you not plan all of this in your mind
so that Odysseus once home might kill them all?   480
Do what you wish but I will tell you what is right.
Odysseus has made the suitors pay the price.
Have them swear an oath to let him rule forever
while we make them forget the slaying of their sons
and brothers. They shall live in harmony

as they used to, prosperous and in peace."

So he spoke and urged on Athena who longed
for this. She sped down from the heights of Olympos.

Meanwhile having sated their love of good food,
artful Odysseus began to speak to them: 490

"One of you see if they are coming near."

So he spoke. A son of Dolios went to
the threshold. From there he saw them coming near.
He called out to Odysseus these winged words:

"They're almost here! Let us arm ourselves at once!"

So he spoke. Jumping up, they armed themselves:
Odysseus with his three men, the six sons of
Dolios, who donned his armor with Laertes:
gray though they were, warriors by necessity.
Once they had prepared themselves with flashing bronze,   500
they went out with Odysseus leading.

Zeus's child Athena then came near them.
She appeared like Mentor in shape and voice.
Seeing her, noble Odysseus rejoiced
and said this to his son Telemakos:

"Telemakos, here you will be tested in
the fighting of men where the best shall win.
Let there be no shame on the tribe of our fathers
who excel all on the earth in strength and valor."

Then wise Telemakos answered him: 510

"Father mine, you shall see that I have
the spirit not to shame our tribe, as you put it."

So he spoke and Laertes rejoiced and said:

"Great gods! What a day for me! I'm rejoicing!
My son and grandson vie for battle honor!"

Then bright-eyed Athena stood near him and said:

"Arkeisios' son, my friend among all men,
pray to the bright-eyed child and father Zeus,
then whirl back and let fly your ashwood spear."

So speaking, Athena breathed great strength into him   520
while he was praying to the child of mighty Zeus.
Quickly then he hurled his long ashwood spear
and it struck Eupeithes on his bronze cheek plate
which did not stop the spear which went straight into him.
With a thud he fell, rattling his bronze armor.

Odysseus and his son fought those in front,
striking with swords and spears sharp at both ends.
They would have killed them all, no homecoming for them,
had not aigis-bearing Zeus's child Athena
cried out in her own voice, stopping the fighters:*   530

"Cease now this horrible fighting, you Ithakans!
Move apart! Let there be no more bloodshed!"

So spoke Athena. Green fear seized them all.
From fear their weapons fell from their hands and they
dropped to the ground when the goddess shouted out.
Fearing for their lives they turned to run townward.

Suddenly Odysseus cried out. Crouching,
he swooped on them like an eagle from the sky.
But Zeus hurled his smoking thunderbolt
that fell in front of his own bright-eyed child.   540
And so Athena called out to brave Odysseus:

"Zeus-born Laertes' son, artful Odysseus!
Cease! Stop now this strife so like a war
or you will anger Kronos' son who sees all!"

So spoke Athena. He heard, his heart rejoicing.
Then she, Pallas Athena, child of Zeus,
bound both groups with an oath forever forward
and she was like to Mentor both in shape and voice.

Endnotes

Italicized quotations are excerpts from this translation.
All other quotations are from authors cited in the endnotes.

BOOK 1

25   In ancient Greece a hecatomb was a sacrifice to the gods of 100 cattle. In practice as few as 12 cattle could make up a hecatomb.

36   Atreus' son's is Agamemnon, king of kings of the Greeks in the Trojan war and brother of Menelaos. His wife is Klytaimnestra.

90   Akaians are the Greeks or Greek speakers, used interchangeably with Danaans and Argives.

111 "The common Odyssean formula ... seems to imply some kind of folding table, a type known from Hittite monuments, though no Greek example has been found." (Heubeck, West, and Hainsworth 1988)

138 The maid poured water over their hands and the basin collected the water.

173 *"I do not imagine that you came here on foot"* is an islander's joke repeated a number of times in the Odyssey.

188 Guests or strangers, they went through the rites hosting each other.

240 The bodies of the heroes were burned in pyres and a mound was heaped up to remember them.

283 *"Zeus' rumors"* means "[a] rumour of which the origin cannot be traced." (Heubeck, West, and Hainsworth 1988)

291 *"His best loved goods"* means roughly to perform the funeral rites. In the memorial mound would be placed all the things he loved best as a memory or to help him on his journey.

327 The lesser Aias tried to rape Kassandra in Athena's temple. Her anger was caused by the Akaians' lack of punishing him for this act. (Adapted from Heubeck, West, and Hainsworth 1988)

380 Compensation could be given to a family for a killing; here the suitors may be killed but their families would have no compensation—or so Telemakos wishes. (Adapted from Stanford 1996a)

440 *"Slatted bed"* is a bed where the sides and end are perforated or corded, presumably to let air circulate under the bed.

442 I use rod for crow's beak. "The bolt was inside, with a strap fastened to the end, which passed through a hole to the outside; pull the strap and the bolt runs home inside. The door-handle is the crow's-beak; the islanders still use the term crow (koraki) for a drop catch at the top of a casement window." (Rouse 1937)

BOOK 2

18 The story of the Cyclops is related beginning at Bk 9:106.

23 His son is lost in the same sense that Odysseus is, that is, he has been away twenty years and has not returned.

64 Note that Telemakos is speaking to the entire adult male population, not just the suitors, and the you he appeals to is the entire adult male population.

66 Here he "appeals to the three main constraints on conduct in the Heroic Age 'nemesis' (a sense of fair play and indignation at unfairness ...), 'aidos' (a sense of shame at wrong-doing or disgrace), and the fear of the gods." (Stanford 1996a)

68 Themis, Law or Laws, the received body of normal ways of just interactions among men. Themis called and ended assemblies. (Adapted from Stanford 1996a)

154 Toward the right (as if facing north) is the eastern side, the side of good fortune. (Adapted from Stanford 1996a)

300 The goats half-flayed or skin partially loosened as part of the cooking process, the hogs singed to remove the bristles. (Adapted from Heubeck, West, and Hainsworth 1988)

362 There are many uses of the phrase *"winged words"* in the Odyssey and little consensus on what this actually means; I choose to leave the words and let the reader apply the meaning.

409 *"God-protected"* is how I translated the Greek "sacred strength" here. It is thought to be an archaic formula perhaps from Mycenaean times referring to the divine status of kings and has symbolic meaning much like "His Royal Highness." When used about Telemakos I use *"god-protected"* since Athena is protecting him (seven times), about King Alkinoös (six times) I use *"mighty,"* and of Antinoös I use *"princely"* (one time). (Adapted from Heubeck, West, and Hainsworth 1988)

BOOK 3

6 Earth-shaker is an epithet of the god Poseidon.

42 Aigis-bearing Zeus' maiden is Athena; the aigis is the storm shield Zeus carries; aigis-bearing is also an epithet of Zeus.

68 The Gerenian horseman, from Gerenios, "a town in Messina, to which Nestor is said to have fled when Herakles was ransacking Pylos." (Stanford 1996a)

73 In Homeric times piracy was no more dishonorable than trading. Odysseus himself was a pirate when he sacked the Kikones' town (Bk 9:39). (Adapted from Stanford 1996a)

134 Zeus' maiden is Athena.

167 Tydeus' son is Diomedes.

177 Geraistos is the southern most point of Euboia.

280 *"With gentle arrows slew"* means death from disease or unknown causes; Apollo slew the men, his sister Artemis the women. (Adapted from Stanford 1996a)

332 The sacrificial tongues are from the bulls killed earlier.

378 Tritogeneia or Trito-born is an epithet only of Athena, but the significance is not known.

382 The cow is an ox cow.

420 Disguised as Mentor, Athena came to Poseidon's feast the day before.

441 The sprinkling of barley grains was part of the ritual for sacrifices. (Adapted from Stanford 1996a)

465 It was the custom for the youngest daughter of the house to bathe the guest. (Adapted from Stanford 1996a)

BOOK 4

4 Hermione is the name of Menelaos' daughter. His son Megapenthes was born of a slave mother because the gods would not permit Helen to bear another child after Hermione (see Bk 4:11–14).

5 Akilleus' son was Neoptolemos who now ruled the Myrmidons.

24 *"The people's shepherd"* is a standard epithet applied to kings, here to Menelaos.

66 The ox chines, the pieces alongside the spine, were considered best; thus to be given the chine was an honor.

91 The man is Aigisthos and Menelaos' brother is Agamemnon.

184 Zeus in the guise of a swan raped Leda and fathered on her twin girls, Klytaimnestra and Helen.

188 The son of Eos, Dawn, is Memnon. The ghost of Antilokos appears in Bk 11:468.

261 The madness sent by Aphrodite is "ate ... blindness of the mind sent by the gods, a divine perversion or deception of the mind leading to evildoing or mischance." (Cunliffe 1963)

276 After Alexander was killed, Helen wed Trojan Deïphobos.

349 The Old Man of the Sea is Proteos here.

369 Fishing and eating fish were uncommon among Homeric heroes. They preferred roasted meat, perhaps following the cattle-raising history of their ancestors.

526 A talent weighed 57.75 pounds or 26 kilograms, the amount equal to the mass of water needed to fill an amphora.

718   "To sit on the ground was a conventional posture of grief."
(Stanford 1996a)

802   The only opening seems to be where a bolt is thrown with a
leather thong to lock the door, presumably equivalent to going
through a keyhole.

BOOK 5

73   The word translated as parsley is thought to mean water-parsley
or smallage (*Apium graveolens*), a plant cultivated since antiquity
and thought to be the wild ancestor of the plant the we now eat
as celery. (Adapted from Stanford 1996a)

93   Ambrosia and nectar are the traditional food of the gods.

109   "This is the only passage where Homer specifically says that the
return of Odysseus was hampered by the wrath of his divine
supporter, Athena." (Jones 2004)

110   *"All his men perished, he alone survived"* does not agree with the
story that Odysseus tells the Phaiakians in Books 9 to 12.

127   The word thrice-plowed "... perhaps refers to a ritual ploughing
of three furrows to mark the opening of the ploughing season."
(Stanford 1996a)

275   *"She alone does not bathe in Okeanos."* That is, the constellation
is always in the sky, never sinking below the horizon into the
ocean. These are the constellations of the Pleiades, the seven
sisters and Boötes, the Plowman.

309   Peleus' son is Akilleus; when he was killed, Odysseus fought to
preserve Akilleus' armor and he himself was almost killed—but
at least that death would have been a glorious one.

346   This shawl, veil, headdress, or mantilla is not much as a life pre-
server but it is immortal, so perhaps a floating version of the
fabled flying carpet.

BOOK 6

10   The task order for new colonies: build the walls first, then the hous-
es, then temples and allot the land. (Adapted from Sanford 1996a)

17 The gods were considered to be taller and more beautiful or handsome than mortals.

137 The Greek word for mingle often has sexual undertones. Odysseus mingled with Kalypso in her caves (see Bk 5:226–227).

143 Wrapping the arms around or approaching the knees of a person was how one came to beseech another.

209 An important role of Zeus was that of the god of guests and beggars.

BOOK 7

59 "The Giants are only mentioned by [Homer] here, in [line] 206 below and [Bk] 10:120. It is uncertain whether [Homer] knew the legend or their unsuccessful battle against the gods, as described in Hesiod's *Theogony*. But perhaps there is an allusion to it in [line] 60." (Stanford 1996a)

62 Nausithoös fathered Rhexenor and Alkinoös. Rhexenor fathered Arete, so Alkinoös married his niece. Apollo slew Rhexenor with his arrows which usually means death from disease.

137 Hermes is the keeper of dreams.

167 See note on Bk 2:409.

183 The ritual drops for the libation are the first to be poured out.

197 "... [O]ne's destiny is spun at the moment of birth ... in Homer, and is no way different from that dispensed by 'fate'." (Jones 2004)

BOOK 8

75 "Nowhere else in Greek literature is there a story of a quarrel between Achilleus and Odysseus." (Jones 2004)

80 Pytho is an old name for the oracle at Delphi. (Stanford 1996a)

164 "The typically aristocratic and Greek scorn of the man who earns his living by trade ... the travelling merchant." (Stanford 1996a)

269 See note on Bk 6:137.

285 "The equipment is golden because it is divine." (Heubeck, West, and Hainsworth 1988)

476   *"Who had just cut from the white-tusked pig's back a piece of meat that had rich oil around it,"* that is, Odysseus gives the bard the chine, a favored cut.

BOOK 9

202   For the worth of a talent, see note on Bk 4:526.

266   See note on Bk 6:143.

483   This line is the same as line 540. "The line is absurd here: a stone falling in front of the ship would not nearly touch the steering oar" which is at the back of the ship. (Stanford 1996a)

BOOK 10

136   Gods had special, non-human voices.

179   "They had covered their faces as a sign of sorrow." (Stanford 1996a)

235   "This alarming mixture is offered with an onion at *Iliad* Bk 11:629–40, where it acts as a restorative to Nestor and Machaon. There is no such place as 'Pramnos' known to us, though it is assumed the name originally indicated origin. Prehistoric man seems to have been keen on mixtures of alcohol and grain. So are the Scots: Atholl Brose is a mixture of whisky, cream, honey and oatmeal." (Jones 2004)

238   On Kirke's rod or staff: "it is better to take it as merely a rod for controlling her animals ... Circe is not a northern witch or fairy but a pharmakis, a semi-oriental potion-enchantress, like Medea. She needs no magic wand; but she does need a stick to manage her menagerie." (Stanford 1996a)

305   "Where divine names are given for objects the human name is also usually given in Homer. Since moly is given only its divine name here, it must belong entirely to the realm of gods. Hence the difficulty, or danger, for men in digging it up ... But armed with this root, what does Odysseus *do* with it? Nothing, is the answer. It gives some mysterious 'automatic' protection to its bearer." (Jones 2004)

BOOK 11

74   See note on Bk 1:240.

270   *"Amphytrion's mighty, tireless son"* is Herakles, the foster son of Amphytrion.

280   Erinys, the Furies or Angry Ones, goddesses "who avenged offences against blood relations, especially against one's mother." (Stanford 1996a)

288   A fragment of a tale known to the audience but less to us, continued in Bk 15:225 and forward. The seer is Melampous.

304   Kastor known as the horse-tamer, brother of boxer Polydeukes, son of Leda and Tyndareos; the brothers share a single mortality, one alive above earth, the other below, and then they switch; thus they have a certain immortality like the gods.

312   A cubit, approximately the length of the forearm, say 18 inches, so 13½ feet wide; a fathom is 6 feet, so 54 feet tall. (Adapted from Jones 2004)

316   These are all high mountains: Mt. Ossa, Mt. Olympos and Mt. Pelion.

318   Leto bore Apollo to Zeus; Apollo slew these gigantic children.

325   Not the usual story of Ariadne, but part of some lost fragment. Dia is thought to be modern Standia, an island just north of Krete. (Adapted from Stanford 1996a)

327   Eriphyle accepted a bribe of gold for her to persuade her spouse Amphiaraos to join the expedition of the Seven against Thebes though he knew he would be killed there. (Adapted from Stanford 1996a)

521   King Priam sent Eurypylos' mother (who was Priam's daughter) a gift of gold to help persuade her to send her son and his companions to defend Troy. The Keteians were a people led by Eurypylos. (Adapted from Stanford 1996a)

577   The word translated as a rood, a quarter of an acre, in Greek is a pelethron, an ancient Greek measure estimated to be 400 feet, so some 3,600 feet, a true giant at almost two-thirds of a mile tall. (Adapted from Stanford 1996a)

622 The lesser man is "Eurystheus, for whom, owing to Hera's jealousy, Heracles had to perform his Twelve Labors, including capturing the watch-dog of Hades," later known as Cerberus. (Stanford 1996a)

BOOK 12

61 *"Wanderers"* are large rocks jutting out from the sea that move and destroy ships.

65 When one of the doves that bring ambrosia to Zeus is caught in the Wanderers, Zeus adds another dove to the flock *"to keep the number."*

72 Hera protected Iasion in the Argonaut saga much as Athena protects Odysseus in the Odyssey.

194 Nodding the brow was a formal sign in ancient Greece, a command or oath, often meaning yes or affirmed.

BOOK 13

106 Cave stone is presumably stalactites and stalagmites.

343 Polyphemos the Cyclops, who was blinded by Odysseus, was the son of Poseidon.

BOOK 14

55 This is one of the few times in the Odyssey where Homer uses direct address, you.

69 Loosed the knees here means caused them to die.

103 *"Far and wide"* presumably means they feed where they can on the hard, meager island.

165 See note on Bk 14:55.

181 *"To make nameless"* means to kill all living male members of Odysseus' bloodline.

190 See note on Bk 1:173.

327 Dodona is an oracle of Zeus in a sacred oak. (Adapted from Russo, Fernandez-Galiano, and Heubeck 1992)

437 See note on Bk 4:66.

BOOK 15

18   The bride gifts go to Penelope, the bride price to her father.

225   The first part of the seer's story begins at Bk 11:288.

363   Ktimene is only mentioned here but, apparently, Odysseus had a younger sister.

411   Apollo kills the men, Artemis the women; the gentle arrows are not felt, a peaceful, quiet death—or a natural death as we might say. (Adapted from Jones 2004)

480   This is a possible reason epic heroes did not eat fish. (Adapted from Stanford 1996b)

BOOK 16

57   The Greek word is atta, a word used in addressing an elder. I have used uncle to preserve the familiarity and respect though Telemakos is unrelated to Eumaios.

59   See note on Bk 1:173.

130   See note on Bk 16:57.

223   See note on Bk 1:173.

267   *"The strong trial of Ares"* means the test of fighting and battle. Ares is the god of war.

293   Iron weapons belong to the iron age, the age of Homer, not the bronze age of the epics. This is likely a proverb. (Adapted from Heubeck and Hoekstra 1989)

BOOK 17

222   *"Never sword nor cauldron"* refers to what a lord might ask for and be given as a guest gift. (Adapted from Stanford 1996b)

272   See note on Bk 14:55.

311   See note on Bk 14:55.

380   See note on Bk 14:55.

383   Hired means workers for the people, that is, skilled workers, those not tied to some great house in slavery but hired by those who can pay them, a rather short list, expanded later to include

another: heralds (see Bk 19:135). (Adapted from Stanford 1996b)

448   *"Reach a bitter Egypt or Kypros"* presumably means sold there as a slave.

545   *"Sneezes at my words."* "Anything unexpected or involuntary stood a chance of being of divine intervention (how else explain it?), and hence an omen in the ancient world." (Jones 2004)

BOOK 18

7   *"Because he carried messages when bid."* "[T]he messenger goddess of the greeks was Iris. Iros would be the masculine form." (Jones 2004)

85   Eketos, an unknown king, perhaps mythical of the kind parents have always used to scare disobedient children. (Adapted from Stanford 1996b)

162   The fact that she thinks of her spouse being there has been put to many causes: Athena put it in her mind, Homer's slip, multiple earlier versions of the story, or perhaps, just intuition.

328   Then as now in cold weather beggars and the homeless seek warm places to sleep, a blacksmith's, or safe, public places. This also implies that Odysseus' return is in late fall, in winter or in early spring when the weather is still cold.

BOOK 19

92   *"Wiping this off your own head."* This may refer either to custom of wiping off the blood of sacrificial animals on their heads or else to a similar custom where a murderer wipes the blood on the victim to show he deserved to die. (Adapted from Stanford 1996b)

163   Sayings such as this one, *"from some ancient oak or rock,"* give the sense of a yet more ancient world of proverbs. The sense seems to be: "You must have some relatives if you're not a freak." (Stanford 1996b)

179   A disputed passage, but it seems to relate to ancient agrarian calendars and cycles of kingship, so Minos perhaps renews his kingship then. (Adapted from Stanford 1996b)

206 East wind and west wind, Eurus and Zephyros in the text: the west wind brought the winter storms and snows, at least to Asia Minor, Homer's land, and the east wind brought the thaws. (Adapted from Sanford 1996b)

296 See note on Bk 14:327.

363 *"You, child"* is the long absent Odysseus whom she is addressing here, that is, both the stranger and the supposedly far-off Odysseus.

396 These favors of thievery and oaths (swearing oaths that can be gotten out of by trickery) made Autolykos the prototype trickster. (Adapted from Stanford 1996b)

407 *"Angry at many"* may also mean having angered many or hating many or hated by many. The Greek for this is obscure and it is cognate, enough to be a pun, with the name Odysseus. This pun has been used several times in the Odyssey but only made explicit in this passage. (Adapted from Stanford 1996b)

457 *"Staunched the blood with an incantation."* "A 'sing-over,' the noun refers to a blood-staunching spell chanted over the wound, a practice known in many parts of Europe. I have heard a circumstantial description of the process from a Russian cavalry officer who witnessed an immediate stoppage of blood from a saber-wound in this way." (Stanford 1996b)

519 Pandareos' child has been turned into a nightingale. This is thought to be a variant of the Philomela story. Here the nightingale, daughter of Pandareos, king of Krete, married Zethos, king of Thebes. She had only one son while one of her sisters-in-law, Niobe, had many. Jealous, she meant to kill Niobe's eldest son but killed her own son instead. Zeus, pitying her, turned her into a nightingale. (Adapted from Sanford 1996b)

575 The props are "stays or trestles supporting the keel of a ship under construction." (Cunliffe 1963)

BOOK 20

51 *"Still you'd drive off all their oxen and their sheep."* That is, he would gain the victor's booty after having won the battle.

62   Artemis' arrows were the way women died (of disease, etc.), men from Apollo's arrows.

65   Okeanos was conceived as a river that flowed back into itself after its flow around the world. (Adapted from Stanford 1996b)

78   The Erinys (the Furies) were also called avengers.

156   This *"public feast day"* is a feast day dedicated to Apollo. (Adapted from Jones 2004)

158   *"Black water"* was the deepest water, hence clear and clean. (Adapted from Stanford 1996b)

187   *"Brought by ferrymen"* that is, from the mainland or another island to Ithaka. (Adapted from Stanford 1996b)

204   *"I sweated when I saw this one"* where to sweat is "a symptom of overwhelming emotions ..." (Russo, Fernandez-Galiano, and Heubeck 1992)

210   The Kephallenian towns are the towns on all the local islands and parts of the mainland ruled by Odysseus. (Adapted from Stanford 1996b)

350   "Here follows the only clear example of ecstatic prophecy in Homer: elsewhere in the Iliad and Odyssey all foretelling is effected by omen and interpretation." (Stanford 1996b)

BOOK 21

4   The gray iron refers to the twelve axes for the contest. To wed Penelope a suitor must string the bow and shoot an arrow through all twelve iron axes. Although there is much speculation how this might be accomplished, there is no suggestion of magic in the Homeric text here. (Adapted from Stanford 1996b)

23   *"And hard-working suckling mules."* The product of wild asses and mares; mules were valued for their strength.

308   See note on 18:85.

395   The bow was made of or tipped with horn, presumably. (Adapted from Stanford 1996b)

BOOK 22

30   The worst death was when the body remained uncared for and was given to vultures. (Adapted from Stanford 1996b)

57   "The 'worth of twenty oxen' was also the high price of Eurycleia's purchase as a slave. A hundred oxen would buy a male prisoner or a suit of golden armour, twelve a large tripod, nine a suit of bronze armour, four a skilled female slave (*Il.* 23, 705). A vestige of the widespread use of oxen as a standard of value is preserved in the Latin word for money, *pecunia (pecus),* English 'fee' (German *Vieh* 'head of cattle')." (Stanford 1996b)

290   The guest-gift of the ox hoof is what Ktesippos threw at Odysseus (see 20:296).

298   See note on Bk 3:42.

408   This cry that Eurykleia begins and Odysseus holds her back from is likely the ululation, a cry of rejoicing often still done at weddings in some countries in the Middle East.

473   "Hanging was always considered a dishonorable and shameful death by the Greeks." (Stanford 1996b)

BOOK 23

190   The olive tree serving as the first of four bedposts, anchoring the bed to the earth.

BOOK 24

1   Kyllenian, an epithet of Hermes, is a mountain "in Arcadia where Hermes was believed to have been born." (Stanford 1996b)

23   "*Met their fate in the house of Aigisthos*" refers to the story of Agamemnon's return. Aigisthos with Klytaimnestra, Tyndareos' daughter, planned and carried out the murder of Agamemnon on his return from Troy.

199   See note on Bk 24:23.

205   The three who went with Odysseus were Telemakos, the swineherd and the oxherd.

211 The Sikels were thought to be the indigenous peoples of Sicily. (Adapted from Stanford 1996b)

225 Penelope had sent Dolios to Laertes to tell him that Telemakos had gone to Pylos and Sparta. Evidently he took his family with him and stayed, all except Melanthios and Melantho, the bad offspring killed with the other servants.

305 Fictitious names, all, and their meanings are contested.

306 Another fictitious name for Odysseus.

331 For the full story of the gifts and scar of Odysseus, see Bk 19:393–412.

355 See note on Bk 20:210.

452 "Note that the ancient Greeks regarded the past as what lay before them, the future as what lay behind; i.e., their mental orientation was toward the known, the traditional and customary, unlike the modern 'progressive' outlook which tends to turn its back on the past and its face toward the future." (Stanford 1996b)

530 Earlier Athena had used the voice and form of Mentor to speak; here she speaks in her own voice, the awful voice of a god, terrifying to humans.

Select Bibliography

GREEK TEXT

Stanford, W. B. 1996a. *Homer, Odyssey I–XII, Edited with Introduction and Commentary*. London: Bristol Classical Press. This impression published in 2004.

———. 1996b. *Homer, Odyssey XIII–XXIV, Edited with Introduction and Commentary*. London: Bristol Classical Press. This impression published in 2004.

Crane, Gregory R. *Perseus Digital Library*. Tufts University. www.perseus. tufts.edu.

COMMENTARIES

Heubeck, Alfred, Stephanie West, and J. B. Hainsworth. 1988. *A Commentary on Homer's Odyssey Volume I, Introduction and Books I–VIII*. New York: Oxford University Press, Clarendon Paperbacks.

Heubeck, Alfred, and Arie Hoekstra.1989. *A Commentary on Homer's Odyssey Volume II, Introduction and Books IX–XVI*. New York: Oxford University Press, Clarendon Paperbacks.

Jones, Peter. 2004. *Homer's Odyssey: A Commentary based on the English Translation of Richmond Lattimore*. London: Bristol Classical Press.

Russo, John, Manuel Fernandez-Galiano, and Alfred Heubeck. 1992.

A Commentary on Homer's Odyssey Volume III, Introduction and Books XVII–XXIV. New York: Oxford University Press, Clarendon Paperbacks.

Vivante, Paolo. 1985. *Homer*. New York: Yale University Press.

West, M. L. 2014. *The Making of the Odyssey*. New York: Oxford University Press.

TRANSLATIONS

Hammond, Martin. 2000. *Homer: The Odyssey*. London: Gerald Duckworth & Co.

Lattimore, Richmond. [1967] 1999. *The Odyssey of Homer*. New York: Harper & Row. Perennial Classics.

Rouse, W. H. D. [1937] 1999. *The Odyssey of Homer*. New York: Signet edition.

Shaw, T. E. (Col. T. E. Lawrence). [1935] 1966. *The Odyssey of Homer*. New York: Oxford University Press. Galaxy 9th printing.

THE LANGUAGE & CONTEXT OF
THE ODYSSEY, ANCIENT AND MODERN

Bell, G. [1911] 2014. *Amurath to Amurath*. Cambridge: Cambridge University Press.

Bittlestone, Robert. 2005. *Odysseus Unbound: The Search for Homer's Ithaka*. New York: Cambridge University Press.

Bradford, Ernle. 1963. *Odysseus Found*. New York: Harcourt, Brace & World, Inc.

Cline, Eric H. 2014. *1177 B. C.: The Year Civilization Collapsed*. Princeton: Princeton University Press.

Cunliffe, Richard J. [1924] 1963. *A Lexicon of the Homeric Dialect*. Blackie and Son Limited. University of Oklahoma Press.

Drews, Robert. 1993. *The End of the Bronze Age: Changes in Warfare and the Catastrophe CA 1200 B. C.* Princeton: Princeton University Press.

Finley, M. I. 1954. *The World of Odysseus*. New York: Viking Press. This impression 2002.

———. 1970. *The Ancient Greeks, An Introduction to Their Life and Thoughts.* New York: Viking Press.

———. 1973. *The Ancient Economy.* Berkeley: University of California Press.

———. 1977. *Aspects of Antiquity.* New York: Penguin Books Ltd.

Fox, Robin L. 2008. *Travelling Heroes in the Epic Age of Homer.* New York: Alfred A. Knopf.

Hall, Edith. 2008. *The Return of Ulysses: A Cultural History of Homer's Odyssey.* Johns Hopkins University Press.

Kirk, C. S. 1965. *Homer and the Epic, a shortened version of 'The Songs of Homer.'* Great Britain: Cambridge University Press.

Kitto, H. D. F. [1951] 1991. *The Greeks.* New York: Pelican Books. Penguin Books.

Liddell, H. G. and Scott, R. [1843] 1966. *Greek-English Lexicon.* New edition Jones, H. S. and R. McKenzie. 1940. Ninth Edition.

Murray, G. [1925] 1955. *Five Stages of Greek Religion.* Garden City: Beacon Press. Doubleday Anchor.

Murray, O. 1980. *Early Greece.* Stanford: Stanford University Press.

Nicolson, Adam. 2014. *The Mighty Dead: Why Homer Matters.* New York: William Collins.

Severin, Tim. 1987. *The Ulysses Voyage: Sea Search for the Odyssey.* New York: E. P. Dutton.

Stanford, W. B. 1963. *The Ulysses Theme: A study in the Adaptability of the Traditional Hero.* Ann Arbor: Basil, Blackwood & Mott Ltd.

———, and J. V. Luce. 1974. *The Quest for Ulysses.* New York: Praeger Publishers.

Taylor, Charles H. 1963. *Essays on the Odyssey: Selected Modern Criticism.* Bloomington: Indiana University Press.

Whitman, Cedric H. 1965. *Homer and the Homeric Tradition.* W. W. Norton & Company, Inc.

Glossary of Names

This glossary cites the first encounter of a name in the text but this is not an index listing each encounter. Greece is sometimes used to designate the location, but there was no Greece in the times described in Homer. If there is a common or Latin version of a name, it is in parentheses immediately after the transliterated Greek name. In general, I have used the Greek name. Notable exceptions include Penelope in place of Penelopeia and Cyclops instead of Kyklops.

Adreste. Handmaid of Helen (Bk 4:123).

Agamemnon. High king of the Greeks in the Trojan War who on his return was murdered by Aigisthos, consort of his wife, Klytaimnestra, (Bk 1:30).

Agelaos. Son of Damastor, a suitor (Bk 20:321).

Aiaia (Aeaea). [1] Island home of the goddess Kirke (Bk 9:32). [2] Dancing ground of Eos, goddess of Dawn, the place of Helios' rising (12:3).

Aiakos (Aeacus). Father of Peleus, grandfather of Akilleus (Bk 11:471).

Aias (Ajax). [1] Son of Telemon, a hero in the Trojan War who killed himself when Odysseus won the contest for the armor of Akilleus (Bk 3:109) [2] Locrian Ajax, son of Oileus, assaulted Kassandra in Athena's shrine and thus caused Athena's wrath. The other Greeks failed to punish the outrage so Poseidon raised a storm at Athena's request. Since this is unexplained in the text, Homer probably presumed his listeners knew the story (Bk 4:499).

Aietes. Brother of Kirke, son of Helios (Bk 10:137).

Aigas. Poseidon's palace, thought to be on the coast or under water somewhere in the Aigian Sea (Bk 5:381).

Aigis (Aegis). Aigis-bearing, a word of uncertain meaning, possibly connected with the Greek word for goat as in a goatskin shield, the 'storm shield' of Zeus or the sacred 'goat-skin shield.' It sometimes seems to mean an armor breastplate. Its use is restricted to Zeus and Athena (Bk 3:42).

Aigisthos (Aegisthus). Son of Thyestes, lover of Agamemnon's spouse, Klytaimnestra, and murderer of Agamemnon (Bk 1:30).

Aigyptios. Elder of the Ithakans (Bk 2:15).

Aiolia (Aeolia). Floating island home of the king of winds, Aiolos (Bk 10:1).

Aiolos (Aeolus). [1] King who ruled the winds (Bk 10:2). [2] Father of Kretheos (Bk 11:237).

Aison. Son of Tyro by Kretheos (Bk 11:259).

Aithiopians (Ethiopians). People living far away (Bk 1:22).

Aithon. Fictitious name Odysseus uses in conversation with Penelope before he reveals his true name (Bk 19:183).

Aitolian (Aetolia). Land on the northern part of the Corinthian gulf (Bk 14:379).

Akaia (Achaea). Land of the Akaians (Bk 11:166).

Akaians (Achaeans). The name used in Homer to designate the Greek peoples, alternately with Argives and Danaans (Bk 1:90).

Akastos. King of a land in the west of Greece (Bk 14:336).

Akeron River. River of woe in the underworld of Hades (Bk 10:513).

Akilleus (Achilles). Son of Peleus and the sea goddess Thetis; a great hero and chief protagonist of the Iliad who chose a short glorious life with fame over a long life without fame (Bk 3:106).

Akroneos. Phaiakian man (Bk 8:111).

Aktoris. Handmaid of Penelope who is, in addition to Odysseus and Penelope, the only other person to know the secret of Odysseus' bed (Bk 23:228).

Alektor. Spartan man whose daughter married Megapenthes (Bk 4:10).

Alkandre. Wife of Polybos, who lived in Egyptian Thebes, (Bk 4:125).

Alkimos. Father of Mentor (Bk 22:234).

Alkinoös. Son of Nausithoös, king of the Phaiakians, married to Arete and father of Nausikaa (Bk 6:12).

Alkippe. Handmaid of Helen (Bk 4:124).

Alkmaios. Son of Amphiaraos and Eriphyle, brother of Amphilokos (Bk 15:248).

Alkmene. Famous queen and wife of Amphytrion, mother of Herakles by Zeus (Bk 2:120).

Aloeus. Husband of Iphimedeia, foster father of Ephialtes and Otos (Bk 11:305).

Alpheios. God of the river Alpheios in the western Peloponnese, grandfather of Ortilokos, great grandfather of Diokles (Bk 3:489).

Alybas. Town Odysseus pretends to be from, of unknown location (Bk 24:304).

Amnisos. Port of Knossos in Krete (Bk 19:188).

Amphialos. Phaiakian, son of Polyneos (Bk 8:114).

Amphiaraos. Seer, son of Oïkles, spouse of Eriphyle who accepted a bride that caused his death. He was one of the Seven against Thebes (Bk 15:244).

Amphilokos. Son of Amphiaraos and Eriphyle, brother of Alkmaios (Bk 15:248).

Amphimedon. A suitor of Penelope, son of Melaneos, (Bk 22:241).

Amphinomos. Suitor of Penelope, son of Nisos of Doulikion (Bk 16:350).

Amphion. [1] Son of Antiope; he built Thebes with his brother Zethos (Bk 11:262). [2] King of the Minyans in Orkomenos, father of Kloris (Bk 11:283).

Amphithea. Wife of Autolykos, maternal grandmother of Odysseus (Bk 19:416).

Amphitrite. Goddess of the sea and the consort of Poseidon (Bk 3:91).

Amphytrion. Husband of Alkmene (Bk 11:266).

Amythaon. Son of Tyro by Kretheos (Bk 11:259).

Anabesineos. Phaiakian man (Bk 8:113).

Andraimonos. Father of Thoas, a warrior at Troy (Bk 14:499).

Ankialos. [1] Taphian, father of Mentes (Bk 1:180). [2] Phaiakian man (Bk 8:112).

Antikleia. Mother of Odysseus, wife of Laertes (Bk 11:85).

Antilokos. Son of Nestor; killed at Troy (Bk 3:112).

Antinoös. One of the leaders of the suitors (1:383).

Antiope. Child of Asopos; mother of Amphion and Zethos (Bk 11:260).

Antiphates. [1] King of the Laistrygonians (Bk 10:106). [2] Father of Oïkles (Bk 15:243).

Antiphos. [1] Son of Aigyptos, companion of Odysseus, killed in the Cyclops' cave (Bk 2:17). [2] An elder of Ithaka (Bk 17:68).

Apeire. Unknown place, home of Eurymedousa, possibly on the mainland of Greece (Bk 7:8).

Apheidas. A fictitious name Odysseus uses when speaking to his father (Bk 24:305).

Aphrodite (Venus). Goddess of love, married to Hephaistos (Bk 8:267).

Apollo. God, son of Zeus and Leto. His arrows kill silently, bringing sudden and painless death as do the arrows of Artemis (Bk 3:279).

Ares (Mars). Appears as the god of war in the Iliad, but here he appears as the lover of Aphrodite (Bk 8:267).

Arete. Wife and niece of Alkinoös, queen of the Phaiakians (Bk 7:54).

Arethousa. The name of a spring near the swineherd's hut on Ithaka (Bk 13:408).

Aretios. Father of Nisos, grandfather of Amphinomos, from Doulikion (Bk 16:395).

Aretos. A son of Nestor (Bk 3:414).

Argives. The name used in Homer to designate the Greek peoples, alternately with Danaans and Akaians (Bk 1:211).

Argo. Ship of the Argonauts (Bk 12:70).

Argos. [1] Town and land in the north of the Peloponnese (Bk 1:344). [2] The name of Odysseus' dog (Bk 17:292).

Argos-slayer (Argus-slayer). Epithet of Hermes. The Greek word, 'argeiphontes' has disputed meaning, but most commonly interpreted as the slayer of Argos, the hundred-eyed dog (Bk 1:38).

Ariadne. Daughter of Minos; killed by Artemis (Bk 11:321).

Arkeisios. Laertes' father, an ancient king in Ithaka. Men of this tribe only sired one son each. His only son was Laertes, who sired one son, Odysseus, who sired one son, Telemakos (Bk 4:756).

Arnaios. The beggar who is called Iros by the suitors; he picks a fight with Odysseus (Bk 18:5).

Artakie. Fresh water spring in the land of the Laistrygonians (Bk 10:108).

Artemis (Diana). The Archer, goddess of the hunt, child of Zeus. She slew Orion. Her arrows kill silently, bringing sudden and painless death (Bk 6:102).

Arybas. Phoinikan, father of the woman who was nurse to Eumaios (Bk 15:426).

Asopos. Father of Antiope (Bk 11:260).

Asphalion. Servant of Menelaos and Helen (Bk 4:216).

Asteris. Small island between Ithaka and Samos (Bk 4:846).

Athena. Goddess, child of Zeus, often called the warrior goddess or by the epithet 'Pallas.' Protector of Odysseus (Bk 1:44).

Atlas. Titan, father of the nymph Kalypso (Bk 1:52).

Atreus. Father of Agamemnon and Menelaos (Bk 1:36).

Atrytone. Epithet of Athena, its meaning is unknown (Bk 4:762).

Autolykos. Father of Antikleia, Odysseus' mother, thus maternal grandfather of Odysseus (Bk 11:85).

Autonoë. One of Penelope's handmaids (Bk 18:182).

Boethois. Father of Eteoneus, retainer of Menelaos (Bk 15:95).

Boreas. God of the north wind (Bk 9:67).

Cape Sounion. Cape at the southernmost tip of the Attica peninsula (Bk 3:278).

Chios. Island off the coast of Troy (Bk 3:170).

Cyclops, Cyclopes (plural). Race of ferocious one-eyed giants. Odysseus and his men blinded the Cyclops Polyphemos, child of Poseidon, causing the rage and hatred Poseidon had for Odysseus (Bk 1:69).

Damastor. Father of the suitor Agelaos (Bk 20:321).

Danaans. The name used in Homer to designate the Greek peoples, alternately with Argives and Akaians (Bk 1:350).

Dawn. The Goddess Eos (Bk 2:1).

Deïphobos. Son of Priam and the second Trojan husband of Helen (Bk 4:276).

Delos. Island in the Aigian Sea famous for being sacred to Apollo (Bk 6:163).

Demeter. Goddess, sister of Zeus, who loved Iasion (Bk 5:125).

Demodokos. Bard in the palace of Alkinoös the Phaiakian king (Bk 8:44).

Demoptolemos. Suitor of Penelope (Bk 22:242).

Deukalion. A king in Krete and father of Idomeneus (Bk 19:180).

Dia. Island in the Aigian Sea (Bk 11:325).

Diokles. Lord in Pherai, a town between Pylos and Sparta (Bk 3:488).

Diomedes. Son of Tydeus and a hero in the Iliad (Bk 3:181).

Dionysos. God of wine who accuses Ariadne who is then killed by Artemis (Bk 11:325).

Dmetor. King of Kypros, son of Iasos (Bk 17:443).

Dodona. Site of an ancient oracle of Zeus in northwestern Greece (Bk 14:327).

Dolios. Slave of Penelope given to her by her father (Bk 4:735).

Dorians. People on Krete (19:177).

Doulikion. Island near Ithaka (Bk 1:246).

Dymas. Phaiakian shipwright, father of Nausikaa's friend (Bk 6:22).

Earth-shaker. Epithet of Poseidon (Bk 3:6).

Eidothea. Goddess, daughter of Proteos, the Old Man of the Sea (Bk 4:366).

Eileithyia. Ancient Great-Goddess figure, goddess of childbirth. In a cave in Krete there was a long-standing cult to her (Bk 19:188).

Ekeneos. Old and wise leader among the Phaiakians (Bk 7:155).

Ekephron. Son of Nestor (Bk 3:413).

Eketos (Echetus). Unknown king, perhaps mythical, of the kind parents have always used to scare disobedient children (Bk 18:85).

Elatos. Suitor killed by the swineherd (Bk 22:268).

Elatreus. Phaiakian man. (Bk 8:111)

Elis. Area in the northwestern corner of the Peloponnese opposite the Ionian islands and Ithaka (Bk 13:275).

Elpenor. Companion of Odysseus who died on Kirke's island having fallen from the roof (Bk 10:552).

Enipeus. Beloved of Tyro and eponymous god of a river in Thessaly (Bk 11:238).

Eos. Goddess of the Dawn. Tithonos was her consort (Bk 5:1).

Epeians. People who ruled in Elis (Bk 13:275).

Epeios. Builder of the wooden horse that allowed the Greeks to sack Troy (Bk 8:493).

Eperitos. Fictitious name Odysseus uses when he speaks with Laertes (Bk 24:306).

Ephialtes. Brother of Otos and son of Iphimedeia and Poseidon, slain by Apollo before he reached manhood (Bk 11:308).

Ephyre. Unknown location in western Greece (Bk 1:259).

Epikaste. Mother of Oidipodes (Bk 11:271).

Erebos. The 'dark place' to the west and a primordial god who is the personification of the darkness and shadows that inhabit the nooks and crannies of the world (Bk 10:528).

Erektheus. Hero king of archaic Athens (Bk 7:81).

Erembians. Unknown people visited by Menelaos (Bk 4:85).

Eretmeus. Phaiakian man (Bk 8:112).

Erinys. Furies or Angry Ones, goddesses who avenged offences against blood relations, especially against mothers (Bk 2:136).

Eriphyle. Wife of Amphiaraos. She accepted a bribe of gold to persuade her husband to join the expedition of the Seven against Thebes though he knew he would be killed there (Bk 11:326).

Erymanthos. Mountain in the Peloponnese (Bk 6:103).

Eteokretans. True Kretans (Bk 19:176).

Eteoneus. Retainer or servant of Menelaos (Bk 4:22).

Euanthes. Father of the priest Maron in Ismaros (Bk 9:197).

Euboia. Large island close to the Greek mainland (Bk 3:175).

Euenor. Father of the suitor Leokritos (Bk 2:242).

Eumaios (Eumaeus). Loyal swineherd of Odysseus (Bk 14:55).

Eumelos. Husband of Penelope's sister Iphthime (Bk 4:798).

Eupeithes. Father of Antinoös (Bk 1:383).

Euryades. Suitor killed by Telemakos (Bk 22:267).

Euryalos. Phaiakian man, son of Naubolos (Bk 8:115).

Eurybates. Odysseus' herald on the trip to Troy (Bk 19:247).

Eurydamas. One of the suitors (Bk 18:297).

Eurydike. Wife of Nestor, daughter of Klymenos (Bk 3:451).

Eurykleia. Slave, daughter of Ops and nurse of Odysseus (Bk 1:429).

Euryloxos. Odysseus' companion though often opposed to him (Bk 10:205).

Eurymakos. Son of Polybos, one of the two leaders of the suitors (Bk 1:400).

Eurymedon. King of the Giants, father of Periboia (Bk 7:58).

Eurymedousa. Captive slave of Alkinoös, possibly of royal birth, now the nursemaid of Nausikaa (Bk 7:8).

Eurynome. Housekeeper for Penelope, nurse of Telemakos (Bk 17:495).

Eurynomos. Son of Aigyptos and one of the suitors (Bk 2:22).

Eurypylos. Son of Telephos and leader of the Keteian contingent in the Trojan War (Bk 11:520).

Eurytion. Kentaur who imbibed too much becoming famously and madly drunk (Bk 21:295).

Eurytos. Archer from Oikalia who challenged Apollo and was killed by the god; also the father of Iphitos (Bk 8:224).

Furies (Erinys). Goddesses who avenged offences against blood relations, especially against mothers (Bk 2:136).

Gaia (Earth). Mother of Tityos (Bk 7:324).

Geraistos. Southernmost point on the island of Euboia (Bk 3:177).

Gerenian horseman. Epithet of Nestor (Bk 3:68).

Gorgon. Dreaded monster, not necessarily one of the Gorgons of Hesiod (Bk 11:635).

Gortys. Cliff somewhere in Krete (Bk 3:294).

Graces (Karites). Goddesses of beauty (Bk 6:18).

Gyrai. Rock Island in the Aigian (Bk 4:501).

Hades. King of the underworld of the dead, brother of Zeus and Poseidon, married to Persephone (Bk 4:834).

Halios. Phaiakian man, son of Alkinoös (Bk 8:119).

Halitherses. Ithakan seer who read omens (Bk 2:157).

Hebe. Daughter of Zeus and Hera, wed to Herakles (Bk 11:603).

Helen. Wife of Menelaos, cause of the Trojan war when she ran off with Alexandros (Bk 4:12).

Helios. God of the Sun, son of Hyperion (Bk 1:8).

Hellas. [1] Generally, the land of the Hellenes or Greek speakers (Bk 1:344). [2] One of two parts of the kingdom ruled by Akilleus' father Peleus in Thessaly; the other is Phthia (Bk 11:496).

Hephaistos (Vulcan). Lame god of the forge, married to Aphrodite (Bk 4:617).

Hera (Juno). Spouse and sister of Zeus, and queen of the gods (Bk 4:513).

Herakles (Hercules). Son of Alkmene and Zeus, a great hero and a great archer (Bk 8:224).

Hermes. God and messenger of the gods; also called Argos-slayer (Bk 1:38).

Hermione. Daughter of Helen and Menelaos (Bk 4:13).

Hippodameia. One of Penelope's handmaids (Bk 18:182).

Hippotades. Father of Aiolos, the king of the winds (Bk 10:2).

Hylax. Father of Kastor of Krete (Bk 14:204).

Hypereia. Former home of the Phaiakians of unknown location (Bk 6:4).

Hyperesia. Town in Akaia, home of Polypheides (Bk 15:254).

Hyperion. Father of Helios (Bk 12:176).

Iardanos. River in Krete (Bk 3:292).

Iasion (Jason). Hero, captain of the Argo, loved by Demeter (Bk 5:126).

Iasos. King of Kypros, father of the current king Dmetor (Bk 17:443).

Idomeneus. Greek hero of the Iliad (Bk 3:191).

Ikarios. Father of Penelope (Bk 1:329).

Ikmalios. Noted craftsman in wood (Bk 19:57).

Ilios (Ilion, Ilium). Alternate name for Troy (Bk 2:19).

Ilos. King of Ephyre (Bk 1:259).

Ino. Daughter of Kadmos, once mortal now a goddess (Bk 5:333).

Iolkos. Land of Pelias, somewhere in Thessaly (Bk 11:256).

Iphikles. King of Phylake who held the seer Melampos captive (Bk 11:290).

Iphimedeia. Wife of Aloeus, mother of Ephialtes and Otos by Poseidon. (Bk 11:305)

Iphitos. Son of Eurytos; he gave the famous bow to Odysseus (Bk 21:14).

Iphthime. Sister of Penelope (Bk 4:797).

Iros. The name given by the suitors to Arnaios the beggar (Bk 18:7).

Ismaros (Ismarus). Town of the Kikones in Thessaly (Bk 9:39).

Ithaka (Ithaca). One of the Ionian islands off the west coast of Greece, home of Odysseus (1:18).

Ithakos. The eponymous founder of Ithaka, brother of Neritos and Polyktor (Bk 17:206).

Itylos. Son of Zethos, killed accidentally by his own mother (Bk 19:522).

Kadmeians (Cadmeans). People of Thebes (Bk 11:275).

Kadmos (Cadmus). Founder of Thebes and father of Ino (Bk 5:334).

Kalkida. River in Krounoi on the western coast of Greece (Bk 15:295).

Kalypso (Calypso). Daughter of Atlas, nymph who loves Odysseus and keeps him on her island (Bk 1:14).

Karybdis (Charybdis). A monster in the form of a whirlpool (Bk 12:104).

Kassandra (Cassandra). Daughter of Priam, seer, Agamemnon's captive slave (Bk 11:422).

Kastor (Castor). [1] Known as the horse-tamer, son of Leda and Tyndareos, brother of boxer Polydeukes; the brothers share a single mortality, one is alive above earth, the other below, and then they switch; thus they have a certain immortality like the gods (Bk 11:300). [2] Son of Hylax of Krete, fictitious father of Odysseus in one of his tales (Bk 14:204).

Kaukonians. People near Pylos mentioned by Athena when she is disguised as Mentor (Bk 3:366).

Kentaur (Centaur). Greek mythological creatures with the body of a horse and the head and arms of a human (Bk 21:296).

Kephallia, Kephallenian. General term for all the subjects of Odysseus' realms, the islands and parts of the mainland (Bk 20:210).

Keteians. People led by Eurypylos who fought on the Trojan side (Bk 11:520).

Kikones (Cicones or Ciconians). People of Thessaly with a town at Ismaros (Bk 9:39).

Kimmerians (Cimmerians). People living near the land of the dead (Bk 11:14).

Kirke (Circe). Daughter of Helios, goddess of the island Aiaia, turned men into animals (Bk 8:448).

Kleitos. Son of Mantios (Bk 15:249).

Kloris. Daughter of Amphion, wife of Neleus (Bk 11:281).

Klymene. Dead soul seen by Odysseus in Hades (Bk 11:326).

Klymenos. Father of Eurydike who was the wife of Nestor (Bk 3:452).

Klytaimnestra (Clytemnestra). Daughter of Zeus, sister of Helen, wife of Agamemnon, lover of Aigisthos; with Aigisthos she plotted the murder of Agamemnon upon his return from Troy (Bk 3:266).

Klytios. Father of Peiraios (Bk 15:540).

Klytoneos. Phaiakian son of Alkinoös (Bk 8:119).

Knossos. City in Krete (Bk 19:178).

Kokytos (Cocytus). River of wailing in the underworld of Hades (Bk 10:514).

Krataiïs (Crataeis). Mother of the monster Skylla (Bk 12:124).

Kreion. Father of Megara (Bk 11:269).

Krete (Crete). Island home of Idomeneus (Bk 3:191).

Kretheos. Husband of Tyro (Bk 11:237).

Kronios. Son of Neleus and Kloris, brother of Nestor (Bk 11:286).

Kronos. Father of Zeus (Bk 1:81).

Krounoi. Land on the west coat of Greece (Bk 15:295).

Ktesios. Father of Eumaios, king of the island kingdom of Syria (Bk 15:413).

Ktesippos. Wealthy suitor from Same, son of Polytherses (Bk 20:288).

Ktimene, (Ctimene). Odysseus' younger sister, only mentioned here (Bk 15:363).

Kydonians. Presumably another early Kretan people (Bk 3:292).

Kyllenian (Cyllene). Epithet of Hermes from a mountain in Arcadia where Hermes was believed to have been born (Bk 24:1).

Kypros (Cyprus). Large island off the coast of Syria, home of Aphrodite (Bk 4:83).

Kythera (Cythera, Kithira). Island southeast of the cape at Maleia (Bk 9:81).

Kythereia. Aphrodite, a name either from the town Kythera in Krete or from the island Kythera (Bk 8:288).

Laerkes. Goldsmith in Nestor's kingdom (Bk 3:425).

Laertes. Father of Odysseus (Bk 2:99).

Laistrygonians (Laestrygonia). Race of giants who are cannibals and feast on Odysseus' men (Bk 10:81).

Lakedaimonia (Lacedemonia). Land in the south Peloponnese; Menelaos ruled there from the town of Sparta (Bk 4:702).

Lamos. Laistrygonian town (Bk 10:82).

Lampetia. Daughter of Helios and Neaira; she and her sister Phaesousa were shepherdesses for Helios' herds (Bk 12:132).

Lampos. One of the two foals with Phaeton who pull the chariot of Dawn, called foals presumably because they are forever young (Bk 23:244).

Laodamas. Favorite son of the Phaiakian King Alkinoös (Bk 7:170).

Lapiths. People ruled by Perithoös (Bk 21:297).

Leda. Wife of Tyndareos, mother of horse-tamer Kastor and boxer Polydeukes (Bk 11:298).

Lemnos. Volcanic island in the Aigian, favored haunt of Hephaistos (Bk 8:283).

Leodes. Son of Oinopos, a suitor who led the sacrificial rites and had some skill reading signs, the first after Telemakos to try the bow (Bk 21:144).

Leokritos. One of the suitors killed by Telemakos (Bk 2:242).

Lesbos. Island off the coast of Troy (Bk 3:169).

Leto. Mother of Apollo and Artemis by Zeus (Bk 6:106).

Leukothea. The White goddess Ino (Bk 5:333).

Lotus Eaters. An unknown people visited by Odysseus and his men (Bk 9:84).

Libyans. People of North Africa visited by Menelaos (4:85).

Maia. One of the Pleiades, the seven daughters of Atlas and Pleione; by Zeus the mother of Hermes the patron god of shepherds (Bk 14:436).

Maira (Maera). Nymph of Artemis; she broke her vow of chastity and the goddess killed her (Bk 11:326).

Maleia. Cliff on a cape in southeastern Greece dreaded for its storms (Bk 3:287).

Mantios. Son of Melampous and brother of Antiphates (Bk 15:242).

Marathon. Area near Athens favored by Athena (Bk 7:80).

Maron. Priest of Apollo among the Kikones in Ismaros (Bk 9:197).

Mastor. Father of Halitherses who reads omens (Bk 2:157).

Medon. Herald of Odysseus in Ithaka (Bk 4:677).

Megapenthes. Son of Menelaos by a slave (Bk 4:11).

Megara. Wife of Herakles and daughter of Kreion (Bk 11:269).

Melampous. Famous seer (Bk 15:225).

Melaneos. Father of Amphimedon who was a suitor of Penelope (Bk 24:103).

Melanthios. Son of Dolios, a slave servant in Odysseus' palace; he sides with the suitors (Bk 17:212).

Melantho. Daughter of Dolios, sister of Melanthios, untrustworthy handmaid of Penelope (Bk 18:321).

Memnon. King of the Aithiopians, son of Eos (Dawn) and Tithonos, killed by Akilleus (Bk 11:522).

Menelaos. Brother of Agamemnon, husband of Helen, king of Sparta (Bk 1:285).

Menoitios. Father of Patroklos (Bk 24:77).

Mentes. Taphian lord; Athena took the his form to speak to Telemakos (Bk 1:105).

Mentor. Loyal friend of Odysseus to whom he left the safeguard of his house; Athena frequently impersonated him when speaking among mortals in Ithaka (Bk 2:224).

Mesaulios. Slave owned by Eumaios (Bk 14:449).

Messene. Land in southwest Greece (Bk 21:15).

Mimas. Headland on the Anatolian coast (Bk 3:172).

Minos. Brother of Rhadamanthys, son of Zeus and Hera, king of Krete, and later, judge in Hades (Bk 11:568).

Minyans. People in Orkomenos ruled by Amphion (Bk 11:284).

Moulios. Herald of Amphinomos of Doulikion (Bk 18:423).

Muse. One of the nine goddess who presided over the arts and inspiration; Kalliope was said to be the muse of epic poetry and thus is invoked here (Bk 1:1).

Mykene (Mycenae). [1] Famous queen (Bk 2:120). [2] Town of Agamemnon in Argos (Bk 3:304).

Myrmidons. People of Thrace; Akilleus was their king and when he was killed, his son Neoptolemos became king (Bk 3:188).

Naiads. Fresh water nymphs (Bk 13:104).

Naubolos. Phaiakian, father of Euryalos (Bk 8:116).

Nausikaa. Phaiakian princess, daughter of Alkinoös and Arete; she helped Odysseus in the Phaiakian lands (Bk 6:17).

Nausithoös. Leader of the Phaiakians when they settled in Skeria, son of Poseidon, father of Rhexenor and Alkinoös (Bk 6:7).

Nauteus. Phaiakian man (Bk 8:112).

Neaira. Wife of Helios, mother of Phaesousa and Lampetia (Bk 12:133).

Neion. Mountain on Ithaka (Bk 1:186).

Neleus. Ruler of Pylos, father of Nestor, son of Poseidon by Tyro.

Tyro was married but Poseidon, disguised as the river god Enipeus, fathered on her two children, Pelias and Neleus (Bk 3:4).

Neoptolemos. Son of Akilleus; after his father was killed he became king (Bk 11:507).

Nerikos. Town, the location of which has caused much discussion (Bk 24:378).

Neritos. [1] Brother of Ithakos (Bk 17:207). [2] Mountain in Ithaka (Bk 9:21).

Nestor. Famous Greek hero and king of Pylos; his epithet is the Gerenian horseman (Bk 1:284).

Nisos. Father of the suitor Amphinomos (Bk 16:395).

Noemon. Son of Phronios (Bk 2:386).

Notos (Notus). God of the south wind (Bk 12:289).

Ogygia. Island home of Kalypso (Bk 1:87).

Oidipodes (Oedipus). Hero of Thebes (Bk 11:271).

Oikalia. Town in Thessaly, home of Eurytos (Bk 8:224).

Oïkles. Son of Antiphates, father of Amphiaraos (Bk 15:243).

Oinopos. Father of the suitor Leodes (21:144).

Okeanos (Oceanus). Ocean river surrounding the world (Bk 3:1).

Okyalos. Phaiakian man (Bk 8:111).

Old Man of the Sea. Proteos, a god (Bk 4:349).

Olympos (Olympus). Mountain home of the gods (Bk 1:27).

Onetor. Father of Phrontis (Bk 3:282).

Ops. Father of nurse Eurykleia (Bk 1:429).

Orestes. Son of Agamemnon, killed Aigisthos to avenge his father's murder (Bk 1:29).

Orion. Hero loved by Eos, the goddess of Dawn, killed by Artemis (Bk 5:121).

Orkomenos. Minyan town in Boiotia (Bk 11:284).

Ormenios. Father of Ktesios, grandfather of Eumaios (Bk 15:414).

Orsilokos. Son of Idomeneus of Krete according to Odysseus (Bk 13:260).

Ortilokos. Father of Diokles who hosted Odysseus (Bk 3:489).

Ortygia Island. [1] Where Artemis killed Orion, location unknown (Bk 5:124). [2] Unknown island, possibly the same as in Bk 5, in the east near the island called Syria (Bk 15:404).

Ossa. Mountain in Thessaly (Bk 11:315).

Otos. Brother of Ephialtes, son of Iphimedeia and Poseidon, slain by Apollo before he reached manhood (11:308).

Paieon. Greek physician who heals the wounded gods in the Iliad (Bk 4:232).

Pallas. Epithet of Athena, of unknown meaning (Bk 1:125).

Pandareos. Father of a woman who was turned into a nightingale; his daughters were taken up by a storm (Bk 19:518).

Panopeos. Land on the border of Phokis and Boiotia (Bk 11:581).

Paphos. Town in Kypros (Bk 8:363).

Parnassos (Parnassus). High mountain in Greece (Bk 19:394).

Patroklos (Patroclus). Hero in the Iliad, close friend of Akilleus (Bk 3:110).

Peiraios. Trusted companion of Telemakos (Bk 15:539).

Peirithoös. [1] Companion of Theseus (Bk 11:631). [2] King of the Lapiths who punished Eurytion the Kentaur (Bk 21:296).

Peisandros. Son of Polyktor, a suitor killed by the oxherd (Bk 18:299).

Peisenor. [1] Father of Ops, grandfather of nurse Eurykleia (Bk 1:429). [2] Herald in Ithaka (Bk 2:37).

Peisistratos. Son of Nestor, accompanies Telemakos in his travels in books 3 and 4 (Bk 3:36).

Pelasgians. Presumably earlier inhabitants of Krete (Bk 19:177).

Peleus. Father of Akilleus (Bk 5:309).

Pelias. King of Iolkos, son of Poseidon and Tyro (Bk 11:254).

Pelion. Mountain in Thessaly (Bk 11:316).

Penelope. Wife of Odysseus and mother of Telemakos (Bk 1:223).

Periboia. Mother of Nausithoös, daughter of Eurymedon (Bk 7:57).

Periklymenos. Son of Neleus and Kloris in Pylos, brother of Nestor (Bk 11:286).

Perimedes. One of Odysseus' companions (Bk 11:23).

Pero. Daughter of Neleus and Kloris (Bk 11:287).

Perse. Mother of Kirke and Aietes, daughter of Okeanos (Bk 10:139).

Persephone. Goddess, wife of Hades, queen of the dead (Bk 10:491).

Perseus. Son of Nestor (Bk 3:414).

Phaedra. Daughter of Minos, wife of Theseus (Bk 11:321).

Phaesousa. Daughter of Helios and Neaira; she and her sister Lampetia were shepherdesses for Helios' herds (Bk 12:132).

Phaeton. One of the two foals with Lampos who pull the chariot of Dawn, called foals presumably because they are forever young (Bk 23:245).

Phaiakians (Phaeacians). People close to the Gods; they are described in book 6, lines 3-12 (Bk 5:35).

Phaidimos. King of Sidon (Bk 4:618).

Phaistos. Small cape on the north side of Krete (Bk 3:296).

Pharos. Island off the coast of Egypt (Bk 4:355).

Pheai. Land on the western coast of Greece (Bk 15:297).

Pheidon. King of the land of Thesprotia (Bk 14:316).

Phemios (Phemius). Bard in the palace of Odysseus (Bk 1:154).

Pherai. [1] Town between Pylos and Sparta, home of Diokles (Bk 3:488). [2] Town in Thessaly (Bk 4:798).

Pheres. Son of Tyro by Kretheos (Bk 11:259).

Philoitios. Oxherd faithful to Odysseus (Bk 20:185).

Philoktetes. Hero in the Iliad, son of Poias, a famous archer (Bk 3:190).

Philomeleïdes. Wrestler who lost a contest to Odysseus (Bk 4:343).

Phoibos (Phoebus). Epithet of Apollo, of unknown meaning (Bk 3:279).

Phoinikans (Phoenicians). Inhabitants of the west coast of the island called Syria (Bk 4:83).

Phorkys. Another Old Man of the Sea, likely pre-Greek in origin (Bk 1:72).

Phronios. Father of Noemon (Bk 2:386).

Phrontis. Son of Onetor, pilot of one of Menelaos' ships (Bk 3:281).

Phthia. One of two parts of the kingdom ruled by Akilleus' father Peleus in Thessaly, the other is Hellas (Bk 11:496).

Phylake. Land of Iphikles (Bk 11:289).

Phylakos. Hero who imprisoned Melampous (Bk 15:232).

Phylo. Handmaid of Helen (Bk 4:125).

Pieria. Mountainous district in Macedonia (Bk 5:50).

Poias. Father of Philoktetes (Bk 3:190).

Polites. Companion of Odysseus (Bk 10:224).

Polybos. [1] Father of Eurymakos, one of the leaders of the suitors (Bk 1:400). [2] Husband of Alkandre, a lord in Thebes in Egypt (Bk 4:126). [3] Artisan who made the ball used by the Phaiakian dancers (Bk 8:373). [4] One of the suitors, killed by Eumaios (Bk 22:243).

Polydama. Lady in Egypt, wife of Thon (Bk 4:228).

Polydeukes (Polydeuces, Pollux). Known as the boxer, son of Leda and Tyndareos, brother of horse-tamer Kastor; the brothers share a single mortality, one alive above earth, the other below, and then they switch; thus they have a certain immortality like the gods (Bk 11:300).

Polykaste. Youngest daughter of Nestor (Bk 3:464).

Polyktor. [1] Brother of Ithakos and Neritos (Bk 17:207). [2] Father of Peisandros (Bk 18:299).

Polyneos. Phaiakian, son of Tekton, father of Amphialos (Bk 8:114).

Polypemon. Fictitious name Odysseus uses when talking to his father (Bk 24:305).

Polypheides. Son of Mantios, a seer (Bk 15:249).

Polyphemos. Cyclops blinded by Odysseus in his island cave (Bk 9:403).

Polytherses. Father of the suitor Ktesippos (Bk 22:287).

Ponteus. Phaiakian man (Bk 8:113).

Pontonoös. Herald in the palace of Alkinoös (Bk 7:179).

Poseidon. God of the Sea, one of the three most powerful of Greek gods with Zeus and Hades; he hated Odysseus because Odysseus blinded his son, the Cyclops Polyphemos (Bk 1:20).

Priam. King of Troy, father of Hector, Alexandros and others, brother of Tithonos (Bk 3:107).

Prokris (Procris). Daughter of Erektheus, ancient king of Athens (Bk 11:321).

Proreus. Phaiakian man (Bk 8:113).

Proteos (Proteus). God, the Old Man of the Sea (Bk 4:365).

Prumneus. Phaiakian man (Bk 8:112).

Psyra. Small island off the coast of Troy and Chios (Bk 3:171).

Pylos. Town and palace of Nestor on the southwest shore of the Peloponnese (Bk 1:93).

Pyriphlegethon. River flaming with fire in Hades (Bk 10:513).

Pytho. Apollo's oracle at Delphi (Bk 8:80).

Raven's Rock. Rocky outcrop near the spring Arethousa on Ithaka (Bk 13:408).

Rhadamanthys (Rhadamanthus). Ruler in the Elysian Fields, a type of paradise for heroes related to the gods (Bk 4:564).

Rheithron. Cove on Ithaka large enough for a ship (Bk 1:186).

Rhexenor. Son of Nausithoös, father of Arete (Bk 7:63).

Salmoneos. Father of Tyro (Bk 11:236).

Same or Samos. Island near Ithaka (Bk 1:246).

Sidon. Town of the Phoinikans who were famous for their metal work (Bk 4:84).

Sidonia. Ancient name for Tyre, home of the Phoinikans (Bk 13:286).

Sikania. Thought to be Sicily, after the early Sikel population (Bk 24:307).

Sikels. People of Sikania (Bk 20:383).

Sinties or Sintians (the Raiders, the Plunderers). People known as pirates and raiders, likely the early, pre-Greek inhabitants of Lemnos (Bk 8:294).

Sirens. Dangerous singing sea creatures, often portrayed in later images as having the body of a bird and the head of a woman; Homer implies that there were only two (Bk 12:39).

Sisyphos (Sisyphus). Hero eternally punished in Hades; the cause of this punishment is uncertain (Bk 11:593).

Skeria. Land of the Phaiakians, no known meaning or location (Bk 6:8).

Skylla (Scylla). Monster who eats men; her name means 'she who rends or flays' (Bk 12:85).

Skyros. Island off Euboia where Neoptolemos was being raised (Bk 11:509).

Solymoi. People visited by Poseidon, supposedly in Lycia in western Anatolia (Bk 5:283).

Sparta. Town in the kingdom of Menelaos in the southern Peloponnese (Bk 1:93).

Stratios. Son of Nestor (Bk 3:413).

Styx. River of hate in the underworld of Hades (Bk 5:185).

Syria. Island far to the east, of unknown location, original home of Eumaios (Bk 15:403).

Tantalos (Tantalus). Hero punished by being eternally tantalized in Hades (Bk 11:582).

Taphos, Taphians. People of unknown location, presumably on the western coast of Greece (Bk 1:105).

Taÿgetos. Mountain in the Peloponnese near Sparta (Bk 6:103).

Teiresias (Tiresias). Blind seer in Hades who tells Odysseus his future (Bk 10:492).

Tekton. Phaiakian, father of Polyneos (Bk 8:114).

Telemakos (Telemachus). Son of Odysseus and Penelope (Bk 1:113).

Telemon. Father of Aias (Bk 11:543).

Telemos. Seer who prophesied that the Cyclops Polyphemos would be blinded by Odysseus (Bk 9:509).

Telephos. Father of Eurypylos (Bk 11:519).

Telepylos. Town of the Laistrygonians (Bk 10:82).

Temese. Unknown location where Mentes (Athena) claims to be going (Bk 1:183).

Tenedos. Island off the coast of Troy (Bk 3:159).

Terpias. Father of Phemios the bard in Odysseus' palace (Bk 22:330).

Thebes. [1] Town in Egypt (Bk 4:126). [2] Town of the Kadmeians in Boiotia (Bk 15:247).

Themis. Goddess of Law or Laws, the received body of normal ways of just interactions among men; Themis called and ended assemblies (Bk 2:68).

Theoklymenos. Seer of the family of Melampous, a fugitive from Argos whom Telemakos befriends (Bk 15:256).

Theseus. Founder of Athens, hero who took Ariadne from Krete (Bk 11:322).

Thesprotia. Land in Epirus, on the northwest coast of Greece (Bk 14:315).

Thetis. Sea goddess, mother of Akilleus by the mortal, Peleus (Bk 24:91).

Thoas. Warrior at Troy, son of Andraimonos (Bk 14:499).

Thon. Lord in Egypt, husband of Polydama (Bk 4:228).

Thoön. Phaiakian man (Bk 8:113).

Thoösa. Nymph, mother of Polyphemos, daughter of Phorkys (Bk 1:71

Thrace. Land of northern Greece, favored haunt of Ares (Bk 8:361).

Thrasymedes. Son of Nestor, brother of Peisistratos (Bk 3:39).

Thrinakia. Island of the sun god Helios where his sacred cattle live (Bk 11:106).

Thyestes. Father of Aigisthos who murdered Agamemnon (Bk 4:518).

Tithonos (Tithonus). Consort of Eos, the goddess of Dawn; Priam's brother from the royal house of Troy (Bk 5:1).

Tityos. Son of Gaia, punished in the underworld for raping Leto (Bk 7:324).

Trito-born. Epithet of Athena (Bk 3:378).

Troy. Site of the Trojan War, also called Ilios (Bk 1:2).

Tydeus. Father of the hero Diomedes in the Iliad (Bk 3:167).

Tyndareos. Husband of Leda, father of horse-tamer Kastor and boxer Polydeukes, foster father of the daughters of Leda and Zeus, Helen and Klytaimnestra (Bk 11:298).

Tyro. Famous queen whose dead soul spoke to Odysseus (Bk 2:120).

Wanderers (Plantae). Rocks that move and destroy ships, near Skylla and Karybdis (Bk 12:61).

White Rock. Seemingly familiar but otherwise unknown landmark on the way to Hades, not mentioned elsewhere in Homer (Bk 24:11).

Zakynthos. Island near Ithaka (Bk 1:246).

Zephyros (Zephyrus). God of the west wind (Bk 4:402).

Zethos. [1] Son of Antiope; he built Thebes with his brother Amphion (Bk 11:262). [2] Father of Itylos (Bk 19:522).

Zeus. Son of Kronos, the most powerful of the gods (Bk 1:27).

www.ingramcontent.com/pod-product-compliance
Lightning Source LLC
Chambersburg PA
CBHW071730110726
47908CB00006B/1556